I0691441

Moonstone & Mugwort

Julie Embleton

Oath & Legacy 1

To Marianne, aka Athena.

'No endeavour could halt this girl woven in bronze and ink.'

1

Ava O'Keefe bristled against covetous ghouls and their incessant spying.

Although not entirely unexpected, she'd anticipated the stalking to begin mid-April, not the second week in March. But driven by the rarity of the incoming celestial event, the spooks had slunk into town early, disturbing her peace. Curiosity and annoyance urged her over to the window, where a peek through the slit between lace and glass revealed a slice of the street below.

Lunchtime traffic clogged Calnaloch harbour. Souls brave enough to face the brazen wind belting in off the Irish Sea huddled around the tables outside Jack's Fish Shack, warming their bones with chunky seafood chowder. Further along, the Lighthouse Cafe had a queue snaking out its door, the line filled with shuffling caffeine addicts, hunching against the cold as they awaited their afternoon fix.

1

Cars occupied the stretch facing the water. Where a frisky tide lapped the wall, seaweed and broken shells littered the path. During the summer months, when patrons spilled out of the bars to savour warm evenings, the low wall doubled as seating. That afternoon, seagulls were the only souls perched on the damp stone.

Craning further, Ava noted only one figure standing out amongst the bustling; a traffic warden scouring for missing parking tickets. But *'The Sneak,'* as locals dubbed the official, wasn't who disrupted her afternoon. She couldn't pinpoint who *did* spy on her, but their presence seared, manifesting as a hot prickle between her shoulder blades.

Whomever—whatever—it was, she'd soon learn. Once they were ready, or desperate enough, they'd make themselves known. With a tut, she released the curtain and faced the room.

Candles and string lights had the cosy space glowing. Rose incense smoke drifted in lazy ribbons, hanging above the table where her tarot deck waited. The round table claimed the floor closest to the window. Although paired with two mismatched chairs, twin tasselled cushions decorated the seats. She'd planned to paint the chairs the same teal as the feature wall, but so far, the task had remained on her 'long finger' list.

A clear quartz sat on top of the tarot deck, and beside it, a labradorite tower paired with a chunk of hematite; both gifts from her friend Iseult Boleyn who owned The Cauldron, one of the town's most popular tourist attractions. Although the tourists brought a steady trade to Iz's shop, they weren't her best customers; albeit discreetly, the local witch community kept her friend's business thriving.

Another much beloved treasured draped the table; a fringed cloth Ava's gran had gifted her. A little faded in places, and noticeably scorched from where a candle once toppled over, the black silk, woven with fine silver thread, hung in a graceful waterfall. Tiny glass beads threaded through the fringe reflected the surrounding candlelight, adding to the

2

otherworldly atmosphere. Clients wanted the whole package when they came for a tarot reading, but decor too witchy or woo-woo could scare them off. Ava liked to think she had the balance just right, and she hadn't experienced a client stepping over the threshold only to freeze, shriek, and bolt—not yet, anyhow.

Ava's gran, Evelyn O'Keefe, had taught Ava how to read tarot. She'd gifted Ava her very first deck on her thirteenth birthday. In the year after, Ava hadn't once missed their eleven o'clock class on a Saturday morning. Ava's mum would drop her off, and she'd duck around the side of her gran's thatched cottage to clamber into the magical world inside her beloved traditional caravan. With its curved turquoise roof, yellow wagon-wheels, and ornate exterior paintwork and trim, teenage Ava honestly believed it a portal to an alternate universe. The caravan had succumbed to age years ago, but she could still picture the dim interior strung with dried herbs and fairy-lights. Candles had crafted dancing shadows that flickered against the purple and indigo walls, while fringed velvet cushions and tasselled throws layered the narrow seats. Sometimes, when she caught a ghostly whiff of her gran's verbena perfume, it took her right back to the magical sanctuary.

Although Evelyn had taught Ava how to read tarot, her gran's special gift lay in palm reading. Ava wanted to learn, too, but Evelyn had refused. *'When you're older,'* she'd said every time, and on the few occasions Ava had stolen through her gran's hidden book stash, she'd never found a single title on palmistry.

Evelyn O'Keefe also knew the strain of being coveted. She'd lived with the curse for sixty-eight years.

The unwanted legacy had then passed to Ava's mother, Aoibheann, and far too soon, inherited by Ava herself; only five weeks after her eighteenth birthday, a few short days after her mum planted a kiss on her head before skipping out the door to meet friends for lunch.

3

Aoibheann had never returned. A week later, fishermen found her body off the coast of Waterford.

Aoibheann's premature death explained why Evelyn hadn't wanted Ava to learn palm reading. Only when Ava held her mum's icy hand in the morgue did she first notice her stunted life line.

After Aoibheann's death—and although legally an adult—Ava wasn't ready to fend for herself. With her father long gone, and no siblings to lean upon, her mum's older sister, Nessa, *'the crazy one'* stepped in.

The O'Keefe's possessed powerful witch blood, and Nessa was no exception. With her long grey hair, flowing skirts, jingling bracelets, and a way of looking through a person that'd put the heebie-jeebies up them, she embodied the cliche of crone to perfection. Folks gave Nessa a wide berth, but Ava knew who hid behind the wild mountain crone persona. Tucked inside her rambling cottage hidden in the Ballinastoe Woods near the Sally Gap, Nessa tended her herbs and worked her medicinal magick in peace. People from all over the country availed of her cures, and when they needed something beyond herbal salves or teas, Nessa spun her unfailing magick.

Although Ava's mum had taught Ava a lot during her teen years, Nessa quickly built upon Ava's foundational witchcraft and greatly enriched it. They didn't always see eye-to-eye, and more than once over the years, Ava had stormed off to live with Iz for a while, but she always returned. Even though Nessa drove her nuts, and point-blank refused to accept Ava's opinion of her inheritance, she was her only remaining family.

'It's not a curse, it's a gift,' Nessa always insisted. *'One that can do great good in this world.'*

But great good or no, Ava silently despised the damned legacy.

Fourteen years later, she hadn't changed her mind, and at times like these, when forces gathered to claw for the power she protected, she

4

wished she could simply tear the curse from her life and fling it out to sea.

"Focus." Ava reeled herself back to the present, and scanning the room to ensure she, and it, were ready for the reading, grabbed a box of tissues off the dresser and tucked them behind the candle on the table. Without needing to ask the client why she'd come today, she could already sense the sting of heartache from the young woman waiting outside.

One hour, and a few tissues later, her client rose from the table, still teary-eyed, but happier. Ava gifted her a rose quartz crystal from the basket of mixed tumblestones she kept on the dresser.

"Keep it close for the next while. It'll help to heal that bruised heart," she told her as they emerged onto the landing. "Tuck it in your pocket or bra, and give it a quick cleanse in the evening to recharge it," she added, throwing Kate a quick reminder about how her website included a section on crystal care. Folks often found themselves too preoccupied with what they'd learned in their tarot reading to remember everything, so her website helped with after-care. Kate called up another thank you and a cheery wave in response.

With a final goodbye, Ava returned to her room. Iz texted just as she swung the door shut.

Iz: Lunch?

Yes. I'm starving

Iz: Jack's or the Lighthouse?

5

LH. Craving soup.

Iz: 2 mins.

Ava gathered up the dealt cards, and sliding them back into the deck, shuffled as she lapped the room to blow out candles. As she returned to the table, a card snapped free, landing face down on the cloth. She automatically reached for it, but despite her mind on the Lighthouse lunch menu, and a mental note to book her car in for a service, intuition stalled her hand.

"Don't," she said aloud, fingers already curling into her palm in retreat. "Do *not* be what I think you are."

Because if it was, it would be the seventh appearance of the Knight of Wands this week alone. The tarot card had been stalking her for two weeks solid; jumping out of decks, appearing as she scrolled through social media, or popping up in conversation on the tarot podcasts she listened to while cleaning her apartment or driving to Nessa's.

"Something else, please?"

But the passionate, risk-taking, sexy charmer smiled up at her when she flipped over the card. Ava grunted in frustration. "I see you," she said, slapping the deck onto the table. "But get to the point already." Like the out-of-sight stalkers skulking around outside, she'd rather if everyone just said what needed saying instead of annoying her with their cryptic, sneaky ways.

Grinding out the remains of the burning incense, she made a final check for fire hazards, flicked off the lights, and locked the door behind her.

The Giddy Goat bookshop occupied the ground floor. Ava had been renting her room upstairs from its owner, Anna, for the last two years, and within that time, had built a steady and reputable business. Prior

6

to having a dedicated space, she'd slung cards from home, travelled to psychic fairs, and read tarot online, all while holding down a HR job she'd secured straight out of college.

After her mum had died, and she'd woken days later to find herself suddenly manacled by the O'Keefe legacy, Ava had worked hard to shove down her witch abilities. Whatever grand plan The Fates cooked up for her, she no longer cared. She wanted to be a normal non-witchy being; work an interesting job, rent a decent apartment, own a cute cat, cut loose on the weekends, date, fall in and out of love, and enjoy a yearly holiday in the sun. So, a week after the funeral, Ava stuffed her tarot decks, grimoires, crystals, and tools into a plastic bag and threw the entire lot out. In September of that same year, she enrolled in Trinity College, Dublin, where she studied Human Resource Management, all the while doing an impressive job of ignoring how denying the family legacy, and her gifts, fractured the peace she fought to attain. She moved into her dingy student accommodation in the midst of a violent thunderstorm, celebrated her independence with a meal where every liquid on the table iced over, and woke the following morning to find her plants and three goldfish dead.

A week and many elemental flare-ups later, Nessa arrived, packed Ava's suitcase, ignored all protests—along with the self-combusting mirrors—and hauled Ava to her forest hideout in the back arse of nowhere. There, Nessa delivered a few home truths, yanked the rescued decks and grimoires out from under the stairs, and set Ava straight about her duty.

It took almost three months for Nessa to re-calibrate the power Ava had denied. Rebalanced, she caught up with her studies, completed her course, and after graduation, accepted a HR role in a hotel, all the while quietly practising her craft. Twelve years of hard slogging later, she quit the HR work, and with the money she'd inherited from her mum, a few wise investments, and a frugal lifestyle, bought her own home. She

7

now lived comfortably in a beautiful apartment she wholly owned, and worked a stress-free twenty hours a week.

But would she sacrifice it all to rid herself of the curse? Without a doubt.

Ava crossed through the shop, threw a wave to Anna, and bracing for a belt of wind, stepped outside.

Iz already approached. She sped up on the footpath, hooked Ava's arm, and clutching her scarf to her chest, shook herself against the icy breeze. "That wind would skin a bishop."

Heads down against the gale, they walked to the Lighthouse. With the earlier rush over, they had a choice of tables in the cosy cafe, so selected one by the generous bay window. Seagulls raised a racket as a fishing trawler chugged into the harbour. Seals followed, their bald heads glinting as they bobbed in the boat's wake.

Ava shrugged off her coat, scanning the specials board on the wall behind Iz. "Ooh, cream of chicken," she read aloud from the chalked menu, but as she hummed approval, the prod of a watcher poked again. Only a faint nudge this time, but enough to dampen the anticipation of comfort food.

"How's your day going?" Iz asked, tugging off her moss-green scarf. She stuffed it into the sleeve of her coat before hanging it over the back of her chair.

"Good. I have a client at three-thirty, and then I'm done. You?"

"It's a quiet one. I might make a date with my couch and close early."

Ava cast a quick glance out the window. Unless the elderly woman walking a Yorkshire Terrier strapped into a tartan coat happened to be a grey-haired, supernatural creature, the true lurker hid from sight. "A night in sounds good."

Iz caught the surreptitious sweep. She scanned the stretch of harbour on view with a quiet, "Ava?"

8

Iseult Boleyn had once held the title of Ava's Greatest Enemy. She'd skipped into Ava's life with her dazzling blonde hair, angelic blue eyes, and runners with flashing lights in the soles, and in the space of a week, stole Ava's first love and knocked off her *'Who Can Shove The Most Grapes Into Their Mouth At Once'* crown. But Ciarán Egan turned out to be a twit, and having a big mouth wasn't something a mannerly young lady should flaunt. Twenty-three years later, the friendship they'd forged as nine-year-old schoolgirls remained as unshakeable as ever. Iz was one of the very few who knew about Ava's legacy, and just as clued-in to the approaching date as Ava, didn't need to add anything further to her query except for an, "Already?"

"Eleven days now—that I know of."

Ava had first sensed curious eyes on a Saturday afternoon as she'd filled her car with petrol before heading off to visit Nessa. Saturday the 18th. She'd noted it in her journal, along with a comment about how stalkers may have been on her tail undetected long before then, which hadn't been a comforting thing to admit.

Iz folded her arms on the table and leaned in. "It's too early. The eclipse is weeks away."

"I know. April twentieth. Three weeks and two days, to be exact."

Their server appeared, order pad and pen cocked and ready. Iz waited until they'd placed their order and were alone again before making a pointed sweep of the few stragglers walking the harbour path. "How many?"

"Two. One's more persistent than the other."

"And they've made no approach?"

"Nope."

"Hmm." Iz popped the flip-top cap on the bottle propping up the menu and poured them both a glass of water. "Does Nessa know?"

9

"Not yet." But Ava would call her later and tell her. She could place a-dozen-and-one effective protection spells around herself and her apartment, but Nessa always had something more potent up her sleeve.

Lunch passed without further intrusion. They returned to their respective businesses, armed with takeout coffee and a treat for the three o'clock slump.

By four-thirty, Ava had snuffed out the candles and incense, tucked the deck in its silk wrap, and flicked off the lights. She walked home with a brisk pace to stave off the cold, her path taking her through the town, across Rune Park, and out the far side to where her cosy home beckoned.

Situated on the land rising above Calnaloch, the apartment complex gifted its residents with a stunning view. From the balcony skirting her top-floor apartment, Ava regularly admired the stretch of Calnaloch's harbour and its pronounced curve. Originally called Caladh na Cailleach, the Irish for *Haven of the Witch*, locals referred to the crook of land as the Hag's Nose. Witch references littered the town, and although Caladh na Cailleach had evolved into Calnaloch over the centuries, many of the town's original families insisted on using the old Irish name.

Further out from the coastline, three small islands rose out of the water. On the left, the Heath, derived from heathen, meaning a person not belonging to an organised religion—typically Christianity in Ireland's case. Historical records detailed incidents of witches being imprisoned on the island as punishment for their practices. Abandoned to survive by themselves, the 'heathens' were damned whether they lived or died.

To the right of the Heath sat The Hearth, where legend claimed one crafty witch escaped from the Heath and swam to safety to live alone in the island's abandoned Martello tower. Lured by the glow of her fire, authorities would sail to the island, but they never found the wily witch. Present-day rumours whispered tales of full moons, a roaring bonfire, and a witch leaping its flames. Those who claimed they got close

10

enough reported a ghostly form exploding into a colony of bats. Ava could sympathise with the beleaguered witch. Somedays, she'd happily embrace the ability to burst into a flock of bats to avoid people.

The third island, and a considerably larger one, lay further out.

Privately owned, it stirred constant gossip in the town. Its original name; Dún na Farraige, meaning *Fort of the Sea*, added to the intrigue. Rumours bounced between the owner being an Irish rock star, a disgraced Bolivian prince, and, for a while, Elvis Presley. Drones had captured footage of an elaborate mansion set amidst stunning gardens, but Ava had never set foot on the island, and as water terrified her, the idea of clambering into a tiny boat promised she never would. Mansion or no, Elvis and his buddies could keep their swanky, private island to themselves.

She arrived home without being followed. Grateful for the small mercy, Ava locked and bolted her outer door, flicked on lights, and quickly drew the curtains in her bedroom and the guest room. The heating had switched on half an hour earlier, and with the open plan living space toasty, she relished a cosy night in with a book and a glass of wine.

As chicken korma cooked on the stove, Ava changed into comfy sweats and thick socks. The post she'd scooped off her welcome mat waited on her hall table, and on her way from the bedroom to the living room, she grabbed the bundle, tutting at the amount of junk mail.

With a glass of chilled Pinot Grigio, she stationed herself at the small island in her kitchen and worked through the pile; one bill, a reminder from her dentist of an overdue check-up, a newsletter from a local politician, a bunch of random flyers insisting she needed their products, and a subscription renewal for the gym.

She winced at the gym form.

Iz had talked her into signing up for spin and salsa classes in February. Ava had much preferred the fun salsa classes to the agonising spin, but

11

with both classes now over, she hadn't crossed the gym's threshold in over six weeks. "I'll deal with you later," she told the letter, and taking another sip of wine, turned to the final flyer.

"Paladino Insurance," she read aloud, and with a muttered, "No way," rolled her eyes at the illustration of a knight astride a chestnut horse and how it mirrored the imagery of the Knight of Wands tarot card. *'We protect what matters most!'* the tagline declared. Although the image bore no wands or representations of fire, she couldn't ignore the significance of the knight.

"Huh," she added as the intrigue deepened. The company was UK-based, and even more curious, the flyer had a firm crease mark and a tiny coffee stain darkening one corner. Paladino Insurance wasn't papering the east coast of Ireland with flyers, but this random sheet had somehow found its way across the sea into the Irish postal system to be shoved through her letterbox. "Whatever," she muttered, and scrunching up the sheet, gathered the other unwanted pieces, hopped off her stool and threw them into the recycle bin.

A wet and windy night had rolled in by the time Ava had cleaned up and retreated to the couch with a book. Caught up in the latest release from her favourite crime thriller author, she was deep in the snowy Scottish Highlands trying to figure out whodunnit when her phone rang. Slotting her bookmark in place, she answered with a smiling, "Hi, Nessa."

"Hello, pet. How are you?"

"Good. You? Are you calling me from home? The signal is strong."

"I popped down to see Ruth," Nessa told her. "Brought her a few eggs. She's making tea, so I thought I'd slip out to her conservatory and catch up with my niece. How's work? I hope you're not overdoing it?"

"No, it's steady, but not heavy."

"You've been on my mind."

When Nessa dropped a statement such as this, Ava knew better than to fob her off. The O'Keefe family were all blessed with a robust sixth sense. When someone called to say they'd been thinking of you, it demanded an explanation. "It started."

Nessa grunted. "I thought so. When?"

"Eleven days ago—the 18th," she told her, reaching for the nearest cushion, one with a colourful dragonfly pattern. "Two, so far."

"Did you catch sight of them?"

"No."

Nessa sighed. "It's early, pet."

"Yeah. I thought I had a while yet," she agreed, resting her chin on the cushion as she cuddled it to her chest.

"Well, it's a powerful eclipse—the most significant in a while. You can expect those in the know to be plotting already."

"Maybe I'll hide up in the mountains with you," she half-joked. "The feckers might get lost in the bog."

"You're more than welcome. I'll throw up more wards, and we can add a few extra bottles along the perimeter." Nessa referred to the witch bottles she used for protection. Filled with hair, nails, urine, rusty nails, broken glass, and protective herbs, she'd buried the glass bottles around the exterior of her home to keep unwanted energies out. "What have you in place?"

Ava glanced in the direction of her front door. "Mugwort, vervain, black salt; the usual."

"And the balcony?"

13

"Nessa," she said, smiling, "if a witch can't protect her own home, she has no business calling herself a witch, right?"

"Yes, pet, but on occasions such as this, a sprinkle of herbs won't cut it."

"I've wards in place. Don't worry."

"But I *do* worry," Nessa said, affecting her fussy aunt voice, the one she used when trying to make light of something.

"I'm always open to suggestions."

Nessa accepted the appeasement with a little croon of satisfaction. "I'll see what I have at home."

"Thanks, Ness."

They chatted for a short while, and with a solemn promise to stay in touch, Ava ended the call.

Disconnected from Nessa, the apartment expanded around her. Silence thickened and shadows darkened as Ava observed her living room. For once, she regretted her polite, quiet neighbours and the lack of noise they produced—although it would be hard to hear creeping stalkers if loud music thumped. She'd checked the windows earlier, right? And drawn all the curtains?

"Now you're being an eejit," she muttered at herself, and swinging her feet to the floor, threw aside the cushion, and brought her empty wine glass into the kitchen.

Rattled by Nessa's concern, Ava peered beyond her reflection in the balcony doors to where Calnaloch twinkled under heavy rain. She hated hiding the panorama, but too spooked for her own good, the exposure made her nervous.

"*Definitely* being an eejit," she said, trying to soothe herself.

Yet, as she unhooked the tiebacks to yank the curtains together, an unwelcome prod told her she wasn't a fool.

In the dark, wet night, someone watched.

14

2

With her first client booked for two o'clock in the afternoon, Ava enjoyed a lazy lie-in the following morning. She rolled out of bed at nine-thirty, threw on sweats and blew out the cobwebs with a bracing walk along the beach. After a shower, scrambled eggs on toast, and another chapter of her book, she tidied the apartment and shoved a load of laundry into the washing machine. She also made an appointment for a dental check-up—and cancelled the gym membership. "That's enough adulting for one day," she announced to no-one.

Just before one-thirty, she locked her outer door, surreptitiously testing the air around the doorjamb with her palm. A warm tingle confirmed the strength of her protection ward. Alongside, she had pouches of herbs stuffed into the soil of the planters, and a row of hematite and selenite crystals lining the top ledge of the door frame. It gave her confidence in her home's security, but she wasn't foolish enough to place full faith in her magick workings. Desperate beings with greater power could override her conventional measures. Crystal and herb spells gave her a solid seventy percent cover, but now trouble loomed, she'd have to turn to her grimoires for the other thirty.

After a cool morning, the afternoon had brought in warmer temperatures. Ava loosened her scarf as she left the complex, taking the narrow pedestrian laneway leading to Strand Street, where she cut off to enter Rune Park.

A modest haven of green in the town, Rune Park formed a wonky 'S' shape, with an oval duck pond at the south end, and a playground at the north. Joining the two, a wide path flanked by rowan, ash, and willow trees provided a pleasant walking route. Smack bang in the middle, and overhung by an enormous protective oak, sat the ancient rune after which locals had named the park. The local council had erected a metal fence around the boulder years ago, and while it prevented people from rubbing the stone for good luck, those who valued its history made petitions to their deities by tying coloured ribbons to the railings, lighting candles, burning incense, and gifting the earth with crystal tumblestones. The witch community monitored the monument, ensuring litter didn't sully the park or endanger wildlife. As Ava neared, she spotted loose paper and the stump of a black candle inside the railing. She crossed the waterlogged grass, gathered the leftovers, and carried them to the bin further along the path.

Just as she threw the remnants away, the skin between her shoulder blades tingled.

While subtle, she knew by the weight of the pressure that Stalker #1 hovered nearby. Although less persistent than Stalker #2, the vibe carried a more menacing prickle. Tempted to wheel around and catch whoever it was, she knew it would be safer not to engage, so resumed her walk.

17

But #1 followed, trailing her through the park, along Raven Row, and all the way through the town until she reached the harbour.

As she put her shoulder to the door of The Giddy Goat, Ava finally dared a glance. A male; tall, whip-thin and fair-haired, faltered on the path not ten metres behind her. His most noticeable feature—a full-length black coat swamping his narrow frame—flapped in the breeze despite his sudden rigidity. With the grace of a brick, he spun and ducked into the charity shop. Ava glared after him, sorely tempted to follow and confront him in the clothes aisle. But truth be told, she didn't have the balls.

Officially across the border of freaking-out territory, Ava prepared for her two o'clock client with a distracted mind. Downstairs had been unusually quiet when she'd walked through the book stacks, and except for the cry of hungry gulls patrolling the harbour, silence pressed down upon her little room. Although she always kept her phone off during readings, she tapped open the radio app and turned up the volume on her favourite rock station. Would #1 dare to creep upstairs after her? She hoped not. Yes, she had defences, but without knowing her opponent and his abilities, she risked using her magick ineffectively.

The track playing faded to an end as she contemplated which tarot deck to use. "Nine Inch Nails," the DJ announced, "with Various Methods of Escape from their 2013 Hesitation Marks album, featuring bass by the gifted Pino Palladino. Two o'clock headlines coming up, followed by your chance to win tickets to this summer's hottest rock gig."

Ava stilled as she unwrapped the chosen deck. *Palladino.* An unusual name, and twice within twenty-four hours. Coincidence or synchronicity? "Once is a coincidence, twice is a pattern," she reminded herself.

A light tread on the stairs leading up from the bookshop flicked her attention to the door. The quiet cough that followed announced her

18

client had arrived. Ava turned off her phone, and with the deck still in her hold, gave it a quick shuffle as she surveyed the room for readiness.

Before taking a moment to ground and centre, an annoying intuitive poke urged her to draw the top card. She hadn't used the deck in over two weeks; her last reading with it had been a tough one, so she'd made a point of recharging it in a bowl of sage, rosemary, and rice since. The insistent nudge won. Already guessing which card waited, she tried to be sneaky by doing another quick shuffle and plucking a random card from the middle. But the Knight of Wands smiled up at her when she flipped it over. "Go screw yourself, mister," she whispered.

After her second client left, Ava called it a day. She craved heat, caffeine, and sugar, so locked up, hurried downstairs, and swung right out of the bookshop to head up the harbour towards the Lighthouse. She slowed near the curved window, relieved to note a handful of customers inside. Those stalking her weren't stupid enough to approach, threaten, or snatch her in broad daylight before witnesses. Right?

Once inside, Ava ordered a cappuccino and a slice of carrot cake at the counter. The l-shaped area herded customers under a brick arch, down three steps, and onto the main floor. There, pale stone walls, parquet flooring, lots of healthy plants, and an abundance of lighthouse and seaside-themed knickknacks delivered a cosy atmosphere. The owners had allocated one expanse of wall for local artists to display their work. Ava owned a stunning watercolour painting of the harbour, and automatically scanned the gallery for the elusive artist's work as she chose a seat.

19

Her selected table afforded her the best view of the floor. Tugging off her gloves and scarf, she took a quick inventory of the customers. Four women at one table; definitely tourists. An elderly man squinting at his phone, two teenage school girls sharing a serving of chocolate cake and gossip, and Larry Hayes from the jewellers. Safe, normal people. "Ava, stop," she murmured to herself. Paranoia had taken a tighter grip than she'd realised.

The server approached with her order balanced on a tray, offloaded with a smile, and pivoted away to gather up empty plates and mugs from the tourists' table. Ava inhaled the inviting steam, sprinkled a portion of brown sugar over the cinnamon and cocoa dusting, and watched it dissolve into the foam. Hot caffeine and delicious cake; just what she needed.

But then, "Just what I don't need," she murmured as an unwelcome prod sent a shiver scuttling down her spine.

A merry jingle announced another customer. Teaspoon hovering above her waiting coffee, Ava waited for their appearance as the patch of skin on her back grew warmer.

A man came into view. He strolled up to the counter, perused the menu boards on the wall, and ordered. Facing away from her, she couldn't gauge much except for his height and build. Tall-ish, broad-shouldered, but not muscle-bound, #2 wore a smart black suit, pale blue shirt, and pristine black shoes. But despite the Baltic weather, no coat, scarf, or gloves.

While not as skilled at deciphering the telltale energies of supernatural folk as Nessa, Ava claimed a fair-to-middling ability. Although disinclined to engage with #2 at any level, she reached out with her senses to send a tentative query in his direction.

A sludgy, disjointed undertone answered. Startled fingers dropped the teaspoon into her coffee.

Vampire.

That explained the lack of outerwear; they didn't feel the cold. And apparently, this one didn't feel the sunlight either, which meant he was an Old One—the ancient, powerful kind she absolutely did *not* want stalking her.

#2 had a newspaper tucked under his arm. With his order paid, he turned away from the counter, but the leaves of a gigantic Kentia palm overhanging the archway hid his face. Reluctant to be too obvious, Ava resisted staring as he settled at a table in the corner farthest from her. Before she could glimpse anything beyond what she'd already seen, he whipped out his paper, snapped it open, and hid behind the broadsheet.

Ballsy. She'd give him that. #1 at least had the sense/manners to scuttle in the shadows. Not this one, however. The audacity twisted her concern tighter. If the old one was this brazen about closing in on her so far out from eclipse day, there'd be chaos on April 20th.

But screw him. She hadn't forked out six euros to ditch her coffee and cake. She could be brazen, too, even if her hand shook when she retrieved her spoon and stirred her cappuccino. Shifting to angle herself more towards the window, Ava steadied her nerve with a quiet inhale and took her first sip.

Who was he? If she was genuinely brave, she'd shove back her chair, march over, wrench his paper down, and demand an introduction. Instead, she honed in on her cake—even though her favourite treat had already lost its appeal. The first forkful slid down her throat as a mouthful of bland goo. Chasing it down with a gulp of coffee, she forced herself to scoop up another bite.

A faint rustle announced a page-turn from her stalker. Ava dared a peek. The server had delivered his order while she'd been pretending not to notice him, but he ignored the pot of tea in favour of world news.

Maybe she had it wrong. Perhaps he was simply a passing business man, gasping for a cuppa on a wintry day. In response to her musing, the spot between her shoulder blades stung. Ava wriggled against the reprimand, surrendering with an internal sigh.

Fork by fork, and sip by sip, she got her six euros worth, despite an inner freak-out swamping her armpits. What would she do if he followed her home? Mugwort debilitated vampires efficiently, but only the common-or-garden vampire. The ancient, too-clever-to-be-ashed old ones demanded wards and spells far more potent.

A gentle clink announced his final sip of tea. #2 folded the newspaper, stood, slid it under one undoubtedly bone-dry pit, placed a tip beside the saucer, and left the cafe. All she caught as she ducked to peep through Kentia fronds was a side profile flashing a jaw shadowed by stubble, a high cheekbone, and thick black hair. Unfortunately, #2 swung a right out the cafe door, following the coast path. If he'd turned left, she would have got a proper eyeful of him as he walked by the window. But then, he knew that.

Slumping into her chair, she contemplated her next move. He'd made the first by announcing his presence without being an ass. He probably believed his placid introduction as respectful, but she had to hold firm. Eventually, he'd declare his problem by claiming how she—through the power of the O'Keefe legacy—was the only one who could help, and once she turned him down, the threats would begin.

Ava cradled her mug, drumming her nails on the chunky pottery. It would be foolish of her to head straight home. She needed to delay and consider her own tactics. Although gone cold, she tipped back the dregs of her cappuccino before fishing out her phone to text Iz.

Can I hang out with you for a bit?

22

Iz replied as Ava gathered her coat and bag.

Iz: Sure. You can help me count. Inventory time.

Need coffee?

Iz: No thanks. X

No warning prickle poked as Ava exited the cafe and left the harbour behind. She headed for the town centre, turning into Keystone Alley, where, left under the arch, she entered Merchant's Square. Tucked into the west corner, The Cauldron, with its purple door displaying a pretty eucalyptus wreath, promised sanctuary.

Although the *'The Witch is Out'* sign faced her, Iz hadn't turned the latch. Ava pushed through, setting off the overhead bell. She butted the door shut with her ass, checking the square for black-suited men as she firmly turned the latch. "Iz?"

"Right here." A blonde head popped up from behind the cash desk. Iz scanned her quickly, rising to full height with a worried frown. "What's up?"

"Number two came into the Lighthouse."

"Oh, shit."

"Yup." Ava rounded the counter, snagging the stool Iz kept for when her feet had enough. She propped herself on it with a sigh. "I think I seriously need to consider heading up the mountains."

"I do, too."

"Whoever he is, he has a pair of brass balls on him. He just marched in and made himself comfy with his Irish Times and pot of tea."

23

"Did he approach you?" Iz scratched the side of her head with a pen. A clipboard waited on the counter, the wad of pages listing the stock requiring counting.

"No. I didn't even catch him looking at me. Although, to be fair, I ignored him with equal efficiency."

"It's too early, Ava—way too early for this to be kicking off with such intensity."

"I know." Ava peeled off her gloves and gestured for Iz to hand her the clipboard and pen. "You count, I'll write."

"Are you sure?"

"Yes. I need the distraction. Oh, and mugwort. As soon as I get home, I'll triple line every window and threshold with a foot-deep barrier, and then I'll cook myself up an anti-compulsion charm."

An hour into counting, a firm rap on the outer door startled both women. Iz motioned for Ava to stay behind the crystal display rack, out of sight of the caller. When Iz tutted, Ava peeped around the wooden shelf to see who had disturbed them.

Detective Finn Delaney. *Great.*

Ava hadn't seen Finn since she'd bumped into him in the Black Raven three weeks ago. Slightly inebriated, he'd been wholly invested in holding her in a deep-and-meaningful conversation which began with; *'I want us to try again. I know you have commitment issues, and that I pushed too hard the last time, but you're the only woman for me, Aves, and if you'd simply let your guard down, and me in, you'd see it yourself.'*

24

Bracing for the incoming awkwardness, Ava cringed. She did have commitment issues, but as Iz had wisely said, if Ava really wanted Finn Delaney in her life, he'd be in it.

Iz unlocked the door. "All out of magic handcuffs, detective," she teased. "Sorry."

Finn drawled a, "Ha, ha," as he shut the door behind him. Ava didn't hear the latch click. "Saw the lights on," he explained. "Thought I'd take a chance."

Ava remained hidden by the display as he further elaborated on how he'd just been to Fisher's Cove and wanted to check something with Iz. Iz's family dated back generations in Calnaloch. When it came to the history of the locals, especially those in the supernatural community, Iz was a walking encyclopaedia.

"Come on in, Finn."

The longer Ava remained hiding, the more awkward it would be. Mouthing a *'Shite'*, she pasted on a perky smile and stepped out. "Finn, is that you?"

"Oh." Finn paused mid foot-wipe, gaze lifting to where she'd appeared. "Ava. Hi."

"Hi back. What brings you here?"

"A case." Cool blue eyes skated over her, accompanied by a flicker of longing and regret before he looked away. "Another missing person," he said, tugging at his left earlobe as he cleared his throat.

Yup. As she'd predicted; awkward.

Ava genuinely liked Finn. He was a good guy with decent morals, a great sense of humour, and an intelligent mind. But she'd learned six months too late they were better off as friends.

Thanks to the O'Keefe legacy, Ava lived a carefully structured life. Routine shaped her days. One centred around her business, another her downtime, and a third surrounded her practice. Finn knew all about her

25

witchery, but he'd blown into Calnaloch only three years ago, innocent to the supernatural past of the town—and the thriving community in its present—and thought the whole thing asinine.

They'd first met when someone smashed Iz's shop window. The brick used had a disturbingly elaborate note wrapped around its width, and the threat had badly shaken Iz. They'd been sweeping up the glass when Finn had arrived in full Garda mode. Ava had sat with them while Iz gave her statement, and then a week later crossed paths with Finn again when he'd bumped into her in the Lighthouse—literally—and upended her coffee. He'd made up for it by buying her another, staying to chat while she drank it, and after, kept popping up in the places she and Iz frequented. Ava had assumed he was chasing Iz, but he'd soon set her straight by asking her out to dinner. She'd refused at first, knowing their worlds could never mesh, but he'd persisted.

Eventually, she'd caved, because as Iz had said with an eye roll, *'It's just a meal, Ava. Go. Enjoy adult conversation, and be a normal human being for a couple of hours.'*

So, she had, and a few weeks later, found herself being introduced to Finn's friends and family as his girlfriend, and for a while, had believed *'normal'* an easy kind of fun.

As she'd suspected, Finn had assumed the witchcraft history of Calnaloch as nothing more than a clever tourist magnet. He thought her practice daft, to the point where it prompted sigh and eye-rolls. But in time, as he got to know the community and dealt with cases that occasionally swung aside the veil, his mild amusement shifted to distrust, which, bolstered by ignorance and a refusal to believe, soon created a chasm between them.

People typically had one of three reactions when they learned how Ava made a living. One: The assumption she was a tree-hugging, patchouli-scented, free-living spirit who wouldn't budge out of

26

the house without knowing what that day's astrology chart prophesied. Two: A Satan-worshipping, goat-sacrificing, tattooed wild woman who'd hex whoever looked crooked at her. Or three: A kooky kinda gal, who'd always have a spooky tale to tell and/or reveal scarily accurate psychic insights, along with being a freak in the sheets.

Finn's friends had slapped label one on her, his mother, an immediate label two, and Finn himself, the cute and kooky aspects of number three. If he'd hoped her a freak in the sheets, she'd let him down. As time passed, gnarly witch politics, his attitude towards her practice, and the truth she kept hidden, quickly eroded their relationship.

Ava had never told Finn about her legacy. The appropriate time had never presented itself, and with no eclipse events during their brief relationship, she hadn't felt the need. Also, as Finn found himself further wading—involuntarily—through witch politics, and continued to struggle with respecting the centuries of tumultuous history tangled within those politics, he began questioning why she couldn't just *'Not be a witch.' That* comment had sparked the beginning of the end. He enjoyed being the guy with the kooky girlfriend, but when shit got real and his linear way of thinking couldn't process her world, her abilities—and all the inexpiable things that came with it—his simple solution was for *her* to quit. During a blazing row, he'd even suggested he'd transfer out of Calnaloch, buy a house, get her settled in a *'proper'* job, get married, and have kids.

The proper job/wife/mother prospect had swamped Ava in a cold sweat. That life had never—and would never—be an option for her. Her legacy insisted on it. A husband and children demanded a commitment she couldn't give. Her own mother had died at the hands of creatures scrambling for the O'Keefe legacy. Why in the hell would Ava be selfish enough to bring a child into this world knowing it could be orphaned or worse, because of her duty?

27

Perhaps she should have laid all her cards out, revealed the entire sombre truth, but Finn wouldn't have believed it, and even if by some chance he had, he wouldn't have accepted it. He would have told her to take off the necklace—because yes, he'd assume it that simple. So, for reasons she couldn't truthfully explain to him, she'd ended their relationship.

Finn fought against her decision, blaming himself for pushing too hard and too soon. Although they'd broken up in November, four months later, he still cradled the hope they'd get back together. Hence the deep-and-meaningful conversations, doleful glances, and mournful sighs. Both of which he aimed her way as Ava asked, "Another missing person? Is it anyone we know?"

"Kathleen and Paul Brady's daughter; Ciara."

"Ciara Brady?" Ava quickly forgot about the hovering awkwardness. "Since when? I only saw her the other evening."

"You did? Where? What evening?"

Ava quickly worked her way back through the days. "Saturday. She was in the queue ahead of me in Casey's."

"Was she alone?" Finn had already dug out his notebook. Ava met him by the counter as Iz stood on his other side, her count of spell candles forgotten.

"Yes. She bought milk. Karen served her. She seemed fine. She saw me when she was leaving and we waved at each other. When I came out, I didn't see her, but I wasn't looking for her, so . . ."

"What time?" When Finn had his detective cap on, he was all business. She mostly preferred that side of him; the no-nonsense, non-emotional one.

Ava had to think. "After five, and before six-fifteen because I was home by then. So, probably six-ish? Yes, it was actually six," she recalled. "The church bells were ringing as I walked up the town."

"When did she go missing?" Iz asked.

28

"Monday night. She went out to meet friends and never came home after."

"The Willow Coven meets on a Monday night," Iz told him. "Ciara wouldn't miss a coven meeting to hang out with friends."

Finn clucked his tongue in annoyance. "Her parents said she was out with friends."

Iz propped one elbow on the counter with a, *'Whose fault is that?'* expression.

She wasn't wrong. If Finn showed a little more respect towards the witch community, he wouldn't find himself in situations where people kept him in the dark.

"If it would help," Iz said, "I can talk to her parents." Finn grimaced, hesitant to accept the offer that would only highlight his failings, but Iz ignored his reluctance. "Finn, Ciara's a third-generation witch."

"Shit. She is?"

"The same as Owen Egan and Katy Horgan."

Finn cursed, and backing away from the counter, flipped his notebook shut.

"That's three third-gen witches now missing from the town," Ava stated the obvious. "Something nasty is most *definitely* brewing."

3

Iz stocked an impressive collection of herbs in The Cauldron. Ava perused the sachets, adding a packet of blackthorn to the basket hooked over her arm. She'd gathered a healthy anti-vampire arsenal, but until she got close enough to identify Stalker #1's kind, couldn't stock up on what would repel him.

The previous evening, she'd carefully made an extract of mugwort. Blended with a dash of extra-strong vamp-repelling ingredients, the highly potent liquid now filled the glass tear-drop pendant hanging around her neck. To prevent it from being torn off, she'd also wrapped the charm in protective magick. The charm didn't have the power to stop nefarious old ones from annoying her, but it would protect her from their compulsion. Otherwise, one simple request, and she'd be doing their bidding.

Iz dealt with two teenage girls at the till, politely explaining the dangers of love spells as she added their red candles and rose petals to a paper bag.

"It's not to spell someone specific," the taller of the pair stated. "We know not to do that."

"Good. Because what goes around comes around, right?"

"Right," they echoed.

Ava plucked a sachet of lavender off the shelf and tipped it to her nose. She'd never mess with another person's will, but an anti-love spell *would* get Finn Delaney off her back. *Tempting*, she smiled to herself.

The overhead bell announced the departure of the teenage witches. Ava hunkered to root through the lower shelf, and as she did, Iz loudly greeted the customer who had slipped in as the girls had exited.

"Felicienne, hi."

Ava tensed against the warning. If she'd been out back where Iz kept the more serious goods, she'd have been out of sight, but on the main floor, Felicienne would see her once she neared the counter.

Felicienne Alarie, High Priestess of the Rowan Temple coven, the most influential coven in Leinster, had self-claimed the title of Aoibheann O'Keefe's Best Friend. The women had met in their twenties, and Felicienne had quickly recruited Aoibheann into her coven at the time. Ava suspected Felicienne had sensed Aoibheann's power, or had some knowledge of the necklace, because Ava could never understand how her gentle, kind-hearted mother had clicked with the cold and waspy Felicienne—or joined her tribe of judgemental, arrogant witches. By the time Ava turned eighteen, Felicienne knew all about the O'Keefe legacy, and somehow assumed Ava would bound through the doors of the Rowan Temple on her birthday and declare gushing readiness to join the coven. But with her mum gone, and Ava a staunch solitary witch, there'd been zero bounding. Felicienne had come knocking on Ava's door instead, incredibly put out when Ava set her straight.

31

'Hostile, with a side of loathing' was how Iz described their fractious relationship.

Yes, Ava disliked Felicienne, but Felicienne openly despised Ava. The daughter of her *'Most precious friend'* had *'Deprived the community of a great power'*, one Ava knew damn well Felicienne had banked on using for her own benefit. She'd raged like a lunatic when Ava had politely informed her she would never join her coven, nor give her first dibs on the magick that rose during eclipses, and all these years later, the bitterness continued to make Felicienne seethe.

So, as per normal, Ava refused to turn and greet her. She'd tried playing nice, but it had got her nowhere, and preferring to avoid the negativity, she'd decided long ago to simply ignore Felicienne whenever possible.

The High Priestess hadn't spotted her. Habitually dressed in flowing dark clothing hiding her five-foot-nothing frame, Felicienne approached the counter with a warm greeting for Iz. Boasting a stunning head of glossy chestnut curls that tumbled all the way to her lower back, Ava thought Felicienne an incredibly attractive woman—but only when she wasn't trying to puncture Ava's brain with an icy glare or muttering spiteful curses under her breath. Unaware of her nemesis' presence, Felicienne chatted away, laughing when Iz told her a funny anecdote about an earlier customer.

Hoping to hide behind the bookcase homing tarot literature, Ava tiptoed away from the herbs display. But Felicienne noted the movement. A glare immediately buried itself in the rear of Ava's skull.

"So, what can I help you with today, Felicienne?" Iz leapt in before Felicienne could launch into a hate attack.

Felicienne murmured something about a tincture. Iz busied herself with finding it, blabbering away so Felicienne wouldn't get a word in. While she fussed about, Ava ducked into the history section. Sometimes

Felicienne chose not to engage with her. She hoped today would be one of those occasions.

But apparently not.

"You've heard the awful news about Ciara Brady, I presume?" Felicienne asked Iz with pointed loudness.

"I have," Iz replied, unlocking the ornate wooden cabinet holding tinctures and potions. Painted a deep shade of aubergine, it matched the shop frontage, and Iz's favourite nail varnish. "It's such a worry for the Bradys."

"Detective Delaney isn't doing much."

"He's taking it seriously, Felicienne. He's doing what he can."

Felicienne sniffed. Ava didn't need to look to know she'd flicked a length of hair over her shoulder along with it. "The witches of this town are best equipped to handle these sensitive matters. We can take care of our own."

"We can."

"Of course, it's probably linked to the upcoming eclipse."

Ava mouthed a, *'Here we go'* and rolled her eyes.

"It wouldn't surprise me to hear that whoever has our children seeks a sizeable ransom—something only our community can pay. Those who possess the power to make that payment should step up, or at the very least, use their gift to locate our missing children and bring them home safely."

Iz returned with the requested tincture to where Felicienne waited. "Can I get you anything else?"

"No. Thank you."

Iz rang the purchase through the till, took payment, and saw the High Priestess out with more kindness than deserved. She sighed as the door clanged shut behind her. "That woman would try the patience of a saint."

33

"The coast is clear?" Ava came out of hiding.

Iz crept towards her, shoulders hunched and fingers wiggling. "Join us," she whispered. "Join us, Ava. We want your power."

"I'd rather shit in my hands and clap, thanks," Ava replied as Felicienne's clip-clop across the courtyard faded.

Iz plucked the incense stick burning beside the crystal display out of its holder. She wafted it around the till area with a ,"Be gone, negative energy!" accompanied by a dramatic swish.

Ava plonked her basket on the counter. "Do you think she's right?"

"About what?" Iz queried, securing the incense into its holder once more.

"That there's a connection between the missing witches and the eclipse."

Iz tutted as she rounded the counter, but glanced at Ava all the same. "Do you?"

Ava shrugged. "It's worth considering. Maybe they want the necklace as ransom, or for me to work a spell using eclipse energy."

"Well, demanding your necklace is pointless," Iz said, removing Ava's purchases from the basket to scan the barcodes. Iz knew Ava couldn't simply divest herself of the damned legacy. It would snare Ava's neck until she took her last breath, and only then would it magickally unhook itself and find a new host to curse. "And if it is a case that someone's jonesing to piggyback on your magick," Iz added, "well, that decision will be yours alone to make."

"I was hoping you'd answer with a defiant *no*."

Iz smiled as she unfolded a paper bag and motioned for Ava to fill it with her purchases. "Friends don't lie."

"But they can sugarcoat."

"When have you ever known me to sugarcoat? That'll be twenty-two seventy-five, please."

34

Ava dug out her phone and held it to the card reader. "I'll never hear the end of it if the abducted witches are a play for the necklace."

"You'll never hear the end of it full stop," Iz replied, ripping off the customer receipt and popping it into the bag. "Lousy weather, late buses, inflation, missing kids—it'll always be your fault, thou, oh bearer of the cursed jewellery."

"You're such a comfort." Ava lifted down her bag.

Iz flashed her a bright smile. "I have faith in you, my witchy friend. You've got this. So, ignore all the peripheral bullshit." A flap set the fine gold bangles on her wrist jingling. "These things play out the way they're meant to. All you have to do is stay true to yourself."

"You've been snorting the positivity powder again, haven't you?"

Iz laughed. "Lunch tomorrow?" she called as Ava held open the door for a customer stepping in.

"Yeah. See you then, Iz."

"Safe home!"

Even before Iz's order had finished ringing out, Ava caught movement across the courtyard; someone ducking under the archway. Unfortunately, it wasn't Felicienne loitering to throw more barbed insults. Stalker #1 had returned.

The flicker of a dark coat-tail announced his swift departure, but his unwelcome presence loitered, skittering over Ava's skin with a wave of stinging bumps.

The unnerving sensation clung as she walked up the town towards Rune Park. Forcing herself to maintain a steady pace, #1 followed, but once she reached the longest stretch of open path near the rune stone, slowed to pretend something on her phone demanded her focus. When she came to a stop, he did what she'd hoped; crept a little closer, just enough for her to get a read on his energy.

35

Briefly closing her eyes, she mentally reached for the edges of his signature. Not a vampire; the energy moved too fast. The answer came when her mind's eye conjured up an image of wispy clouds skimming across a sky; air—which she associated with fae.

Not wanting to delay, she quickly resumed walking, her tentative energetic grasp fading as she widened their distance again. So, a fae stalked her, but one with a clumsy aura. Either a young fae, or one who meddled too much in human matters.

The fae kept to themselves for a reason. When they mingled amongst those outside their community, it messed with their auras. Like magnets for dirt, fae sucked up the heavier, sticky energies of other supernatural beings—and humans. Judging by the leaden foot of her stalker, and the stodginess polluting his aura, he busied himself with both, meaning it wasn't likely he coveted the necklace for himself. "No," she murmured, peeking over her shoulder to realise she'd completely lost hold of his location. This fae did the bidding of another.

With the weather unkindly cold, the park lay empty. Ava scanned the perimeter, and although she knew better than to dally, slowed to pinpoint movement. Vacant paths suggested he'd scarpered. But why follow her this far only to vanish? Turning to hurry on, she grasped her bag tighter—and pivoted into a wall of black.

While she'd been dawdling, the fae had skirted around her, and now blocked her path.

He lurched for her.

Ava jerked aside, aiming her elbow upright as he lunged, slamming the curve of his chin with her boniest appendage.

The blow tripped his feet. Squealing from the insubstantial whack, he staggered sideways.

36

"Stay away," she warned, standing her ground with confidence. Judging by his instability, she had more than enough physical strength to fight him off—and she knew all the best places to kick.

The creature flung her a nasty glare. Built like most fae, Stalker #1 stretched close to six feet, but made entirely of skinny bone and only a lick of meat, a stiff breeze could blow him over. Unlike other creatures, fae possessed no bulk and were easily hurt. As chalky green eyes watered with pain, Ava noted his stereotypical fae features; pale, lank hair, wild eyebrows, and a face angled like an anvil.

Hateful glare narrowing, he rasped a demanding, "Give it."

"Nope." Ava gathered energy from within, drawing on the element of earth to weigh down his fae abilities. A hefty blast of heavy, grounding energy would drop him to his knees.

"*Give it*," he said again, flicking spindly fingers with wicked-looking nails at her.

"It doesn't work that way, you twit. Back off, or I'll—"

To her surprise, the fae sprung.

Ava threw out a retaliation. The surge slammed into him, knocking him straight onto his bony ass a few metres away. Now pissed, she snapped a, "Who sent you?" while maintaining the safe distance.

"He wants it, and he'll get it," #1 said, lumbering onto knees before returning to his feet.

"He—whoever he is—won't," she assured him. "Now piss off or I'll hit you hard enough to knock your skinny ass into next week."

Ava rarely got mad. It took a lot to get her temper fired up, but for some unknown reason, fear liked to possess her tongue and set it flapping with brazenness. She'd crossed paths with many unpleasant supernatural beings over the years, and it never failed to shock her how sassy comments flew while in the thick of battle or a precarious stand-off. If she didn't learn how to control it, one of these days, she'd land herself in serious trouble.

#1 fought to catch his breath. Doubled over, hair curtained his face as he wheezed. A hand drifted up to sweep it aside, and fractionally too late, Ava saw the sparkle of dust escaping skinny fingers. As she wheeled away, throwing up one arm to cover her mouth and nose, the dust enveloped her in a cloud.

Her attempt to escape fae glitter backfired spectacularly.

Ava's heel caught on the grass verge, tipping her sideways. Knees first, she hit the grass, cracking teeth together. Scrambling to kick him off, hold her breath, swipe aside the glitter bomb, and defend herself, she flailed like a drunk octopus.

Grabbing the advantage, the fae swooped in. He snatched her wrist, yanking hard to uncover her face to deliver another blast of glitter. But before she could aim another strike of her own, a screech announced his sudden—and violent—involuntary departure.

Although she'd inhaled only a tiny amount, the dust already had Ava's vision spinning. Rolling onto her stomach, she caught a revolving view of the fae bolting out of the park with a pronounced limp. "Chicken shit!" her possessed tongue yelled as the sky and grass swapped places.

Spotless shoes moved into her swirling eye-line. "Miss O'Keefe?" a smooth voice queried.

Ava sneezed. Disabled by the spins and the intoxicating effects of the glitter, she could only grunt as her uncoordinated hands, elbows, and arms struggled to hoist her upright. Annihilated balance dumped her onto the grass again.

"Allow me, please?" The stranger leaned in. A sparkling gold watch clasped his wrist. Butting against it, a blinding white shirt cuff, edged by a deep-as-night navy suit sleeve.

Drunk on glitter, Ava tried to push away the offered help, but her body failed to function. She landed face down on the cool grass where the sweet, juicy green blades tickled her nostrils.

As the world spiralled into black, a concerned, "Miss O'Keefe? Miss O'Keefe, are you okay?" faded with it.

When Ava opened her eyes again, she no longer chewed on grass. Instead, she found herself propped against the front door of her apartment, handbag beside her on the welcome mat, along with her bag of supplies from The Cauldron.

Confused, she blinked down at her splayed-out legs, up to a darkening evening sky, left and right to assure herself of her surroundings, and then down again. All limbs and clothes were present and correct. No blood, no wounds, no immediate sign of grave injury. But pain most definitely thumped the backs of her eyeballs. Stalker #1 had left her with a blinding fairy dust hangover. "Winged bastard."

It took several deep breaths before Ava organised unwilling limbs to haul her into a precarious upright position. Clumsy fingers struggled to pluck her keys out from the jumble in her handbag; a tricky feat with everything sparkling. Another battle followed with the insertion of key into lock. Finally victorious, she shouldered open the door, kicked her bags over the threshold, and stumbled in after them.

Staggering down her hallway, she made a beeline for her bedroom and flopped onto her bed like a dead fish. "Bastard," she groaned again, and surrendering to violent spins, buried her face in the pillow. Given the choice, she'd pick tequila poisoning over fairy dust every time.

39

Just after midnight, Ava woke with a desert squatting on her tongue.

Almost in control of all her faculties, she rolled off the bed and made her way into the kitchen. Once she'd guzzled two pints of water, she peeled off her clothes and stood under a hot shower for twenty minutes.

After, she stuffed everything she'd been wearing into the washing machine—except for her boots and coat, which she flung out onto the balcony. She also carefully removed her bedspread and dumped it outside, too. Struggling to stand upright, she surveyed the night, her grip tight on the balcony railing. The worst of the headache had gone, but her vision remained wonky. As if viewing the world through a filter, everything glittered. She would have thought it pretty, only the reflected night light burned her retinas.

A muttered vow about raiding Iz's shop for every anti-fae herb, crystal, potion, and lotion in stock drifted into the sparkling night. "If that fae comes at me again, I'll turn the rangy bastard into goblin food."

4

Ava never took a sunny day for granted, but when she parted her curtains the next morning and brightness instantly shrivelled her eyeballs, she mourned for the absence of dull, wet weather.

She'd slept, but the aftereffects of the glitter left her headachy and sensitive to light and noise. Thankfully, she had no clients booked in, so had the day to recover.

Craving caffeine, she abandoned her bed for the kitchen, sympathising with vampires when the daylight brought her to a skidding stop in the doorway. Through streaming eyes she rooted out her shades from the hall-stand drawer, and moments later, when the clatter and wheeze of the kettle set her teeth on edge, slapped on headphones, too.

She sipped at the hot coffee while sitting at the island, and for good measure, swallowed two painkillers. Human medicine wouldn't do much against fae magick, but until she got to The Cauldron, she desperately needed something to numb her body. Many questions surrounding the previous afternoon's events swirled through her aching skull, but she wasn't ready to consider them just yet; she required a cure and Iz first.

The rescue placed her in a supremely awkward position. #2 had earned major brownie points for chasing off #1 and bringing her home safely. The Old One could have taken full advantage of the situation and whisked her away to his vampire lair, but instead, he'd made a smart move. Yes, his game demanded her co-operation in return, and without doubt, he'd remind her of the fact—ad nauseum—when bargaining.

Vampires were a manipulative, conniving lot. Throughout the spectrum all supernatural creatures, she'd pick any other kind over vampires when it came to trust. The way they manipulated minds for personal gain disgusted her. When he presented himself, which he would, she'd need to remain hyper-vigilant.

"These circumstances call for diplomacy," she warned herself while clasping her mugwort pendant. Whatever about the fae and whoever jerked his strings, she couldn't stir trouble with an old one. She'd need tact—in spades. Simply refusing the vampire wouldn't cut it, and the one thing she and Calnaloch couldn't afford as the eclipse approached was a Witch versus Old One death match. "Goddess. Why me?" she groaned against the burgeoning predicament, and shoving aside her mug, dropped her forehead to the granite.

After another shower and more coffee, Ava felt almost ready to face the world. With her shades firmly in place, she left her apartment, hoping #1 wouldn't try his luck a second time.

42

Thankfully, a parent and toddler group claimed the grass where she had passed out in Rune Park. The small crowd soothed her worry. No-one would risk jumping her in front of so many witnesses, and two of the parents she'd shared a subtle nod with were both witches, so if trouble struck again, she had backup.

Following the curving path, Ava stepped aside for a jogger and a man pushing a twin buggy. Now she'd braved the outdoors, the fresh air cleared her head. Calnaloch continued to sparkle around the edges, but she no longer had the desire to fork out her eyeballs—or stick a hot poker in her ears.

Before she could fully exhale a quiet sigh of relief, a warning prodded. Gritting against the urge to scream, spin on the balls of her feet and march home, Ava held her ground, lifted her chin, and rounded the bend.

Ensconced on a bench further ahead, as if posing for the cover of a highbrow men's fashion magazine, #2 reclined, pretending, once again, to inform himself of world events.

Instinct yelled for Ava to take another route out of the park, but more pissed off than afraid, she bit down and marched on.

With every step bringing her closer, she expected him to lower the paper, but #2 didn't budge an inch as she walked by—she was the one who faltered.

Up close, his aura, and its strength, caught her breath. If power had a scent, she imagined his laced with leather, freshly printed money, and the earthiness of fertile earth.

Pushing ahead, she struggled not to steal a peek at where the broadsheet hid his face. Four, six, ten feet widened between them, but as distance grew and his opportunity to speak shrank, silence firmly held.

43

Ava smirked as she exited the park. So, the vampire wanted to play games? Fine. She'd play along. But he underestimated the stubbornness of his opponent.

Iz was serving when Ava pushed through the door of The Cauldron. She paused mid-chat, gaped at Ava, narrowed her gaze, and with a jerk of head, sent her to the back room. Ava ducked through, went straight for the high-backed armchair upholstered like a Gothic throne, and dropped into it. From the main shop floor, she heard Iz bustling the customer out, locking the door, and flipping around the sign. "What the actual fairy-fuckery happened to you?" she yelled.

Ava waited until Iz dived through the curtain before replying, "Fairy-fuckery is actually very apt."

"Are you okay?" Iz leaned over her, taking her chin to tip her head up as Ava gingerly removed her shades. "What did they use?"

"Glitter."

"Those bloody fae! Was it bad?"

"My thirtieth birthday hangover was a day at the spa compared to last night."

Iz hooked the nearest box with her foot and dragged it over to sit. "Tell me," she demanded.

Ava filled her in on the events, including how #2 likely still posed on the bench in Rune Park. "Why go to the trouble of hauling the fae off me yesterday, only to ignore me today? What kind of tactic is that, huh?"

"Sneaky, up-to-no-good vampire tactics," Iz answered. "So" —she slapped her knees before getting to her feet— "we're dealing with fae *and* vampires. Well, first things first. You need a cure."

"Yes, please." Ava rested her weary head against black velvet padding as Iz returned to the shop floor. A snick of metal announced her unlocking the purple cabinet.

"Does Nessa know?" Iz called in.

44

"Not yet."

"Who's behind the fairy stalker, I wonder?"

Out of Iz's sight, Ava shrugged to herself. "I asked, but I didn't get an answer."

"Probably wouldn't have told you, anyway. Stick on the kettle, will you? I have a tea here that will help. Is everything still sparkly?"

"A little." Ava heaved herself out of the throne and slipped through the beaded curtain hiding Iz's kitchenette. A half-eaten croissant lay waiting for Iz's next break. Ava plucked a corner off, realising she hadn't eaten since lunchtime the previous day—unless the blades of grass she'd face-planted on counted.

Iz brewed her a tea that smelled of crusty socks. A light brown scum floated on the surface, and when Ava grimaced, she got a short and snippy, "Drink it" in response. Halfway through the torture, a knock rattled the outer door just as Iz suggested they try to find out to which family the Old One belonged—or ruled.

"Read the sign, folks," Iz muttered.

The caller persisted.

Iz swooped up off the box, and going no farther than the plum curtain, peeked through the gap. "Finn."

"Don't let him in," Ava pleaded, allowing her head to fall back against the padded headrest again. "I don't have the bandwidth for him right now."

"Me neither," Iz agreed, returning to her cardboard seat. "Okay. So, I'll discreetly ask around about your stalkers, and while I do, you need to leave town."

"I do." As much as Ava resented the fact, Calnaloch wasn't safe. If fae and old ones already gathered, she dreaded to think who and what the following weeks would bring.

45

"As soon as you've finished that tea, go home, pack, and get the hell out of here. Number two might have saved your beautiful ass last night, but you're right; he's only doing it to earn grace. Vampires and fae love nothing more than keeping score, and right now, he's a solid one to your big fat zero."

Ava swirled the final inches of sludge around the mug. Despite how foul it tasted, she already felt like herself again.

"Knock that back." Iz stood. "I'll walk you home."

Ava just about held down a gag as the last, gritty mouthful swirled down her throat. Shaking off a shudder, she returned to the kitchenette, rinsed out the mug and flipped it over on the draining board. "Can I steal this croissant? I need to get rid of the taste of crusty socks."

Iz cackled.

Ava crammed the entire half portion into her mouth, and swiping crumbs off her lips, followed Iz out. She'd already put her coat on and had turned off the shop lights. "Iz, stay. You're losing out on business."

"Shut your hole," she replied kindly. "You're way more important."

Iz hadn't even the chance to fully tug the door over before Finn appeared from the Turkish barbershop on the opposite side of the courtyard. He whistled over at them, a loud shrill demanding they not scuttle off.

"Shite," Iz muttered.

"Don't breathe a word," Ava quickly whispered as Finn jogged over.

"Hey, ladies. I knocked earlier," he said.

"You did?" Iz twisted the lock home. "We were out the back, sorry."

"Aves?"

Finn hadn't used her nickname in a while. Tensing against his softly-softly tone, Ava almost wished one of her stalkers would appear and provide a distraction against whatever he felt the need to discuss so damn urgently.

"I heard you were attacked in Rune Park last night."

Iz dropped the keys. They landed with a clatter. As she bent to scoop them up, Ava met her *'what the hell?'* glare with her own *'oh, shit'* one.

Ava forced out an impressively decent fake laugh. "I wouldn't say *attacked*."

"The woman who reported it said otherwise. Are you alright?"

She motioned at herself. "Do I not look alright?"

"Aves, don't play dumb with me." Finn pointed at where Iz clutched the keys. "Can we go inside and talk, please?"

"There's nothing to talk about. I had a run-in with a disgruntled client, is all."

Finn whipped out his notebook from an inside pocket. With a pointed clearing of throat, he flicked through a ream of pages. *"'After the woman struck the man, he knocked her down. I could be mistaken, but it looked like he blew glitter in her face. She fell onto her side, covering her eyes, but he tried to pull her up. Another man appeared. He seemed to come out of nowhere. He pushed the first man, but it didn't just nudge him back. He actually flew through the air and landed almost thirty feet away'."*

"Okay, okay." Ava flapped at Iz to unlock the shop. "Fine, we can talk inside."

Iz drummed her nails against her folded arms as Finn attempted to interrogate Ava. He read through the entire eyewitness account once more, enunciating *'blew glitter in her face'* along with, *'he seemed to come out of nowhere'* and, *'flew through the air'*.

"Um, Finn?" Ava leaned in to wiggle a finger at the accurate report. "It sounds to me, that whoever made this, was snorting their own brand of glitter last night."

Finn gave her a blank look.

"The Devil's Dandruff, you know? A little White Dragon?"

"Jesus, Aves. How do you even know those names?"

Ava pleaded with the ceiling for patience as Finn stashed the notebook in his jacket pocket.

"Look, just tell me what happened—what really happened. The truth, okay?"

"Seriously, Finn?" Iz butted in. "You want the truth?"

Finn glared at Iz.

"Let me tell you how that will go. You'll listen, then tell us we're taking the piss."

"I won't."

"Okay, well, here's what happened. Our girl, Ava, has a magick necklace."

"Iz!" Ava yelped.

Iz flashed a 'shut up,' palm. "It feeds off eclipse energy, and with the next eclipse coming in a few weeks, the assholes of our supernatural community are already gathering for its power. Ava's being stalked by a fairy and an old one. That's a term for ancient vampire, those who—excuse the pun—are so long in the tooth, they can swan around in full daylight without puffing into dust. The fairy attacked her in the park last night and blew glitter in her face, basically rendering her unconscious. The vampire sent the fairy packing and brought Ava home. He's now sunning himself in Rune Park, waiting to bargain his way into getting Ava to work some wickedly powerful magick."

Finn shifted his weight.

Iz held his stare. "Comments? Queries?"

Finn turned to Ava. "Aves, you know you can talk to me. Tell me what happened."

Iz threw up her hands and wheeled away.

Ava offered a one-shoulder shrug. "I read his wife's cards last week, told her a few home truths about the domestic violence issues she's having with him. He confronted me in the park because she left him. I

48

did hit him, he did push me, I fell, and yes, some guy appeared and hauled him off me. I thanked the guy, brushed myself down, and went home. I can't explain superhero strength, glitter bombs or people materialising out of thin air, sorry."

"Why didn't you report it?"

Out of Finn's sight, Iz gesticulated her impatience once more. "I didn't see the need," Ava told him. "It was nothing."

"Aves."

"Finn." Iz pushed by him to unlatch the door. "Ava didn't file a report, so you've no right to be grilling her on what happened. We have somewhere to be, so if you're finished with the interrogation, we'd like to go."

Finn relented, and with a heavy sigh, stepped aside to free up the exit. "Wait," he demanded before Ava could skirt him and flee. "I'll walk you home. If that guy's pissed with you, he won't stop at one attack."

"I don't need you to walk me home." Ava met Iz's look of panic. Finn wouldn't wave goodbye at her complex. He'd insist on coming in, delaying her escape from Calnaloch, and potentially coming face-to-face with her stalkers.

"She's not going home." Iz jumped in. "She has a client waiting. Actually—now that you're here, is there any update on the missing witches? I thought you might like some insider info to pad out your inquiries."

Finn weighed up the offer. As he did, Ava made a point of checking her phone. "I'm running late. I'll catch up with you both later, okay?"

"Call me later," Iz said, doing a fine job of hiding her concern. "Okay?"

"Of course."

"We're not done talking about this," Finn told Ava. "I want your client's name so I can have a word with this guy."

"No can do, detective. Client confidentiality and all that."

49

"Ava."

"Bye, Finn," she called, scurrying out of the shop, sure another commanding whistle would follow. But Iz distracted him with more important business than walking his ex-girlfriend home.

Ava hurried under the arch, and once out on the main street, picked up her pace. Instead of cutting through Rune Park, she took the longer route home, weaving through lanes in the housing estates. She approached her complex from the road leading to the golf club, taking a shortcut through its carpark where she had to hop a low wall to reach the grounds. Once over the wall, she landed on grass, and ahead, as soon as she skirted a bank of hydrangeas, the entrance to her building waited only twenty metres away.

But between it and her, #2 loitered.

Ava staggered to an ungainly stop on the grass. #2 wouldn't allow her to pass without conversation this time. Pushing himself away from the shiny car he'd been leaning against, he walked towards her.

The Old One oozed an imposing vampire aura, one laced with Mediterranean sex god vibes. With his dark hair, chiselled jawline, and aquiline nose, a horny adolescent corner of her brain sniggered, *'Bam chicka wow wow'* as he approached. All the scene missed was a thumping sexy beat—and maybe a wind machine.

Vampire thrall! she yelled at stupid herself. *Don't frickin' stare at him!* "What do you want?" she snapped as he neared, inwardly taken aback by her cutting tone.

"Miss O'Keefe."

At some point between ignoring her in Rune Park and deciding his next move would be to harass her outside her home, #2 had ditched his suit jacket. Slowing six feet away from her, he slid his hands into his tailored pants. The action strained a pale blue shirt across his chest, highlighting how his body matched his magnificent face. Somewhere, a museum held an ancient marble statue in his likeness. It wouldn't have surprised her if Michelangelo had carved it.

"How are you?"

"Fine."

"Allow me to introduce myself."

"Don't bother," Ava cut him off before he could offer a name along with the hand he extended. "I have no interest in who you are. I also don't care to waste any more time with this bullshit, so let me set you straight. The necklace is not for sale, loan, rent, or *taking*. Whatever dire circumstances bring you to this town, I will have no part in them. Your problems are not my business, so leave me alone."

The proffered hand graciously withdrew. "I see."

"Thank you for intervening yesterday. I do appreciate your help, but if you were planning on using the heroics to start a scoreboard, don't bother. I don't owe you anything."

The Old One flicked a smouldering stare beyond her shoulder. "*I* am not keeping score."

"Good."

"*He* is, however."

Ava almost followed his lift of chin, but remembering how stupid it would be to take her eyes off a vampire, listened instead. A rustle, accompanied by a familiar nudge, warned of the return of #1.

"Aeylor. Servant of Manus Larsen," #2 announced quietly.

"Is that supposed to mean something to me?"

"Aeylor is the fae who attacked you last night. He's here on behalf of Manus Larsen, a skilled necromancer."

Manus Larsen. The name rang a bell. A low, mournful, bring-out-your-dead kind of bell.

"Aeylor," he called out. "Be gone. Miss O'Keefe is under my protection."

51

"I most certainly am *not* under your protection!" Ava yelped.

But a puff of woodsy air announced his supersonic departure. Ava didn't turn to where the shrubbery at her rear shook. Instead, she bolted off the grass, onto the path, and across the carpark fronting her building. She bounded up the steps, slammed in the code to the main door, and taking the stairs two at a time, hightailed it to her apartment.

Once inside, she turned every lock and secured every chain, which amounted to one of each.

"Fuck!" Old ones, fae, and now a necromancer? Shit just got too real.

5

Ava hauled her suitcase out of the coat press in the hall, threw it onto her bed, and flung open her wardrobe. She grabbed whatever hung nearest, hurled the bundle into the case, and spun for her dresser, where she scooped out two handfuls of underwear.

A buzz from her pocket alerted her to a call as she dropped half the pile; Nessa. Jamming the phone against her ear with her shoulder, she continued to scoop and dump. "Packing as I speak."

"Ava, pet. What's going on down there?" Nessa referred to any place a mile out from her home as *down there*. "Are you okay?"

"Trouble, that's what's going on. I'll be out of here in fifteen minutes."

"Pet, the line is bad. Can you hear me? Are you okay?"

53

Now was not the time to be dealing with Nessa's shitty signal issues. "Ness? I'm here, I can hear you."

"Ava? What happened? Can you hear me?"

"Nessa?" Ava checked the screen. The call had dropped. She quickly fired off a text, hoping Nessa would read it once she got a signal, then returned to packing, ducking into the bathroom to gather toiletries. When she returned, Iz had messaged.

Iz: 911. Call me!!

Iz answered within two rings. "I just heard the Paladinos are in town."

Ava had to scramble through an already chaotic brain to make the connection. When it came, she snatched the metal curve of her bed end, and slowly turned to plant her ass before her knees could buckle.

She'd missed the glaring message: The damn Paladino insurance flyer, and the Pino Palladino/Nine Inch Nails reference had all but screamed at her. "*The* Paladinos?" she queried all the same, hoping a different, saner, less murderous family of vampires existed. But no such luck.

"The very ones," Iz told her. "Enzo and Cyrus. Maybe Martha too, although Felicienne didn't know for sure."

"*Felicienne* told you?"

"Ava, you need to pack up your shit now. Call Nessa and get your ass up the mountains."

"The Paladinos," she murmured as Iz continued to bark out orders. Which meant #2 was Enzo, the not-so-violent one. Cyrus, the crazed and incredibly violent one, wouldn't have chilled with a newspaper and tea in the Lighthouse, or politely allowed her to walk by in Rune Park.

Powerful supernatural beings had hassled her over the years, but the Paladinos took it to a whole new level. They were *old* old ones, dating back centuries, possibly even millennia. Their Italian origins remained cloaked in mystery, and the lore surrounding their family grew legs with every whispered telling, but exaggerated or not, if she had the Paladinos hankering after her necklace—

"Ava. Are you listening to me?"

"Yes. Yes, I need to . . . um, I need to . . ." Ava sucked in a thin stream of air. "He was here when I got home, waiting in the carpark."

"Oh, shit. Which one? Cyrus?"

"Enzo."

Iz cursed, blaming Finn for Ava having to walk home alone. Ava told her what happened, clutching at where her heart jack hammered as she recounted the information about Manus Larsen.

"Enzo Paladino will be back," Iz warned.

"He will," Ava agreed, twisting to face her bedroom window, fully expecting to see him squatting on the outer sill like a gargoyle.

"Have you enough petrol in the car to get to Nessa's without stopping?"

"Petrol?" She was supposed to remember whether she had a full or empty tank?

"Come on, Ava, focus."

"I think so, yeah. Actually, I do. I filled it last week."

"Okay. Good. Finish packing and get out of there as soon as you can. Don't stop until you reach Nessa's. Even if he follows, he won't be able to cross her boundary line."

"Okay." Ava squeezed her eyes shut, fighting a wave of icy panic. The thought of Manus Larsen had scared her, but the Paladinos were a whole different ballgame—one in which she wanted no part.

"Call me once you're in the car. I'll stay on the line with you the entire way."

"Yeah, okay."

55

"You've got this, Ava. Do you hear me?"

"Yeah. I'm okay. I am," she lied, hearing the tremble in her voice. "I'll—I'll finish packing."

"Okay. Talk to you in a few."

Ava hauled herself up on wobbly legs, forcing herself to focus on the suitcase. She'd packed enough clothes and toiletries. If she needed more, Nessa had plenty. But her most precious tarot deck and grimoire she wouldn't dare to leave behind, or face into whatever came at her without their guidance. "You've got this," she muttered, hunkering to reach the bottom drawer of her dresser. "Just breathe."

With her case hastily zipped, she wheeled it into the kitchen, parked it beside the island, and hurried over to slide open the balcony door. She'd left her favourite boots out to air, and sure they were now free of fae glitter, shoved her feet into them. As she laced them up, she glanced over her plant collection. She could be gone for weeks, and in that time, the herbs she'd spent hours carefully nurturing would die if neglected. Once she got to Nessa's, she'd post Iz her keys and ask her to care for them.

Another task for Iz presented itself when Ava returned to the kitchen; empty the fridge she had filled with fresh food only two days ago. She could quickly bag the groceries and run up and down to the car to load them, but were vegetables and milk worth giving Enzo Paladino or Manus Larsen a chance to pounce?

As Ava mourned the stocked shelves with a, "No," her stomach growled. When had she last eaten? Suddenly light-headed from hunger, a glitter hangover, and panic, she realised it wouldn't be wise to get behind the wheel of her car with such low blood sugars. "You need food," she told herself, grabbing bread, mayonnaise, a fresh block of cheddar and punnet of plum tomatoes.

As Ava flung the snack together, she tried Nessa again. The call went straight to voicemail. "Uh, Ness," she said, craning to see the time on the

56

microwave, "it's just gone four. I'm making a sandwich to go and then I'm out of here. I should be with you by five-thirty, six at the latest. If I'm not, send the cavalry," she half-joked. "I'll call you again from the car."

Chances were, Nessa was already on her way to her nearest neighbour whose location provided a better signal. "She'll call in five minutes," Ava assured herself, twisting to release the phone. But distracted and jumpy, her move to free the phone and catch it while flicking tomato snots off her finger failed.

The phone slipped through loose fingers, hit the counter edge, and with a dramatic bounce, flipped and spun.

Ava lunged, but not fast enough to catch it. However, the device landed safely, screen up, on the rug. "Yes!" she rejoiced. But at that very moment, slippy fingers lost their grip on the knife handle. The steel implement shot free, dropped, and with defiant intent, struck the phone right in the middle of the screen.

"No!" Even before she stooped to snatch it up, the damage was obvious. Despite the screen protector, the glass had shattered into a chaotic mess. "Son of a bitch!" she yelled. "The worst possible timing!"

A light cough jerked her around.

Ava spun so fast, her hip bashed the island's edge. Although pain sharp enough to make her double over burned, shock rendered her rigid and upright.

On her balcony, propped nonchalantly against the railing, stood Enzo Paladino.

Horror stilled everything—except her tongue. "You can't come in!" it blurted.

"I have no intention of asking for an invitation, nor intruding upon your home, Miss O'Keefe," a caramel-smooth reply came with an equally sweet smile.

57

Although free to invade her balcony, magick prevented the vampire from stepping inside her home. But carelessly, Ava had left the doors open to allow a final wash of air into her apartment. Without the protection of double-glazed glass, nothing but air hung between them.

Ava maintained their stare-off while slowly bending rubbery knees. A blind pat located the fallen knife. The old one watched, a slightly bored expression sending one eyebrow higher than its counterpart. Yes, she knew a knife held as much use as a wet dishrag against a vampire, but as she returned to standing with it in her grasp, she felt less vulnerable. "What do you want?"

"You already know."

Yes, she did. And she needed to calm down, because panic wouldn't serve her right now.

He watched, amused, as she sucked in a bracing breath.

One inhale wasn't enough; she needed a thousand to calm her thundering heart, but as the second exhale hissed out, a, "How dare you come to my home!" rushed free with it. Not how she thought she'd transition from pant-crapping anxiety, but anger would serve her better over fear right now.

Courage had somehow crept into her feet, too. With two brave steps, they carried her past the corner of the island. "How dare you threaten me!"

The waiting vampire palmed his chest with a blink of practised innocence. "Have I threatened you?"

"Don't do that" —she jabbed the knife at him— "don't you dare stand there and play word games with me. You're on my damn balcony, so what the hell do you think you're doing? Admiring my plant collection?"

"Well, the rosemary is lush."

Before Ava registered the involuntary thought, or the sudden whine of steel cutting air, he caught the knife she'd flung.

58

A force had overtaken her body, the one that only ever appeared when it found itself under attack. *Back off!* she yelled at it. *Firing knives at Enzo Paladino is not a wise move!*

With a clear of throat, the old one uncrossed his ankles, pushed himself away from the railing, and calmly set the knife down on the glass top of her little bistro table. "I am not here to threaten you. I merely wish to hold a conversation."

"I already told you no."

"You did, but you didn't give *me* a chance to speak. And considering I've had a knife thrown at me, surely I deserve at least five minutes of your time?"

Great. The scoreboard now read a solid two to her persistent big fat zero. "Two and a half minutes," she countered, folding her arms in fear they'd involuntarily launch another kitchen utensil. "Then you leave."

With paralysing panic easing, Ava's awareness expanded beyond the crafty vampire on her balcony. She'd parked her suitcase on the far side of the island. From his position, it sat out of sight, but she needed him gone before he did spot it. If he discovered she was planning on leaving Calnaloch, he'd likely abduct her.

"My niece is missing."

A quick grope through her scrambled brain and Ava recalled his lineage; Martha Paladino, sister to Cyrus, niece to Enzo. Reportedly, one of the saner Paladinos. "If it's a locator spell you need, there are a dozen witches in this town who'd gladly assist you."

He hadn't moved farther than the metal table holding a healthy basil plant. Affecting an amenable pose, he slid one hand into his pocket. "Someone hides Martha far beyond the limits of a simple locator spell."

"Well, then—a hundred witches outside this town who are more advanced than the locals. There's a powerful coven in Cork," she said,

59

hoping to entice him away from Calnaloch—and the province of Leinster. "I'm sure they could help."

"Twenty-nine failed attempts would suggest otherwise."

"I'm sorry for your troubles" —Ava gestured at herself— "but failed attempt number thirty stands right here."

"Miss O'Keefe."

"*Ava*," she snapped. And then immediately regretted it. But hearing *'Miss O'Keefe'* on repeat reminded her of Gregory the Groper, a sleazy colleague with whom she'd once had the misfortune of sharing an office space. When Enzo Paladino said it, his Italian lilt made it sound a hell of a lot sexier.

"Ava." He smiled. "We both know the power you're capable of raising—with and without the necklace. Don't underestimate yourself, or me, please."

"And I'm sure you're also aware that killing me renders the necklace useless."

Distaste scoured his expression. His relaxed pose stiffened. "You will come to no harm by my hand. That, I promise you."

Ava snorted—loudly. "Vampire promises hold as much weight as gnat farts."

Her declaration incited an impatient mutter, one delivered so silently, she barely saw his lips move.

A pained buzz broke the tension; her banjaxed phone. She'd left it beside the chopping board and abandoned sandwich. Fractured light filled the screen, but with the glass crushed, Ava couldn't answer the call. It had to be Nessa, and the longer Ava took to reply, the more her aunt would freak out.

She turned to an intact phone being held out—on his side of the invisible barrier. "May I assist?"

"No, thank you." Did he take her for that much of a fool? "Look." Focusing on ending their cosy chat so she could get the hell out of dodge, Ava firmed her stance. "I can't help you, Mr Paladino."

Something beyond her hearing whipped his focus away. His casual lean against her chair shifted. Suddenly alert, he pressed a finger to his lips, motioning for silence. Sound deciphered, he announced, "You have company."

For once, Ava appreciated Finn's unannounced arrival. "You should go. If Finn sees you here, there'll be trouble."

"It's not Detective Delaney. Manus Larsen has arrived."

"M—Manus Larsen?"

"Yes. Invite me in, Ava."

Fucking vampires and their sneaky tactics! Wise to his game, Ava reached behind for the support of the island. "Nice try," she said, glaring at where he'd moved to stand at the metal strip dividing private from public territory. "But I'm not stupid enough to fall for your lies—or extend a warm welcome to you. *Ever.*"

"This is no ruse," he assured with a biting tone. "Invite me in. You cannot defend yourself against Manus Larsen."

Patience finally drained. Temper scalding, Ava snapped a, "It's time for you to leave, Mr Paladino. Get the hell off my balcony!" and to accentuate her demand, flung the jar of mayonnaise at him.

Of course, he ducked the missile with impressive ease. The jar flew straight over the railing and into the night. A faint rustle announced it landing in shrubbery.

Up to that point, Enzo Paladino had worked the controlled, respectful old one routine to perfection, but darkness carved his features as he blurred to the opening. "Invite me in."

"Not in a million fucking years."

"Ava!"

61

An explosion from beyond the kitchen swallowed Enzo's murderous roar. Splintered wood flew the entire length of Ava's hallway, clattering against the wall outside her open kitchen door. Following close behind, the thud of approaching intruders.

"Invite me in!"

Chaos erupted too fast for Ava to make any sense of what happened next.

Three large men swarmed her kitchen. One of them slammed a wad of cloth over her mouth, filling her throat with a sweet chemical taste. Rough hands wrenched her off her feet, and in a jumbled mess of being hoisted over a shoulder, Enzo Paladino hollering, and a whoosh that sounded like an inferno igniting, she blacked out.

6

G ritty eyes parted to reveal grainy light filtering through cloth.
Pain drilled Ava's brain, but the rest of her body felt strangely numb. A squirm told her why. Someone had tied her to a chair; bound her ankles to the legs, and her wrists to the armrests. She jerked against the restraints, and hoping to knock off whatever covered her face, shook her head. All it did was increase the throbbing in her skull. "Hello?" she croaked, squirming against cruel binds. "Hello? Is anyone there?"

A scuff of soles announced an approach. Ava stilled, bracing for whoever neared. They ripped the covering away, yanking hair with it. The yelp that followed quickly died in her throat.

Stationed on a platform, what she guessed to be an abattoir spread out below her. Cages flanked the outer walls, while suspended from the ceiling, vicious hooks dangled the entire length of the room. Beneath them ran an open channel speckled with lumpy dregs.

Ava bucked against restraints as the figure blocked her view of the horror to hunker by her knees. Stalker #1's angular face dropped into her line of vision. "Now you'll give it."

"You piece of shit!" she hissed. "Go fuck yourself."

Pale eyes narrowed. "Rude." Aeylor fished in his back pocket. A dirty rag appeared. Before she could protest, he shoved it in her mouth.

Ava choked against the sudden intrusion, working her tongue to spit it out, but he had a second strip, and quickly gagged her, wrenching the loose ends together with a vicious yank behind her head.

Assured of her silence, Aeylor stepped aside, and propping his elbows on the railing surrounding the platform, watched her struggle with a blank expression.

After a few minutes, Ava gave up squirming and screaming. The rag had soaked up all her spittle, and every time she tried to swallow, it made her retch. Unable to do anything but listen to angry breaths streaming through her nostrils, she waited.

A groan of aged hinges announced another arrival less than five minutes later.

Aeylor perked up. "Awake," he said to whoever approached.

"Wonderful," they replied.

Pain thumped mercilessly at Ava's skull. This was the part where she was supposed to engage her smarts and cook up a clever escape plan involving a safety pin and a breath mint, but all she wanted to do was pee herself and beg for mercy. Securely gagged, she couldn't croak out a hex, and bound to the chair, her numb fingers lacked the power to flick out magick.

Aeylor stepped aside to allow the newest attendee to move in. Of short stature, but wide and blocky, the man slowly lowered to his hunkers. "Ava O'Keefe," he stated, balancing elbows on his knees as he studied her.

64

Eyes as pale and cold as ice roamed her face. Although albinism gave him an almost angelic look, Ava saw beyond the purity of white skin, eyelashes, brows, and hair. Manus Larsen reeked of death. Depravity oozed from him, creeping around her like a freezing fog.

Manus clicked his fingers. Aeylor stepped in to untie the gag before wrenching out the rag he'd stuffed into her mouth.

"Where is it?" Manus asked.

"Where's what?" she croaked, trying to produce enough spit to form a swallow.

"Let's not play games, witch. Tell me where the necklace is. Aeylor here will fetch it, and then you shall be my guest until the eclipse."

For all their dastardly planning, it never ceased to surprise Ava how the evil overlords neglected to do their research. But she couldn't tell Manus Larsen the necklace currently lassoed her neck and magick prevented him from seeing it. "At—at home."

A slow shake of head sent fine hair swishing around his face. "I'll ask one more time. Answer me truthfully, or the drain under your chair won't remain redundant."

Ava hadn't thought to look down up to that point. A glance revealed how he'd stationed her over a perforated grid. Remnants clung to the metal; stringy pieces of dried flesh that almost made her gag. "It's hidden. Only I can get it."

Manus grabbed her right hand. Bound firmly at the wrist, she had no wriggle room when he clutched her little finger and bent it back at a ninety-degree angle. Pain shot through her delicate tendons. "We searched your apartment. It's not there. Tell me where you've hidden it."

Ava squeezed her eyes shut. Cold sweat layered her skin. This wasn't how she wanted to die, but the magick protecting her legacy prevented the wearer from revealing its presence. Manus could break all ten of her fingers, and whatever else he fancied. But he'd never get the answer.

65

Impatience won. With a jerk, he snapped her little finger.

Ava screamed as the fragile bone cracked.

He grasped her ring finger next, and before she could suck in a breath, broke it, too.

"Enzo Paladino!" she gasped. "I gave it to Enzo Paladino!"

"Vampír," Aeylor snarled with disgust in his native Irish tongue.

"When?" Manus demanded, circling her middle and index fingers next.

"Just—just before—you came." Darkness already feathered the edges of her vision. Bile climbed up Ava's throat as she struggled to swallow. She'd lie rings around herself until her heart stopped beating. Powerless against the magick safeguarding the necklace, if Manus persisted, she'd likely end up naming Iz and Nessa too. "At my—my apartment."

"Where is that son of a bitch?" Manus rounded on Aeylor.

Aeylor spread his hands in ignorance, but added, "Will find."

"The necklace is no good to him without you," Manus reminded her. "So you'll stay here until we find him and it. And in the meantime." The pale agent of death reached for his rear waistband. He withdrew a blade housed in a curved ivory handle. Ava whimpered when he rested the cold tip against her cheek. "He'll need an incentive to co-operate."

"*He* is already here."

Aeylor and Manus wheeled to where Enzo Paladino's voice echoed from the rear of the abattoir. Ava also strained to find him, but with Manus blocking her view, sweat stinging her eyes, and pain making everything spin, her rescuer remained out of sight.

Aeylor leapt off the platform. As he shot down the aisle, Manus flipped the knife, quickly severing the binds on her wrists. "Find him!" he roared at his fae slave, using the sliced rope to tie her hands together with a cruel knot. He cut her ankles free next, and fisting a handful of her hair, hauled her to her feet. With an angered grunt, he kicked the chair

66

aside, reached up, and, yanking her bound hands over her head, secured her to the hook hanging from the roof.

Strung up like a heifer, toes barely skimming the grate, Ava screamed. She lashed out to kick Manus, but he grabbed the filthy cloth and rammed it into her mouth again.

Darting around her, he pressed the knife to her jugular, and roared, "Paladino, I'll gut your witch like a pig!"

The icy sting of parting skin ramped Ava's panic up to maximum level. Every twist sent pain spearing up her arms, but with adrenaline pumping, it bolstered her panic to break free.

Manus snared a chunk of her hair again. "Hold still, you stupid bitch!"

Aeylor reappeared from the gloomy shadows—but in full flight. Layers of loose clothing hanging off his thin frame flapped like broken wings as he descended from ceiling to ground. He landed with a sickening crunch, face down in the channel.

"Paladino!" Manus seethed. "I'll kill her. I will!"

Heat washed Ava's neck as the blade bit deeper. What a shitty way to die; trussed up like a Sunday roast, bleeding out and squealing. If she survived, she'd never eat meat again.

A blast of air, followed by a pained grunt, and she abruptly swung alone.

From her rear, a deafening clang announced a body slamming into a cage wall.

Ava tugged harder at the rope binding her wrists, ignoring how it tore her skin. Blood accelerated down her neck, quickly changing her shirt a warning shade of scarlet. *Home!* every fibre of her being pleaded. *Get out of here!*

But diving blood pressure swarmed her brain, stealing strength, and pinching out her vision. As bone-tiredness claimed her, Ava's chin sank to meet her chest. She fought against it with a pitiful cry and final pathetic squirm, aware her life-force dripped through the grate below her feet. *I don't want to die!*

Enzo Paladino roared her name.

The stinking abattoir fluttered into blackness.

7

Enzo Paladino stared into the night, arms folded, nails digging into skin, jaw locked. Although he faced where the land beyond the house swept down to the shoreline, the wild view didn't register. The heartbeat he'd latched onto since arriving at the abattoir continued to beat, but until green eyes fluttered open and the witch returned to denying him help, he feared it would slow to a stop. If it did, decades would slide by before he found the necklace's new host.

Hope—and his plans—would be crushed by then.

Despite showering and changing into fresh clothes, the scent of her blood continued to taunt. He'd scrubbed his skin, turning it raw in places, yet the perfume lingered, burning his throat and making his gums prickle. When he'd untied her limp form from the meat hook in the abattoir and carried her out to his car, he'd had to pierce his own tongue to prevent it from trailing up her neck to feast. Witch blood held the power to drive a vampire insane, and his sanity certainly neared complete disintegration as her scent filled his nostrils all the way to the hospital.

In an attempt to stave off the primal urge, Enzo had fed while doctors tended to the witch—and twice since returning home. But even now, from across the landing, her witch blood called to him; a maddening, sensuous hum. Closing his eyes, he grunted against the craving.

A chime from his inside jacket pocket loosened his rigid stance. Grateful for the interruption, he whipped it out, but gratitude drained when he saw the name. "Waylen Kane." He sighed.

Kane: Progress?

Some

Kane: Time is against us.

"I am aware," Enzo muttered as he typed.

The matter is in hand.

A click of latch announced a door opening. Enzo slid his phone away, crossing the room to step out into the landing. The nurse he'd compelled to attend from the hospital reported the patient coming round. "Wait here," he told her.

Hooked up to a drip, a thick wad of gauze covering her neck, and the two fingers of her right hand splinted, the witch had seen better days.

Enzo stood a safe distance away from the end of the bed as she slowly roused herself awake. Confusion rendered her mute while she blinked at the strange surroundings, but when her sweeping gaze reached him, she jerked to sit upright. A yelp sent her sinking into the pillows again.

70

"You should lie still," he told her.

"Where the hell am I?"

"My home."

"What is this?" She tried to sit up once more, but only made it halfway as she motioned at the drip. "Are you drugging me?"

"Please." Enzo came to her side, palming where she already scrambled to peel away the sticky bandage holding the cannula in place. "Hydration. Nothing more. The hospital gave you pain relief earlier, and blood."

"Blood?" Remembrance hit. Her good hand flew to her neck. "Manus—the abattoir. He—I didn't die? I'm still alive?"

"Very much alive." All things considered, he'd expected a more violent reaction. So far, so good. "Shall I fill in the blanks?"

Scanning the room once more, wariness clouded her expression. "Please do."

Enzo recalled the events of the abattoir, and how he'd brought her to the hospital after. He detailed her injuries, the treatment she'd received, how he'd compelled a nurse and medical equipment to ensure safe recuperation in his home instead of a public hospital, informed her of her expected full recovery, and the estimated time it would take. "You received pain relief in the hospital, but I guessed you'd rather administer subsequent doses yourself."

The witch muttered agreement, but it turned into a sudden gasp. "You didn't—you didn't feed me your blood, did you?"

"I did not." His blood in her system would mutate her witch powers. If he'd been any later reaching the abattoir, the situation could have called for such drastic action, but thankfully, he'd wrenched her out of Manus Larsen's filthy hands in time. "I took the liberty of bringing your suitcase here," he said, gesturing to where he'd placed it beside the wardrobe. "You were planning on leaving town?" He knew exactly to where; her aunt, Nessa O'Keefe, and her fortress of a home in the

71

Wicklow Mountains. Once safely over the impenetrable boundary line, the witch would have been completely out of his grasp.

A familiar scowl appeared. "How did you get inside my home?"

"I didn't. I had one of my men fetch the case for you. They're repairing the fire damage as we speak, and replacing your front door."

"Fire damage?" Another wince as she shifted position.

"Larsen threw a fireball at me. I'm afraid it scorched several plants, along with a section of your kitchen."

Her already pallid skin paled further, accentuating the freckles dusting her nose and cheeks. As her lips formed a silent 'what?', he inwardly tensed against the odour of stale blood. Despite his request for the hospital to clean her, residue matted the light brown hair tangled around her neck. He casually clasped his hands behind his back, driving nails into his flesh to overwhelm the thirst scalding his throat.

"Is it bad? Is my apartment ruined?"

"No. It's nothing that can't be repaired."

With a heavy sigh, she sank into the pillows. "Could this day get any shittier?"

For him, it only improved. Not only had he cut Manus Larsen out of the game, but the witch was now safely bound within his home and under his protection. But he kept the gratitude to himself as she murmured something that sounded like, 'ten-nil'. "Excuse me?"

"Nothing."

"Miss O'Keefe, I need to apologise."

Curious eyes narrowed at where he continued to stand at the foot of the bed. "For what?"

"When I confronted Aeylor outside your complex, it goaded Larsen into retaliating. I would not have come to your home had I known it would entice him there."

"Chances are he would have come at some stage. And if you hadn't arrived," she said quietly, diverting her eyes as she fiddled with the splint, "things might have turned out a lot different."

Enzo had known exactly how enraged Larsen would become once Aeylor told him Enzo Paladino had claimed the witch under his protection. He'd been wise to bet on the necromancer coming for her. But he hadn't foreseen the violence Larsen would inflict. Any other witch would have bound Enzo with curses and hexes for his meddling, but over the last few weeks, he'd discovered Ava O'Keefe an admirably centred woman. He motioned to where she lay. "I shall leave you to rest now."

"Wait."

Enzo stalled.

"Is he . . .is Manus . . ?"

"Larsen is no longer a problem."

She didn't reward him with a sigh of relief. "You killed him?"

"It was you or he. Now, please," he said, not wishing to hold a debate about the morals of ending a lecherous necromancer, "rest."

"Thanks," she said, wincing as she kicked off the bedcovers, "but I'd rather go home."

"That's not possible, I'm afraid."

The witch ignored him, of course, her focus on ensuring she didn't catch the tube snaking down from the drip bag as she shuffled to the edge of the mattress. But as the hospital had warned, it would take a day or more for her to recover.

Enzo caught her before buckling legs crumpled her to the floor. "You must rest. Your body needs to heal."

A bony elbow jabbed his ribs. "I don't want to be here."

"Which I appreciate. But until your strength has returned, my conscience cannot agree to you refusing care."

73

"Your *conscience*," she snorted, slapping him away as he tried to steer her towards the pillows. "Don't take me for an idiot. And get your hands off me."

"Very well." Enzo backed away, flexing the fingers that had inadvertently neared her pendant.

He'd tested her mugwort charm in the hospital, tempted to learn of its strength, but she'd bound the glass vial with a magick that prevented his touch by delivering a wicked scorch. He should have ignored reason and heeded the urge to compel her the night he'd pulled the fae off her. It would have saved him a lot of trouble. "Please rest."

"As soon as I can, I'm leaving here. Understand?"

Once she roused the strength to explore, the witch would realise leaving wasn't an option. Enzo predicted a violent retaliation to the discovery, but that was a problem for tomorrow. "I understand."

"As soon as I can!"

Enzo left the room, not missing her mutter of, "Fucking vampires". With a gesture to the waiting nurse, he took her aside, out of the witch's earshot. "Sedate her," he said, hooking the woman into his intent stare.

"Sedate her," she replied with a slow blink.

"Tell her it's an antibiotic to counteract an infection in her neck wound."

"An antibiotic."

Enzo turned for the stairs, but at the last second, added, "And watch over her for the night. Notify me if her condition changes."

"Yes."

74

Ava gingerly raised her right arm, wincing against the sight of her splinted, aching fingers. Where Manus cut her neck also complained; a tightness that didn't respond well to movement. It stung as she carefully reached up to pat where throbbing pulsed above her left ear. A grape-sized swelling protested against the light touch.

Despite her injuries, the bigger picture glowed with positivity. She could have been a lot worse. Broken bones and swollen skull aside, she'd been lucky.

Enzo Paladino raced ahead on the scoreboard. He'd racked up a solid ten points to her obstinate zero, but that didn't mean she'd use her necklace for his benefit. No, sir. If he thought all his good deeds were about to be repaid with super-duper magick, he was about to be disappointed.

Something about his apology didn't sit right with her. She hadn't considered how manipulating Aeylor could have provoked Manus into abducting her, but knowing how cunning vampires were, she wouldn't disregard the suspicion Enzo Paladino had played a dangerous move. If she learned for sure that he'd purposely dangled her as bait, she'd hex him with a century of plague and pestilence.

"Fucking vampires," she muttered, clasping her mugwort charm. Comforted by its presence, it had surprised her to find it intact. Between the manhandling she'd suffered, and everything that had happened since, she'd expected it to be gone. Had Enzo tried to remove it? If it were her in his shoes, she would certainly have tried to yank it off. Hopefully, it had scorched him good and proper.

Somewhat assured he didn't plan to harm her just yet, Ava considered her precarious position. She had no phone, no idea where in the world

75

he'd whisked her to, and right now, possessed a body capable of nothing more than laying horizontal. Attempting to escape was pointless; she doubted she'd even make it to the door of the fanciest bedroom she'd ever clapped eyes on.

But just because a self-rescue lay beyond her capabilities, it didn't mean a failure.

Iz and Nessa would know something had gone spectacularly wrong by now. They'd probably already found her with a locator spell. At any moment, the cavalry would charge in and haul her out of the Paladino lair. In a few hours, she'd be snug in Nessa's house, laughing at Enzo Paladino's loss as she toasted her freedom with a crisp Pinot Grigio and a greasy pizza.

The door to the room opened, but neither Nessa nor Iz appeared. A navy-uniformed nurse entered, crossing straight to a desk at the far side, where she busied herself with the medical items arranged across its surface.

"Hi," Ava said, straining to see what had her busy—hopefully preparation to unhook her from the drip. Enzo said he'd compelled the woman here. Had he also ordered her to remain mute?

Apparently not.

"Hello," she replied, throwing a quick smile over her shoulder.

"I'm Ava."

"I'm Geraldine. How are you feeling?"

When she turned to approach, Ava stiffened against the syringe in her hand. "What's that for?" she queried, eyeing the needle with sudden dread.

"It's an antibiotic. There's a risk of infection from your neck wound." Noting her cowering, Geraldine smiled again. "It goes in here," she said, indicating the drip.

76

"Oh." Ava exhaled with relief as Geraldine administered the dose through the bag's injection port, and not one of her veins. She had a serious needle phobia. "How much longer do I need this?"

"I'll remove it in an hour. Do you need to use the bathroom?"

"No," she lied. It would be easier to move about once free of the drip stand, and until then, her bladder could wait.

"Now. All done." Geraldine finished her business and returned to the desk, where she deposited the empty syringe in a metal dish. "How's your pain?"

"Manageable."

"Good. Well, all you can do for now is rest. I'll be outside if you need anything. Just shout."

"Can you not stay? It would be nice to have company."

"I must wait outside."

Judging by the robotic tone of Geraldine's *I must wait outside*', Ava guessed their host had ordered it. She watched as she left the room, and once alone, settled against the bank of plump pillows. Vampires. They *never* missed an opportunity to manipulate.

Silence clung as she stared at the unfamiliar space. Maybe she was wrong to assume Iz and Nessa were on their way. Considerable time had passed between Manus abducting her and now. If they hadn't located her, it meant she needed to work a little communication magick of her own.

From the huge bed, Ava hunted for items representing the element of air, but grew quickly distracted by Enzo Paladino's fancy place. With hints of soft ocean blues, the room embodied a colonial vibe with its vaulted ceiling, dark wood floor, and pale fabrics.

To her left, a handsome fireplace with a marble surround graced the wall. Opposite her, judging by the volume and length of fabric, cream drapes hid what she guessed to be an enormous window. The desk Geral-

77

dine had commandeered for her medical supplies sat beneath it, and to its right, a bank of built-in wardrobes in warm wood. Two impressive monstera plants, joined by a lush palm, added a healthy splash of green to the space. Along with the elaborately framed artwork, mirrors, and modest collection of knickknacks—which probably cost more than her apartment—it rivalled any five-star hotel.

Tiredness tugged. Ava's gaze drifted up to the vaulted ceiling, eyes growing heavy as she mentally scrolled through her repertoire of communication spells. With zero supplies to hand, she'd have to be creative. She also needed to learn her location, because depending on who within the cavalry was geographically closer, it would be more efficient to aim her intent specifically.

The day's events caught up with her. Ava cupped her charm and closed her eyes. A quick snooze, and then she'd find her way out of Paladino Palace. "Sleep," she murmured. "Then home."

8

The sharp need to pee woke Ava. She blinked to awareness to find the drip and Geraldine gone. All her medical paraphernalia had vanished with her.

Stiff and disobliging limbs complained as she sat up in the bed. Immediately checking for her charm, she found it tangled in her hair. "Okay," she said, settling it in place before throwing off the covers. "Take two."

This time, the room didn't dip or her vision blacken as she carefully rose to standing. Her fingers hurt and her neck itched, but the thumping pain in her head had ceased. Where one of Manus's brutes had hoisted her over a shoulder, her ribs ached, but beyond those minor aches and pains, she believed herself fit enough to get the hell out of Paladino Palace. "But first, the loo."

The ensuite prompted a low whistle of awe. Claw tub bath? Check. Walk-in shower with more dials and knobs than a submarine? Check. Double sinks with marble vanity? Check, check.

79

Once she'd dealt with her aching bladder, Ava stood at the sinks, baulking at her reflection.

Where Manus had cut her neck, blood left a chunk of her hair stained and crusty. In dire need of a brush, strands stuck out at all angles. Twin bruises formed a purple eight on her forehead, while a scratch marred her right cheek. All in all, she resembled someone dragged through a ditch backwards. "Or hung like a pig in a slaughterhouse," she muttered, leaning in to examine the gauze over her wound. Carefully peeling it away, the tug to the laceration beneath roused a hiss. It wouldn't do to get the wound wet, but the need to wash away the prickle of sticky hair—and what she could of yesterday's trauma—had her ready to climb out of her own skin.

Returning to the bedroom, Ava dropped to her knees before her suitcase. "Am I happy to see you," she whispered, flipping it onto its side to unzip it. The idea of strange people marching all over her apartment at Enzo Paladino's bidding continued to anger her, but right now, for sanity's sake, she would park her annoyance and focus on bathroom tactics instead.

Aware of how both her neck wound and finger splints needed to stay dry, she reckoned a bath offered the most sensible solution. Loaded up with shampoo, body lotion, and a fresh set of clothes, she returned to the bathroom and filled the deep tub to the brim, hoping she drained every drop of hot water from the palace tank. Although, knowing vampires, they probably preferred ice-cold showers.

A long soak and a good scrub later, the water had turned a disgusting shade of rust. Ava grimaced as it swirled down the drain, then rinsed her hair under the tap to wash away any lingering residue.

All the awkward reaching and twisting left her exhausted, but the effort was worth it. Clean, dressed in fresh clothes, and ready to find

80

a way home, she began with the voluminous drapes. A tug of cord whooshed them apart—and sucked the air out of her lungs.

"Fuck. No," she whispered when she could catch her breath again. "No, no, no!"

Water—everywhere. Lots and lots of water.

Paladino Palace, according to the view, nestled on an island out in the goddamn middle of the sea. But what sea? Or was it an ocean sparkling under bright sunshine? The Atlantic Ocean? The Pacific? The Indian? "This is not good."

Ava backed away from the watery scene, heart hammering. Yes, she only had one viewpoint from this giant single window, yet with how the water reached the horizon in every direction, she didn't think the other palace windows would reveal the property somehow edged a bustling town—or any location with an efficient transport system that could whisk her home to Calnaloch.

A yank swung the door open to reveal a generous u-shaped landing outside her room. Decorated just as plushly as her bedroom, the polished woods, rich rugs, and antique furniture screamed old money; the kind the Paladino Clan had undoubtedly amassed over centuries. Ava stepped out, noting a room left of hers, and opposite it, a door set into a wall displaying an enormous oil painting of a city in ruins. "Cheerful," she muttered at the dismal scene. "Sodom or Gomorrah?"

Guessing the same layout appeared on the other leg of the U, she swung her attention to where a wide, curving staircase invited her to the level below. As she tiptoed towards it, not a sound came from the depths of Paladino Palace. Vamps had bionic hearing, so if Enzo Paladino was home, surely he'd heard running water and her gasp of horror when she'd gaped at the view?

Maybe his absence was an offer of space. Or maybe he'd simply dumped her here and absconded.

Slowly descending, Ava's palm grew slicker on the banister with every step. What if he had vamoosed? *No*, she tried to calm herself while peering over the railing at the gleaming floor below. He wouldn't go to the trouble of saving her from Manus Larsen, bring her to the hospital, and then care for her in his home, only to leave her alone. He needed her; he wouldn't abandon her. "Definitely not," she whispered, just to break the heavy silence.

But *where* had he brought her? She could be anywhere in the world. For all she knew, he'd trapped her on the coast of some tiny private island tens of thousands of miles from Ireland. No wonder Iz and Nessa hadn't shown up.

Her sole met the tiled hall floor. Utter silence swamped the house. Not even a tweet of birdsong, or sigh of wind—which there should be this close to the sea.

Solid double entrance doors waited across the hall. Void of panes, they offered no hint of what lay beyond. Above, a stunning iron and glass dome arched out of the ceiling, but it displayed a clear sky that could hang over any corner of the globe.

Ava crossed towards the main entrance. The heavy handle in the towering blond wood doors turned, but the latch didn't engage. "Damn you." He'd locked her in.

Seven doors waited in the hallway. She chose the one on her right to begin. When she nudged it open, a Dickens scene unfolded before her. Dark, but not gloomy, all four walls held floor-to-ceiling shelves stuffed to the brim with books. The upright between each section held a candle safely housed in a glass bulb. Almost two dozen tapers lit the space, their flutters throwing dancing light over the book spines. Two ox-blood leather couches faced each other in the centre of the floor, divided by a mahogany coffee table sitting on a rug woven in shades of burgundy and gold. With all walls occupied by shelves, no art graced the room, but free surfaces displayed ornaments, clocks, and even more dusty books.

Ava snapped her mouth shut. Although tempted to have a good root around, she turned to where the front-facing window waited.

A brass claw held teak shutters in place. She unhooked it, wincing against a creak of protest as she eased them open, but she only needed to part them a few feet to get the answer to her question.

Yes; an island.

Enzo Paladino had squirrelled her away on a goddamn island.

"Mr Paladino!" she yelled, flinging the shutters together before wheeling away. "Mr Paladino! A word, please!"

If he heard, he ignored her yell. Ava strode out into the hall, clamped her hips, and stared around. "Where are you? And where the hell am I? Is this your idea of a joke? We're out in the middle of nowhere!!"

Nothing.

"Mr Paladino! Stop being an ass. I want out of here, now!"

Silence stoked her rage all the higher as she pictured him hanging upside down from the attic rafters by his toes, smirking at her annoyance. Yesterday, when she'd said she wanted to leave, he'd replied, *'That's not possible.'* Now she knew why. The smug bastard.

One by one, Ava burst into each room, leaving doors swinging in her wake as she hunted her elusive abductor.

He lived in a bona fide palace. After marching into what she could only guess to be a third reception room, she scoffed at another display of fine antique furniture. "This is ridiculous, do you hear me? Who lives like this? What in the hell could you want with all this space? And furniture?"

Only one door remained, but as she strode towards it, the click of a latch from somewhere above skidded her to a halt. Ava dashed to the foot of the stairs. "Are you up there?"

83

No reply.

"Mr Paladino. Are you up there? Stop being a monumental ass! You need to explain what I'm doing here!"

But she already knew. Adjusting her demands, she took the steps two at a time.

"Fifteen minutes ago you had a ten percent chance of me helping you, but now it's a big fat zero. You cannot abduct me and expect me to comply with your wishes!" she yelled.

Tender ribs protested to the burst of action with a vicious stab. Ava grasped her side and halted halfway up the Gone With the Wind staircase. The sudden motion hadn't done her head any favours either. "Shit." Sinking onto one of the wide steps, she clutched the hot ache. "Are you up there? Can you please come down and talk to me?"

Frustration, throbbing pain, and mounting fright stung her eyes. Inhaling against the threatening tears, Ava warned herself to steel her resolve. This wasn't the time to get emotional. Calm reasoning would help her figure out a way home, not tears and ranting.

Think, Ava, she ordered herself, resting her head against the railing spindles. Although she wasn't well enough to try anything too elaborate, she did have the strength to work simple magick. All she needed was a map. The Dickens library surely held an atlas amongst its collection.

With the pain in her side easing, Ava slowly returned to standing. Her bolt up the stairs had set her vision spinning, and still feeling woozy, she kept a firm grip on the banister to make her way down. "Asshole. Conniving, mercenary, vampire *asshole*."

"Good morning."

The unexpected greeting stumbled her feet. In the same moment Ava spun to gape up at where Enzo had materialised, she missed the waiting step and pitched forward. Before she could even gasp against the

84

sensation of falling, Ava found herself at the foot of the staircase, safely cradled in her abductor's arms.

Eleven-nil. Goddamn him.

"Put me down!"

With the exact smirk she'd pictured him wearing from his rafter perch, the old one carefully lowered her feet to the floor.

"Where am I?" she demanded, widening the space between them as she straightened her clothes.

"My home."

"Where? *Where* is your home? Because all I can see out there is water! You've taken me to the middle of nowhere. I want to leave. Now."

As if abducting witches featured daily in his life, Enzo Paladino smiled, gestured towards the only door off the hallway not swinging on its hinges, and asked, "Are you hungry?"

"No!" She almost stamped her foot. "What in the hell is wrong with you?" Ava darted to the front door and jiggled the useless handle. "Open this door. I'm leaving."

"The door is open."

"No, it is not." Another violent rattle of the handle proved his lie.

"Allow me," he said, and gesturing she step aside, he approached. With another smug smile, the owner of Paladino Palace took hold of the handle, turned it, and swung open the grand door.

The first thing that struck Ava was the silence.

Steps led down from the entrance to a sizeable circular driveway, complete with a trickling stone fountain occupied by bathing birds. Flanking the gravelled circle, a bank of ash and birch trees swayed gaily in the breeze. Overhead, gulls surfed the currents, hovering effortlessly in place.

But the view was silent.

No wind whispering through leaves, no roar of the surrounding ocean, no melodic tinkle of water or chirping of happy birds. And where fresh sea air should have washed over her face and stirred her hair? Nothing. As if she stood behind a thick wall of glass, none of the outside breached the threshold of Paladino Palace.

"I'm trapped," she realised aloud. He'd locked her inside with magick—shelter wards, to be exact.

"You're safely contained in my home," he corrected.

"You *kidnapped* me."

"I *rescued* you."

"I want to leave."

"I need you to stay."

"Let me *go*."

"You should eat." The door slammed shut, cutting off the silent view. "Come."

"No." Ava folded her arms as he walked away. "I want to go home."

With his back to her, Enzo Paladino came to a stop, tipped his face towards the elaborate plasterwork ceiling, and slid his hands into the pockets of his charcoal pants. Today, he wore just a shirt, no tie or jacket. Casual Friday? Maybe he had plans for a takeaway and tequila later.

Despite her silent scoffing, Ava braced. She had to remember who and what stood across from her, clearly struggling to keep a lid on his temper. An old one had abducted her. He'd already killed Manus Larsen—without a flicker of remorse—so what would one more death mean? Sociopaths like him didn't put all their eggs in one basket. Right now, she may be the most convenient way to fix whatever problem he had, but she wasn't the only solution. If she pissed him off, he'd likely dump her in whatever strange city lay beyond the island and leave her to fend for herself.

He'd also been conniving enough to secure her inside his home with shelter wards, meaning not only could she not get out, but neither could

86

magick get in—specifically the kind of magick that Nessa and Iz would work to locate her.

Shit. The cavalry would not be breaking down the door anytime soon. Pizza was definitely off the menu for later.

"Miss O'Keefe." Enzo turned to face her. His serious tone matched the dark scowl bunching his generous eyebrows together, brows that crowded towards velvety brown eyes. "Manus Larsen was only one of many who covets your necklace. Yesterday, he demonstrated his capabilities. Those who already gather shall do the same—and worse. Yes, I want your help, and yes, I'm hoping you will freely give it, but do not mistake this" —he gestured at their plush surroundings and the doorway warded to keep her indoors— "as cruelty, nor me as a patient man. In my home, you will be cared for and protected. When our time is done, I shall return you to your home—with a generous settlement for the inconvenience caused. Until then, this is where you shall stay. Do you understand?"

"What I understand is that you've abducted me and plan to force me to do magick for you."

"I'm hoping you'll revise your thoughts on that once we've spoken."

"I'll revise my thoughts when you let me go."

"You cannot leave. The sooner you accept the fact, the easier it will be. For both of us."

Molars grinding, Ava pleaded to the same ceiling for patience. It appeared to work.

The minute's pause gave her an idea; she needed to come at Enzo Paladino from a different angle. He'd been clever enough to erect shelter wards which meant he knew more about witchcraft than the average, plus, someone had placed the wards for him, so he clearly had witches or warlocks on his payroll.

"People need to know I'm here. If word gets out a vampire has abducted a witch, there'll be hell to pay."

87

"I agree. I will notify your friend and aunt. But in exchange, you shall cease insisting I *abducted* you. The fact is, I removed you from a potentially life-threatening situation, and am now gracefully allowing you to recuperate in my home."

Vampires and their damned word play. "Fine. But I want to speak to Iz. She won't accept a message. She'll need to hear my voice."

He nodded. "I shall arrange it. Now, please. You must eat."

"Wait." Ava winced at her bravery. Her *'non-abductor'* visibly clenched. "Just one more question. Where am I?"

"I'll show you." Leading the way, he brought her around the staircase and entered the only door she hadn't flung open. A stunning kitchen spread out before her, all dark woods, duck egg blue walls, and cream granite. French doors showed off another impressive view, framing a garden lush with spring greenery. He gestured she follow him to the edge of the left pane. "Stand here," he ordered.

Ava complied, noting the wall of foliage blocking whatever view he wished her to see. But he instructed her to peer through a specific gap between the rhododendron and hydrangea bushes. As she angled herself into position, leaves gave way to land in the distance—not a whole lot from her viewpoint—but enough to recognise a church spire.

"Oh."

He hadn't shipped her to the other side of the globe.

Although needle-thin, the spire's welcome familiarity had her scanning right where she quickly picked out recognisable boxy shapes following a curve of land. "The Hag's Nose," she whispered, and then, "We're—this is Dunfarr? I'm on the island? This is your home?"

"Does that soothe your worry?"

Calnaloch lay across the water. The old one had taken her less than a mile off the coast. Ava O'Keefe, nil. Enzo Paladino, twelve.

No wonder Nessa and Iz hadn't located her. This close to home, a locator spell would have her lit up like a beacon in seconds. Whoever had cast the shelter wards had ensured her well and truly cloaked.

With Calnaloch blurring, Ava swallowed. She had to accept she wasn't leaving his house—not just yet, anyway. Obviously, Enzo Paladino hadn't stalked her on a whim. He'd carefully planned her abduction and confinement. She just needed to out-plan him.

Discreetly swiping tears, Ava glanced to where the man in question bustled around the kitchen. She'd play along for now. He hadn't threatened or hurt her, and she didn't think he would, but vampires were vampires, and she'd be a fool to hand him even an ounce of trust.

When she fully turned away from the comfort of a distant Calnaloch, he had unloaded the fridge. An array of food lined the ivory granite counter; bread, cheeses, eggs, meat—all for human consumption.

The bastard had never doubted he'd get her in his home.

"Why do you have all this? You don't eat," she queried innocently.

An impatient look flicked her way. "We occasionally entertain human guests."

"We. That's you and Cyrus, right?" Cyrus The Madman. Ava had heard gruesome stories of his wickedness. She wondered if he was in the house now, and without thinking, glanced up at the ceiling.

"He's not here presently. But he shall be in a few days—once I know you've settled. What are you hungry for?"

The sliced meats he'd uncovered made her stomach turn. The thought of eating something that had died in an abattoir had flashbacks assaulting her senses.

"Soup," he said, as if reading her thoughts. "That would be best. Tomato and basil?"

Ava nodded, unsure of what to do with the sight of an old one folding up the sleeves of his spotless white shirt, retrieving a copper saucepan from an overhead rack, plonking it on the stovetop, and then rooting out a carton of soup from the fridge. He gave it a thorough shake before opening.

"You cook?"

He poured the contents into the saucepan. "Heating is not cooking. Sit, please."

A large table sat to one side of the glass doors. Flanked by built-in cushioned benches, the open sides offered free-standing chairs. Ava perched on the bench offering her a clear view of the kitchen, and the vampire preparing her meal. "How long have you owned this house?"

"A while now."

Enzo stirred the pot with concentration. A muscle ticked in his jaw as he ground his teeth. Did he hold back a comment or question? Or did the smell of human food make him want to barf?

Where folded shirt sleeves revealed bare forearms, Ava noted his sallow skin dusted with dark hair. Sinew flexed as he tended to the soup, dragging her eyes to a well-proportioned hand with clean, trim nails.

"Is it just us here? You said you have people working for you. Are they staying in the house, too?"

"We're alone for now. When my nephew returns, they'll come with him."

To keep Cyrus in check? To prevent him from going on a murder spree in Calnaloch? "Do they know I'm here?"

"Yes."

So what was to stop Cyrus from blabbing? Or selling her off to the highest bidder?

"Ava," he said, halting her panicked thoughts without taking his eyes off the soup. "You are under my protection. Under my roof, I promise your safety."

Under my roof. A subtle way of warning she'd be a sitting duck if she found a way to breach his wards. And who had crafted those wards for him? It took experience to bind an entire home, and the added layer that prevented her from hearing or feeling anything beyond the threshold? Well, that demanded a specific power. "Felicienne," she realised aloud. *That* was how she knew the Paladinos were in town.

Enzo glanced over. Was that a flicker of regret?

"Does she know I'm here?"

"No."

"Are you sure? Because Felicienne wants my eclipse magick more than you do. If she gets wind you've squirrelled me away in this house, she'll rip down those shelter wards before you can blink."

Steam rose from the pot. "So you'd rather assist me than her?"

Ava silently corrected her earlier oath. Okay, so, yes; she'd help Enzo Paladino quicker than she would that spiteful mare Felicienne Alarie, but *he* didn't need to know that. "I'd rather not assist anyone," she told him truthfully. "I prefer to stay out of these damned situations. There's never anything but trouble, and someone always ends up hurt."

"I'll do my best to ensure there's no trouble."

"Right," she said with a snort of disbelief. Vampires, witches, eclipse magick? They already brewed disaster. "So, when are you going to tell me what it is you want?"

"Soon."

Enzo left the soup to retrieve a bowl from a cupboard. He placed it on the side and busied himself with returning the food to the fridge. "Would you like bread?"

"Yes, please."

"Butter?"

"Thank you."

91

So civil. *Yes, please. Thank you. How do you do? How may I assist? Isn't the weather delightful?* Ava slumped against the padded backrest. She'd landed in a fucked up situation and it had her head thumping. "How soon can I talk to Iz?"

"Once you've eaten."

"And then what?"

"And then" —he almost smiled— "we begin."

9

Enzo left her alone to eat. Ava hoped he'd slunk away to call Iz. Her friend needed to know she wasn't lying dead in a ditch, and although Nessa deserved the update, too, Iz handled these things better, and would pass on the news once she'd found a suitable way to word it.

Nessa would flip her shit when she heard a Paladino had abducted her niece. It *was* actually shit-flipping information, but a Nessa rant wouldn't serve anyone right now; hexes would be thrown.

Although Ava had no appetite, the hot soup warmed her insides. The simple act of sipping and swallowing also centred her racing thoughts. With the kitchen to herself, she picked through her situation, deciding to take a logical approach.

'*It is what it is*', one of her mother's favourite sayings, neatly summed up her predicament. Sometimes, events happened in life a person couldn't control, and spending precious energy fighting the immovable scenarios was a pathetic waste of time. Aoibheann always told her to consider what she *could* control and to focus only on that. Right now, Ava had zero sway over her confinement in Paladino Palace. Even if she did somehow smash through Felicienne's wards, what good would it do? Fifty paces would deliver her to a rocky shoreline.

Ava couldn't swim, and would rather poke out her eyeballs with a hot nail than climb into a boat. And she doubted Enzo Paladino careless enough to leave a boat bobbing on a mooring off the coast of his swanky island, anyway. Even if he had, she didn't know the first thing about sailing.

But what she did possess, was authority over her power, and how much or little of it to give. She also controlled her knowledge. Enzo was ignorant to the full extent of her education, and just how richly the witchcraft in her veins flowed. If she played dumb when necessary, she'd discreetly keep the upper hand.

The crusty roll he'd served with her soup broke apart with a satisfying crunch. While the jury remained out on Mr Paladino's trustworthiness, she wanted to believe he hadn't lied when he said he'd bring her home. To stay on his good side, she'd have to remain composed, and once he revealed his demands, she could more easily manipulate him.

"So, it is what it is," she murmured, dunking a chunk of bread. He'd abducted her. She currently possessed no way to escape. But time and smart-thinking would tip the power in her favour again.

"Good talk," she told the soup.

Once she'd eaten, Ava cleaned up after herself, stealing a quick moment after to poke through the cupboards. A dry goods pantry held a small collection of dried herbs; oregano, rosemary, sage, and even bay leaves. She noted the useful ingredients, along with salt, peppercorns, and a variety of spices. A scan of the garden revealed the welcome sight of

94

rowan, ivy, and nettle. Nature, and whoever it was who enjoyed cooking, had provided her with a decent spell starter kit.

With the dishes dried and returned to their places, Ava took another moment to admire the beautiful kitchen as she folded the tea-towel. The sparkly glass chandelier she'd go without, but everything else made the space a warm, inviting room—even if it did match the footprint of her entire apartment. Murmuring a satisfied, "One, twelve" at how she'd kindly tidied up after herself, she exited the kitchen, wondering to which sprawling corner of Paladino Palace the Master of the House had drifted.

No sooner had she stepped out into the hallway than he called out, "I'm in the library, Ava."

'One is in the library,' she mouthed, rolling her eyes at the pretentiousness of it all, but quickly silenced snarky thoughts when she pushed open the door to find him standing by the window, holding out his phone to her.

"Your friend."

Ava reached for the phone, but he withdrew her connection to the outside world before impatient fingers made contact. 'Don't make me regret this,' his dark scowl demanded.

"You can trust me," she said quietly.

Enzo left the room, closing the door behind him with a soft click.

"Iz?"

"Ava, is that you, really?"

Despite the concern in Iz's tone, Ava closed her eyes, soothed by the welcome comfort of her friend's voice. "Yes, it's me. I'm okay. Everything is fine, I promise."

"Are you sure? Wait—am I sure? How do I know this is actually you?"

"It's me, I promise." A silent pause announced Iz's uncertainty. Afraid she'd hang up, Ava quickly said, "Ask me something only I would know."

"Um. . .what's my guilty pleasure?"

95

"Eating pizza in the bath." Ava smiled. "Which is, and always will be, disgusting."

"Who's my celebrity crush?"

"Kristen Stewart."

"Where's my birthmark?"

"You don't have one."

Iz's exhale of relief came down the line like a hurricane. "Shit, Ava. We've been so worried. We tried every locator spell and couldn't find you."

"You won't. He has me cloaked efficiently."

"Are you sure you're okay?"

Ava relayed the events since she'd left The Cauldron the previous afternoon. Iz listened without interrupting, which Nessa wouldn't have; she'd have butted in, firing off questions and yelling opinions. With the account relayed, and injuries skimmed over, Iz accepted the situation as Ava knew she would; with calm logic.

"He told me you're safe with him. Are you?"

"I appear to be. So far—abduction and confinement aside—he hasn't given me reason to doubt him. I don't want to be here, but right now, I have no choice."

"Has he told you what he wants?"

"Not yet." Ava turned her back to the view of white horses scurrying across the water. If she'd taken the call in the kitchen, where she could peep through foliage to see a slice of her hometown, she'd likely have choked up. "But neither have I agreed to help."

"Have you any choice?" Iz said quietly. "He's an old one."

The leather couch sighed as Ava sat. She grabbed the nearest cushion and clutched it to herself. "We'll see."

Iz hummed approval. "Agree to everything, but promise nothing, right?"

96

"Something like that." Ava glanced towards the door. If she were Mr Paladino, she'd be listening in. But could he hear Iz's voice?

"I'd ask where you are," Iz said, "but I don't think it's a good idea for me to know. Felicienne called to The Cauldron this morning. Two shifters rolled into town last night, and she also reported growing fae activity. I've had double my usual customers today already, so things are definitely heating up. She's looking for you, but I said you've left town. She's assuming you're with Nessa. I said nothing either way."

"Okay. Call Nessa as soon as we hang up and warn her she may have unwanted visitors. You need to be careful, too, Iz."

"I'm fine, really. But there's a potentially bigger problem than Felicienne."

"Which is?"

"Finn. He called to your apartment last night."

"Fuck." Ava thumped her forehead, narrowly avoiding the bruise. "Let me guess. The clean-up crew were there."

"He flipped his shit, Ava. Came to my door like a damn bull hollering about fire damage and splintered doors. I was in the middle of working a locator spell, and when he saw it, he nearly lost the plot."

"Shit."

"Once he hears I've spoken to you, he'll calm down. But he knows something is stirring. For once, he's actually seeing with his eyes and thinking without his stubborn, logical brain getting in the way. He's added you to the list of missing witches and has CSI scouring your apartment for evidence."

"He *what?*" Ava lurched upright, flinging aside the cushion. "He has no damn right to be in my home going through my stuff! Tell him to back off, Iz. Tell him I said he's to get the fuck out of my apartment!"

"I don't think he will."

97

"Make him! Call him as soon as we're done—tell him I'll never speak to him again. He has no right to violate my privacy!"

The door swung open. Ava turned to where Enzo stood in the opening, grip tight on the handle. "The detective is in your home?"

"He and his CSI team!"

"I'll deal with it."

"Wait—Enzo!" A blur of tailored clothes, a slam of a door, and he was gone.

"Uh," Iz said as Ava continued to gape after the dramatic exit. "What was that?"

"I'm not sure, but if he's bolted off to yank strangers away from my belongings and the hell out of my apartment, I'm not stopping him."

"Is he worried Finn will identify him? Do vampires leave fingerprints?"

"Don't know, don't care." Ava plonked onto the couch again. "Look, when you call Finn, tell him I'm sunning myself on a beach somewhere in Europe."

"Should I call him before or after Nessa?"

"Before. Now." Enzo had skedaddled without his phone, and as tempting as it was to make a string of calls, Ava knew it would backfire. She didn't have the full measure of Enzo Paladino yet, but breaking the fragile trust they endeavoured to build wouldn't be a smart move so early on. He'd likely punish her by cutting her off from Iz.

"So, I did some online digging," Iz revealed, "and there's not much to be found on the Paladinos, but if I do come across anything useful, I'll let you know. There's one thing you will appreciate, though."

"What?" Ava queried, wondering what had Iz smiling.

"Remember how the Knight of Wands was stalking you?"

"Uh-huh."

98

"The name Paladino comes from the Franks. It derives from paladin, meaning knight."

Any other day, Ava would have seen the funny side of Iz's discovery. "Of course it does," she said with a sigh instead.

Iz laughed for her. "Stay strong, my friend, do you hear?"

"I will."

"May the Goddess be with you, Ava."

"You too, Iz. Stay safe."

Ava slid Enzo's phone onto the coffee table. Now she'd spoken to Iz, her sense of isolation had eased. But knowing Finn poked through her belongings had her hackles up. If he manhandled her decks or grimoires, she'd hex him. "Oh, shit," she whispered. What if he found her journals?

Moaning, she flopped sideways across the couch, slamming the cushion over her face. She'd filled several pages ranting about him. If he read any of it, she'd die of embarrassment. And the risk he'd discover all the other stuff about her curse, Nessa, and her mum? Ava groaned aloud again. Not for the first time, she wished she could rewind to that wet Friday morning when he'd invited her out to dinner as they'd stood outside the newsagent's on Raven's Row. If she could get a do-over, she'd reply with a big fat no.

Ava dumped the cushion and sat up. Out of curiosity, she reached for Enzo's phone again. Password protected, of course. Leaving it in open sight on a hardback edition of some ancient Italian tome, she decided to nap for a while. Once Enzo returned, they had a negotiation session to tackle, and for that, she'd require a full battery of energy, smarts, and patience.

99

Enzo tracked the witch's heartbeat to her bedroom the moment he neared the house. He entered, checking the library first, where he found his phone waiting on Elsa Morante's 'Arturo's Island'. He checked the call log, surprised to see she'd spoken only to her friend. So, she hadn't taken advantage of his lapse. A demonstration of trust? Not what he'd expected so soon.

Steady breathing from behind her bedroom door confirmed she slept. He lifted his hand to knock, but then decided against it. She had strength and energy to recoup. Their business could wait.

When he'd arrived at her apartment earlier, two men and the detective were inside. Unable to cross the threshold, Enzo had knocked on the jamb of the open door, teeth gritted against the rattle of rummaging. Detective Delaney appeared from a room to the right—the living room. On the opposite side of the hallway, an ajar door revealed a strip of the witch's bedroom. He hoped the search hadn't extended that far. Manus Larsen had failed to find the necklace, but the witch may not have considered warding it against curious humans. Wherever she'd hidden it, the thought of someone else discovering it before he, strained already taut nerves.

'Can I help you?' The detective had asked.

'I'm a friend of Ava's.'

Finn Delaney clearly thought he had a claim on the witch. He flicked a critical look over Enzo, and demanded, 'What kind of friend?'

'One who knows better than to go through her private belongings.'

'One who knows she was attacked and is now missing?'

'*Ava is not missing. I spoke to her five minutes ago, and she's perfectly well.*'

The detective's demeanour changed. '*You spoke to her? Where is she?*'

'*With a friend.*'

'*She's not with Iz.*'

'*No, she's not,*' Enzo agreed.

'*So why are you here?*' Finn Delaney neared by another few steps.

'*I have a message for you from Ava. You're Detective Delaney, correct?*'

'*I am.*'

One more step, and the witless Delaney came close enough for Enzo to latch onto his gaze. '*Leave Ava's home and take your men with you. You will forget everything you saw and leave behind anything you took. Ava is perfectly well. She travelled abroad for a few weeks. She'll be home when she's ready.*'

Delaney blinked. '*Ava is safe and well.*'

'*Yes. Leave her home now and do not come back.*'

'*Don't come back.*'

Enzo had waited in the carpark, watching from the cover of trees. Five minutes later, the detective shouldered his way out the front entrance with two men in tow. '*Sorry about that,*' he'd said as they'd headed for their respective vehicles. '*Crossed wires, it seems. The woman is safe and well.*'

'*That's all that matters,*' one man replied.

Enzo returned to the library and poured himself a large scotch. He'd picked up on fae, shifter, and demon scents in the town. Word of the witch's location had spread quicker than he liked, and he worried digging would trace it right back to the Enclave.

The Enclave governed the supernatural world. Each of the seven factions held a body of three, with the reeve overseeing the entire group.

101

For decades, the warlock Ortega had held the role of reeve in Europe, but with his seat abruptly vacated, every faction now scrambled to fill that seat with one of their own. Alongside Enzo's vampire faction, fae, witches, nymphs, demons, and shifters all craved to have the power tipped in their favour. And with the warlocks now suddenly robbed of that partiality due to the yet unofficially unexplained death of Reeve Ortega, they fought with even greater desperation.

Only the angel faction disregarded the contest; their peaceful nation demanded no governing, so they rarely attended meetings. Enzo worried they might decline to vote altogether, claiming they would prefer the matter to play out without their involvement. Yet, if ever there was a time for divine intervention, this was most certainly it.

The Enclave followed a majority rules system. Each faction voted for or against a ruling. With an uneven number of seats within each faction, two matching votes claimed the majority. From there, the overall majority of yea or nay claimed the tentative result, but the ultimate decision lay with the Reeve.

Shortly after Waylen Kane's arrival six years ago, Ortega began noticeably favouring his warlock and witch kin with that final decision. Up to that point, he'd ruled fairly. But a rot had taken hold within the Enclave, and every instinct screamed that Waylen Kane manipulated the entire situation—including Ortega's death—for personal gain.

Martha's abduction further compounded Enzo's predicament. Her absence stalled the vote for Ortega's replacement, and with the Enclave keen to restore order, they'd voted to rule another member would replace Martha if she failed to return. Martha despised Kane with as much vigour as Enzo. She also agreed with his suspicion that Kane was involved in Ortega's death.

Enzo wanted Martha on the reeve throne. She followed a steady moral compass, and would obliterate the cancer Kane endeavoured to spread.

102

But for Martha to win the vote for reeve, she needed to be present. She also required an edge, something which would transcend the existing abilities of their faction. Enzo knew precisely what that advantage would be, and as he alone held the blame for ripping it from Martha centuries ago, only he could endeavour to make amends now.

He suspected witches lay behind Martha's disappearance, but coven after coven failed to break through whatever magick hid his niece. With time slipping away, and desperation mounting, he'd taken a more aggressive approach. One night, a young and frightened Spanish coven member finally blurted a secret: An Irish witch, possessed the ability to locate Martha. But when the trembling woman explained *exactly* how, Enzo quickly realised this unknown witch held the answer to *all* his problems.

A curious twist came only a day later when Kane approached Enzo, citing concern for Martha's disappearance. He named the Irish witch himself, insisting Ava O'Keefe held the power to locate Martha. In exchange for the *'invaluable information'*, Kane asked for Enzo's vote when he put himself forward for reeve.

'Our factions have butted heads for decades, Paladino. It's time for it all to end,' he'd whispered at the most recent enclave gathering. *'Once I'm reeve, I'll ensure the vampire body gets fairer judgement. Ortega turned his back on you years ago. In the future, you'll have my support.'*

'And you're sure the O'Keefe witch can find Martha?' Enzo had queried, immediately suspicious of Kane's supposed generosity.

'Without a doubt. My advice? Find her. Convince her to co-operate, and when you do, I'll thank her personally.'

Enzo had shaken Kane's hot, moist palm, gushed fake thanks for the tip, and silently vowed to claim Ava O'Keefe as soon as possible. If the warlock knew of Ava's true ability, and how Enzo planned to use it for something far more significant than discovering who had abducted his niece, Kane wouldn't have been so quick to reveal his secret.

Thoughts cluttered by his missing niece, Kane, Ortega, and the machinations churning out of his sight, Enzo wandered to the couch, lowering himself to sit, but the provocative scent of witch nestled in the fibres. With an abrupt turn, he moved to the opposite seat, snorting to rid his nostrils of the gum-prickling perfume.

Swallowing his scotch in one mouthful, burn and frustration roused a grunt. Weeks of close confinement lay ahead; he *had* to learn to tolerate her torment. If he didn't soon adjust, he'd be a danger to himself, her, and those relying on him to succeed. "Maledette streghe," he hissed, forcing himself to once again cross the rug and take his first choice of seat. "Damned witches."

Half a bottle of scotch later, the witch woke. Enzo listened to her moving about her room, and after a few minutes, she came downstairs. He'd left the library door ajar, and when she called out, he answered.

"Was Finn there?" she immediately asked on entering, cradling her splinted hand.

"He was. With two others."

"And? Had he removed anything?"

Enzo was right to suspect she'd hidden the necklace in her home. "Such as?" he queried, feigning concern.

The witch fronted her reply with a shrug, coming to stand at the end of the couch. "Stuff. Books, maybe, or, I don't know, notebooks?"

Had she the necklace concealed inside a book? "I didn't see."

Frowning at him, the index finger of her uninjured hand tapped against the wrist she held. "Why? You were there."

"Ava. I cannot enter your home. I spoke to your detective from outside the door."

"He's not *my* detective," she corrected sharply.

The reprimand gifted him a brief flash of satisfaction. He bet it would pain Finn Delaney to hear her state the fact.

"So, you're not sure if he took anything?"

"If he had, I compelled him to leave it behind and forget everything he'd seen."

Relief softened her features. The anxious drumming ceased. "So, no matter what he might have seen or read, he's already forgotten?"

"Correct."

"Good." The witch perched herself on the couch's padded arm. "What else did you compel him to forget?"

Enzo crossed his legs, shifting position to hold his scotch closer so the alcohol fumes would overpower her scent. What might Delaney have read? Details of where she'd hidden the necklace? But from his surveillance over the last few weeks, Enzo had learned the detective to be a highly reluctant believer. If he barely respected his ex-partner's spiritual practices, Enzo doubted the man was even aware of her endowment. "I told him you're abroad, safe and well, and that you shall return once ready. He won't revisit your home."

"Okay. Good. That's good." Satisfied, and visibly reassured, her gaze drifted to the fading day outside.

Dusk rolled in. Wind had settled, and with the tide out, a tang of brine, rot, and fish layered the air. If he opened the window, it might blanket the call of witch blood.

105

"I'm aware we have business to discuss," she said, making air quotes around the word *business* as she stood. "But I really need to eat. I'm lightheaded."

Enzo surrendered his glass to the coffee table. "I'll prepare you something."

"No, no." Backing away with a gesture he remain sitting, she told him she'd manage by herself. "You don't like the smells," she stated. "It bothered you earlier, so I'll cook for myself."

"It didn't trouble me," he corrected her as she disappeared.

"Oh, I saw you." Amusement rang clear as she crossed the hallway. "You looked *pained*."

Pained was an apt assumption, but the witch wouldn't find it so amusing if she heard it was the scent of her blood that had him close to powdering his molars.

"Cristo." With a grunt, Enzo closed his eyes and petitioned the heavens for divine strength.

10

Ava ate until her stomach hurt. She made pasta with mushrooms, red peppers, and pesto. Fresh bacon waited in the fridge, but the second she saw it, all she could hear was squealing pig. Would she ever be able to eat meat again without thinking of the abattoir? Earlier, although she'd slept, violent dreams of Manus Larsen's pale face sound-tracked by the rattle of metal hooks jerked her awake. The nightmare had swamped her in such a slick, cold sweat, she'd had to shower.

While the pasta cooked, she sliced two doorsteps of bread off a fresh loaf, spread them with garlic and herb butter—heavy on the garlic, just to piss off Enzo—and toasted them under the grill. An impressive rack of wine occupied one corner of the swanky kitchen, and although tempted to savour a Chianti, Ava knew it would be better to keep alcohol out of her system. Witchcraft and alcohol did not great bedfellows make. If she found herself in a situation that called for a sudden spell, she wouldn't risk it misfiring.

Enzo waited patiently while she ate and cleaned up. Classical music floated in from somewhere closer than the Charles Dickens Den, leaving her to wonder if that's what wealthy people did with all their reception rooms; move from one to another according to the sun's location. The thought had her rolling her eyes.

Although curious to finally learn why an old one had gone to so much trouble to nab her, Ava dallied in the kitchen. If Enzo Paladino's business demanded something heinous of her and her magick, it'd be a flat out no. She hadn't pegged him as twisted as Manus Larsen, but old ones didn't reach their antique age by playing nice.

With no other dishes to wash or counters to clean, she dried her hands, told herself to pull up her big girl pants, and followed the strains of Beethoven.

The new room, she nicknamed *The Birdcage*. Feathered beauties featured in paintings and fabrics, while a glass cabinet back-lit by tiny lights, displayed a collection of dainty crystal birds. Tones of gold and dark blue coloured the room, and while it didn't strike her as Enzo Paladino decor—considering the absence of candles—she found it tasteful.

The man himself sat in a high-backed armchair stationed to the right of the hearth. Upholstered in a stunning shade of royal blue, it looked every bit a throne, and he an Italian king as he watched her settle onto the couch opposite.

"So," she said, once she'd cleared her throat. "I'm fed, watered, and ready to listen."

A tilt of head, accompanied by a slow, deliberate blink, came in reply.

She wondered if he ever lost his cool. For an Italian, she found him remarkably composed. "But I have something to say before you begin."

"Speak freely, Ava."

"Terms and conditions apply," she announced. "No matter the personal cost, I do not work magick that will harm another living being."

"*Harm none*," Enzo stated the familiar witches' creed.

"Exactly. So I need to know every detail. If I have a question, you answer. Lie to me, and you'll regret it. Likewise, if you hide something from me. Omission is the same as lying. Got it?"

"I accept your terms."

"Okay," she said, shuffling her butt deeper into the seat. "I'm listening."

Enzo lowered his arms, settling them on the rests. He exuded confident calm as he faced her across the divide, one provided by an iron and glass table littered with chunky books on nature photography, art, and wine. A china ornament sat on one side; a vividly painted parrot. It was pretty, but more like something her gran would have had sitting on her mantelpiece. Saying that, Ava bet it cost a few million euros.

"My niece Martha is missing. She was last seen in Rome three weeks ago. My nephew, her brother, returned to their home to find her gone. There were signs of a struggle. I've worked with several covens to locate her, but they've found no trace."

"Do you know who might have taken her?"

"At this stage, not with confidence."

"Any idea why they want her?"

Enzo slowly rubbed the pads of his index fingers and thumbs in a circle. "Martha comes from a long line of witches."

The first surprising revelation. "So, she's a witch turned vampire?"

"Yes."

"How long is her line?"

"Thirteen generations."

"*Thirteen?*" Martha Paladino was a goddamn *thirteenth-generation* witch?

Ava gaped at where Enzo sat, needing a moment to digest the major plot twist. Did that mean Enzo carried witch blood, too? And was it *her* kin behind the theft?

"Does Martha still practice?" Vampirism would normally have negated Martha's power, but with her being a thirteenth-generation, all bets were off. Yet Enzo replied with a brief shake of head.

So, Martha Paladino had earned herself Unicorn Witch status—a good enough reason to be shanghaied. Was that why she'd been turned originally? Had she volunteered to be changed to escape her lineage, or had someone resented it and turned her without consent? Questions unfolded one after another, but now wasn't the appropriate time for rapid-fire queries. "If her power is disabled, why is her witch heritage an issue?"

"You're familiar with the Enclave, I presume?"

"Of course." The governing body of the supernatural world kept their respective communities in loose order. Ava imagined them as a bunch of ancient males; fat, pompous asses who gathered in an echoing, wood-panelled hall, grumbling about the modern generation and their wild ways as they guzzled brandy and mourned the *'good ol' days'*. When they deemed a being, group, or entire community out of order, they sent their minions in to reprimand those in the wrong, clean up the mess, and deliver a stern warning before departing.

For the most part, the Enclave kept their noses out of supernatural business, but when shit got messy, such as faction to faction fighting—like when demons tried to move in on shifter territory in the Slieve Bloom Mountains five years ago—the Enclave would throw their collective weight around. Punishment came swift and brutal. If you landed on the Enclave's Shit List, you never came off it.

Nessa said the Enclave was a necessary evil. Her mum had used far less polite language. All Ava knew, was that without the Enclave, supernatural beings would struggle to co-exist with humans. Their strict laws served a purpose, and while Ava had never met an enclave member, or had the delightful pleasure of crossing paths with one of their foot soldiers, she had the sense to respect their authority. Even if they were a bloat of hippo-like men.

"Martha holds a seat in the Enclave. If it remains vacant, another will fill it, and we've worked too hard for our faction to risk such a loss."

"Whoa." Ava flapped at him to halt. "*We?*"

Her interruption roused an impressive Italian scowl. "*We* what?"

"You said *'we've worked too hard for our faction'*. Are you also in the Enclave?"

"I am."

"Are they aware you're here with *me?*" Ava pointed at herself, hearing her pitch reach new heights. "Asking for my help? Do they know about me? And can I say no?"

"Is there an order in which you would prefer that slew of questions answered?"

"Can I say no?" she repeated the most important one.

"Yes."

"But I'm on their Shit List if I do refuse to help, right?"

"Their *Shit List*?"

"Are you here on behalf of the Enclave, or is this" —Ava gestured at where she sat on his plush couch with her abductee status— "purely Enzo Paladino business?"

Enzo leaned forward to rest his elbows on his knees. "Does it matter?"

"Yes, it does! I thought this situation was all your doing. But if the Enclave is involved, it makes this whole thing way bigger than anything I'm prepared to handle!"

"I'm asking for your help for personal reasons. It's not enclave business."

"Okay, so, I'm sitting here right now because you, an enclave member, want me to find your niece, who is also an enclave member?"

"Correct."

Already, the scant information didn't add up. Ava shook her head, her quiet laugh mocking her own stupidity, but also how cleverly Enzo Paladino had planned this subterfuge. "You're telling me you want me to work a simple locator spell using the immense power of hybrid eclipse energy?"

"Ava, you're capable of locating her without eclipse energy."

Which she absolutely was. So, what was it he *did* want her to do? Because it damn well wasn't just finding his niece. Spreading her hands in an *'I'm waiting'* gesture, she glared over at him.

"I want you to reactivate Martha's witch power."

A deep inhale just about redacted her reply of, *'what the fuck?'* "You're not serious," she said instead.

Enzo said nothing.

"That involves me tapping into twelve generations of witches. That's an insane amount of energy to call upon, never mind try to corral into one being. Have you any idea how wildly demented your request is?"

"Ava, you are more than capable of—"

"Enzo, you haven't patronised me yet. Please don't start now." A cushion embroidered with kingfishers sat close to her. Ava gathered it into her arms, enjoying the resistance when she gave it a squeeze. "Setting aside your *unhinged* request for one moment, why do you want her witch power restored?"

His first hesitation came with a flex of jaw. "Will you accept enclave business as an answer?"

"For something as simple as finding her, yes. For reigniting her witchery, no way."

112

"My position prohibits me from discussing enclave business with non-enclave members."

"I get that, but you agreed to my terms."

Enzo's long fingers curled around the ends of his arm rests. "The Reeve wants it."

"That" —she lifted her chin at him— "was your first lie." Enzo's scowl returned. Luckily for him, his vampirism meant the furrows wouldn't permanently score his face. "I told you. If I want an answer, you give it to me. I need to know why you want Martha's power restored. Otherwise, I'm out." She already inched to exit stage left. Restoring such a formidable creature meant someone gaining an unconquerable advantage. No-one hankered for such a win without cradling nefarious intentions.

Another bout of jaw grinding followed before he said, "I'm not at liberty to reveal enclave business."

"Well, I'm not prepared to put myself through the agony of dialling into twelve generations of witch power, flipping on your niece's witch switch, and frying my circuits in the process without a damn good reason. And by damn good reason, I mean saving millions of lives, ending world hunger or reversing global warming. I won't risk my life for someone's selfish whim or personal gain. No way."

Behind Enzo's throne, a sizeable sideboard held an array of alcohol. Ava spotted her poison of choice; tequila. Enzo tracked her longing gaze, twisting to see where it landed.

Tea would be a far more sensible alternative, she told herself. Tea and trauma went hand in hand. Shite day at work? Have a cup of tea, love. A bout of explosive diarrhoea? A strong cuppa will cure that, girl. Death in the family? Sip on this tea, pet. The Enclave want you to reactivate a Unicorn Witch? I'll stick on the kettle, hen.

113

Enzo abandoned his throne to cross to the sideboard, where he plucked up the bottle of Fortaleza tequila. Ava could almost taste its smooth, sweet spice as he held it up in offering.

"No, thanks." She watched as he took his time pouring his own poison; a solid three fingers of scotch. Did he purposely dally so he could concoct a new lie? Or did he debate over telling her the truth? As he stalled, she ran her fingertips over the cushion's stitching, tracing one bird's wing. "If this is going to work, we have to trust each other," she reminded him.

"In that case, trust me when I tell you that restoring Martha's power will not serve maleficence—quite the opposite, in fact."

"I still need to hear why you want it."

A quiet sigh whispered.

With his back resolutely turned to her, Ava wondered what expression he held. "Have I given you a reason not to trust me?"

"No. Yet you mistrust me," he said, returning to his throne. He pointed to her neck as he sat. "That, for example."

Ava grasped her mugwort charm. "Because I know how easy it would be for you to compel me into doing your dirty business."

"My business is not dirty, and neither would I compel you. I followed you for weeks. At any point, I could have compelled you. But I didn't."

"So, you want me to take this off as proof that I trust you?"

"No," he decided after a pause, gaze flicking to where his index finger stroked the lip of his glass.

"You don't trust yourself?"

Enzo took a large mouthful of scotch. "Witch blood, Ava. As old as I am, I'm not immune to its lure."

"Right."

"So, it appears," he said, crossing his legs, "that we have not yet formed a mutual confidence in each other."

114

"I've been in your company for. . .how long?" Ava glanced at the carriage clock on the mantelpiece. At that moment, she realised what the room missed—in fact, what every room she'd so far seen within his enormous house lacked; photos. She had no idea what Martha or Cyrus Paladino looked like. Or a younger Enzo Paladino. She guessed him to have been changed sometime around his early, maybe mid-forties. If he'd lived as a vampire for the centuries legend whispered, cute baby Enzo photos certainly didn't exist, but what about when cameras finally did appear? For a family who had likely seen every last square inch of the planet, weren't they at least tempted to display pictures of their travels and experiences?

"Just over twenty-four hours," she answered her own question after a rough calculation. "It typically takes more than one day to build trust."

"It does. However, we don't have the luxury of time."

"Okay, well, here's the first reason to trust me: I didn't abuse the fact you left your phone behind earlier."

"I rescued you from the abattoir."

"I didn't tell Iz where we are," she volleyed in return.

"I had the damage in your apartment fixed and sent your detective on his way," he parried.

She tutted at his insistence on calling Finn hers. "I haven't worked any defensive magick against you. Yet."

"I ensured you received the best medical attention, brought you to my home for safety, and haven't deprived you of anything. *Yet.*"

"Fine." Ava flung aside the cushion. "You win." She shuffled to the edge of the plump seat and stood. "You've earned lots of trust points. But that doesn't mean I'm agreeing to anything without knowing the why."

Enzo sipped in silence as she strolled a lap of the room, surveying the art, ornaments, and books.

115

Trailing her finger along a row of book spines, she asked who the bird enthusiast was. The books shared a shelf holding a record player, but vinyls were absent.

"Cyrus."

"Seriously?"

Enzo twisted in her direction to query her surprise with his trademark lift of eyebrow.

"I would have thought his tastes leaned into darker subjects," she replied honestly.

"They do," he said, watching her amble. "Martha encourages him into the light whenever possible."

Was it too soon to ask if all the sordid tales of Cyrus Paladino were true? Although, she'd learn herself once he arrived. "They're close, then—he and Martha?"

"She's the only one who can control him. Another reason I desperately need her home."

With her second lap almost complete, Ava slowed by the cabinet holding the crystal aviary. "You don't get on with each other?" What attracted a brutish vampire like Cyrus Paladino to tiny glass birds? Perhaps he liked to sprinkle them over his breakfast cereal.

"Cyrus and I are polar opposites. What I loathe, he adores. What I strive for, he neglects, and vice versa."

Ava returned to her starting point, but remained standing at the side of the couch. She wanted to ask if she'd still be safe once his savage nephew arrived, but in a polite way.

Enzo anticipated the unspeakable question. "My nephew enjoys vampirism. He revels in what he believes are the loose morals it bestows. As a human, he suffered with his mental health, and his troubles only compounded once he was turned. He listens only to Martha, and her disappearance has caused him great distress. I'd prefer his absence while

116

we're working together, but I can't afford to leave him out there without her supervision. Once he arrives, he will behave, and I promise, he will cause you no harm."

"But?" she said, when his statement trailed off without the usual Paladino confidence.

"He will disrupt the house."

"You make him sound like a hormonal, sulky teenager. Does he stomp around in combat boots, black jeans and tatty rock t-shirts yelling, *'It's so unfair'?*"

Enzo Paladino laughed. He actually threw back his handsome Italian head and laughed aloud to the ceiling. The sound curled her toes. Hail the Goddess for blessing her ears with such a rich, throaty laugh.

"That," he said, saluting her with his scotch, "is my nephew in a nutshell."

Ava sat, retrieving the cushion. To hell with all their eclipse business. What did she have to do to make Enzo Paladino laugh like that again? "Leaving the why aside for now, is Martha stable enough to handle being a witch *and* a vampire? The transition back to witch could take years."

"She is," Enzo replied, a faint smile still tilting his generous lips.

"What about Cyrus? Did he inherit the witch gene?"

"No. He was wholly human."

But what kind of human to make him as wicked as he was now? Or had tongues exaggerated the tales of his wickedness over the centuries? Ava hoped so. She faced being locked tight inside this house with him for weeks. "And you?" she dared to ask.

"No," he said decisively. Enzo studied where he swirled the remaining half inch of scotch around his crystal tumbler. "So. Are we at an impasse?"

Ava sighed. "If you refuse to tell me why you want Martha's witch switch flipped, then yes."

117

"I see."

"And even if you do tell me, I have to be honest about something." Enzo met her gaze.

"Hybrid eclipse magick is potent stuff. I'm not sure I'm a strong enough vessel to hold it while channelling twelve dead witches *and* feeding their power back into your niece. I don't even know how to begin working that kind of magick. And another thing?" Aware she thought aloud, Ava didn't bother filtering. She needed clarity. If she ended up bowing out of the agreement, she wanted to be sure all her cards lay face up on the vampire's table. "Calling on deceased witches demands dark magick. I don't practice that branch. If I agree to this, once I research the how, if the only way is through degenerate methods, I won't do it."

Enzo nodded. "I understand."

"And I want an iron-clad guarantee that the Enclave won't punish me if I do back out."

"They won't," he said without hesitation.

"Or you."

He almost looked wounded. "I won't."

"Okay. Well, I guess that's all we can say for now, then."

With their business concluded for the evening, Ava decided to make tea. She also needed a painkiller. Her broken fingers throbbed. Tomorrow, if she woke feeling stronger, she'd concoct a balm and try a little healing magick.

Dismissed from the throne room, she returned to the kitchen where the walk-in pantry gifted her with a selection of teas. She chose chamomile, and locating the cupboard with mugs, set about filling the kettle.

Iz had told her Paladino translated as knight, but Ava couldn't equate Enzo with her Knight of Wands stalker card. The steady, subdued Knight of Pentacles yes, but not the wilder, more passionate nature embodied

118

by Wand energy. Enzo was more uptight than easy-going, and definitely not an emotional type of man—even for a vampire. Perhaps Cyrus was the Paladino the cards strove to warn her about?

Enzo rounded the kitchen door, resting one shoulder against the jamb. "I have a suggestion."

Ava set the kettle on the stove and located the switch for the burner. A ring of pretty blue teardrop flames sprung up under the kettle's base. "Let's hear it."

"Agree to find Martha, and in the time it takes, trust will hopefully build between us enough for you to accept my silence on why I need her power restored."

Ava considered the proposal. She could say no, but then what? If he kicked her out, she'd be back to square one, dodging evil stalkers by hiding in the Wicklow Mountains. If she played her cards right, she could stretch out her stay in Paladino Palace until after the eclipse. At least then she'd be safe. Well, safer. Okay, maybe just safe-ish. "What if trust doesn't build?" she asked, folding her arms as she rested one hip against the counter's edge. "What if we remain in this impasse, where you withhold the why, and I refuse to siphon eclipse magick?"

"Then you have my word. I shall return you to your home safely."

"But you won't get what you want."

"I have other options."

But options he'd have to chase and nail down. Right now, he had her in his lair, right where he needed her witchy prowess. "Are you afraid of me knowing your top-secret enclave business, or is that you already know I'll refuse to flip Martha's witch switch when I hear the why?"

"The former," he answered with such defiant honesty, it almost had her accepting his offer right there and then.

Instead, she said, "Let me sleep on it."

119

11

Thanks to the industrial-strength painkillers prescribed by the hospital, the trauma her body and mind had suffered evaporated as soon as Ava's head hit the pillow. Although she wanted to pluck through the evening's discussion, consciousness shut down. It didn't even reboot during the night to throw frightening replays of the abattoir. The following morning, she woke slightly disorientated, struggling to remember her location, why she was there, and what day of the week it was.

Once re-calibrated, she rolled out of bed and headed for the bathroom. The wound on her neck had healed well enough to leave it bandage-free. A fine, crusted line marked where Manus's blade had sliced. Ava peered at it in the mirror, hoping it would fade. Her hair would hide it for now, but if it left a scar, she'd forever be reminded of what happened. She'd also have to come up with a story to answer nosy questions. Finn's especially once he saw it, which he would, because he never missed a thing. "Not today's problem," she told her reflection.

A rummage under the sink produced a roll of plastic bags someone had stowed away for the pedal bin. Ava carefully wrapped her hand, tutting at the annoyance of having to put up with two splintered fingers for the next few weeks. She wondered if Enzo would permit her to send a shopping list to Iz for healing supplies. To find his niece and work nuclear-strength witchcraft demanded a seriously larger arsenal than her current. One grimoire and tarot deck wouldn't cut it.

With hair elastics holding the bag in place, Ava undressed and fired up the Niagara Falls shower. Washing with only one hand proved tricky, and her ribs still ached when she stretched, but the powerful water jets made light work of rinsing the suds out of her hair without her needing to reach up and scrub.

Once dressed, she settled into the plump armchair situated to the left of the window. Overhung by a palm, it promised a nice nook to meditate, but the painkillers lingered in her system, threatening to send her to sleep after five minutes. They also blanketed her connection to spirit with a thick fog. Much like Felicienne's shelter wards, Ava couldn't reach across the divide for the familiar energies. She opted for simple breathing instead, doing nothing more than focusing on the temperature of air entering and exiting her nostrils. When her stomach interrupted with a loud complaint, she gave up, deciding to turn to her tarot cards.

Her most reliable and precious deck waited for her in its silk wrapping amongst the clothes she hadn't yet removed from her suitcase. Ava kissed it, murmuring a hello to the cards and the spirit of her gran. What would Evelyn O'Keefe say if she appeared before her granddaughter at that moment? Ava smiled as she lowered herself to sit cross-legged on the floor. No sane-minded person in the entire witch community would

121

react with anything other than horror to hear an old one had trapped a witch in order to reinstall negated witch power.

The deck, her beloved Rider Smith Waite, showed its age. Years of shuffling and handling had the edges worn. Time had washed it with a faint yellow stain Iz called *'antique white'*. Ava would continue to use the cards until they crumbled away to powder. They'd been through a lot together since she'd first yanked off its cellophane wrapping on her thirteenth birthday and gushed tearful thanks to her gran.

With the silk spread on the wooden floor before her, Ava closed her eyes and shuffled. A simple and to-the-point reading would serve her best; her choked mind wouldn't benefit from a slew of messages right now. "Three cards," she said to herself. "Current path, what is hidden, what lies ahead." With an inhale to block out mental chatter, she shuffled, and when ready, cut the deck and dealt out three cards.

The 2 of Swords, the Moon, and the Tower faced her.

"Indecision, illusion, and upheaval," she summarised her answers aloud. A sigh followed.

Indecision she agreed with. Both she and Enzo battled uncertainty. The message of illusion from the Moon worried her, because if Enzo had lied beyond claiming Reeve Ortega wanted Martha reactivated, she hadn't picked up on it. Perhaps the deception came from other forces; the Enclave, maybe?

Finally, the Tower promised chaos, an unexpected change that would bring everything crashing down.

Ava grimaced at the sombre spread. She hadn't expected a reading of sunshine and happiness, but it would have been nice. Out of curiosity, she flipped the deck over to check the shadow card; the one on the underside, which provided clarity to a reading. The 10 of Swords faced her; *a painful ending*. Ava grunted dismay, and returning the cards to the deck, reshuffled, and stowed it back in its silk wrap. "Tequila for breakfast, I think."

Half way down the stairs, she slowed to peer up at the gunmetal grey sky showing through the dome. Rain splattered against the glass, but no sound accompanied it. "Still as weird as it was yesterday," she whispered.

Downstairs, the interior of the house hung equally quiet. Fresh bread waited on the counter for her; warm to the touch. Ignoring the sausages and bacon in the bottom of the fridge, she gathered ingredients to make a cheese, mushroom, and tomato omelette instead.

As Ava cooked, she drew up a mental list of items for healing magick. Turmeric, cloves, lavender, and rosemary would all help with pain relief. The chamomile tea bags she would re-purpose for a salve, and if she was lucky, mallow might have found its way into the palace grounds to enhance the balm. As the wards kept her locked indoors, she'd have to ask Enzo to hunt for the plant. The pretty purple flowers wouldn't bloom until June, but with a picture for reference, he'd recognise it by its leaves—which was all she needed. Once boiled, strained, and added to the chamomile, she'd have an effective ointment to treat her neck wound. Comfrey and boneset would help to heal her broken fingers, but they were harder to find growing wild. If Enzo agreed to a shopping spree, she'd ask Iz to add tinctures to her basket. Nettle tea for calcium, too.

With her list growing, and her omelette almost ready, Ava quickly hunted for a pen and paper. Both she unearthed in the dresser, laughing to herself at the discovery that even the Paladinos had a kitchen junk drawer. Shoved inside, she spotted wine corks, odd screws, plastic cutlery, receipts, two batteries, and a box of matches. So, Enzo Paladino wasn't as organised as he liked to portray. Who would have thought?

123

'Enzo, caro mio. Dove sei?'

Enzo rolled over, responding to the gentle call, hand sliding through his sheets in search of soft skin. "I'm here, Giulia," he murmured, his forage rewarding him with nothing but cold cotton. "Giulia?"

Absence jolted him awake. He hadn't dreamt of Giulia in a long time; centuries, perhaps, and the echo of her voice rendered him disorientated and uneasy—as did his utterance of her name. Already upright, he scanned the room.

Definitely alone.

A wider search located the present witch downstairs, cooking. She hummed to herself; the soothing melody that had invaded his dream.

"Of course." It made sense now. He battled with the beckoning of witch blood, and confining himself in such close quarters with the O'Keefe witch had unlocked old and painful memories.

The witch's scent laced the air with stronger intent every day. Enzo inhaled, hissing as fangs slid from hiding. Caught off-guard by a long-ago love and the craving to savour Ava O'Keefe, his head fell back as lips parted and tongue curled in anticipation. He could almost taste her, feel the rush of hot, silky blood washing over taste buds, cascading down his throat, and satiating his desire.

An irritating buzz wrenched him out of the stupor. Enzo snapped his mouth shut, wincing as fangs pierced his inside lip. From under the sheets, arousal strained. Palming himself, he reached for the phone. Two messages waited, both from Waylen Kane.

124

Kane: Any luck?

Kane: I hear trouble is brewing in Calnaloch. Are you there?

Enzo turned the phone off. He had no desire to deal with Kane so early in the day. Tonguing away his own blood, he sank back into the pillows.

Only Martha had the wit to help Enzo navigate this unorthodox and challenging situation. While just he and the witch occupied the house, he somewhat managed, but once Cyrus arrived—along with the entourage essential to keep him under control—his ability to remain level-headed would likely crumble. He barely maintained patience now. With Cyrus's mood swings, temper, and penchant for trouble, he'd be demonic within minutes of his nephew's first blood-encrusted sole swinging across the threshold.

Cyrus had been waging a bloody retaliation throughout Europe since Martha's disappearance. Without his sister, he spiralled. Enzo's men did their best to keep Cyrus distracted, and for the last ten days, it appeared to be working—along with the company of the woman to whom he'd taken a fancy. Enzo didn't want a stranger entering his home, especially a witless human female, but if she calmed Cyrus, he'd suffer the intrusion, and perhaps the distraction was what exactly he needed; if focused on keeping his crazed nephew out of trouble, he wouldn't have time to think about the witch.

When Enzo eventually roused the strength to share space with his house guest, he found the witch at his kitchen table. Stationed facing the glass doors, she'd shoved aside empty plates to work. Unaware he watched from the doorway, she busied herself with writing, her attention moving between page and garden. The earlier rain had passed, leaving

125

behind a sky dotted by puffy clouds. As a bank parted, bright rays poured down, casting a tawny glow on her hair. Where sunlight caught her eyes, pale green turned aquamarine.

Injured fingers left her with a clumsy grip on the pen. "Marigold," she murmured, and adding the entry, tutted at the graceless writing. "Okay. What else?" Absorbed in thought, the witch absentmindedly lifted the pen to her mouth, tapping its end against her bottom lip.

Enzo honed in on the plump pinkness. Entranced by the sight, and lured by her scent, he found himself halfway across the kitchen before snapping out of the daze. "Good morning."

Startled, she jumped. The pen fell, bounced off the edge of the table, and hit the floor. It rolled to a stop at the lip of his shoe. Enzo picked it up and set it beside her notepad. "I do apologise."

An exhale steadied her breath. "Thanks. But could you make a bit more noise when you wander about? Cough, or shuffle your feet, maybe?"

Enzo complied with a comical clearing of throat, surprising himself.

"Much better," she said, smiling. "Good morning."

"What's this?" he asked kindly.

"A shopping list."

Enzo leaned in, wondering what he'd neglected to provide that she wished to eat, but quickly realised she had demands of a different nature. He anticipated her question before she could finish tucking hair behind one ear and aiming a pleading look up at him. "I suspect this requires an order to be placed with The Cauldron?"

Ava nodded, relief softening her eyes.

Enzo pulled away, remembering another's eyes stirring such a strange feeling within him; a pair close to cornflower blue. When they'd feigned love and adoration, he'd fallen straight into their vivid depths. Clambering out of them had cost him his life.

126

"Is there access to the internet in this house?"

"No," he answered, positioning himself at a safer distance beside the stove, where the scent of cooked food masked the call of her blood. He retrieved his phone and turned it on, needing the distraction. "Why?"

"I've only got one grimoire here. I'll need more to work on finding Martha. But online research would help, too."

"You'll have to manage without the world wide web," he said, quickly typing he had no update yet in reply to Waylen Kane. If he kept the warlock at bay with ambiguous messages for as long as possible, Kane would find out too late about Enzo's true plan. "There's an extensive collection of grimoires here. I'm sure they contain suitable spells."

"You have grimoires? Whose?"

"Martha's." Enzo looked up from the screen to find her gaze glued to him. "And her ancestors. Some are in English, but the majority are Italian."

"Oh." A grimace followed. "The only Italian I know is *'ciao, bella'*, *'grazie'* and a few expressions too rude for your ears."

Enzo wondered who'd been teaching Ava O'Keefe foul Italian. "I can translate," he assured her.

"Okay. But I need other things, too. Starting with this list." She tapped the page. "The painkillers are too strong for me."

"They're upsetting your stomach?" Enzo put his phone away.

"No. They're making me woozy. I can't work magick with a fuzzy head."

"I'll make the call to Iseult once you've compiled your list."

"Thanks."

But she hadn't finished with her requests. A shy smile queried his willingness to grant her more. "What else?" He'd found it easier to remain aloof with her yesterday; a sudden benevolence had possessed him today.

127

"Would you be okay with searching the gardens for a few plants? They'll help with my healing."

"Which plants?"

"Comfrey, mallow, boneset. They're not that common, so I can draw you examples."

"They're all here. I can gather whatever you require."

Lips that hadn't caught his attention before today formed a small *'oh'*.

"Martha keeps the gardens of all our homes stocked with healing plants. She can't work magick, but she can certainly craft balms and poultices. There are dozens here, including a few rare varieties she grows in the greenhouse."

"There's a greenhouse? Accessed directly through the house?" Ava half rose from the bench with breathy awe. "Please say it is, so I can see it."

"Unfortunately not," he told her, looking away before the shining disappointment in her eyes could prompt him to command the entire glass structure uprooted and re-positioned to grant her entry. "But whatever you require, if it's there, I'll fetch it for you."

The witch dropped into the seat again. "Okay. Thanks."

"I'll be in the library."

Waylen's reply came in as Enzo crossed the hall, mind tangled by the witch in his kitchen and the one in his dream.

Kane: Is the formidable Enzo Paladino losing his touch?

Enzo waited until he'd shut the library door behind him before replying.

128

Everything worth having is worth the wait.

With a smirk, Enzo threw down the phone and dropped onto the couch. It was imperative he centre himself, and fast. Time slipped away, and now the witch had agreed to find Martha, he would have to learn to endure her presence for extended periods.

During the night, he'd wandered about Martha's room, contemplating the array of grimoires lining her shelves—along with the power they contained. The test of mutual trust would soon begin. With a wealth of magick at her fingertips, Ava could negate the wards in no time, overcome him, and escape.

Her inability to swim didn't mean she couldn't wade through the water at low tide; at its highest point, it wouldn't rise above her shoulders. Regardless of whether Ava knew of the tidal nature, in order for this tentative agreement to work, it was critical she trust in his protection—and he in her acceptance. If either made a move against the other, all hell would break loose.

Closing his eyes, Enzo dropped his head against obliging leather. His history with witches had branded him distrustful and hateful of their kind. It was unfair to paint them all with the same brush, but he'd suffered their cunning and lost so much because of it, he couldn't help but cling to his prejudices. Ava O'Keefe hadn't yet showed Giulia's traits, but he'd devoted himself to Giulia for almost three years before seeing beyond her deception. He didn't trust the witch under his roof, but neither could he trust *himself* at this point. Ava and he faced each other across a fault line, and one tremor from either's actions could be cataclysmic.

Light footsteps announced her approach. Enzo sat up, grabbing the nearest book. When she knocked and entered, he took his time lifting his gaze from the page.

The sheet she'd torn from the notebook hung between them. "If it's too much, I understand. The first ten items I definitely need, the eight beneath them, I can go without, but would prefer not to."

Enzo took the paper, scanning it for anything unusual or dangerous. He'd learned enough from his niece over the years to recognise trouble, but the list contained items to help with healing, and a few to aid psychic vision.

"How does this work?" she asked, taking a seat on the couch opposite him. Gently clasping her splinted fingers on her lap, a tiny wince suggested they continued to cause her pain.

"Iseult will box the orders in three separate parcels for three different addresses. I'll have each one collected and brought to a new location, and once assured no-one is tracking the couriers or parcels, I will collect them."

"That sounds good. I'm worried about Iz being targeted."

He nodded in understanding. "Calnaloch grows busier by the day. Iseult is already under observation, but I have eyes on her, too. I'll keep her safe, I promise."

"Who knows you're here?"

"It matters little. We're protected," he said, lifting his chin towards the window, where, beyond, an invisible shield netted the entire building.

Ava accepted his answer in silence, but motioned to the list. "Will it be a few days before I can get these?"

"Not days. I should have them here by nightfall."

Tense shoulders softened. "Good. That means we can get started."

"It does. And if you're ready now, I'll show you where we'll be working."

"Now?" Excitement already shining, she stood. "Sure."

Wishing her anticipation didn't have his lips wanting to mirror her smile, Enzo returned the unread book to the table.

The burn of torment already scalded. As Ava exited the room before him, he paused to briefly remind himself he had both the ability and patience to suffer this trial. But as he followed her, inadvertently passing through the trail of her scent, Enzo caught himself purposely inhaling.

12

Although Ava wanted to snoop through every room in Paladino Palace, she'd so far resisted, so when Enzo led her past her bedroom and further down the corridor, anticipation sparked a thrill. The door located beside Sodom and Gomorrah didn't hide another guest suite. Instead, an enclosed staircase rose behind it.

"This way," he said quietly.

She followed.

They emerged into a large airy room, a stained glass dome above, and even more light pouring in from the French doors leading to a balcony on her right. The expansive space didn't match the colonial style of the downstairs. Patterned fabrics and rugs brought warmth and cosiness, while the overall vibe declared organised chaos. Shelves bowing under the weight of their load, bookcases stuffed to the brim, surfaces littered with piles of paper, loose books, jars, and crystals. The scene was more than she could absorb.

Unable to move beyond the top step, she took a slower sweep of the room. To her left, a tall apothecary cabinet claimed a length of wall. Nestled beside it, a working table, scorched and stained in places. The corner homed a robust ficus. Positioned so its occupant could enjoy the view beyond the balcony doors, a handsome desk paired with a padded leather high-backed chair. Books, crystals, gizmos and whatnots cluttered both the desk and working table, while to the desk's left, and dividing the room to the midpoint of the parquet floor, a ceiling-high freestanding bookcase formed a partition. Curious to see what lay behind it, Ava stepped up and moved further into Martha's space.

The u-shape created by the dividing bookcase held more of the same floor to ceiling storage, along with an armchair straight out of a cottagecore setting. Tucked into the corner, someone had paired it with a matching footstool. Where shelves ran along the outer wall, they ended at the halfway point to accommodate a fireplace with a cast-iron fire surround. Vertical to the black marble hearth sat a dainty floral-patterned couch, covered in the same cute fabric as the armchair and footstool. A pine coffee table waited beside it. Several colourful cushions and a fluffy throw invited her to flop down and get comfy.

"Wow," she said, in complete awe. For the first time since waking in Paladino Palace and clapping eyes on all its finery, she found herself in a space where she didn't feel under-dressed or awkward. If Enzo had opened his bargaining by showing her this room first last night, she'd have blurted out an emphatic yes without thinking.

Adding to the sense of stepping through a door and arriving home, sage and sandalwood flavoured the air. Aged books hung amongst the scents, too, the distinctive aroma of old paper, tired bindings, and cracking leather.

Ava turned on the spot, believing all her Christmases and birthdays had come at once. "This place," she said, wonder delivering her statement in a breathy sigh. "It's beautiful." Unlike the splendour she'd so far seen in the house, this room revelled in its own simplicity, happy to be its own quirky self. It was, without doubt, absolutely perfect.

Enzo had positioned himself by the hearth of the compact fireplace. "Are the desk and table sufficient?"

Ava rounded the bookcase to admire the working area again. "Yes," she said immediately. The desk provided more than enough space to spread out books and papers, while the working table would allow her to prep ingredients and work magick without having to shove things aside.

Distracted by the view framed by the balcony doors, Ava crossed towards them and grabbed the twin handles. But they turned without engaging, robbing her of the pleasure of flinging them wide open to soak up a blast of pure sea air. "The wards," she realised aloud.

Enzo looked genuinely pitiful when she glanced over at him.

But look at all you have in its place, she told herself, admiring what waited. As if she'd stumbled into a movie scene, she expected a robed sorcerer or his bumbling apprentice to appear. "This is all Martha's?" And did it not break her heart to be amongst such vibrant witchery with her abilities voided?

"It is. There's not usually this volume stored here, but I gathered as much as I could from her homes. Hopefully, it's everything you will require." Where Enzo stood, he half blocked a squat cabinet, the ebony doors inlaid with what she guessed to be ivory.

Ava neared, palms lifting of their own accord as if approaching a roaring fire on an icy day. "What's in there?"

Almost as if wishing to hide the pretty piece of furniture, he shifted to his left. "Books."

Smiling at his elusiveness, she asked, "What kind of books? Grimoires?"

"Yes. But the type with which you've already stated you'd rather not engage."

The suddenly curious gaze he pinned on her, darted her attention to the locked cabinet again. "Dark magick?"

"Yes."

Huh. It didn't feel like dark magick. It reminded her of the lure of a hot bath with her favourite jasmine scented bubbles, the first mug of steaming coffee in the morning, a greasy pizza the night after a few tequilas too many, and the now lost promise of security when stepping into her mum's arms for a hug. *Are you sure?* she itched to ask, but decided against it. Once alone, she'd pick the lock and see for herself.

"Okay." Ava set her sights on the comfy desk chair calling to her derriere. "First things first. You filled this room with Martha's belongings, but I need something more intimate of hers; hair, nails, blood."

Enzo snapped out of his Doberman impression to cross the room, aiming for the apothecary cabinet housing rows of cute drawers. He opened one and withdrew a small zip-lock pouch. "I pulled these from her hairbrush."

Ava noted the tiny scattering of long, grey locks. She'd imagined Martha as a young, dark-haired beauty, perhaps in her twenties. Taking the bag from Enzo, she held it up to the light. Definitely grey. So, someone had turned Martha years after Enzo? "This is perfect," she said, instead of firing off two dozen questions about him and Martha and their journey into immortal beings.

"What else do you require?"

"For now, nothing. I'll start with a simple locator spell, try to discern what type of energy is blocking me, and go from there."

Hoping he'd leave her to work in peace, Ava approached the rugged desk. The urge to throw herself into the chair, fold herself across the polished surface, and say hello with a hug had her almost giddy.

135

"Can you estimate a time-frame?"

"Not yet," she told him, taking hold of the high-backed chair. "It's like peeling an onion. I can only strip off one layer at a time. It could take a few days before I get to the core and form a clear idea of what's cloaking her energy."

Enzo nodded in acceptance, threw a glance around the room, and taking the hint, inched towards the staircase. "If you need me, please call."

"I will. Thanks."

He was nervous. She was, too.

But his hesitation to leave came from distrust, a fear that she'd craft a spell to break free of the wards and escape. Her anxiousness spiked over the worry she'd be unable to breach whatever cloaked Martha. Five minutes in her beautiful, inspiring room, and Ava wanted to meet the woman in person. She already felt a kinship with Enzo's niece, even if Martha was more vampire than witch.

Enzo departed. Ava waited until she heard the click of latch from the door at the foot of the stairs, and breathing in, closed her eyes.

The zing of energy saturating the entire room brought her back to her gran's caravan. It sang as delightfully as Nessa's home, Iz's shop, and the section of her own bedroom in which she'd set up her altar. Spiced with magick, mystery, and the endless loop of the witches gone before and still to come, Ava spread open her arms, welcoming them and herself home.

An hour later, after a thorough tour of the room and its contents, including the mystery cabinet which she quickly realised had been locked by magick, Ava had the desk tidied, ingredients laid out on the table, and her head in the game. Grounded and centred, she threw up a protective shield and set to work.

Reaching out to Martha mirrored shouting into an abyss.

With each attempt, Ava met nothingness. She doubled ingredients, swapped them out, altered her chant, powdered one batch of herbs, burned another, ground, chopped, and liquefied, but every try brought the same result; emptiness, a void, a great big nothing.

Satisfied with all she'd done, Ava stepped away from the table, stumbling on heavy feet as if falling out of the in-between and back into reality. Whoever had Martha bound her good and tight. She'd expected as much. Clever magick, enriched by experience and power, hid Enzo's niece. Run-of-the-mill locator spells were pointless.

Thirsty, and in need of her grimoire, she retreated downstairs to the kitchen first. She filled a jug with water, grabbed a glass, an apple, and a tub of cashew nuts she found in the pantry. With pockets loaded, she hurried to her room next, dug out her grimoire from the suitcase, and returned upstairs.

Settled on the couch, she dragged the coffee table closer so she could reach the water and snacks while flicking through the pages. The spell she needed certainly didn't wait within her own grimoire, but Nessa had taught her to search for breadcrumbs; a chant here, an ingredient there, even a sigil could unlock an idea.

As considerations formed, Ava hopped up for a pen and paper, pausing at a shelf housing a collection of Martha's grimoires. Heeding the intuitive nudge, she called upon divine guidance, closed her eyes, and trailed the spines with her index finger, stalling when the urge poked. The chosen book carried the scent of musty lavender. A quick peek inside revealed text in both Italian and English. Tucking it under her arm, Ava swiped a brand new notebook and pen off the desk, and returned to her cosy seat, excited to study the ancient grimoire.

137

Time passed unnoticed as she worked, and it was only when Enzo coughed his arrival halfway up the stairs did she lift her head.

Evening had fallen. A mandarin dusk tainted the sky, the colour promising a fine day tomorrow.

"You haven't eaten," he said, coming off the top step.

"I didn't realise the time." Or how long she'd been sitting in the same position. As she turned to watch him approach, the crunch in her neck roused a wince.

"I've prepared a meal for you."

"You have?"

"It's nothing elaborate," he warned, nearing to peer down at the notes she'd made. "Any progress?"

"Martha's hidden by experienced magick. I can't sense what kind yet, but I'm working on it. I already have a few ideas."

Enzo noted the empty jug and glass, along with the browning apple butt. "Please don't neglect yourself."

"I won't."

"Come. Eat."

He'd lied about the *nothing elaborate* meal. Enzo had prepared thick slices of courgette and aubergine, layered with grilled halloumi, crushed walnuts, and pesto. Served with a side of jasmine rice speckled with tiny cubes of red pepper and mushroom, it was far from simple. Ava stared at the perfect presentation, then up at where he stood, watching her—perhaps waiting for approval. "For someone who doesn't eat solid food, you sure know how to cook it."

"I hope it's to your satisfaction."

"I already know it is. Thank you."

A customary nod followed, and as if unsure what to do with her thanks or praise, Enzo muttered something about needing to make a call and vacated the kitchen like his ass was on fire.

Truth be told, Ava would have preferred him to stay. He seemed to know enough about witchcraft to listen if she chatted about what she'd pulled from the grimoires so far. Even if he couldn't follow the threads she hoped to weave together, speaking her thoughts aloud would have helped her to clarify the muddle in her head. But he probably needed fresh air to purge the stink of food from his nostrils. From tomorrow, she'd watch the time so she could relieve him of human-feeding duty.

Ava enjoyed every mouthful and only realised as she scraped up the last few grains of rice that she'd eaten a meat-free meal. Had he cottoned on to her sudden aversion, or was cooking dead flesh a step too far for him?

He'd left the kitchen spotless, so when she finished, all she had to do was slot the plate and her cutlery into the dishwasher. She made tea, and careful not to slosh any over the rim of her mug and onto the pristine floors, made her way upstairs once more.

With the lights on, candles lit, and the curtains drawn, Martha's room became her new happy place.

Ava curled her feet under her on the couch, and with a wall of cushions supporting her back, and the soft throw draping her knees, cuddled up as cosy as a dormouse. Less than twenty-four hours ago, she would have sold a major organ to escape Paladino Palace, but the prospect of being locked up here for the next while suddenly didn't seem so bad, especially when compared to what waited in Calnaloch. Those skulking around the town, hoping to bully her into doing their bidding, sure as shit didn't have a working space like this. Neither would they treat her as respectfully and non-violently as Enzo had. She had wanted no part in

139

vampire business, but meeting Martha through her precious belongings had changed her mind. Ava honestly didn't think she had what it took to flip Martha's witch switch, but she'd put her heart and soul into finding Enzo's niece—even if it meant siding with the enemy.

Enemy?

Ava grimaced. Okay, so maybe not *all* vampires were manipulative assholes. Maybe Enzo was the exception to the rule. She remained firmly on the fence about his trustworthiness—and still cradled a healthy suspicion about why he wanted Martha's witch abilities restored—but the old one had racked up a few solid brownie points over the last day. Not that she'd tell him, of course.

He didn't reappear again that night. Ava worked into the wee small hours, finally caving at one-thirty. She'd gathered enough to start afresh in the morning, and with a refreshed mind, studying the complicated spells in Martha's grimoires would be easier—hopefully.

Candles snuffed and room tidied, she retreated down to her room. She'd completely forgotten about her order with Iz until she spotted the three boxes neatly stacked outside her bedroom door. Tiredness erased, Ava pounced on the delivery.

Iz had fulfilled her list, but added a few extras: Four bars of Ava's favourite chocolate, jasmine bath bombs, chai tea, a monster pack of fizzy jellies, tampons, and a blank page tucked inside an envelope. Ava held back a squeal at the letter, and in her excitement, had to think hard to remember the unveiling chant she and Iz had crafted between them. As fledgling witches, they'd set up their secret letter system so they could swap notes in school. Assured of their rants remaining private, they'd complained about their teenage woes and crushes. More than once, teachers had called them out on note-passing, only to be disappointed by a blank sheet.

Ava pushed aside everything she'd tipped onto her bed, kicked off her shoes, and dived under the duvet. Two false starts kept the words hidden, but on the third attempt, Iz's neat writing appeared, quickly flowing down the page.

Ava, I haven't hand-written a letter since we were in primary school. The habit of starting with 'Dear Ava. I hope you are well' has me pissing myself laughing. Miss Creedon would be so proud of me. But, seriously, how are you? I really do hope you're well.

Things are heating up around here. Even more strangers have appeared in town, and Felicienne's practically camped out on the doorstep waiting for news of you. She has a face on her like a bulldog chewing a wasp. Finn's no better. He keeps asking who you're in Italy with, and should he be worried? Should he? Wink, wink.

What's with all the healing herbs? You skimmed over what happened on the phone yesterday, but I'm guessing you got hurt. Who do I need to kill, eh?

Can you arrange to get your keys to me? Nessa's coming to town the day after tomorrow to triple-ward your apartment. She's worried about you, but is calm enough—for now. If I can talk to you again, it'll put her at ease, so tell Mr P to grant you phone rights.

Off topic, but guess who called me yesterday? Alice!!! She left the solicitor firm in Kilkenny, and is planning to start her own practice here in Calnaloch. What do you think of that? It was weird talking to her after so long, but nice at the same time. She said nothing about us getting back together, but the suggestion was there, kind of. Anyhow, with all that's going on right now, the complication of a relationship isn't something I want. I'd be happy to hang out with her, but I'm not ready for more at this stage.

Jesus. Here I am, shite talking about my ex and you're being held captive by a vampire. Friend of the year, here.

141

Mr P seems happy enough for you to order off me, so I hope we can keep this system going. I'll stuff every order with your favourite things, but don't be afraid to ask for anything. Do you think he'll allow you to speak to me again soon? I'll feel better when I hear your voice again.

May the Goddess be with you, my friend. Stay safe. I love you.

Iz xxx

Ava swiped hot tears away and read the letter for a second and third time.

Iz and Alice had dated for over a year, but Alice had chosen her career over Iz, and packed herself off to her *'dream job'* in Kilkenny, leaving behind a broken-hearted Iz. The dream job had obviously crumbled. Ava hoped Iz would stick to her word and tread carefully with Alice's return. It had taken her a long time to get over the breakup, and Ava didn't want to see her friend nose-dive into a depression again, especially when Ava wasn't around to care for her.

A careful murmuring of the reversal chant, and the page turned blank again. Ava folded it in four, and tucking it under her pillow, slipped out of bed to undress.

First thing tomorrow, she'd ask Enzo about speaking to Iz again. The last thing he needed was a pissed off Iz and Nessa working hexes against him. So far, things were manageable both on and off the island, and for everyone's sake, it had to remain that way. A lot could go wrong otherwise.

13

Once the witch fell asleep, Enzo spent the night wandering the island. Rain weighted the wind, soaking his clothes and hair, but he ignored the discomfort, preferring to be buffeted by the cruel outdoors instead of the seductive pulsing humming through his home.

She'd sensed the collection of dark magick paraphernalia locked in the ebony cabinet. For a witch who claimed she didn't work with degenerate magick, she'd honed in on it immediately, and the open intrigue lighting her eyes had startled him. If anything, the power should have repelled, not enticed. Why hadn't she recognised the lower vibrations?

"A moth to a flame," he muttered, slowing to face north, where the distant Calnaloch Lighthouse pierced the night with its slow sweep of pale light. The O'Keefe witches stayed away from darker magick, but somehow, it called to Ava O'Keefe.

Martha had pieced the dangerous collection together over two-hundred years. She'd begun in her late twenties, and even after losing the ability to work magick, continued to hunt and gather the grimoires, instruments, and amulets. To the best of his knowledge, his niece had rarely utilised degenerate magick. Martha strove only to stem its insidious growth at a time when factions warred with dirty tactics. Enzo hoped the magick she'd cast to lock the cabinet held the strength to keep his witch out.

Catching himself refer to Ava as *his* witch, he grunted. Should he continue to pursue Martha's restoration through Ava O'Keefe? Perhaps he should simply accept Ava's agreement to locate his niece, and hope that once he had Martha back, they could seek others to assist. But who else out there possessed the power to channel twelve witch lines while feeding off eclipse energy? No-one that Enzo knew of. Agitated by the turmoil of his thoughts, he commenced another lap of the grounds.

Wandering the island allowed him to not only escape the provocative lure of witch blood, it avoided sleep, too. One brief nightmare of Giulia had been enough to leave him off kilter for the day. Should he dream of her in a deeper state of sleep, he might wake believing himself existing at another time—one when his blatant hatred for witches had twisted him into a spiteful, violent man. What if an unconscious revulsion drove him from his room? He couldn't take the risk of hurting an O'Keefe witch. Her clan would retaliate. He'd lose his chance to locate Martha, and worst of all, fail to make amends for an impulsive act he'd regretted for the last five centuries.

A slumbering Calnaloch twinkled in the distance as he rounded the house once more. His earlier visit to the town confirmed an increasing influx of creatures, the majority belonging to the warlock faction. While Enzo despised Waylen Kane, he quietly respected his capacity to keep a finger firmly pressed to the pulse of warlock and witch business. The man knew more of what went on within his faction than any other enclave member. Those creeping through Calnaloch in search of Ava O'Keefe likely believed their presence unobserved, but Enzo would bet his wine cellar in Florence that Waylen knew exactly who slunk through the shadows.

The witch Felicienne certainly knew some faces. He'd called to her home under the pretence of an update on the disappearance of Ava O'Keefe, but in reality, wanted to keep himself informed of town activity. Felicienne liked to think herself the all-seeing eye of Calnaloch and its supernatural happenings, but she hadn't yet suspected she'd warded his island home to keep Ava O'Keefe in, and herself out. Felicienne assumed Enzo sought the witch as keenly as she. And no doubt, already silently swore she'd keep Ava all to herself should she locate her first.

'I have my connections in Italy looking for her,' Felicienne had told him, insisting, as always, on receiving him in a stuffy room devoid of natural daylight. By the light of flickering candles, and an air choked by incense, Enzo suffered their meetings with teeth gritted.

'As do I,' he had replied. *'But she's left no trail behind.'*

'Well, she's definitely not in touch with the aunt, and I've been keeping a close eye on The Cauldron. Iseult has had no contact with her, either. It's typical of Ava. She likes to proclaim Iseult as her friend, yet leaves the girl high-and-dry without so much as a bye-your-leave. She thinks herself too good for this town—and my coven. If her mother were still alive, she'd be both ashamed and broken-hearted by her daughter's contempt.' Felicienne sniffed her distaste and quickly laid the blame for the missing witches, the unwanted Calnaloch visitors, and Iseult's upset on *'Ms O'Keefe.'*

The condemnation had annoyed him, and now he picked at it anew, riled him once more. If *'Ms O'Keefe'* was as selfish as Felicienne lamented, she wouldn't be a somewhat willing prisoner in his home, striving to find his niece while considering risking her life to restore Martha's power.

145

Instead of snapping at the bitter, ungracious woman to be silent, Enzo had tuned her out, allowing his senses to investigate the sprawl of her property. Strangely enough, he sat not three feet across from Felicienne Alarie, and quite happily tolerated her witch blood. In fact, it provoked no hunger in him. Nor that of the other witches spread throughout the covenstead. Their blood sang alright, but not with the enticing melody of his witch's.

Enzo turned away from the view. *Ava O'Keefe's* blood, he corrected himself. "Not *your* witch's, you damn fool."

A glance upward locked onto the window of Ava's bedroom. She already devoted herself to locating Martha. Day one, and she'd worked late into the night, ignored her own needs, and had likely fallen into bed exhausted. Felicienne Alarie didn't deserve such grace and selflessness joining her coven, and should she be foolish enough to air her spite in front of him again, he'd—

"Idiota!" Enzo hollered, closing his eyes as he wheeled towards the sea. The damn lure of witches. Would he *ever* learn?

The science behind sleeping on a problem proved itself overnight.

A busy mind nudged Ava awake, presenting the ideas it had filtered out of her mental jumble. Blinking up at the vaulted ceiling, she grasped the presentation of a new angle. Cloaking magick typically blocked the seeker from locating their target, but if Ava flipped the direction, she stood a better chance of luring Martha towards her.

Immediately intrigued by the idea, she clambered out of bed, stubbing her toe on one of Iz's boxes. She hopped to the bathroom, and after showering and dressing on auto-pilot, hurried to the summit of Paladino

Palace. Newly inspired, she set to work, and within two hours, had a solid beckoning spell pieced together.

Just as she gathered the ingredients, a warning but polite cough declared Enzo's arrival. A waft of freshly brewed coffee came with him.

He didn't look his typical collected self. Ava couldn't pinpoint what it was, not that she dared to stare at him long enough to figure it out. Even though he dressed to his usual perfection, a sense of dishevelment clung. Accepting the out-held coffee with a smile, she said, "I'll be better today. I'll ensure I stop for meals—and *make* those meals."

"It doesn't inconvenience me," he replied.

"The smells bother you." Ava took a sip and sighed at the deliciousness. His coffee was easily the best she'd ever tasted.

"I'm adjusting." With a lift of chin, he shifted focus to the open grimoire. "What are you working on?"

Ava savoured another sip before setting the mug on the working table. "So, I've switched tactics. This is a beckoning spell. Martha is cloaked, but I'm not, so in simple terms, I should potentially be able to entice her energy to connect with mine. I'm starting at a basic level, but will build on it with each attempt. I might have to call on you later for help. Depending on how Martha's cloaked, I may need your blood, or to use you as a conduit." When she looked up from where she'd been gesticulating at her notebook, the gathered ingredients, and a sigil she'd already drawn, Enzo's countenance had shifted from weary dishevelment to hopeful.

"Anything you need." Curious, he came to stand beside her, glancing over her notes. "This is yours?" he asked, pointing at her sigil.

"It is."

"Martha has a persuasion charm," he said, turning to scan the room. "She bought it in Egypt. Allegedly, it belonged to a Pharaoh—Ramesses II, according to the vendor, but we both suspected that a lie. She used

147

it once to find me—in 1537, if I remember correctly. It drew me all the way from Asia to South America."

With so much to unpack from his rushed statement, Ava gaped at where Enzo already searched the apothecary cabinet. A blur and clamour of vampire speed opening and shutting dozens of drawers on sticky runners followed.

"1537?" Her tongue formed first. "You're really that old?"

The blur snapped to a stop. "*That* old?" he queried with mild humour, forearm resting on an open drawer.

"I mean, I just, I wondered, and—there are rumours, you know?"

"Rumours?"

Ava caught the beginning of a smile before the whirlwind kicked off again. When he shot to where she stood, his speed blew her hair away from her face. Two sheets of paper fluttered across the table. She slapped them down before they could skitter to the floor.

"A persuasion charm." Enzo dangled his found treasure before her. Encased within a netting of fine, tarnished silver, a teardrop lapis lazuli crystal hung from a threadbare leather cord. "Perhaps this will assist?"

"It may." Ava took it from him. Although dusty, and definitely in need of a sage cleanse, a zing of magick tickled her palm as she turned it over. If Martha had used this, she'd already forged a connection to the item, boosting its summoning power. "Thanks." She smiled at him. "This will help a lot."

"You haven't eaten yet." Serious Enzo reappeared. "I set breakfast out downstairs. I think it would be best if you eat before you grow too distracted."

For once, he didn't scuttle out of the kitchen while she ate. Instead, he stood by the glass doors with a fistful of almonds and raspberries. Ava watched him eat them one by one as she spread rhubarb and ginger jam

148

across her toast. Had he stalked her well enough to stock her favourite preserve, or was it mere coincidence? "You eat human food?" she asked, caving to her curiosity.

"Rarely. These" —he opened his palm— "I enjoy for the texture only."

He'd answered one question. Might he answer another fifty-seven? Ava plucked a strawberry from the bowl of soft fruits and bit through, leaving behind the frilly stem.

"1525," Enzo suddenly announced.

"1525 what?" she asked quietly, already guessing what it was he'd revealed.

"I was turned in 1525 at the age of forty-five years."

Ava swallowed, lowering the slice of toast she'd been about to attack. 15 goddamn 25. "By choice?" her barely there whisper wondered.

"No. Wrong place, wrong time," he said simply, and tipped the last three raspberries into his mouth.

Ava remembered her phone request just as he reached the kitchen door. She called after him.

"Yes?" he answered from the hallway, out of view.

"May I talk to Iz today? My aunt's coming into town. She'll need to hear I'm okay."

"Leave it with me."

Four beckoning attempts delivered zero results, but confident she was on the right path, Ava persisted. By one o'clock she'd crafted a new version of the spell, but laid her pen down and closed the notebook. She needed to make lunch and chase Enzo about the call to Iz.

149

Both the library and birdcage doors were shut when she crossed through the hall. The kitchen was empty, too. Knowing he'd hear her banging about, she set about making food. If he had something to announce, he'd reappear and say it.

All the meat had vanished from the fridge. Ava glanced over the freshly stocked contents, deciding on a cheese and tomato sandwich, a green salad, and more of the olives he'd served for breakfast. She'd just made herself a mug of tea when a cough announced his approach. Trying not to laugh, she squeezed out the tea bag and deposited it in the countertop bin marked 'compost'. Vampires composted. Who knew?

"Iseult will call this phone at two," he said once he'd rounded the doorway.

He handed her a mobile so basic, even the most technically challenged person could use it. Two buttons; answer, hang up, and one button for each of the zero to nine digits. That was it.

"It's a secure line. The call can't be traced from either end. Iseult has a similar phone. She won't call you on her personal phone again."

Ava took the offering. "Thank you."

"Will you agree to settling on a fifteen minute call once every other day?"

"Yes," she said before he could change his mind.

"Arrange them for different times, please. Don't form a pattern."

"We won't."

"You cannot make outgoing calls from this phone."

He'd thought of everything to keep the communication as guarded as possible, but Ava didn't care. A call every other day to Iz was more than she'd hoped for. It would also keep Nessa's powder dry. And if barring her from making calls kept Iz safe, she welcomed it. "Thanks, Enzo, really. This is more than I expected."

"You're welcome, Ava."

150

Enzo had spoken her name many times before that moment, but it sounded different this time—like he meant it. Or wanted to say it.

"I must rest for a while. Should you require anything, call for me."

Ava nodded, clutching the precious phone to her chest. She remained that way for a while after he left, aware of a subtle shift in him, or maybe between them. But with two o'clock already approaching, she parked the intrigue. Her poor brain could only handle so much in one day.

She and Iz talked for the full fifteen minutes.

Little had changed at Iz's end. Felicienne continued to hover like a wasp at a picnic, and Finn remained fixated on why Ava had vamoosed to Italy, and with whom.

Iz found it hilarious. *'I'm so tempted to say you've nicknamed your travel buddy the Italian Stallion just to piss him off.'*

'Don't,' Ava had begged. She'd tried to change the subject by asking more about the Alice situation, but Iz skipped over it.

'I'll meet Alice for coffee whenever she rolls into town. But I have no expectations or hopes beyond a civil conversation.'

Both assured of the other's well-being, they agreed to four o'clock for their next catch up.

Ava returned to Martha's room feeling less abductee, more slightly restricted house guest. Truth be told, with all the hassle Finn and Felicienne raised, she'd rather be on Enzo's island, surrounded by Martha's amazing collection than dealing with all the bullshit in Calnaloch. Her handsome host wasn't exactly a hardship, either.

151

As she returned to her work, she found herself smiling at the memory of his *'You're welcome, Ava.'* The way he'd said her name had whispered in a loop ever since. Smile stretching wider, heat rose to her cheeks.

"Oh, no you don't," she warned. "Don't you *dare* go there."

But the thought had already rooted.

14

Time slid away in Martha's room, stealing days with it. Ava found herself looking up from whatever grimoire or notebook she'd been engrossed in, to find the hands on the clock had spun forward, weather had changed, or night had crept in over the sea. If it wasn't for Enzo appearing with snacks, tea, and water, or summoning her downstairs for mealtimes, she would have lost track of the days entirely.

From behind warded balcony doors, she admired a calm evening, washed in hazy pink and purple light. The previous day, she'd made decent progress, and determined to finalise a spell, had worked late into the night, oblivious to time, and how—unlike Enzo—her body really did need sleep. At some point, she'd curled deeper under the throw, cuddled into her cushion nest, and fallen sound asleep.

But that morning, she'd woken in her bed.

153

She wouldn't have questioned why until she moved to roll over and realised she still wore her clothes. Understanding dawned, scalding her cheeks; Enzo had carried her down and tucked her under the bedclothes without her stirring awake. He'd even removed her shoes and lined them up neatly by her nightstand. She might have believed she'd stumbled downstairs herself and flopped onto the bed without stripping off, only she always put her shoes away at night.

Dying a slow death all over again, Ava thumped her forehead against the glass. She'd been too embarrassed to say anything to him that morning, and once she realised he was avoiding the subject, too, it only increased the awkwardness. It didn't help that he'd been acting weird with her all day; barely making eye-contact, keeping his distance, and at dinner time, escaping the kitchen with a claim he had *'matters to attend to.'* He'd sat with her without hesitation for meals the days before, happy to let her blather on about her research and ideas. Tonight's absence had left her lonely.

"Shit," she mourned on a sigh, regretting her stupidity. The last three days had been good—great, even. She no longer felt like an abductee, or Enzo, her abductor. He'd loosened up a bit more, and she'd even made him laugh—twice. The Knight of Wands appeared when he did, flashing a brief glimpse of the sexy, charismatic Enzo Paladino he'd been hiding. Although she knew better, she wanted to see more of that Enzo. When he dropped his guard, it gave her a delicious, low-down thrill.

"It is what it is," she said, her disappointment clouding the glass. She swiped it away with her cuff, and noting the time, retreated to the couch to wait for Iz's call.

"Wherever you are," Iz said when Ava asked about Calnaloch, "stay there, girl. It's freak season here. I've never seen so many strangers knocking around."

"It's that bad?"

154

"Yup. Every ingredient suitable for a locator spell has sold out. I swear, if one more stranger comes in here looking for mistletoe or yellow evening primrose, I'll scream. You're safely cloaked, right?"

"I am."

"Good, because the entire lot of them are giving me the heebie-jee-bies."

Besides the influx of creatures hunting Ava, Iz had little other news. Finn continued to push for updates on her, and judging by Iz's naughty snort, she was having too much fun embellishing Ava's fake Italian adventures. "You're heading for the Amalfi Coast," she told her. "And I think it's high time you met an Italian Stallion, so. . ."

"Iz, don't you dare," Ava cut her off. "No sexual escapades, do you hear?"

"You're no fun," Iz tutted. "I'm living vicariously through your travels, and *this* close to getting Finn's ears steaming."

"Iz, come on."

"Alright, alright. I'll tone it down. Hey," her voice softened. "You sound good. I mean, as well as can be expected, all things considered."

"I am. As weird as it sounds, this is where I need to be right now. Enzo is a model kidnapper," she half joked. "I'll be two stone heavier by the time I leave if he keeps feeding me the way he is. I didn't think vampires could cook, but he deserves a Michelin star for the meals he's producing."

"So, he's treating you well?"

"He is. How's Nessa? Is she still threatening to hex him?"

Iz hummed a yes and no. "She's calmed down a bit, but still spitting nails about the whole thing. I'll call her as soon as we're done here and catch her up. Do you need any more supplies—specifically the non-magickal kind? Chocolate, a couple of smutty books?"

155

"I'm okay for now, thanks." Her mind already conjured up Enzo smut all by itself. It didn't need any further encouragement. "Did you hear from Alice again?"

"A few texts. I took my time replying. I think it's best I tread carefully there."

"I do, too. I don't want you hurt again, Iz."

Although a few minutes remained, with no other news to share, they arranged their next call and swapped goodbyes.

Ava returned to the desk, and deciding it would be more productive to bury herself in witchcraft, pushed all other worries aside. Things between her and Enzo would be back to normal tomorrow, and right now, she faced bigger problems—like honing in on the meticulously cloaked location of a sedated vampire-soon-to-be-witch-again.

Laser focus paid off.

A few hours later, Ava made a first tentative link with Martha. Although faint, Martha's energy feathered the edges of Ava's awareness as she sat within a circle constructed of salt, cinnamon, rowan, and thyme. It wasn't hard to recognise Martha's presence. It reminded Ava of late summer; the heady scent of overripe fruits and blooms, wrapped in dry heat and laced with rich sandalwood.

Ava clung to the tentative wisp, and almost as if Martha wanted her to know she sensed it, the fragile cord stretched, reaching out to tap Ava twice on her left shoulder before slipping into the darkness again.

Opening her eyes, Ava returned to a room dim under sputtering candles thanks to the pitch-black night outside. Rain sheeted the glass

156

doors, announcing the descent of a storm, but cut off from sound, it raged in silence.

She'd been sitting in a trance for so long, her legs had gone numb, but unable to hold back her excitement, she tipped onto her side, and yelling for Enzo, scrambled to get upright. The pain of rigid muscle flashed through her neck and shoulders. Ava hissed against the burn, taking care not to smudge the sigil she'd chalked onto the floor—or tread on where Martha's persuasion charm lay in the centre. "Enzo!" she yelled. "We connected!"

The stairwell door flew open, and just as Ava loped to standing, Enzo blurred into the room.

"I connected with her!" Ava moved to step out of the circle, but deadened legs sent her tipping.

Enzo caught her clumsy stumble. She crashed into him, her chest to his, the meeting of her soft warmth against his cool hardness abruptly reducing her awareness to the contrasting temperatures of their bodies, the gentleness in his strength, and how, up close, his scent made her head swirl.

Enzo steadied her. As suddenly rigid as she, he inhaled equally sharply. But his sudden gasp wasn't an aversion to her closeness. Like her hitch of breath, it was an attempt to brace against the flare of electricity between them, a hot flash crafted by the sneaky universe. As if waiting for that moment of physical contact, it exploded, igniting a curtain of stars behind her eyes.

From her stumble to his save, him steadying her and settling her on two feet again, no more than four seconds had passed. But within that whip of time, Ava had registered the chemical shift inside her body. Crowded together—no matter how fleeting—had kicked off a chain of unalterable internal changes.

157

Her apology came out breathlessly as she hopped aside, wincing against returning blood flow delivering a rush of pins and needles. "Dead legs. It's not a good idea to jump up like that after sitting for so long."

Enzo's expression mirrored the silent storm raging outside. For once, he appeared speechless.

Moving further aside, Ava refused to heed the rippling sensation behind her breastbone. To direct Enzo's glare away from her, and marshal her own thoughts into refocusing, she motioned at the circle.

Damn. He smelled so enticing. Not an expensive bottled-scent kind of appeal, but the allure prompted by a serotonin and dopamine rush whipped up by an oestrogen and testosterone-fuelled frenzy.

"Martha—we—I," she tried, but failed to form words with coherence. "I connected with her."

His first endeavour to speak came out as a hoarse murmur. "You did?" he said on his second try, followed by another clearing of throat. Like her, he nailed his stare to the circle, doing just as fine a job with pretending they both hadn't experienced the same rush.

"It was faint, but she reached me." Ava patted her left shoulder. "She tapped me here, twice. Well, not physically tapped, but her energy brushed mine. I didn't actually feel her touch, it was more that she—"

"I understand."

Babble much? Ava took a moment to centre racing thoughts. "Martha knows now," she said after two careful inhales. "She knows someone's reaching out. The link was weak, so tomorrow, to enforce it, I'll need to use you." Heat flared in her cheeks. She could think of a dozen ways to *use* Enzo Paladino, and not one involved magick.

Enzo studied the circle, nodding intently as if giving her request serious consideration. "Of course, whatever you need," he said, tugging at the neck of his fancy grey cashmere sweater.

"Great. Thanks. Um . . .I should tidy up here and get some sleep."

158

"Of course. Goodnight. We'll speak tomorrow."

Ava slammed her hands to her face the second the stairwell door clicked shut. Bone-shrinking embarrassment doubled her over.

Confession time.

Pre-stumble, Ava thought Enzo Paladino too handsome for his own good. As economical as he was with it, she couldn't help but love his caramel-smooth voice, spiced by that sexy Italian lilt. The Gods had crafted his eyes, purely to smoulder a *come to my bed'* look. His lips, when they smiled, promised the kind of wickedness that would keep a girl naked for days on end. And his laugh? Oof. She had no words for that.

But the Ava of now? The Ava who'd had her breasts smushed to his rock-hard chest? Who'd so very nearly traced the tip of her nose up the slope of his throat to breathe in his Paladino-ness? This Ava was well and truly screwed.

"Shit." Ava lowered herself to her knees. This was no vampire-thrall trickery or her sex-starved body craving a hit of cold and delicious Italian gelato. This was something way beyond sexual attraction, a magnetism far more dangerous and addictive. Shifters bonded with their mates, vampires sometimes formed sire connections, but vampires and witches coupling? Nope. They didn't belong together. Everything about them screamed opposition; their blood, their life force, how one fed off life, the other off the earth, how one could so easily manipulate the other, hurt the other, alter their being beyond recognition. Vampires and witches were oil and water. And yet. . .

Ignore it.

Yes. She would simply ignore the draw to Enzo Paladino. It wasn't like she had nothing to distract her. A unicorn witch needed rescuing and reviving. It would take every ounce of her time and energy to figure out how, and as long as she remained up here, and Enzo down there, meeting

159

for the occasional information dump or polite check-in of the other's well-being wouldn't be too difficult.

And, Ava suddenly remembered, carefully rising from her knees, Cyrus would land any day. A vicious vampire trapped in the mind of a sulky teenager would add another level to her distraction.

Standing tall, Ava brushed her palms off. She could do this. In two weeks, if she agreed to restore Martha's power, even less if she decided against it, she'd pack up her stuff, wave goodbye, and return home. The Paladinos would then mosey back to their respective European homes, and all would be forgotten.

Ava surveyed the room as she flicked on the lights before taking her time to snuff out the remaining candles. With the circle still intact, she side-stepped it to close the open grimoires on the table. A quick tidy of the desk left everything ready for another attempt tomorrow. All she needed to do now was return to her room, prepare for bed, retire the energy-zapping day with a little grounding and meditation, and then fall into bed where she'd dream of— "Ignore it. Ignore it, ignore it, *ignore it!*"

Enzo sat on the edge of his bed, elbows ground into his knees, chunks of hair fisted, and eyes squeezed shut. He wanted to label what had happened, but he couldn't, because he didn't understand it. The lure of Ava's witch blood was one thing, but what he'd experienced in that room was something else entirely.

For the last ten minutes, he'd cycled through desperate explanations: Ava had bewitched him with a spell. He'd simply allowed her to get

160

too physically close. Stress corrupted his ability to tune out her witch charms.

But he'd rebutted every one. Ava hadn't cast a spell on him. She wasn't in the business of ensnaring or manipulating. And she certainly hadn't used charms, magick, or any form of clever intent.

Sudden physical closeness didn't explain it either. Enzo had held her before; when he'd saved her from Manus Larsen. Even with her blood driving him to distraction, he'd encountered no abrupt, possessive desire. And last night, when he'd scooped her off the couch and carried her down to her room? At no stage, had cradling her warm, soft body to his chest turned his insides to lava.

So what *had* happened? He knew the flush of falling in love, regularly tangled with the primordial tug of sexual attraction and desire. He'd craved many women over the centuries, courted them with determination to coax them into his bed. But in the few seconds Ava needed him to keep her from hitting the floor, a cellular-deep urge to own her had overwhelmed him. Not in a carnal way, but something far more profound—as irreversible as a vampire sire bond; partnership, unfaltering trust, and devotion.

Enzo rose with a quiet grunt. The craving to protect and provide continued to race through his veins. But he was no primitive human male, thumping his chest to attract a female. He'd lived half a millennium. What need had he for such a binding connection? And with a *witch*?

Enzo crossed to the window, throwing up the pane to welcome in the storm, but not even wind and rain buffeting his face and chest could wash away the ghost of her contact. The brand from Ava's soft breasts continued to sear. The sprint of her startled heart still thrummed in his mind, along with how her cheeks had pinked, pupils had blown, and breaths had rasped. Whatever had occurred, the moment had stunned

161

her as dangerously as he. "No—this cannot be," he insisted to the wild night.

Enzo leapt from the second-floor window, landing on the sodden ground below. He bolted for the shoreline, tearing off his choking sweater. Once at the water's edge, he flung it out to sea. Arms spread, torso exposed, he roared into the wicked wind, venting shock, rage, and confusion. And driving the holler, the agonising desire to slip into Ava O'Keefe's bed, draw her fragile human body against his steel form, and watch over her until dawn.

15

When Ava lifted her head out from under the duvet the following morning, a discernible shift altered the atmosphere of Paladino Palace.

With a gasp, she bolted upright. She and Enzo were no longer alone. Cyrus had arrived.

She took her time showering and dressing, wondering should she wait for Enzo to come knocking, or just wander downstairs herself, stick out her hand and say hi to the vampire whose violent ways marked him as the most unwanted house guest *ever*.

But the second she emerged from her room, the door mirroring hers on the far opposite side of the landing swung open. *Enzo's bedroom?* Ava caught a slice of what lay behind him, but before she could note anything beyond the corner of a four-poster bed, he cut off the view. "Cyrus has arrived."

"I know." Ava glanced towards the hallway below. She preferred Paladino Palace with just one vampire. Cyrus and his party had the air buzzing as if swarmed by mosquitoes.

"Unexpectedly," he added, coming to stand at the halfway point between them on the landing.

Divided by a sea of rich wooden floor, where Enzo stood on a navy and gold rug, Ava nodded over at him. "I guessed as much."

See? It's fine. He's not affected by what happened. And now she'd regained sense, she realised she'd been freaking out over nothing. A day of intense magick had misfired synapses in her brain. She'd simply misinterpreted the awkward collision, conjured something from nothing, and put her knickers in a twist for no good reason.

"Ava."

But no. Just that one soft utterance of her name, and Ava barely stopped her knees from unlocking.

"I forbade him to enter your room and Martha's. Please, stay between both for the next few days. I know it restricts you, and I've already demanded so much, but it's safer this way."

"It's okay. I understand."

"He's—"

"Uncle?" The demanding call came from below, and before she could turn to Enzo for a prompt of what to do, or he even have the chance to tell her, a puff of air delivered Cyrus Paladino onto the landing.

Slouched, Cyrus neared her height, but despite his shorter stature, carried a broad, strong build. He shared Enzo's black hair, but wore it slicked back, layered with a product that gave it an almost blue tinge under the bright sky peeping through the dome. While not unattractive, his features were a lesser version of Enzo's; thinner lips, softer jaw, less

164

pronounced cheekbones, and a stouter nose. Cool, grey eyes flicked over her. Dressed in black jeans, a greying Pink Floyd t-shirt and a pair of muddy combat boots, his outfit and demeanour clashed against the lines showing on his face. Ava guessed he'd been turned at an age similar to Enzo, but he hadn't aged quite as gracefully to that point.

"This one smells delicious."

"Cyrus!" Enzo barked.

The warning went unheeded. Cyrus lounged against the banister, looping the chunky acorn newel with one arm as his gaze raked her from crown to toe. "I'm Cyrus."

"I'm Ava."

"Did you find my sister?"

"I've made a connection."

With a lazy tilt of head, Cyrus swung his attention to Enzo. "Why do I have to be here? This place is boring."

"You know why," Enzo answered, and with a, "Come," gestured Cyrus follow. "Let Ava work."

With a huff befitting a petulant teenager, Cyrus traipsed down the stairs after his uncle. "There's not even anything to do outside."

Ava retreated to Martha's room, surprised to see a key waiting for her in the inside lock. A two-inch piece of steel wouldn't keep murderous vampires out, but Enzo hadn't left it there for nothing, so she twisted it and snapped the latch into place.

Unable to focus on anything but the unpleasant change in atmosphere, and the trouble it might bring, Ava sank into the soft leather chair behind the desk, slouching deep enough to grow a second chin.

Her short-lived contentment had vamoosed with the storm. She'd woken to a new palace, one strained by tension and uncertainty. Enzo hadn't clarified how many made up Cyrus's entourage, but their cosy two's-company status had exploded.

165

"It is what it is," she reminded herself, and sliding upright, wheeled herself towards the desk. She couldn't control who lived in the house, or their behaviour, but she did have charge over what happened in Martha's room. Priority number one; find Martha. Two; avoid Cyrus. Three; forget about last night.

Twenty minutes later, a knock pulled Ava out of her research. She called out as she descended the staircase, and Enzo replied with a low, "It's me."

He'd brought her breakfast; a tray stacked with fruit, toast, coffee, and scrambled egg.

"I can make my own," she insisted as he carried it up ahead of her. "You don't have to keep doing this."

"It's best if you stay away from Cyrus for now." Enzo set the tray down on the table by the couch. "He's irritable."

Why wouldn't he be? "He doesn't want to be here."

"No. But someone has to keep an eye on him."

Ava skirted him to access the couch from the hearth end. The only other option demanded squeezing by him, and that meant physical touch. "How many came with him?"

"Five."

"All vampires?"

"Yes." Stress had Enzo's eyebrows permanently bunched, so she held back on questioning if the entourage were trustworthy enough to keep quiet about the witch working eclipse magick in Paladino Palace to their vampire buddies.

Enzo wandered over to where she'd left the circle intact from the previous night, sliding his hands into his pockets as he studied the sigil drawn in the centre. Either he'd already forgotten about their moment, or, like her, he'd chosen to ignore it. Although, with the new arrivals, they both juggled greater concerns. "His girlfriend, the human, isn't here."

166

Ava looked up from where a sprig of fresh parsley decorated her scrambled eggs. "That's not a good thing?"

His sigh suggested it wasn't. "He said they fought, and that she decided not to come."

"Does she know what he is?"

"No." Attention now drawn to the view beyond the glass doors, he crossed the room, leaving her twisting to follow his movements. "He's compelled Daphne so much that at this stage, I would imagine he's cloaked most of her conscious thought."

"Why didn't he compel her to come, then?"

"Apparently, they fought over the phone."

Ava shuffled around to where the smell of buttery scrambled egg made her stomach growl. Daphne got lucky. Hopefully, she'd stick to her guns and stay away.

"How can I help you today?"

"Um," Ava faltered, swallowing her first mouthful. Enzo stared out to sea, so she kept her attention glued to her food. "I'm not sure yet. I need to do a little more work, but I think the best place to start will be with your blood."

"Call for me when you're ready."

"Okay."

Enzo descended the stairs, pausing at the bottom to call up that she lock the door after him.

Ava hopped up to hurry over to the top step. For the first time since the previous evening, he held her gaze. Heat flashed behind his eyes, quickly shadowed by regret. "I'll lock it," she promised him. "But realistically, a fragile latch won't keep Cyrus out if he wants in."

"No. But it's easier to hear splintering wood than him creeping through an unlocked door."

"Comforting," she muttered.

Enzo agreed with a grunt, and departed.

A frustrating day passed. Ava tried numerous times to draw Martha towards her again, but failed every occasion. Enzo's blood didn't even help. He'd come at her call, silently deposited the drops needed into a bowl, and left again.

Ava could only describe the sensation buzzing in the void as interference. Had Martha's captor discovered the beckoning attempt? Whatever jammed the airwaves suggested they did. The disruption clacked like a rattlesnake's tail, warning her to stay away.

With a call to Iz scheduled for eight, she tidied and retreated to the couch, tugging the cotton throw over her shoulders. A cool night had descended once the sun had dipped below the horizon, matching the tension hovering in the palace.

Iz had updates. Finn had called to The Cauldron that afternoon with news of seven witches now officially missing; three from Calnaloch, two from Kerry, and one each from Galway and Cork. All third-generation witches. As Ava listened, she wondered if the same person lay behind Martha's disappearance.

"My guess," Iz said, "is that whoever it is, they're in need of thirteen witches. I'd put my money on channelling magick. What do you think?"

Adding two and two to make five, Ava leapt to a suddenly worrying conclusion. Thirteen third-gen witches could power a magickal battery strong enough to draw dormant energy from a unicorn witch.

"Ava?" Iz queried her silence.

"Yeah, I'm here, sorry. I'm wondering if they're linked to what I'm working on for Enzo." She hadn't told Iz anything about Enzo's request, and wouldn't either. Iz knew better than to ask.

"Do you think they could be?"

"Maybe. Hey—could you talk to Ciara Brady's parents and ask them for something of Ciara's?" If she tried reaching Ciara with the same beckoning spell she'd been using for Martha, and met the same rattling interference, it would answer her question.

"Yes, of course. Felicienne's probably already taken any hair, but leave it with me and I'll see what I can do."

"Make sure Finn doesn't get wind of it, okay?"

Iz tutted and hummed annoyance.

"What?" Ava popped a square of chocolate into her mouth.

"I preferred him when he refused to believe. Suddenly, he's Mr Open-Minded. I saw him walking through Rune Park with Felicienne yesterday evening, the two of them nattering like best buds. If he gets Felicienne on side, he'll be in on everything."

Including Enzo, Ava realised. When Enzo compelled Finn to get out of her apartment, did it include forgetting Enzo's face and/or name? What if Felicienne mentioned him in conversation?

"He's also still fixated on you being in Italy," Iz added another item to her worry list. "He's been stalking your social media accounts."

"I hardly ever post, so that's no tell," she replied, barely enjoying the crunch of salted caramel. "Does he not believe you and I are talking?"

Iz huffed irritation again. "I dropped in a casual comment about how well it was for some soaking up the hot, dry weather of the Amalfi Coast while we had to put up with storms. But all he did was fire a look at me. He knows I'm bullshitting him."

Ava groaned and sank deeper into a slouch.

"Why don't you give me your login and I'll post something?"

169

It wasn't a bad idea, but how would Iz fake an Italian backdrop? "Post what, though, Iz? For Finn to believe it, it'll have to be a current photo of me *in* Italy."

"Girl. I have editing skills."

"That's true." Iz had built and designed the website for The Cauldron and knew her way around photo-editing software. If anyone could fake a few images of Ava living it up on the Amalfi Coast, it was Iz. "Okay, do it. But just two photos—and only one with me in it. The second should be a food post."

Iz gave a little giggle of satisfaction. "Can I mention your Italian stallion?"

"Don't you dare!"

"I'm kidding, I'm kidding."

Ava called out the login details for her accounts and reminded Iz to say in the caption how much she was enjoying being offline.

"Good point. Finn will probably DM you, and while I'm all up for posting fake pictures, I draw the line at messaging. Oh, hell," she whispered. "Is he a dick pic kind of guy? Because I definitely don't need to be seeing those."

Ava laughed so hard she almost choked.

The subject shifted to Nessa's visit. Nessa had been less murderous than Iz had expected, and although Nessa didn't want Ava anywhere near the *'poisonous Paladino family'*, she accepted Ava's decision and agreed to butt out—for now. But she'd commanded Iz to keep her informed of every conversation they shared, and if Ava failed to call within three minutes of their arranged time, Nessa swore she'd launch all-out war on Enzo's island.

"She's layered your apartment with extra wards," Iz told her. "Said there's a clamour of energies surrounding your complex—mostly fae and warlock."

170

Ava glanced around her cosy, safe-ish space. Yes, she shared a house with an unhinged vampire, but once again, she had to admit she was safer here than anywhere else right now.

Iz went on to tell her some interlopers had been brazen enough to call into The Cauldron enquiring about her, pretending they wanted a reading. "A few of your real clients have been in, too, so I told them all you'd taken a few unplanned weeks off."

"Shit." Ava smacked her forehead. "I forgot about Anna. She'll wonder why I haven't been in."

"It's okay. I spoke to her this morning. Finn freaked her out with a warning you'd possibly gone missing, but I set her straight, so she's now also telling everyone you've skipped off to Italy. She even put a sign in the window saying you weren't taking bookings for the time being."

"So, Finn is the only one not buying the Italy story?"

A tinkle in the background announced Iz entering her kitchen, disturbing the chime hung above the door. The familiar melody had Ava wishing she were sitting at Iz's table, drinking tea and nibbling on chocolate.

"For now. But if he gets into Felicienne's head, she'll start querying it, too."

Every day added a complication to the situation. Ava closed her eyes and threw her feet up on the coffee table. Fourteen days remained until the eclipse. If she refused to flip Martha's witch switch, would Enzo kick her out? If he did, she'd stumble straight into the waiting claws of the growing crowd on Calnaloch's streets.

By the time the call ended, Ava had eaten half the bar of chocolate. As she winced at her piggery, a soft knock announced Enzo.

For the last few days, he'd been slumming it with his casual wardrobe, but finery had made a reappearance; a suit, shirt, and tie—along with a face suggesting he'd been sucking on lemons.

He'd brought a guest. A woman stood behind him. Enzo gestured she wait in the landing, and closing over the door, told Ava they needed to talk.

Cyrus required distracting. Enzo had agreed to take him ashore and entertain him with the nightlife in Dublin city.

In the foot of the stairwell, a cosy five-by-five space, Ava folded her arms. Yes, the palace protected her, and no, loud, sweaty nightclubs weren't her thing, but her own stroppy teenage self had risen from the depths, pissed off that Enzo and Cyrus got to go out while she moped under house arrest. It didn't help that all she could suddenly picture were hordes of women draped over Enzo as he plied them with champagne from a VIP corner of some swanky club.

"I'm leaving Kara and Max here," Enzo said, as if a parting gift of Cyrus's bodyguards somehow made it all better. "Both know to call me if there's a problem."

Afraid she'd spit out a snarky reply, Ava simply nodded, and even managed a one-shoulder shrug.

"I'd rather not leave you," he said, creating a distance between them by backing against the door.

In the few feet of air separating them, a hot current sparked, one that had Ava struggling not to appreciate just how perfect his suit fit, or how damn good he smelled.

"But Cyrus is being difficult."

Maybe *she* should start being difficult. Did she not deserve a little entertainment, or would Enzo refuse to bend to his captive witch's demands? "I understand," calm, mature Ava replied. "I'll be fine here, don't worry."

Enzo's expression darkened.

Ooh, he didn't like her easy surrender. And when he asked if she was sure, she provoked him further by smiling. "Of course I'm sure. Enjoy

172

yourselves. I'll see you tomorrow." As if keen to return to her work, she backed up the bottom two steps. "Don't leave your drinks unattended."

A weak smile appeared at her joke. "I'll see you tomorrow."

"Okay. Bye. Have fun!" Ava turned, and before she'd reached the top step, the door snapped shut behind him.

Out of his sight, irritation hissed out on a sigh. She had no right to be mad, she really didn't, but angry breaths streamed as she bit down the urge to yell what she honestly thought about his *'boys' night out'*. Had he wanted her to plead that he stay because he didn't want to spend a night keeping his wayward nephew out of trouble? Or did he need to hear how an evening heaving with temptation made her blood boil with jealousy?

Aware her reason had skedaddled as efficiently as Enzo, Ava sided with the jealousy option. Even though Enzo wasn't the kind of man who needed his ego stroked, if he truly wanted to stay at home, he'd have refused Cyrus. Clearly, the prospect of strutting his Italian god-self around Dublin city offered more amusement.

Fine. That was his prerogative.

What did she care?

"A lot. That's what I care. A whole damn lot."

173

16

Half an hour passed before Ava gave up trying to pretend Enzo hadn't pissed her off. With Cyrus gone, she had the run of the house, and thinking a distraction would serve her better than seething in Martha's room, she traipsed down the stairwell, wondering if there was even a television under the roof of Paladino Palace. Probably not.

But there were snacks.

She swung open the door to see the woman standing where Enzo had left her on the landing. Not creepy at all. "Oh. Hi."

"Hi. Ava, right?"

Unprepared for such a warm smile, Ava stalled in surprise. "Yes. I'm Ava. You're Kara?"

"I am. Everything okay?"

"Craving popcorn, is all," she said.

"I'll come with you." Kara had an American accent matching her sweet, peppy disposition. "Kansas," she replied to Ava's query. "Junction City, to be exact."

With her perky blonde ponytail, Ava could picture Kara cheering for a college football team, bouncing along the sidelines in a colourful cheerleader uniform. But she didn't ask. For all she knew, Kara could have been turned before the invention of cheerleading.

Downstairs, she met another new face. Kara introduced her to the stocky guy hovering in the hallway. Max wasn't as welcoming. His expression remained coldly blank as he barely graced her greeting with a nod.

"He doesn't say much," Kara confirmed as they headed into the kitchen.

Ava found popcorn kernels in the dry pantry, and with oil and a deep saucepan sourced next, fired up the stove.

"Movie night?" Kara asked from where she'd politely stationed herself beside the French doors.

"I wish," Ava scoffed. "I'll bet there's not even a television in this house."

"Ah. You haven't seen the basement," Kara said knowingly.

Ava wheeled to face her. "There's a basement?"

"Pool, plasma screens, gym—"

Ava flicked off the stove. "Show me. Please?"

Kara led Ava back through the hall, around the bottom of the stairs, past Max the Morose, the Dickens Library, and towards the room Ava had briefly glimpsed on her first day and labelled as another pointless reception space. But she'd missed the door inside, one which Kara opened to reveal a staircase leading to a whole new level of Paladino Palace.

They emerged into a basement with a glass wall on the left framing an indoor pool area straight off the front cover of 'Wealth Beyond

175

Your Wildest Dreams.' Azure blue tiles, underwater lighting, and a casual layout of leafy palms had Ava thinking they'd wandered into the Caribbean.

"Sauna and steam room," Kara said, pointing to the doors behind a row of cushioned recliners. Her grin told Ava she found the whole thing wildly insane, too. "I don't know why," she whispered. "We don't even like the heat."

The tour revealed a games room next, one with a pool table, dart boards, air hockey, and three old-school arcade machines. A state-of-the-art stereo system occupied one corner, with the shelves beside it stuffed with vinyls, CDs, and cassettes. The neighbouring room popped her mouth open wider. A mini movie theatre, tricked out with a dozen plush seats overlooked by a giant screen. "Holy shit."

"There's more," Kara told her lightly.

The next door swung back to reveal a bona fide gentlemen's club. Populated by leather Chesterfields, antique tables and lamps, it boasted a sleek wooden bar better stocked than her local. Ava could picture Enzo holding court in one of the fancy armchairs, swirling a brandy as he contemplated the stock exchange with tweed-suited, pipe-smoking men.

A gym with a treadmill, rowing machine, and weights came next. Neither she nor Kara could identify the rest of the equipment. "Torture devices?" Ava joked.

The final door revealed a graciously lit gambling den with a roulette wheel, poker, and blackjack tables.

Ava threw a limp wave at the sight. "This is impressively ridiculous, and at the same time, ridiculously impressive."

"Right?" Kara giggled.

"Do they even use any of it?"

Kara shrugged. "Mr Paladino seems to be most fond of the bar. Sometimes he plays pool. But only ever at night. Usually while you're asleep."

"Enzo plays pool?"

"Mm-hm. So" —she gestured at the mind-blowing options— "what would you like to do?"

"Honestly, I've no idea. There's too much to choose from."

Had Enzo purposely kept all of this a secret? They hadn't exactly had an opportunity for him to offer a tour of his house, but she'd spent the last few days moving between only four of the bazillion rooms; her bedroom, ensuite, the kitchen, and Martha's room. Would it have killed him to suggest she unwind with a sauna, a movie, or a game of PAC-MAN?

"You know what?" Ava turned to where Kara leaned against the open doorway of the gambling den. "I'd like music. Loud, shake-your-booty music. And tequila." Let Enzo enjoy his night out. She could have just as much fun here.

Kara brought her back into the games room. Ava immediately flicked on the stereo, tuning into a station playing a dance mix for losers like her; sad, lonely women who weren't out in nightclubs on a Saturday night with hot Italian men in designer suits. No champagne for pathetic loners involuntarily manacled with a cursed necklace enticing supernatural villains. No siree.

An unopened bottle of Enzo Paladino's expensive Fortaleza tequila swung into Ava's eyeline. "Hell yes!" she whooped, gratefully accepting Kara's offering.

Kara appeared just as excited about their spontaneous party. "Do you play?" she asked, motioning at the pool table.

"I do."

"Yay!" Kara clapped with joy. "Fun!"

Ava tipped the unopened bottle upside down to wet the cork as Kara set up for a game. Iz had gifted her a bottle of Fortaleza for her thirtieth birthday, and between them, they'd made a balls of removing the fancy

177

agave piña cork. At over one hundred euros a bottle, she hadn't had the opportunity to crack open one since, but she'd made a point of googling how, specifically for a time like this. A careful twist and the cork slid out in one piece. "Kara?" Ava held out the bottle to her. "Join me?"

Kara declined the offer with a swish of pony tail. "I'm working."

Of course she was. "Did Enzo tell you not to let me get drunk?"

"No," she replied with honest-to-goodness innocence. "He said nothing about alcohol."

Because he thought Ava would be a good little girl, squirrelled away in Martha's room for the night. *Ha! Sucker.*

Ava savoured the first mouthful of the spicy vanilla liquor. Layered with sweet caramel, it prompted a loud smack of appreciative lips. " Oof. So delicious!" And so much nicer than the cheap stuff she drank in the Black Raven. "You break."

Three games of pool later, Ava had a sizeable tequila buzz powering her boogie battery.

"It's time to dance!" she declared, holding aloft the bottle. Although she'd been pacing herself, she'd passed Tipsy Junction a while back, and Drunk Station now neared. But she didn't give a shit. Turning up the volume, she began to sway to the beat, and with Kara happy to leave her solo, her vivacious bodyguard retreated.

Nicely toasty, Ava peeled off her cotton sweater, and flung it with an impressive aim. The garment hooked itself on the cue rack. "Not *that* drunk, see?" she told it, toeing off her boots next. Spurred by the deep thump of base, way too drinkable alcohol, the anger that continued to simmer, and a dangerously volatile layer of frustration, Ava surrendered to the music.

Enzo heard the heavy thud of bass as soon as the boat neared the island shoreline.

Cyrus caught it, too. "Your witch is having a party," he said, and with a slow shake of head, tutted disapproval.

Tucked against his side, inebriated from her own partying, Cyrus's on-again girlfriend perked up. "I love parties," Daphne slurred.

The moment Daphne had appeared in the nightclub, eyes glittering with remorse as she rushed into Cyrus's waiting arms, Enzo realised his nephew had hoodwinked him. But Daphne, despite how Cyrus had compelled her mind into occupying no more than a few original thoughts, had a way about her that calmed Cyrus.

Enzo had been prepared for a night of trouble, but could honestly say he'd quickly found himself bored. When Cyrus announced he'd had enough, Enzo had been more than happy to vacate the brash, bright club and its stench of human. If he'd checked his phone once since leaving home, he'd glanced at it a thousand times, both terrified and hopeful Kara or Max would call with a demand for his return.

He hadn't wanted to leave Ava alone. He'd counted on her arguing, demanding he stay. After all, why should he benefit from an evening out when she remained locked inside his home? Instead, she'd shrugged calm acceptance and told him to enjoy himself. He thought he'd glimpsed anger, but her breezy parting comment of, *'See you tomorrow'*, had left him stung by something he couldn't quite name.

The boat reached the small jetty on the western side of the island. Enzo glared up at the house. The lights were off in Martha's room and Ava's bedroom. If the two vampires he'd charged with her care had spent the evening partying, they'd be blowing with the sand in the next three minutes.

Enzo left Cyrus to deal with an uncoordinated Daphne, fury rising as he marched towards the house. He burst through the front door to find Max standing fully sober in the hallway, stationed exactly where commanded. So *Kara* had defied him?

"What the hell is this?" Enzo gestured at the racket filtering up from the basement. "Where's Kara?"

"The basement, sir."

Cyrus came in behind him, Daphne cradled in his arms. "I want to dance!"

"No. You want to sleep," Cyrus told her.

Daphne gusted a loud yawn. "I'm tired. Can we go to bed now?"

Enzo made a beeline for the music. It grew louder with every step descended. He'd misread Kara, and the fact disturbed him, yet as he came down off the final step, the unmistakable scent of Ava O'Keefe and expensive tequila hit him full force. Standing outside the closed games room door, Kara held her post, hands clasped behind her back, sober, alert, and maybe just a little amused.

"Kara?"

"I've been with her all night, Mr Paladino."

"What's going on in there?" But he already knew. Ava sang along, atrociously, to whatever track thumped.

"She's dancing."

"And drinking."

Kara's smile vanished. "You didn't want her drinking? I wasn't aware, Mr Paladino."

"Witches and liquor, Kara. When is that ever a good mix?"

Kara looked ready to cry. "I'm sorry."

"You'll know the next time," he said.

"Yes, sir."

Enzo braced, conscious he required more than his evaporating self-control could provide. Clearing his throat, he briefly closed his eyes, grasped the handle, begged for strength, and opened the door.

Stripped down to a lavender camisole, Ava slowed the enticing sway of her denim-clad hips as she lowered one arm to point at him with a bottle of tequila. "Enzo Paladino!" she sang in greeting. Two-thirds of the bottle remained. But clearly, the third she'd consumed had done enough damage. Approaching him on bare feet, with hair loose and messy, eyes glassy, and cheeks flushed, she purred, "You're home early."

"Good evening, Ava."

"Oh, it's *good evening*, is it?" she asked with more humour than anger. He took it as a positive sign. "*Did* you have a good evening? How *was* your boys' night out?"

Enzo hadn't yet experienced an intoxicated Ava O'Keefe. In the weeks he'd been watching her, she'd displayed little interest in alcohol, so ignorant of what he faced, he chose to remove the root cause of the problem first.

But Ava anticipated his move.

The bottle swung out of his reach. "Nah-ah. This is mine."

"I think you've had enough."

"Nope." Backing away, she clutched it possessively with a slurred, "Even though I am a *little* drunk."

Where dancing had enticed the thin fabric of her camisole to bunch, a strip of smooth, pale skin dragged his eyes down. "More than a little, Ava." Forcing hungry eyes up, they next landed on a tease of black lace peeping out from the scooped neckline.

181

"But do you know why I'm as skunk as a drunk?"

Oh, he could guess, but would prefer not to hear. She told him anyhow.

"This" —she smiled, dangling the bottle between them— "is the *finest* tequila. It pretends to be vanilla-y at first, but after a while, you discover it's oh-so-caramel smooth. And then, once you *really* get to know it, you find out it's actually hiding a delicious hint of spice." The 'spice' she enunciated slowly, closing her eyes as the word trailed off with a sigh of pleasure.

The breathy delight speared him with a shock of arousal. Rooted in place, Enzo faltered.

"It's literally you—in a bottle." With deliberate leisure, Ava lifted the rim to her lips, tipped a generous measure into her mouth, and swallowed with a hum of satisfaction. "Yes, sir. It's Enzo Paladino bottled. And I want to drink it *all*."

"Not tonight." Enzo had his substitute secured before she could lift it to her lips again. Or invite her to taste the *real* him.

"Hey!" She pouted. "That's not fair."

"You'll thank me in the morning."

"Will I?"

Enzo wanted to laugh at her suggestive batting of heavy eyelids, but her humour suddenly vanished.

"Shit. I'm drunk."

"You are."

Ava groaned, and with a huff, muttered, "You went out."

As he guessed. The true reason behind her frustration. "I had to. I'm sorry."

Hugging herself, she glanced around as if suddenly realising her whereabouts. "Where did you go?"

Barely able to hear her above the pounding music, Enzo skirted her to turn down the volume. She visibly deflated as quietness descended. "To a loud, unpleasant club."

"You didn't enjoy yourself?"

"No." But he was enjoying himself now, watching her eyes struggle to hold his and not roam his body. "Ava. Let me take you to bed."

A beautifully offended frown formed. "I am *not* that kind of girl."

"I meant, allow me to bring you to your room, fetch you water, painkillers, and ensure you get into bed safely."

"Oh." She drew in a breath. It did nothing to steady her wavering. Drunk enough for a stiff breeze to blow her over, she appeared ready to topple at any moment. "Did you have champagne?"

"No. I had scotch."

"But I'll bet you had women draping themselves all over you," she muttered, rolling her eyes before turning away.

"I most certainly did not." He'd spent the entire torturous evening picturing her—no-one else. The only woman Enzo wanted draping his body was the inebriated witch before him—but sober. He craved Ava O'Keefe coming to his bed willingly, and with all faculties present.

Wandering on unsteady feet, Ava spotted her sweater. "There it is," she slurred. Once yanked free of the cue rack, she bunched it over her chest before tugging down her camisole to hide showing skin. "So." Flapping at her face, she clumsily swiped wayward strands tickling her cheek. "No draping women?" she asked quietly, propping a hip against the pool table.

Enzo didn't hold much faith in the sturdy furniture keeping her upright. "None," he said, inching closer in anticipation of a tumble.

"Oh."

A strained moment passed with Ava studying her sweater, fingers picking at the hem. Shoulders and eyelids drooping, she shook her head.

183

"This is hard," she finally said, and with a sigh, looked up to gesture between them. "This. Us. You're too—"

Enzo watched her in the pause, hurting for the open regret and confusion dulling her eyes. As if hooked by an invisible cord, he found himself shrinking the distance between them. "Too what, Ava?"

"Too everything," she decided. "Like—why do you have to be so handsome?"

"You're equally distracting," he assured, fingers itching to corral her flyaway strands.

"Yeah," she scoffed. "Right."

"Ava—"

"You know, the thing is, I really *do* want to find Martha," she cut in. "I wasn't so sure at first because of all your secrets, but now I am." She flapped again, but this time at the surrounding air, as if a swarm of insects required dispelling. "Something's blocking me, and I can't think straight today to figure out what. That—that thing that happened last night," she said, gesturing between them once more, but with increased agitation. "It has my head muddled."

Enzo didn't have a name for it either, but the unknown attraction scorched the air between them once more, drawing him within inches of where heat pulsated from her body.

"What happened last night? Was it you doing your vampire thrall thing?" A scowl appeared as she glared up at him. "Because if it was" —she poked him in warning— "you're playing dirty."

Enzo captured her finger, and flinging caution aside, hooked her around the waist, pulling her hips against his. The heat of her skin spread through him as pleasurably as he'd feared. "Maybe it was you casting a witch charm upon me."

"I didn't," she whispered, now frowning at where she grasped his biceps. "And I wouldn't. That would be mean."

184

Enzo smiled down at her. He had about sixty seconds before the tequila stole her consciousness. "I know you wouldn't. And, Ava? I'm not playing dirty either."

"I'm confused." Glassy eyes slid shut, and with her limbs surrendering, she softened against him.

Heat further swarmed his cool flesh, the contrast rousing a delectable shiver. "I am too," he admitted, straining against the urge to dip his head and inhale her delicious scent. Despite the tequila fumes, her witch blood enticed him as acutely as her warm, compliant body.

"This is hard." A wicked little smile appeared as she remained hiding behind closed eyes. "And so are you," she whispered, squirming against his arousal.

The movement enticed a groan he barely silenced. "Ava," he warned kindly. If she were sober, he'd kiss her sass into silence.

"Shit." Coming to her senses, Ava pushed him away. "I'm drunk. I didn't say that, okay? Forget it—forget me, just—" Unsecured, intoxication tipped her sideways. Ava flailed for the pool table, but swiped wide, grasping only air.

Before his inebriated witch could tumble onto her ass, Enzo caught her and scooped her into his arms. "Bed, Ava. Now."

"Uh huh," she agreed, her head lolling against his chest. "Before I do more stupid."

"More stupid?" he asked lightly, crossing the room. If stupid meant speaking her mind, he'd gladly hear more of her confessions.

Ava's splinted hand lifted, and with a swirl, every surrounding bulb glowed up to full brightness. "That." The music suddenly rose again. "And that—ooh, and this." Glittering light trailed from her fingers. She threw the sparks up into the air. As if standing inside a fireworks display, the tiny dazzling lights enveloped them.

Enzo carried her up to the ground floor in a shower of stars and glitter. Lights flicked on and off, and as they neared the open library door, a soft whoosh announced the candles inside igniting. "Impressive."

"I have all the best party tricks," she murmured, and with a final giggle at her antics, passed out.

17

"Kill me now," Ava muttered as she crouched under a hot shower the following morning. Her head pounded, her stomach mutinied, but worst of all, shame had her cheeks peeling off her face.

She couldn't remember it all, but delightful little flashbacks recalled drunk flirting, bad dancing, dire singing, and something about Enzo Paladino being a bottle of tequila. When a memory of how she'd rubbed herself suggestively against him replayed, she groaned in agony.

But the bad behaviour hadn't been entirely one-sided.

As dehydrated and achy as her brain was, it succinctly recalled the desire swirling in Enzo's almost black eyes when she had squirmed against him. And he'd definitely indicated he found her attractive.

She'd thrown up once this morning, but a disconcerting twist of craving and shame threatened round two. Ava inhaled against the lurch

187

in her stomach, and tipping her face into jets of sobering water, squeezed her eyes shut. "Yes. Death, now, please?"

More alert than when she first woke and stumbled out of bed to be sick, Ava noticed the water and pills waiting on her bedside table when she emerged from the bathroom. She swallowed them with an economical sip, hoping they'd stay down long enough to do the trick. If she didn't pull herself together soon, she could forget about working any magick for the day. Not only was it a shameful waste of time, but it left Martha trapped for longer than necessary.

As she dug out her last pair of fresh jeans and a hoodie, she reminded herself to ask about the laundry facilities. Did Paladino Palace even have a washing line erected on its grounds? If it did, she'd sell a piece of her soul to be hung out on it today. What she wouldn't give to have fresh air buffeting her face. Was there a chance Felicienne hadn't warded every single damn window in the house? Perhaps she should spend the day hunting for a missed exit. It would be a great way to avoid Enzo.

Dressed, and unable to avoid the inevitable, she palmed her aching forehead. "Suck it up, O'Keefe. You're the one who guzzled all that tequila. Now it's time to pay the price."

Stony-faced Max seemed to have taken up permanent residence in the hallway. Ava didn't make eye contact as she descended the stairs, but the sting of his scowl stuck to her as she made her way to the kitchen. An excited voice came from its direction. Ava immediately assumed it to be Kara, but as she neared, realised the accent was different; British—Derry, if she wasn't mistaken.

". . .and then we can go sightseeing?"

"Maybe," Cyrus answered.

Ava pushed open the door. Cyrus sat at the table with a young woman on his lap, a stunning Halle Berry lookalike Ava guessed to be in her early

188

twenties. With an elbow propped on his shoulder, the beauty played with his slick locks, a dreamy expression on her face. It took her a moment to register the newcomer.

"Oh, hi!" She perked up. Her pitch pierced Ava's brain. "You must be Ava, Enzo's girlfriend."

"Um, no," Ava quickly tried to correct her. "I'm—"

Cyrus squeezed out an impatient glare demanding, *just go with it*.

"I'm Daphne," Halle Berry's doppelgänger clarified before Ava could correct the misunderstanding. "Daphne Wolcott, and," she added, clasping Cyrus's head to her chest like a doting mother—or a possessive psycho, "I'm *his* girlfriend."

"Hi, Daphne. Nice to meet you."

"Good morning, Ava."

She'd missed Enzo standing by the stove. With most of her shame flushed down the toilet, nothing remained to cringe over Daphne's *'girl-friend'* comment—nor all the blurry events of the previous night, so, "Morning," Ava replied, surrendering to the unavoidable awkwardness. Purposely, she left the *'good'* out, because so far, her morning had been shite.

"How are you feeling?"

"Merda," Cyrus snickered before she could answer.

"Yes," she agreed flatly, sure everyone staring at her had also royally embarrassed themselves at some stage in their life. "I feel like shit."

"Oh, no. Are you hungover too?" Daphne sympathised. "I partied way too much last night. It's just the worst, isn't it?"

"It is."

Enzo looked his usual perfect self. "Drink, please," he ordered, holding out a mug.

Ava grasped the steaming offering, rejoicing at the prospect of a solid caffeine hit. But Enzo had tricked her. He'd brewed something sourced from the juices of the compost bin. "What is this?" It looked like an Iz concoction, complete with unidentifiable brown things floating on the surface.

"A cure of Martha's."

One sniff had Ava wanting to bolt back upstairs to her bathroom.

"And then you'll eat this." Enzo finished buttering toast, and picking up the plate, motioned for her to follow him out of the kitchen. "We have work to do," he told those remaining behind.

Ava trailed him out as Daphne giggled at Cyrus to, 'stop!'

"I can't drink this," she announced as Enzo climbed the stairs ahead of her.

"You'll feel better if you do. Trust me."

Aware she chickened-out by not facing him for the apology, Ava murmured a low, "Um, look, about last night. . ."

His regret hummed quietly. "You disappointed me, Ava."

Behind him, she cringed, cheeks heating again. "Sorry." Goddess. Why hadn't she stayed in her room? Or under the shower?

"I expected more of you." Enzo reached the landing, and turning, nearly sent her tumbling down with the unexpected smile aimed at her. "I've never heard anyone sing so poorly. It was truly awful."

Stalling, her splinted hand took a clumsy grasp of the banister. "I can't hold a tune in a handbag."

"So it would seem. But besides that," he said, stepping down to take her mug, "you have nothing to apologise for." Nudging the toast aside to balance the stinky concoction on the plate, he cupped her elbow with his free hand. "So, that" —his chin tipped towards the kitchen as they came off the top step— "is Daphne."

If he was happy to leave the previous night's shenanigans in the past, Ava was too. "When did she appear?"

"Last night, in the club."

190

Ava faked a shocked gasp. "Enzo Paladino. Did your nephew pull a fast one on you?"

"He did. But I won't complain. He hasn't whined once since she reappeared."

Enzo led the way to Martha's room. Ava took a seat on the couch, clenching against the dread of drinking compost stew. But the look Enzo gave her when she sniffed at it with a mutter, warned she had no choice. The first sip didn't make her want to hurl, so she braved a second, followed by a bite of toast. "So, I spoke to Iz last night. There are a few things you need to know."

Enzo did his usual pacing as she told him her theory about the missing witches and their connection to Martha. He agreed he'd collect whatever sample Iz procured from the Bradys, and that her supposition wasn't unfounded. When she mentioned Finn and how he stalked her on social media, Enzo's pace turned into more of a stomp. She shouldn't, but she kind of liked how the subject of Finn seemed to put his hackles up. When she revealed Finn and Felicienne appeared to be joining forces, he further bristled.

"I'll talk to Felicienne," he said, scowling out at a calm sea with his arms bunched.

While pacing, he'd folded up his sleeves, baring his forearms. Ava slowly chewed her toast, eyes fixed on where sinew flexed as his fingers clenched. What was it with male forearms and rolled-up shirtsleeves? It was the same piece of limb that showed when they wore a t-shirt or short-sleeved shirt, but something about the crumpled cotton bunched around the elbow stirred her lady parts.

"Ava?"

"Huh?" Quickly swallowing the half-chewed mouthful, she tore her gaze up. Whatever he'd been saying, she'd completely missed.

191

A dangerous smile tipped one corner of his lips. "I asked if you are well enough to work today?"

Ava reckoned she'd turned puce more times in the space of the last hour than she had in the last decade. With another flush, this one creeping all the way to the tips of her ears, she scooped up the compost stew again. "I should be. Another hour or two and I'll be fine."

"Cyrus will probably be gone all day. Daphne wants a tour of Calnaloch."

Was knowing she'd be alone with Enzo supposed to help or hinder her concentration? Hinder, definitely. Especially if he kept firing those wicked little smiles at her.

"You mentioned an additional way in which I can assist your connection to Martha. Perhaps we could try it later?"

"Sure. Let me figure out the details first." Ava took a gulp of the wretched brew. Not that she'd admit it aloud, but the taste wasn't too bad when chased down with buttery toast. Now her tongue had woken, she deciphered ginger and turmeric, but the green/brown flecks she couldn't identify. Whatever Martha's recipe contained, it already settled her stomach.

A buzz alerted Enzo to his phone. He took one look at the screen, and slipping on his poker face, announced he had a call to make. "Drink it all," he commanded before disappearing.

"Yes, boss," she murmured once the door below clicked shut.

Feeling less bin scrapings and more human, Ava allowed the *'tea'* and toast to go down before rousing herself off the couch.

Enzo's blood hadn't helped with locating Martha yesterday. She needed something stronger, and reckoned her best option would be to anchor herself in Enzo and reach out to Martha from there. His and Martha's blood connection should assist with drawing Martha out, while his vampire strength had the potential to shield Ava herself from psychic attack.

192

But a *'should'* and a *'potential'* weren't enough. Before risking anchoring herself to or with anyone, she had a lot of research to undertake.

Ava chose a random grimoire from the shelf. Age had the edges of its vellum pages flaking and brittle, so she brought it to the desk, carefully laid it down, and eased open the cover. The intrusion roused a crackle of tired parchment. Although written in Italian, she flipped through it slowly, studying the sigils, illustrations, and diagrams. Wishing she had an Italian/English dictionary, she took out her own notebook and copied whatever caught her eye.

The in-house translator arrived as she pored over a page with a complicated diagram representing an astral journey spell. Enzo came with the announcement he had to go out for a while; Iz had managed to get a small sample of Ciara Brady's hair. "Cyrus is still here, but if he leaves before I return, Kara and Max will remain."

"Will you be gone for long?"

"Hopefully, no more than an hour. If Felicienne is available, I'll speak to her about Detective Delaney."

Not *your* detective, Ava noted. "What will you say to her? Felicienne doesn't take instruction, you know. You can't just tell her to ignore Finn."

"I'll remind her of how she knows her own mind best, and how her wisdom far exceeds that of a human's."

"That" —Ava smiled— "she'll buy."

"I thought so."

In need of water, Ava walked downstairs with Enzo. Max flat out ignored them as they stood in the hall, but the second the door shut behind Enzo, the prod of his glare struck her again. She wondered what his problem was.

Cyrus was in the kitchen. Alone, he lounged on the bench, legs stretched out, socked feet perched on the chair opposite. Dressed in another faded tee and the same black jeans as yesterday, he read a paperback, but had the left side folded over, hiding the cover.

"Anything good?" Ava asked, reaching up to the cupboard above the sink for a glass jug.

"A space opera," he answered. "It's alright." Distracted by her interruption, he threw it down. "You still haven't found Martha."

While not an accusation, it carried enough of an undertone for Ava to consider her answer. "I've connected with her, which is good. But a barrier's blocking me, so I need to find a way through it to reach her again."

"How will you do that?"

"I want to try anchoring myself to Enzo," she answered, watching the jug fill. "He'll act as a weight to keep me grounded, serve as a magnet to draw Martha towards us, and hopefully, shield us both from psychic attack."

"You don't sound too confident."

"Right now, I'm not," she admitted, turning off the tap. Happier to be facing him, she leaned against the counter. "But there are centuries of information contained within Martha's grimoires. The answer lies somewhere amongst them."

"Martha knows everything in those books," he stated proudly. "If she were here, she wouldn't need to look."

Ava smiled, shaking her head in admiration. "There's an incredible amount of knowledge in that room. I'm in awe every time I open one of her grimoires."

A flash of vulnerability crossed Cyrus's expression as he fiddled with a dog-eared edge of the book cover. "Do you think she's okay?"

"I honestly don't know, Cyrus. When we made contact a few days ago, there was a calmness to her energy, which makes me say yes, but that was then. I can only hope she's okay now."

194

"Me too."

He clearly missed his sister, and being packed off to live with his uncle probably didn't help matters. Enzo wasn't the most patient man. He didn't particularly want his nephew here, and Cyrus knew it. "Actually," she said carefully, immediately drawing his attention up. "I could really use your help with something."

"What?"

"I found a spell that appears to be related to what I need, but it's in Italian."

"You want me to translate?"

"You're the only person who can."

Cyrus carried the jug of water upstairs for her. As Ava poured herself a glass, drank it down in one go, and gathered the things she needed, he wandered around Martha's room. He poked amongst the shelves, fiddled with crystals, and rooted through drawers. A nosy teenager trapped in a grown man's body, she smiled to herself.

He'd found a sage bundle, and pulling a leaf out, lit it from a candle on the mantel before fanning the smoke into his face. "This smell always reminds me of Martha."

"Verbena reminds me of my gran. Jasmine, too."

"I like how scents do that," he said, plonking onto the couch. "I sometimes forget things, and then I get a whiff of something, and I remember it again."

"Have you a favourite?" Ava brought the weighty grimoire over to where he sat, setting it down on the coffee table.

"This," he replied, holding up the remnants of the smoking sage leaf. "And the smell of horses."

"Do you ride?"

"No." Bitterness tightened his voice. "Horses spook around me now."

195

Which meant they didn't before he'd been turned. Ava sat beside him, opened the grimoire at the page she'd marked with a blank sheet, and handed it over.

Cyrus placed it on his lap, smoothing his palm with quiet reverence across the stained vellum. "This one's old."

"It is. I'm nervous about handling these older books. The pages are brittle."

"That's why she converted them all to digital format," he said.

"She did?"

"Martha doesn't want time destroying everything she learned. Or her books being damaged."

Ava grabbed her notebook and pen, ignoring the pointed comment. "The more I learn about Martha, the more I like her. I'm really looking forward to meeting her."

Cyrus nibbled the skin at the side of his thumbnail before asking, "What do you want me to translate?"

"The whole page, if that's okay?"

He shrugged, and shifting to get more comfortable, began.

Cyrus translated with more patience than Ava would have expected. He even suggested alternative meanings for some words, as if intimate with how his sister's mind worked. He knew enough of witchcraft to grasp her intention, and what kind of help she needed, so directed her to a shielding spell further ahead in the book.

Ava filled eleven pages with notes, excited by all she'd learned. Once she noted Cyrus growing twitchy, she finished up, thanking him for translating. "Can I ask you something about Martha?" she queried as he closed over the thick grimoire and returned it to the coffee table.

Cyrus rose to his socked feet, scratching behind one shoulder. His grunt she translated as a 'yes.'

"What does she look like?"

196

Busying himself with working another leaf out of the sage bundle, Cyrus described Martha as three inches taller than him, with long grey hair, brown eyes, and a laugh that made everyone smile.

Ava's heart clenched for him as he stared at the curling smoke, a softness crossing the expression he worked so hard to keep guarded.

"She used to have black hair, like me, but after Enzo. . ."

Breath held, Ava silently pleaded with him to finish. After Enzo what?

"Shock bleached it grey," he continued. "She was only twenty-two. Everyone laughed at her."

Ava almost bit her tongue with curiosity. "That must have been so hard for her. How old were you then, Cyrus?"

"Twelve."

Shit. Hard for him, too. "How old was Martha when she—?"

Cyrus's expression suddenly twisted. Anger flashed as he thumped the heel of one hand against his temple.

Enzo had mentioned the mood flips, and Ava abruptly wished she'd kept her mouth shut. "I'm sorry. I shouldn't have asked. It's none of my business."

"No. It's not," he snapped. "But you still want to know, don't you? You want to know how old Martha was when *Enzo* turned her."

Wholly unprepared for both his sudden fury—and the shocking reason behind it—Ava heard her own tight gasp in the demanding pause. This was a hornet's nest she definitely shouldn't have poked.

Cyrus pinched out the burning sage leaf. "Fifty-two. *Enzo* turned my sister when she was fifty-two." A rush of stirred air, a slam of door, and he vanished.

Ava stared after him. She hadn't seen that revelation coming. The Paladino family history had many dark chapters, and this one, she had absolutely no business knowing.

197

"Dammit," she groaned at herself, flopping against the cushions. She'd crushed the sliver of progress made with Cyrus, and learned something Enzo had likely been keeping a secret.

Between this morning and last night's stupidity, she'd really messed up. Where were time reversal spells when a girl needed one?

18

Enzo returned to find Cyrus and Daphne gone. The hair sample Iseult had procured, he brought to Ava. Still suffering the effects of a hangover, her mood was quiet. He suspected she remained embarrassed, too. For the short while he spent recounting his conversation with Felicienne, she barely made eye contact, choosing to focus on the numerous sheets scattered around her desk instead of him.

He left her alone to work, but with a reminder she had to pause for lunch. The mention of food prompted a grimace, so he decided to make a light vegetable broth. With little else to do, it would occupy his thoughts for a couple of hours.

Waylen Kane had texted while he'd been in Calnaloch. Enzo had skirted his questions about Ava by commenting on the growing number of warlocks in the town, and demanding Kane have them moved on.

> They're drawing too much attention. Get rid of them.

Kane: Afraid of the competition?

> Don't flatter your kind, Kane. It's crass.

There'd been no text since.

Felicienne had left Enzo equally irritated.

Iseult was right. The haughty High Priestess and Delaney were suddenly thick as thieves. Only that morning, clearly jealous over his ex's exploits, Delaney had forwarded Felicienne a screenshot of Ava smiling against a backdrop of sparkling sea and a slice of the Amalfi coastline. Felicienne had ranted to Enzo about Ava's selfishness when, *'Half the town's witches are missing'.*

Iseult had added a caption to the fake post, claiming the weather and food were fantastic, but that the Italian men were *'beyond description'.* Enzo had found it difficult to hold back a smile as Felicienne tutted and huffed. He doubted Ava would find it as amusing.

Alone in the library, he watched the bright morning haze over as cloud built, the quiet moment loosening his mind and allowing a memory of the previous night to slip through.

Ava O'Keefe was a complication he didn't need, but one he could no longer deny he unconditionally wanted.

The image of her swaying towards him, flushed, sexily dishevelled, and with hurt pouting her kissable mouth, had him clenching against a wave of desire. The desperate craving to consume her witch's blood had disintegrated. In its place, he craved her, as a woman, *his* woman, *his* witch. If their work to locate Martha crumbled, he'd find an excuse to keep her here. Even if Ava refused to restore Martha's power, he'd insist on her staying until after the eclipse. Greedy creatures skulked the streets of her town, loitering near her apartment, and trailing the paths she regularly trod. The thought of them coveting his witch had Enzo battling a savagery he hadn't experienced since his early days as a vampire.

He didn't want Ava near Felicienne either. Pure spite fuelled the High Priestess; she no more deserved Ava than the detective.

"Enzo!"

Ava's cry spun him away from the window.

When he blew into Martha's room, she was still within the circle, rising unsteadily. Pale and visibly shaken, she reached out for him, allowing him to guide her step over the boundary so she wouldn't break the circle's line. "What happened?"

"It's the same energy," she said tightly. "Like a rattlesnake. Whoever has Martha captured the other witches, too."

Enzo lead her to the couch where she landed clumsily on the seat.

"Shit," she whispered, leaning over to brace her elbows on her knees as she cradled her head. "That was rough. I hadn't expected such a violent retaliation."

Hunkered before her, he grasped her shoulders. Trembles vibrated through her. "You should have waited for me."

"It wouldn't have made a difference, and I didn't think they'd retaliate—not so violently, anyhow."

"Dark magick?"

"Death magick, I'd say." Ava dragged fingers down her throat as if clawing away a bind. "The power cloaking them is heavy and sticky. It's like tar. I couldn't breathe for a second."

"No more," he commanded without hesitation. "We find another way to connect with Martha. I won't have you risking yourself again."

"I already have another way," she told him. She'd been pale this morning, but the meagre colour she'd regained had drained once more. "Earli-

201

er, while you were gone, Cyrus translated passages from one of Martha's grimoires for me. There's a form of journeying I can do. It's loosely based on astral travelling, and I still have to smooth out the details, but it's safer than beckoning. The only thing is, I'll need you to anchor me."

"I'm here for whatever you require, Ava. But only if it's safe for you."

"Enzo." Despite how shaken the retaliation had left her, defiance firmed her tone. "We *have* to find Martha. Whoever has her knows she's special, that's why they're fighting so hard. If it were us trying to stop Martha from being taken, we'd retaliate with everything we have. They're doing the same. We face a dirty fight, but I'm not giving up. No way."

Enzo gathered her hands. Skin as cold as his met his touch. "I shouldn't have brought you into this."

Ava laughed, a slow shake of head rippling her hair. "Oh, it's too late for take-backs now, Mr Paladino. You can't undo what's done." But fear suddenly stripped the humour. Withdrawing, she leaned away from him. "You're not going to send me away, are you?"

His defiant bark of, "Absolutely not!" made her startle. With a pause to soften both his tone and expression, Enzo clarified his reply. "You'll stay here until the eclipse has passed and the damned vultures circling your home have gone. Regardless of whether you work another spell, you shall remain here, with me, under my protection."

"Oh," she said softly. "Okay."

Enzo pinned a questioning but kind look on her. "Do you presume to think I would cast you out onto the street?"

Ava looked down at where tension had turned her knuckles white. "A few days ago, maybe."

"But not now?"

She shrugged, yet a tiny smile escaped. "No. I think you'd miss my delightful singing too much."

Enzo gently rested his finger under her chin, tipping her face up to meet his eyes again. "I'd miss everything about you, Ava. *Everything*."

Enzo had made soup. Ava teased him about denying his culinary skills as he placed a bowl before her on the table. It smelled like heaven. Still shaken from the psychic attack, and not quite over the knee-trembles from how he'd taken her chin, looked deep into her eyes, and said he'd miss *everything* about her if she were gone, the soup spoon wobbled on its way to her lips.

When he queried how Cyrus had come to translate for her, she recounted her morning, leaving out the part about Cyrus's angry departure—and the reason behind it.

He seemed surprised by his nephew's willingness to help.

"He misses Martha," Ava said, not that Enzo needed telling, but she'd been prejudiced enough to allow Cyrus's history to taint her judgement. Although only a brief glimpse, she'd seen beyond his mask that morning. "She's clearly a mother figure to him. I think that's why he's drawn to Daphne. He's trying to replace what's missing."

"Be careful around him, that's all I'm saying," Enzo said, rinsing out the pot at the sink. He'd rolled up his sleeves again, but Ava kept her eyes on her meal. "His mood can change with the wind, and his demons quickly drag him to violent, dark places."

Ava had witnessed it earlier with how Cyrus had flipped from genial to enraged. *Mental note to self; don't poke the Cyrus Bear.*

"Iseult posted on your social media account."

203

Ava looked up from the last inch of the delicious soup. Although Enzo had his back to her, she'd caught the humour in his comment. "What did she do?"

"Posted a lovely photograph of you enjoying the sunny Amalfi Coast, and one of your evening meal."

Photos were one thing, but what Iz had typed in the caption was another. "Enzo. What did she do?"

Enzo turned to face her, grabbing the tea towel to dry his hands. "Apparently, the Italian men are *beyond description*."

Ava threw a groan to the ceiling. "I'll kill her."

Enzo chuckled.

"Wait—how did you see it? Who showed you?"

"Felicienne."

"*Felicienne* follows me?"

"Detective Delaney forwarded her a screen shot."

Ava slumped in the chair. "Which means he's already suspicious. He knows I wouldn't write something like that. Did the photo even look real?"

"Yes. Iseult did a good job," he assured her, gesturing at the remains of her soup.

"What did Felicienne say?" she asked, retrieving her spoon. "Did she query it?"

"She's annoyed to think you're vacationing in Italy while half the town's witches are missing."

"*Half the town's witches.*" Ava huffed in annoyance. If Felicienne could get a taste of the darkness she'd experienced that morning, she wouldn't be so hasty to judge. Although, knowing Felicienne, if she *had* been present, she would have mocked Ava's efforts and detailed every mistake made. Sound-tracked of course, by the Alarie Sniff of Disappointment.

"She's not worth concerning yourself with," Enzo said.

Ava looked up to where he busied himself with polishing a glass. "Can you read my mind?" she queried, half joking.

"I can read your scowl," he replied, slotting the glass into its place in the cupboard. "Ignore Felicienne."

"I will," she decided, mentally flicking Felicienne and her bitchy ways thousands of miles out to sea. Screw the High Priestess and everyone else who assumed her selfish. Once she located Martha and the missing witches, they'd all learn the truth.

After lunch, Ava retreated to Martha's room to go through the notes she'd taken with Cyrus that morning. Enzo came with her. He claimed he wanted to scan the grimoires himself, so parked himself on the dainty couch, the stack of books he piled up testing the legs of the coffee table.

Ava tried to ignore him as she worked, but every little move he made had her awareness flitting over.

She sensed his gaze on her, too. With each sneaky glance and their shared pretence of unawareness growing by the minute, the air practically crackled.

Eyes obediently lowered to the page before her, Ava inhaled determination. Between her drunk tongue and his earlier *'everything'* comment, their toes butted the edge of a dangerous line.

Ignore it, she warned herself. *Ignore the line and whatever lies beyond it.* But butterflies continued to feather her insides, while her mind insisted on replaying the moment; Enzo's touch, the burning sincerity in his eyes, the softness in his tone.

Nope. Deep breaths weren't working.

Ignore it, ignore him, ignore everything!

205

By early evening, despite all the internal distractions, Ava had pieced together a solid working. Although most of what she described went over Enzo's head, she walked through the process with him repeatedly while he cooked, encouraging him to question each step and suggest anything that could go wrong. The danger list, as she'd anticipated, grew with every minute. But O'Keefe's weren't quitters. The lives of abducted witches lay in the balance, and Ava would take whatever risk necessary to free them.

Cyrus and Daphne returned just as she finished eating. The remnants of her hangover, the psychic attack, and a day of intense concentration/ignoring Enzo, had left her mind and body shattered, so when an animated Daphne burst into the kitchen, ready to detail every minute of their day, Ava found her enthusiasm reserves empty.

On entering behind Daphne, Cyrus had flicked a glare at where Enzo sat sipping wine. As soon as Enzo looked up, Cyrus's normal countenance of bored superiority slid into place. His go-to face certainly had a mean edge to it, but Ava reckoned holding a grudge for five-hundred odd years would carve permanent resentment into anyone's expression.

Earlier, Enzo had suggested she take a sauna. *'To leech the last of the tequila fumes out?'* she'd joked. It wasn't a bad idea. With a day of heavy spell-casting looming, she needed to be in good working condition. As Daphne gushed over the *'cutest little witchy shop'* in Calnaloch, Ava deposited her plates in the dishwasher and said goodnight. She paused on the way out, slowing to offer Cyrus a smile. "Thanks for translating this morning. It was a huge help."

He shrugged. "I'd nothing else better to do."

"Well, I appreciate it."

The sauna worked wonders. Ava emerged with muscle and bone turned to putty to find Kara stationed outside. She greeted her with a cheerful, "Hello!" and told her she'd walk her up to her room. "Mr Paladino was called away," she explained.

Too rubbery to care, Ava didn't bother asking to where, or why. If it was something she needed to know, Enzo would tell her.

Halfway up the stairs, Kara cut herself off mid-tell of how she also couldn't swim, to wheel around at where Max occupied his usual dark corner of the hall. She stared him down, and although Ava couldn't hear what he said when his lips moved, Kara certainly did. She hissed at him like a feral cat, and for the first time, Ava saw beyond the petite, cheery vampire to the wild creature beneath.

"What was that about?" Ava whispered when they emerged onto the landing.

"Don't worry. I'll deal with it."

Bundled inside her room, Ava also decided she was too tired to care about Max and whatever problem he had. Armed with her healing salve, she stood before the bathroom mirror.

Her neck wound had healed to form a tiny pink line. Satisfied with how it faded by the day, she applied a layer of balm, then turned her attention to the splint. Once unfastened, a cautious flex confirmed the herbs doing their job. The joints were notably stiffer yesterday. Another week or two, and she'd hopefully be able to ditch the cumbersome splint altogether.

207

Heat from the sauna lingered in her bones as Ava savoured the comfort of her bed. Toasty, rubbery, and deliciously sleepy, she melted into the mattress. Sleep teased like the tide, tugging her under, then nudging her awake. Under the lull of heavy slumber, when a touch brushed her waist, followed by fingers ambling along the curve towards her hip, she found herself unable to stir.

Lips skimmed her neck. A cool graze eased her hair aside, exposing hot skin. *Enzo*, she tried to murmur. He splayed her lower belly with one hand, and with a possessive tug, hooked her to him.

Their bodies found their place against each other with ease. Sweeps of hungry lips had her quickly delirious. Ava wanted to turn and face him, suggest they shouldn't confuse such an already complex time by rushing into anything, but his chilly strokes burned delightfully.

With her voice thieved, Enzo's hums of pleasure a lullaby, and her self-control vanquished, heat built between her legs. High on Enzo Paladino, she couldn't even budge to reciprocate his caresses. With every sense soaring, she turned to liquid in his arms.

His covetous touch moved lower, trailing the inside of her thigh. *Yes,* she wanted to plead, *yes!*

Enzo's teasing lifted away. His weight evaporated. Suddenly in possession of her mind and body again, Ava snapped her eyes open.

She lay alone, the pillow beside her smooth and undisturbed. With a kick, she untangled herself from the smothering duvet and sat up. "Great," she panted. "Now I'm having Enzo Paladino sex dreams."

The following morning, Ava skipped breakfast, taking only hot water with lemon. She'd woken early, her busy mind rattling her awake as it ran through the memorised steps of the pending working. In need of calm, she meditated for half an hour, sitting peacefully under the palm as she sensed the nearness of her mum and gran. Her usual one-sided chatter wasn't necessary; she simply drew from their faint presence, mentally charging her psychic battery.

With the house quiet, and no sign of Enzo, she climbed the stairs to Martha's room, more optimistic than pessimistic about what lay ahead.

Ava had cleansed the space, prepped the circle and herself, and lined up everything needed before Enzo appeared. Standing before her in all his handsome Italian glory prompted an immediate sex-dream flashback, but resolutely pushing the warm squirmy feeling down, she jumped straight into business.

"A final run-through," she told him. "Step by step. And if you think of anything, speak now. We can't hit pause once we're in that circle."

"Have you eaten?" he asked, propping himself on the edge of the table where the ingredients waited. The arms which had enveloped her so desirously in her dream folded, flexing biceps.

Ava tsked at him—and herself—as she wafted the sage bundle again. "Questions about the working, not me."

"You *are* the working," he informed her, watching her avoid eye-contact.

She really didn't need the distraction of spicy dreams today. Such lousy timing. "No. I haven't eaten. I prefer not to for work this intense. My body will already be under enough demands without having to deal with digesting a meal."

Enzo made no further comment. Keen to get started, she covered each step of the process again, and with no obvious errors, and everything ready to go, hauled in a deep breath. "Okay. So I guess this is it."

Enzo held out his hand.

209

She slid hers into it without a second thought, inwardly clenching when he interlaced their fingers. Dream Enzo had done the same last night. "Let's begin."

19

Both cross-legged on the floor and facing each other inside the circle, Ava held out her hands to Enzo.

Nerves had her heart rapping as his cool fingers slid around her warmth. Unlike the beckoning spell, this journey would take them across a divide. Together, they'd travel an astral highway, where Enzo would act as the wheels, keeping her safely stuck to the road.

On the floor between them, Ava had nestled Martha's persuasion charm amongst the crystal and herbal ingredients. The gemstone would assist with reaching out to Martha, while Enzo's familiar energy would strengthen the link. Hopefully, Martha would be able to flash a visual clue of her whereabouts, or even a glimpse of her captor. On paper, the working seemed simple enough; make a psychic connection, have a quick chat, vamoose. But in reality, a lot could go wrong.

Ava rolled out her shoulders, drew in a deep breath, and grounding in Enzo, began.

Travelling through the astral plane with an undead being on board didn't make for smooth passage. As if riding a violent roller-coaster, blindfolded, clashing energies raged. Ava focused on only two things; her hold on Enzo and linking with Martha. But the constant battering left her grip on him tenuous. It slipped numerous times, yet Enzo yanked her back to him on every occasion.

When Martha's presence finally wove through the clamour, her hesitant whisper came loaded with warning. Ava honed in and mentally grabbed on. They'd found each other, and she now needed to solidify the connection with the utmost care.

The first image Martha sent flashed a dark space with grainy light coming from above. Ava noted a dull brick wall, a layer of moisture coating the grey stone.

Martha's courage wavered. She slid away, but Ava held her ground as passing traffic continued trying to shunt Enzo off the road.

Another image; a circular wall; no end or beginning.

Martha retreated again.

Left hanging once more, Ava strained to maintain a grip. Her strength already waned. The shielding spell surrounding her and Enzo faltered. In her mind's eye, she envisioned jagged cracks scurrying over its intangible form, threatening instability. '*We don't have much time!*' she warned Martha.

Enzo's niece returned. She shoved her way through with a force that swamped Ava in a sticky heat, but through the feverish cloak, she saw a woman before her, just as Cyrus described. '*I see you!*' Ava called out.

Chaos surrounded Martha; cries of fear, shouting, the low chant of summoning. '*Our,*' Ava heard on repeat. '*Our!*' The prickle of Martha's anxiety increased. With one last thrust, she pushed herself forward.

212

Ava reached for her. Despite only a fingertip maintaining her purchase on Enzo, she clambered to the very edge.

His responding yank urged her back, but Martha stretched as desperately as she, spurred by the fear of their link snapping.

Two things happened at once: Enzo climbing to meet her, and Martha smashing through the barrier separating their consciousness. Three words rang out. *'Tell Enzo it's—'*

Brutal, sharp pain severed the connection.

Whiplash speed wrenched Ava from the depths of the in-between, straight back to Martha's room. Slammed by the retaliation, her head and shoulders hit the parquet floor with a cruel smack.

Winded and dazed, Ava gaped up at the spinning ceiling, fighting not to panic as the spasms in her diaphragm choked off her lungs.

As soon as the contractions ceased, she gulped in a breath. "Enzo!" wheezed out on its release.

Over and over she had warned Enzo not to reach with her. *She* was the witch, not he. Employing a car metaphor, she'd told him that no matter what, he must remain inside the vehicle, hands on the wheel. Instead, he'd leaned out the window with her. "Enzo, why did you do that?"

He didn't reply.

Ava scanned her body. No serious pain. A metallic taste declared her teeth had drawn blood, but beyond that, when she cautiously propped herself up on her elbows, everything responded as it should.

Enzo lay sprawled opposite her. Eyes closed, his lower half remained inside the circle, the upper beyond its perimeter.

"Enzo," she croaked, lurching sideways before clumsily rolling onto her knees. "Wake up." Crawling through the scattered remnants, she reached his side. He didn't move when she shook him. "Enzo?"

Why wasn't he opening his eyes? He was the vampire—the being fifty times stronger than her. He should be on his feet already.

Ava shuffled closer and patted his cheek. Her touch shifted his head. It tilted, revealing the unnatural angle of his neck and where broken bone pierced skin. Blood trickled from the wound, forming a sticky puddle beneath his hair.

Cyrus heard her screams. He pulled her off Enzo's static form, yelling at her to shut up. It wasn't until he shook her hard enough to make her teeth rattle that shock finally waned. "Stop fucking screaming! He's had his neck broken, that's all!"

"That's all?!" Ava yelled back at him, hearing herself, but in zero control of her tongue. "*That's all!?*"

"He's a vampire. He'll wake up. Calm the fuck down, will you?"

Ava shoved Cyrus with an angry shriek. "*You* calm the fuck down! And stop cursing at me! It's not like I see broken necks every day of the week! Of course I'm panicking. I thought he was dead!"

"No such fucking luck," Cyrus muttered.

"Fuck you!" she snapped, and clearly possessed, slapped Cyrus hard across the face.

He barely flinched, but his pupils blew, filling his eyes with rage.

"He's like this because he's trying to get your sister back! The least you could do is be grateful!"

"*He*" —Cyrus pointed viciously at his unconscious uncle— "is the reason my sister's gone in the first place. *He* turned us. *He* fucked our lives up. We didn't want this, but he gave us no fucking choice. If it wasn't for him, this—" he hissed, now jabbing his skull, "fucked up brain of mine would have been put out of its misery five centuries ago."

Still heaving for breath, Ava held Cyrus's glare over Enzo's motionless body. The stand-off lasted for a long, tense moment before Ava gathered the sense to back down. The last time she'd lost her shit around an old

214

one, she'd been lucky he hadn't retaliated. Cyrus was no Enzo; he was way too loose a cannon to provoke. "I saw Martha. She's okay."

Cyrus deflated. As if a pin popped his rage balloon, he shrivelled into calm. "She's okay?"

Ava nodded, swallowing down the final dregs of panic. "I couldn't make out where she is; somewhere dark, grey brick, grainy light. She spoke to us. She said, *'Tell Enzo it's'* and then we got cut off, violently."

Cyrus glanced down at Enzo. "They snapped his neck to break your connection."

"That's what happened?"

"Yeah. He was your anchor. Whoever it was, cut him down to cut you off."

It made sense. Ava clutched her neck, aware it could be her lying in a pool of blood. To breach her shield within the astral plane and inflict bodily harm on another demanded serious power. Whoever took Martha clearly worked with the darkest of magicks. They could have easily snapped her neck. In fact, why hadn't they? The severance would have been permanent, and— "Shit. They know who I am," she realised aloud. And whoever *they* were, they needed her alive.

Ignoring her murmuring, Cyrus asked what Martha meant by, *'Tell Enzo it's'.*

Shoving aside the new serving of distressing thoughts, Ava focused on the present. "I guess she was trying to tell us who took her, or where she is. She also said *'our'* on repeat. Does it mean anything to you?"

"No."

"Is it an Italian word—or part of an Italian word that might suggest where she is?"

He shook his head.

Adrenalin trickled dry. Where she'd smacked off the floor—and where Cyrus had grabbed her—pain throbbed. Thinking she'd be safer on the ground, Ava dropped to her hunkers. But closer to Enzo, the protrusion of broken bone threatened to make her faint. Looking away, she focused on her breath as grey clouds infiltrated her vision. "How long before he wakes up?"

"A while. An hour or two." Cyrus lowered himself to her eye-level. "Look," he said with obvious begrudgery, "he's fine, okay? He'll wake with a sore neck, but he's had worse, believe me."

Worse than his spine sticking out of his neck?

"I'll carry him down to his room—if you want."

"Good idea." Better Enzo on his bed than the hard floor.

Cyrus grabbed Enzo's feet, and, hauling him up like a sack of potatoes, flung him over one shoulder. Before Ava could yell at his carelessness, Cyrus had already vanished.

When she caught up with him, he'd thrown Enzo onto his bed. Standing over him, Cyrus's hands flexed as he formed and loosened fists. Whatever he whispered to his uncle, Ava couldn't hear.

Unsure about entering Enzo's bedroom uninvited, she hovered in the doorway. "Is he okay?"

"He will be," Cyrus said, and leaning in, poked the protruding bone back into place.

Ava gagged.

Cyrus turned at the noise, and with a sigh of impatience, motioned to where Enzo lay. "He'll be fine there. Stay with him if you want, but he'll come round with a jerk, so I wouldn't get too close."

"Okay."

"I'm going back to bed," he announced. "I'd appreciate it if you didn't wake me with screaming again."

Ava waited until he'd brushed by her before mouthing a *'fuck you.'* And worried she really was about to faint, braced against the wall and lowered herself to the floor.

216

She stayed there until fuzzy vision and the urge to puke passed. Enzo didn't move once during the long while, and the complete stillness creeped her out. Did he lie so rigidly when he slept, or was this stiff as a board situation only for when he'd been . . . what? *Semi*-murdered?

Ava slowly got to her feet and approached the bed. Where Cyrus had flung Enzo down, one arm had landed awkwardly, half draping Enzo's face. "Enzo? I'm going to move your arm," she whispered. "So don't wake up and freak out, okay?"

He didn't budge when she took his wrist, nor when she settled his arm in a more comfortable pose. Where his shirt had bunched up from Cyrus's mishandling, she tugged it back down over his waistband.

Impressed with herself for ignoring the temptation to trace the edges of abdominal muscle, Ava braved another peek at his neck. The bulge of broken bone had vanished. Skin had healed too. Only for the blood matting his hair, no sign of injury remained.

Curious fingers itched to slide through Enzo's thick hair and coax it into shape. Ava whipped them behind her back, clenching them tight. If Enzo woke to find her fiddling with his hair, she'd have to kill herself.

Thinking it would be best to withdraw fully from temptation, she retreated to the doorway. Should she wait in his room or hers? Cyrus suggested she could stay here, but Enzo might not appreciate the intrusion into his personal space—the decor of which she only now noted.

Although a copy of the layout and size of her bedroom, Enzo's differed. A sombre palette of dark woods and navy fabrics drenched the room in night vibes. Where her white vaulted ceiling threw down reflected light, his hung as black as a moonless sky. His bed, a huge four-poster affair, dangled swathes of inky blue fabric tied at each post. Lush jacquard drapes framed his windows, accompanied by fitted plantation shutters.

217

The dark never bothered her, but Enzo's dark was the kind where she reckoned she'd literally be unable to see her hand in front of her face.

Across the room, the smaller of the two windows placed her position as directly off the gable end of the house. At this height, she'd have a distant but unobstructed view of Calnaloch. The promise enticed her to stay. That, and the fact that when she'd woken from Enzo's abattoir rescue, he'd been watching over her. She could now repay the favour.

Skirting the foot of the bed, Ava tiptoed towards the window, positioning herself to admire the view of Calnaloch on her left, and the sleeping vampire on her right.

Enzo found himself staggering through a forest, aware he raced to find Martha, but too dazed to recall the events that had led him to the Italian countryside. Quiet unease twisted his gut, a sense he should be elsewhere, but he followed the pull tugging him forward on clumsy feet.

Time shifted, delivering him to the forest's edge, where through thinning trees, he saw Martha struggling to free herself. Her captor had tied her to a wooden post; part of a fence surrounding an overgrown vegetable garden. Where she sat on muddy ground, Martha twisted against the binds, her screams muffled by a strip of rag.

Giulia had gagged his niece to prevent her from crying out a hex or curse. Wherever the witch hid, Enzo knew she waited for him.

Silently breaching the treeline, Enzo stepped onto rough earth, immediately recognising Giulia's homestead. The simple cottage with its crooked chimney and small outhouse had deteriorated since he'd first visited to meet his new wife's parents.

Urgency rose through him again, an unnerving sense he was needed elsewhere. Enzo peered over his shoulder, scanning the dark forest for a clue of what called for attention. Only the distant cry of a fox responded.

Foolishly, he'd believed Giulia long gone from their lives. When he'd left her thirty years earlier, staggered away from their home that fateful night, heart crushed and spirit broken, he'd pleaded to the heavens to never lay eyes on her again. Hours later, as rabid creatures tore his flesh and drank his blood, he'd found peace in the agony: Death would irrevocably sever him from the witch who had betrayed him so cruelly.

But the beasts hadn't taken his life. They'd simply transformed it.

Revived as an undead creature, vengeful, furious, and insatiably hungry, Enzo had returned to their former home three days later to discover Giulia already gone, her most precious treasures taken with her.

As he'd stood in their bedroom, the evidence of his wife's hasty departure scattered around the dirty floor, his first thought had been Martha. It was his niece who Giulia had coveted all along. Giulia sought him out, charmed him with her wicked wiles, fooled him into believing he could trust her, *love* her. And once he'd fallen under her spell, she'd tricked him into bringing his orphaned niece and nephew to their home.

Giulia had used Martha to compensate for her juvenile power. Martha didn't like or trust her, but Enzo's selfless wife had put a roof over their heads, food in their bellies, and calmed Cyrus's wild temper with a routine of schooling and labouring on their small farm. Bewitched by Giulia, Enzo hushed Martha whenever she whispered her concerns. He wouldn't tolerate an unfavourable word against his wife.

But Martha persevered.

She woke him one night, urging him to follow her outside. Their only mare was due to foal, and Martha enticed him towards the ramshackle barn, pleading for quiet so Cyrus wouldn't wake. Giulia was already

219

tending the horse, she'd whispered, explaining his wife's absence from his bed.

But Giulia tended no four-legged animal. Through a gap in the barn's slats, Enzo heard grunts and cries of pleasure, and when he'd dared to put one eye to the breach, saw what had truly urged his wife out of their marriage bed and into the night.

The horror hadn't ended there.

In his state of shock, he'd missed Martha slipping away from his side. She burst in on the adulterous scene, threatening to reveal Giulia's dirty secret.

Unaware of her husband's presence, Giulia mocked Martha, promising she'd drown Cyrus in the river if Martha dared to utter a word. As she shamelessly fixed her undergarments and dismissed her lover, she scoffed further, revealing all Martha warned Enzo of as being true. Giulia had bewitched him to gain access to his niece. With just a few sentences, the scornful woman Enzo watched through a slice of rotting wood made a mockery of everything he'd believed good in his life.

Once Enzo had settled Martha and Cyrus in a new town hundreds of miles from the home he'd shared with Giulia, he said farewell. The uncontrollable chaos and violence of his unsolicited new life threatened their safety. Martha's witch blood called to him constantly. Cyrus's childish behaviour and volatile temper stoked a dark desire to physically harm the boy.

Confident he'd hidden his niece from the treacherous witch, Enzo left Italy, determined to learn a less violent way to navigate his vampirism.

Three decades later, he'd barely learned to control those wild impulses when Giulia returned, and once again, threatened Martha.

Enzo crouched, waiting for Giulia to appear from the remains of her childhood home. Martha continued to struggle, shaking her head in a bid to loosen the rag. She hollered and raged, but her choked curses would bear no weight unless spoken freely.

A log settled on the fire pit in the clearing. As flames sprung anew, orange light bathed Martha's face. She'd once prided herself on her thick, coal-black hair. As a twenty-two-year-old woman, her beauty had drawn attention from many suitors. But when she'd learned of Enzo's fate, shock had bleached it grey overnight. Thirty years later, the volume and length remained—the silver, too. But time had aged the youthful face Enzo remembered. Skin had softened and lines had formed. In 1555 Italy, few lived long enough to reach Martha's age of fifty-two, but he wouldn't allow Giulia to take his niece's life before her intended time. He would end the witch himself that night, and if she took him to hell with her, so be it.

Enzo twisted against an unsettling déjà vu.

The scene played out with strange familiarity; Giulia emerging from the hut, Martha continuing to wrestle against her binds, his booted feet skimming the ground as he sped towards the clearing.

As the events unfolded, he already knew the outcome: Giulia would strike him, he would fall, clothes catching alight as Martha screamed.

But the fire wouldn't consume him. Martha's struggle would pay off. She'd spit the cloth free, holler to the skies, and snap the magickally crafted ropes. Giulia would then rush to retaliate, but Martha possessed greater power and speed. The flames consuming his ice-cold flesh would evaporate. Giulia would come for him again. And then, rushing his senses, blinding him to everything, the maddening perfume of freshly spilled witch blood.

"No." Enzo fought against the ache in his throat, the pinch of descending fangs, and the saliva already washing his parched tongue. Not this time. He wouldn't—couldn't—not again!

221

But he watched, severed from his body, a viewer, not a participant, as the other he crawled on hands and knees to where Martha had sliced her forearm open with a piece of jagged rock.

"Come, Enzo, come," Martha pleaded, one hand splayed as she kept Giulia at bay. The witch hung in midair, scrabbling at her throat as an invisible force held her aloft.

Enzo reached his niece's side, tears already pouring for the inevitability of what was to come. Martha displayed her torn and bloody skin, telling him to drink, to make her like him, and end her cursed witch line with the gift of immortality.

It's not a gift! Enzo wanted to roar, but disconnected, could only watch as the lure of witch blood overpowered his infantile vampire restraint. *No!* he screamed at himself, head snapping back as warmth flooded his mouth.

Instinct took over.

He ripped and tore, guzzling down the ecstasy, aware the rapping of his niece's heart slowed.

Enzo slid his fangs from Martha's arm, gasping against the high as he tilted his face towards a full moon. Blood coated his chin. It swarmed his neck and chest in a sticky heat. His belly already swelled, but he needed more, craved the pulsing flow from an artery. He grabbed Martha's neck, and, ignoring her soft cry, leaned in.

But it wasn't Martha.

Ava's terrified eyes met his as she pitifully cried his name.

"No, Ava, *NO!*" Enzo reared as a guttural roar of pain reconnected thought to limb. He swooped to gather Ava up, but her body shed its form. She dissolved before him, crumbling to cold ash, meeting his lap and the earth in a sheet of coarse powder.

222

Enzo clambered from choking confinement with a holler. He found himself standing at the end of his bed, in the bedroom of his Irish island home.

Disorientated, he staggered sideways, crashing against the dresser. Items toppled to the floor and smashed.

Chaos claimed his mind, throwing a manic jumble of memories; Giulia's sneer as she righted her clothes, Ava taking his hands as she sat opposite him in the circle, Martha's soft pleas as she enticed him to drink her blood, Ava in his arms, laughing as she bathed them in glittering sparks, and then her body softening into ash. What was real? What had he dreamt?

"Enzo?"

Enzo jerked away from the gentle call, shielding himself in fear of seeing Ava before him, but an Ava who would crumble into grit.

Where she stood by his window, silhouetted against the late morning sun, he feared the face hidden in shadow. Did it already powder?

"Enzo. It's me, Ava."

"Ava?"

"Yes, it's me."

He blinked as she neared with careful steps. She looked whole, safe, unharmed.

"You had your . . . We had a little trouble with the journeying," she said.

As sharp and swift as a whip crack, the confusion in his head cleared. He remembered it now, the neck pain, the brutal disconnect that ripped him from Ava. In that split second, he'd thought *her* taken, *her* life severed. But she stood before him, backlit by a blue sky with lazy gulls wheeling in the distance.

"Oof!"

223

He snatched her to him. Desperately needing the warmth of her body, the thump of her beating heart, and the swirl of her luscious witch scent to confirm her presence, he clutched her tight. "You're not hurt? You weren't injured?"

"Enzo, really, I'm fine, but you're squeezing me a bit too tight. Can't breathe here."

"You're not hurt?"

"No, I'm not, I promise."

He softened, easing off just enough to cup her face and scan her for signs of injury.

"You're the one who had his neck broken. Are you okay?" she asked.

"Ava, are you sure?"

"Look at me." Warm hands unhooked his. She stepped back, and gestured at herself with an, "All present and correct. I'm a little bruised from the hard landing, but otherwise, I'm fine. You, however" —she poked him kindly— "scared the shit out of me. I thought you were—" The sentence choked off. Eyes suddenly glistened. "I thought you were . . ."

"I'm not." Enzo motioned at his own present and correct self. "I'm right here."

Ava closed the small distance she'd created, slid her arms around his waist, and pressed her cheek to his chest. "Don't ever do that again."

Enzo rested his chin on the crown of her head, aware of how perfectly she fitted against him—how perfectly they fit *together*. "I won't."

20

Enzo announced a ban on witchcraft for the remainder of the day, and Ava happily conceded. He helped her to disassemble the circle and tidy up, after which they retreated to the library. He ordered her to sit while he disappeared into the kitchen, and on his return, presented her with a tray holding chamomile tea and a slice of fresh carrot cake.

"You like carrot cake," he told her, when she stared at the offering.

She did. She loved it. But it took her back to that day in the Lighthouse when he'd sat across the floor, hiding behind the Irish Times. Did all stalkers pay such close attention to the cake preferences of their prey? "I'm not sure whether I'm flattered or creeped out by how much you know about me."

Enzo lowered himself into the opposite couch, crossing his ankles as he stretched out. Instead of commenting, he delivered a coy smile, playing up to his role of Mr Enigmatic.

"How are you feeling now?" she asked, forking a piece of the treat.

"Sto perfettamente bene."

"I recognise *bene*, so does that mean you're okay?" The cake was delicious. She hadn't enjoyed her favourite indulgence since that Wednesday at the end of March. This time, despite the company being the same, she could actually taste and savour the flavours.

"I am perfectly well. What about you? You're still pale, Ava."

"Because I got a fright. Well—" she corrected herself, "more than a fright."

"No more journeying."

She hummed around a mouthful of sweet goodness, the reply neither a yes, nor a no. Enzo wouldn't listen if she suggested they try again—not this soon, anyhow. Now she'd connected to Martha, it would be easier on round two, and the next time, she'd hyper focus on learning where Martha was, and who had nabbed her.

While tidying, they'd spoken about the images Martha had psychically sent, but couldn't make sense of the image of an endless wall. Neither could Enzo shed light on Martha's cry of *'our'*.

"Do you think she was trying to tell us she's in a place familiar to you both? Maybe that's why she was saying *'our'*. And also" —Ava swapped her fork for the mug of tea— "saying, *'tell Enzo it's'* means it's definitely someone or a location you're familiar with."

"It is," he agreed, "but after five centuries, we share hundreds of friends—and foe. Without more information, the frame of reference is too vague."

So let's try again, Ava itched to say.

The door swung open.

226

Cyrus appeared with Daphne in tow. He flicked a quick glace at where his uncle sat, fully revived. "See?" he said, swinging the smirk to Ava. Amusement twisted his mouth, but she immediately recognised how he laughed *at* her, not with her. "Told you he'd be fine."

Twitchy energy rolled off him. Ava sensed it the kind that preceded trouble. Enzo thought so, too. Although he didn't budge, comfort shifted to wariness.

"Ooh, cake," Daphne said from behind Cyrus's shoulder. She had a coat and hat on. "Can we get cake when we're out, Cy?"

"You're going out?"

Cyrus plastered on a bored expression. "We are," he replied to his uncle, tone sharp with challenge.

"Where?"

Ava inwardly tensed. Enzo's snappy query was exactly what Cyrus expected, and didn't need to hear. *'You're not the boss of me,'* she expected him to snarl

Instead, Cyrus shrugged. "Wherever the wind takes us."

"The zoo," Daphne announced, clapping her gloved hands. "We're going to Dublin Zoo!"

"Cyrus," Enzo warned, expression further darkening. "No. I forbid it."

"Shh!" Cyrus loudly hushed, driving a knuckle into his temple. "I want to go. You can't stop me."

"They feed the penguins at half-two," Daphne butted in, drawing Cyrus's hand down to clasp it between her own. "So, we shouldn't delay."

"Cyrus." Enzo tried again.

"They're my favourites," Daphne gushed on, obviously recognising the knife-edge on which Cyrus teetered. "Do you like penguins, Ava?"

227

"I do," Ava answered. Carrot cake lodged in her stomach as Cyrus tugged at the neck of his sweater. "I haven't been to the zoo in years, though. I couldn't tell you when I last saw a penguin."

"Would you like to come with us?"

"She can't." Cyrus spun, and tugging Daphne with him, ushered her out into the hall ahead of him. Daphne asked why, but the front door slamming cut off whatever reply he made.

Enzo stared after them. "Merda."

"What's the problem with the zoo?" Ava asked quietly, palming her chest to calm her heart.

"Animals spook around us," Enzo replied, sitting forward as if preparing to stand. "Cyrus goads them. He stares them down. There was an incident with a leopard in Berlin a few years ago that ended badly."

"Maybe with Daphne there it'll be different?"

"Maybe," he said, staring after his departed nephew. "And the others are with him, too. Hopefully, that'll inspire him to behave."

Ava returned to her cake. Enzo had five centuries of dealing with Cyrus. It wasn't her place to make suggestions, and a handful of conversations certainly hadn't made her an expert on how Cyrus's mind worked.

Medicine didn't recognise personality disorders in the 1500s. Whatever Cyrus had suffered in human form, Enzo believed to be exacerbated by his vampirism, but she wondered had Enzo or Martha considered identifying the disorder. Enzo had mentioned mood swings, poor social skills, violence, a lack of empathy, and a fear of abandonment. With Martha gone, Cyrus had to be incredibly anxious, heightening his stress, which in turn, would cause him to lean into his other tendencies.

"What happened between you two earlier?"

Ava looked up from licking a blob of cream icing off her fork. "What do you mean?"

"Unless you somehow gained the ability to carry a one-hundred-and-eighty-pound dead weight overnight, I'm assuming Cyrus brought me to my room."

"He did." When Enzo spread his palms to indicate he needed more than her two-word answer, Ava set the fork on the plate. "He heard me, came upstairs, calmed me down, and told me you'd be fine. I told him what had happened, and then he carried you—"

"Ava, I don't want the PG version," Enzo butted in. "Not an hour ago, Cyrus told me you were a wildcat. Why would he say that?"

He had to hear her heart thumping. Even now, thinking about how she'd slapped Cyrus had her realising she was lucky to be sitting on a comfy couch enjoying a carrot cake high. "I was freaking out. He was . . . I don't know, annoyed, I guess, and between us, things got a bit . . ."

Enzo turned static again. Although not prone on the floor this time, he looked as rigid and lifeless as he had earlier. "Did he *touch* you?"

"What? No!" Ava flapped off the notion, grimacing at the thought. "He was cursing at me, telling me to shut the fuck up, so I told *him* to shut the fuck up, or calm the fuck down—I can't quite remember. And then he said—well, it doesn't matter, he was being an ass, and I was already wound up, so I somehow ended up slapping him across the face. I shoved him, too. But that was all."

In one fluid movement, Enzo rose, crossed the divide, and sat on the couch beside her. He framed her cheeks with his cool palms, jaw ticking as he visibly strained to control himself. "Ava. You *cannot* provoke Cyrus."

"He started it!" Did she really just whine that? "Look—I was freaking out. I tend to do stupid shit when that happens—like slapping vampires or throwing knives at them, remember?" Her attempt to make light of the situation failed miserably.

229

"But I would never, ever have harmed you, Ava. You could have thrown a hundred knives at me on your balcony that night, and I would not have retaliated. Cyrus, however, is entirely different."

"I know, I know." Ava took hold of his wrists to ease his careful touch away. This close, the air between them fizzed. Pulled into the impossible brownness of his eyes, everything but the couch space they occupied dissolved into nothingness.

Three days had passed since that moment in Martha's room. In the aftermath, Ava had sensed the connection between them solidify. She wanted to deny it, laugh it off as Stockholm Syndrome, or Enzo's inescapable vampire handsomeness. But when she did, she could hear the universe snickering. It didn't make a lick of sense; she and Enzo were opposites in too many ways, especially in the most fundamental, but hour by hour, whatever unseen binds trailed around and between them, they tightened.

Life had taught Ava independence. She prided herself on being a resilient woman who relied solely on herself—and rarely failed in that task. But Enzo Paladino enticed her into surrendering her oneness. She longed to lean in, rest her head on his shoulder, and not be the only adult in charge of her life. He offered things she didn't need, but suddenly wanted; security, comfort, affection, trust. She no longer doubted the why behind his reason for Martha's power to be restored. Whatever it took, she would give her all to grant his request. But—and here lay the grounds for why she couldn't have him touching her, or looking at her the way he did at that moment—they lived in a bubble right now.

Encased in his fancy home, their only focus aimed at rescuing Martha, reality existed in some other far off dimension where the daily humdrum of earning a living, paying bills, booking dental appointments, and remembering to get the car serviced, weren't of concern. But in eleven days, they would. On April 21st, astrological forces would resume

230

normal service, power-hungry creatures would slink away, Felicienne's wards would come down, and Ava would return home. What would happen then? She and Enzo would meet for drinks in the Black Raven on Friday nights? Rotate between Calnaloch's restaurants every Saturday, occasionally joined by Iz or Cyrus and Daphne? Would they sit over coffee on a Sunday morning, studying their respective diaries?

'Sorry, darling,' Enzo would say. *'But I have enclave business all week. Let's schedule a movie night for the following Wednesday.'*

'Hmm,' she'd say. *'Wednesday evening doesn't work for me. What about Thursday? Actually, no, scratch that. It's eclipse season. I'd best go into hiding for a month. Can you fit me in towards the end of September?'*

If she caved to her heart now, it would only complicate an already problematic affair. To sail through these muddy waters, she needed to treat Enzo and his request as a business transaction. In return for his protection, she would locate his niece and reignite her witch power. No matter how her heart—and body—ached to abandon themselves to her client, she had to resist. As crass as it was, the, *'don't shit where you eat'* proverb applied exactly to this kind of situation. So yes, even though she thirsted for Enzo's touch, got a deep, low-down-thrill from his protectiveness—and that hollow at the base of his throat where a few curious chest hairs peeped up from under the soft cotton of his black shirt—she had to push it all away.

But while she'd been inner monologue-ing, he'd already moved, and now busied himself with watching where he threaded her hair through his long fingers. The other hand had slid to her hip, his thumb brushing slow strokes.

"Where did your mind go?" Enzo murmured.

She'd also missed him shifting closer, sneakily parting her knees with one of his. Crowded this near, his scent worked as cleverly as his gentle touches, enticing her to drift behind closed eyes and melt into his lap.

"Nowhere. Look, Enzo."

"Yes, Ava?" A tiny exhale of appreciation escaped as he stroked the curve where her neck dipped to her shoulder.

"This—" Ava wanted to motion between them, but at some unknown point, her hands had found their way onto his body; one clutching the hardness of his arm, the other fisting his shirt. Where her knuckles brushed his marble abdomen, muscle contracted in response. "We don't need this complication. It's a bad idea."

"I disagree." Curious fingers traced the length of her spine.

"You're distracted by the lure of my witch blood."

He laughed, a dangerously wicked chuckle that ignited fiery sparks in her lower belly. "It no longer lures. Your blood *sings*, Ava, welcoming me home." Enzo lowered his head, his hair brushing her chin as he leaned in to inhale the skin below her ear.

With her eyes almost rolling back to last week, Ava lost all power over her body. An obliging head tilted aside to invite Enzo's exploration. Cupping the rear of her neck, he gently tipped her onto the couch cushions.

The weight of his body on hers, the ease with which they fit together, it all felt so perfectly right. To hell with all her arguments; she had been crafted for him, he for her.

Around them, naughty little cupids high-fived in celebration of a job well executed. Did Ava not appreciate the painstaking work that had gone into pairing a five-hundred-year-old vampire and a cursed O'Keefe witch? Could she not marvel at all the strings they'd had to manipulate, untie, weave, and pluck to manifest this anomalous connection?

Enzo's lips brushed her jaw. Pleasure hummed, just as she'd dreamt, but in reality, it came in surround-sound, bone-melting music.

232

Enzo shifted, propping himself up on one elbow. As he peered down at her, loose locks hanging over his forehead, eyes black with desire, Ava forgot what it was she was supposed to be denying.

Generous lips hovered inches from hers. She licked her own, anticipation catching her breath.

"Does this feel wrong?"

"No," she said on an exhale of anticipation.

"Then don't fight it."

Fight what? Why are you talking right now? Use your mouth for what it was intended and kiss me!

A shrill ring tone sledgehammered their cocoon into a million pieces.

Logic slammed into place.

Ava curled her lips in, preventing them from crossing a line she absolutely needed to remain unbreached. Where hungry fingers had already slipped under the hem of Enzo's shirt to savour the broad, steely stretch of his back, they quickly retreated. "No," she said, wriggling to escape. "We can't do this."

Enzo rose, balancing upright with one knee between her thighs as his left foot met the floor. "Ava."

"Your phone is ringing."

"Fanculo il mio cellulare."

"I know what *fanculo* means." A squirm with more intent slid her high enough to pull up her leg and leave Enzo half-kneeling as she clambered off the couch. Tugging down her top, she cleared her throat with a sharp cough, and with a pat to tousled hair, said, "I need to be somewhere you're not." And with that, wheeled away, left the room, and escaped upstairs.

233

21

Just as Ava contemplated diving under a cold shower, she realised the time. She and Iz had a call scheduled for two o'clock—less than three minutes away. If she'd been in a deep lip-lock with Enzo Paladino, the call would have rung out, and Iz would have launched into panic-mode, eventually prompting a full-scale Nessa attack.

Slumped in the armchair, Ava groaned quietly to herself. How in the hell would she navigate another eleven days in Enzo's orbit? Every part of her wanted to scurry back downstairs and kiss him until her lips turned numb. "Stupid, stupid, stupid!" she berated herself.

Enzo's spy phone rang before she could finish sighing. She tried to answer with a chirpy tone, but failed miserably. *Just like you did with resisting Enzo Paladino.*

Iz immediately pounced on her sombre tone. "Oh, crap. What's up? You don't sound good."

"I'm fine. It's just—it's been a hard day."

"It's only two o'clock. What happened to have you sounding this rough so early?"

Ava pulled her knees up to her chest. "A tough working this morning. It went a little askew."

"How askew? Are you okay?"

The Cauldron didn't open on a Sunday, so Ava guessed the sound of birdsong came from Iz's back garden. Although a small space, Iz kept a stock of herbs in a raised bed against the south-facing wall. Ava wished she were there with her, sitting on the edge, wailing about her woes while Iz weeded. "Enzo got hurt. I freaked out. And we didn't get the clarity we needed."

"How hurt?"

"He had his neck broken."

"What kind of working were you doing for that to happen? For fuck's sake, Ava!"

Ava tutted at herself in agreement. "I know, I know."

"He's alright, I presume, being unkillable, and all that?"

"Yeah. I got such a fright, though. I screamed the house down. If anything happened to him, I'd . . . shit. I don't know what I'd do." Iz held silent. Ava translated it as free rein to vent. "Seeing him like that; so . . . dead-looking. It was awful. I never want to experience it again. I was so relieved when he woke. Thankfully, he's fine, but I'm still shaken."

"Oh, no," Iz said with open dread.

"Oh, no, what?"

"Tell me I'm not hearing what I think I'm hearing."

"What is it you think you're hearing?" Ava asked, surprised by the anger creeping into Iz's tone.

235

"Ava, no. Just no. He's a—dammit!" Iz snapped, a scuff announcing her getting to her feet. "Do I actually have to spell this out for you?"

"Uh, I think so, yes."

"Did that damned vampire compel you? Are you still wearing your mugwort charm?"

Ava unfolded her legs, shifting to perch on the edge of the seat. "No, Enzo didn't compel me, and yes, I am wearing my charm. Iz, there's nothing—"

"We've been friends for twenty-three years. I know you. And I recognise that tone. You've fallen for him, haven't you?"

If Ava had been sitting in Iz's garden, she'd have firstly asked where in the hell Iz's sudden aggression had come from, and then argued and denied her assumption about Enzo. But she had less than fifteen minutes of airtime with her best—only—friend, and wouldn't waste it lying. "Shit," she surrendered with a sigh. "Iz, I don't know how it happened. I can't help it."

"Oh, sweet Goddess."

"Do you think I want this?" Ava whispered, remembering to keep her voice low. "I'm acutely aware of how messed up it is, trust me, but I can't pretend I don't feel what I feel!"

"He compelled you. That sneaky bastard compelled you."

"He didn't. Enzo's just as confused as I am about what's happening between us!"

Iz snorted. "Yeah, right. He planned it, Ava. He bloody well planned it!"

"He didn't! Look—Iz, you've got it wrong. I don't want to waste our few minutes fighting, but I—"

"You're making a huge mistake. He's a goddamn Paladino. An *old one!* His nephew is psychotic, and he's probably no better. He stalked you—remember? He knows exactly how to get under your skin and

236

make you trust him. What's to say he didn't compel you weeks ago, long before you had your charm, huh?"

"He didn't," Ava insisted, temper fraying. "I know he didn't."

"Well, if he compelled you, you wouldn't think so, would you?"

"Iz." Ava got to her feet, marched into her ensuite and slammed the door. She twisted the sink tap on full flow. "He did *not* compel me. This is *not* a one-sided thing."

"End it," Iz snapped, as if Ava turning off her feelings was as simple as operating the faucet she clenched. "Tell him you're done and that you want out of there today. Nothing but bad, *bad* trouble hangs around the Paladinos, and I will not stand by while my friend gets tangled up in their bullshit. Have you forgotten you're a witch, huh? Witches and vamps don't belong together, never did. Whatever it is you think you're feeling, lock it away, stamp it down. You and that bastard are not going to happen. No way, no how."

"I'm a grown woman," Ava reminded her sharply, shocked she and Iz were actually fighting. "I'm more than capable of deciding who I want to be with."

"Not when it's someone like Enzo Paladino. Fuck, Ava! I'd rather see you with Finn than him!"

Ava inhaled against a rising wave of fiery anger and icy hurt. "You don't mean that."

"Like hell I don't! Why in the hell would you do this to yourself? You're already on dangerous ground. Why would you make everything worse?"

"Did you make a conscious decision to fall for Alice? No. It just happened. That's how attraction works, Iz."

"Don't bring her into it." A distinctive ping marked metal hitting concrete as Iz flung down the trowel. "Alice and I, and you and Enzo? Two very different things, my friend."

237

"Enzo and I—"

"Don't!" Iz ground out. "Don't you dare start a sentence with *'Enzo and I'*. Nessa's going to lose her shit when she hears about this."

"What?!"

"She needs to know."

Ava grabbed the cool marble counter-edge to counteract her world spiralling out of control. "It's not any of Nessa's business! And since when are you a tattle-tale?"

"It's not tattling. It's a goddamn *intervention!*" Iz yelled, and with that, the line went dead.

Ava lifted the phone away from her ear. Although it had no screen, she still stared at it in disbelief. "What the hell?"

Both rattled and outraged, she clutched at where her heart galloped. A ball formed in her throat, quickly sending prickling tears to her eyes. She and Iz rarely fought. In fact, it had been at least ten years since they'd last swapped testy words. Iz was the sane, logical one, not the furious, judgemental person who'd just severed their call.

Ava threw the phone down. It skittered across the counter, hitting the tile wall with a thud. Turning her back to the mirror, she ground the heels of her hands into her brow bones. Iz was wrong. Enzo hadn't compelled her. Of course Ava knew she walked on treacherous ground, and no, she couldn't just douse her feelings and/or announce she wanted to leave. "Fuck!" she whispered as hurt and fury leaked from her eyes in hot streams. Could today get any worse?

Enzo couldn't help but overhear the distinct rise and fall of an argument coming from Ava's room. She'd obviously scheduled a call with Iseult, and for whatever reason, they'd fought. Perhaps they'd quarrelled about that morning's journeying. If Enzo had known an aggressor could physically harm either of them in their travelling state, he'd have refused to allow Ava to work the spell. He doubted Iseult would react any differently.

The call that had disrupted their earlier passionate moment remained unanswered. Two text messages had followed, also ignored. But as Ava's bathroom door slammed and the tap suddenly ran at full force, yet another text came in.

Enzo quit his pacing to snatch up the phone. Waylen figlio di puttana Kane. For robbing him of tasting Ava's sweet mouth, he'd rip Kane's throat out the next time he saw him.

Kane: Why didn't you tell me?

Enzo stilled.

Kane: Paladino. Call me.

Kane: CALL ME.

Silence fell upstairs. Enzo glanced at the ceiling, then down to where Kane's demand flooded his gut with unease.

I can't talk right now. What do you want?

Only seconds passed before Kane's answer came in.

239

Kane: You have her.

Not a question, nor an accusation, but a statement of fact. When Enzo learned who had disclosed his business to Waylen Kane, they'd be truly sorry.

Yes, I do.

Kane: Has she located Martha?

She's working on it.

Kane: Time is running out.

"I am aware, you cretin."

Kane: The reeve vote will take place in 12 days. If Martha doesn't return, Alistair Worthington will take it.

"Over my cold ash," Enzo snarled, stabbing a reply.

Rest assured. Martha will return.

Kane: I'm not the one who needs convincing.

Kane disconnected. With his imperious warning twisting Enzo's concern tighter, Enzo tipped his face to the ceiling in pleading. He and Ava had eleven days before the eclipse hit. Neither expected the time between then and now to pass without trouble, but he hadn't anticipated eruptions this far out.

Kane had the inside track on something, and undoubtedly, already connived to twist the situation to his advantage. Edyta Majewski, the third vampire holding a seat within their faction, would know what menace stirred within the Enclave. Someone pushed for Martha's seat to be filled, and Enzo guessed Kane behind that shove. But before making any calls, he needed to check on Ava. After all that had happened in the last few hours, he didn't want her brooding alone in her room. Perhaps he could entice her downstairs with food.

Enzo's phone burst to life again. A blocked number. Tempted to ignore it, his thumb hovered, but instinct told him to answer. "Pronto?"

"Enzo Paladino?"

"Si."

"Aurelius Soto."

Aurelius Soto. General Dogsbody to the Reeve, Enclave Transcriber, and Bringer of Bad News. Enzo slid behind closed eyes, struggling to temper his patience. "Good afternoon, Aurelius."

"Your presence is requested at an enclave meeting tomorrow morning at ten o'clock sharp."

"What is the nature of the meeting?" But he already knew. Waylen Kane sprinted steps ahead of him.

"You have a witch in your possession, one you've allegedly abducted in order to locate Martha Paladino. The warlock council demand an explanation."

"I see."

241

"Ten o'clock, Mr Paladino. Bring the O'Keefe witch."

To hell with this day.

Ava didn't respond to his soft knock. He tried once more, and noting how his rap didn't even hitch her breathing, inched open the door. The sight of her slight form curled in the centre of her enormous bed twisted his lifeless heart. Stepping inside, he quietly rounded the bed.

Damp cheeks and a fistful of tissue confirmed she'd been crying. Had she fought that bitterly with Iseult? Or had the morning's events finally crashed down upon her? If he hadn't pushed her earlier, succumbed to his desire, she might have sought comfort from him. Instead, he'd forced her into shouldering the upset alone.

For the first time in more decades than he could count, Enzo admitted his control slipped. The strings he meticulously plucked and knotted to conduct his life unravelled around him. An abducted niece, a feral nephew, a corrupted enclave, and a witch who had woken feelings he had long thought impossible. No matter how he scrambled to prevent the fraying, he watched it all come undone.

Suddenly exhausted, he made his way to the armchair. Everything hinged on Ava restoring Martha's power, but how could he demand such a tremendous and dangerous undertaking of her? What if the transfer proved too much for her body or mind? It might maim her magick, or at the very worst, kill her. Added to the threat, how in just over twenty-four hours, she would stand before the Enclave, defend his actions and lie on his behalf. If they learned of her deception, they'd deliver a vicious punishment his witch didn't deserve.

The whip of separating strings filled his mind with chaos. Enzo leaned forward, and clasping his skull, bit down against a building roar.

Ava woke just as he made the final arrangements for their travel. She scowled at where he sat, her sleepy eyes blinking displeasure. "What are you doing in here?"

"I came to check on you. You were asleep. I wanted to stay." What had he left if not honesty?

Ava sat up, wincing against the afternoon brightness. "What is it? You have bad news written all over your face."

But honesty didn't extend to further overloading her mind. "You and I have a trip to make."

Sleepy green eyes narrowed. "We do? Where? And why?"

"The Enclave wish to meet with you."

Ava laughed, but without humour. "Eh, thanks, but no thanks," she said, swinging her feet to the floor.

"It's not a request," he informed her with soft regret.

"Let's pretend it is. Anyway, I'm stuck here, right? You can't ask Felicienne to drop the wards or she'll discover you've got me squirrelled away here in Paladino Palace."

"*Paladino Palace?*"

"Well, it's not exactly a poky three-bed semi-detached," Ava pointed out, reaching back to rub her left shoulder.

"Are you hurt?"

"I hit the floor pretty hard this morning, but I'm okay." Reluctant as he to stand and face their pending journey, she sighed over at him, shoulders slumping in defeat. "Do we have to go?"

"I'm afraid so. When the Enclave call, one must answer."

Her kneading ceased. "Why did you tell them I was here?"

"I didn't." Enzo got to his feet. "We'll be away overnight, so pack accordingly. I'll make you something to eat while you do."

"Cool your jets there one second," his witch demanded, halting his attempt to escape. "How do they know I'm here? What are you not telling me, and how come I can leave this house all of a sudden?"

Enzo turned away from the door. The time for secrets had passed. He wouldn't risk Ava walking into the Enclave, ignorant of its web of deceit. As much as he didn't want to drag her into dirty business and pile on further terror, he had to reveal the truths he'd hidden.

Before the insistence demanding he hold his tongue could take full control, he blurted out his first secret. "Reeve Ortega is dead."

Ava's lips parted into a shocked 'oh'.

"There's a scramble for his seat, and enclave members are playing dirty to claim the throne. Martha deserves it—in fact, the future of the Enclave depends on her taking it. If she can return as a functioning thirteenth-generation witch, she'll win the majority vote and put an end to the corruption eating the Enclave from the inside out. But if I can't prove you can locate and bring her home, they'll fill her currently vacant seat and she'll never set foot inside the enclave court again.

"Waylen Kane is a member of the warlock faction. He incited the cancerous rot, and is playing an angle to secure the reeve position, but I can't figure out his play. My guess is that he's reported me, and is using the fact that I've abducted you as a ploy to have us both brought in. And the reason you can leave this house, is that I left one door free of wards in case of emergency."

For a long moment, Ava simply stared at him, shock blanching her already pale complexion. And then she laughed—once—a short huff of disbelief. "This day. Seriously. This *fucking* day."

244

22

Ava endeavoured to process Enzo's information dump as she picked at the sandwich he'd made her. Freeing a piece of tomato from between cheddar and lettuce, she barely registered its taste as she chewed.

The urgency and significance behind his motive to restore Martha's power settled upon her like a leaden cloak. If she couldn't locate Martha, the Enclave would fill Martha's seat and corruption would win. If Ava did find Martha, but botched reanimating her abilities, the failure would mean every supernatural community potentially crumbling as the Enclave disintegrated. Why had this landed on *her*? How could Enzo have burdened her with such a substantial load?

Eyes downcast with guilt, Enzo sat across from her, hands clasped and resting on the table. So far, he hadn't refused her an answer. Nor had he tried to hoodwink her with vague replies.

"So, you think it's this Waylen Kane guy behind Reeve Ortega's death?" Ava asked, picking through her thoughts and sandwich.

"I have no proof, but instinct tells me yes; he's involved," he replied with unfaltering honesty.

"Because he wants to be reeve."

"Yes. Ortega was a warlock. Within months of Kane joining the Enclave, Ortega's favouritism began swinging in favour of the warlock faction. Either Kane blackmailed him, or he promised Ortega something that transcended his pursuit to maintain the Enclave's integrity. If it's the latter, it could only be one thing; power. Martha believes so, too. She was the first to question Ortega's sudden bias."

Ava set down her sandwich, the neat triangle bearing only one small bite. "Are you in trouble for kidnapping me?"

"If you refer to this" —Enzo gestured at their unorthodox situation— "as 'kidnapping' in front of the Enclave, then yes."

"So, I need to say I agreed. That you approached me, and I voluntarily came here to find Martha."

He nodded, and glancing at her abandoned plate, reached across to nudge it closer. "Eat, Ava, please."

"Will the Enclave take my word? I mean, will it just be a case of they ask, I answer, they accept? Or will it be like a lie-detector machine situation? Because if so, you and I both know they'll—"

A crash from the hallway—one that announced the front door slamming against the inside wall—cut Ava off. Enzo stood, the drag of his chair legs against the tiles emitting a low groan. "Cyrus."

"I said let me go!" a bellow came from the hall, confirming Enzo's guess.

One second Enzo was there, the next gone. Ava scrambled to follow.

246

Kara, Max, and two of the other three vampires she hadn't until that point met, struggled to keep Cyrus between them as they scuffled in the hallway.

Blood coated Cyrus's jacket. It streaked his face and sheeted his chin. He looked like he'd been scuba-diving in human insides.

Behind him, resembling a Stepford Wife with her mannequin-still pose, thin smile, and vacant gaze, Daphne simply stared ahead. Blood stained her, too; ugly splashes streaked the front of her coat.

"Mr Paladino." Kara spoke first, holding firm against Cyrus's struggle. "There was an incident."

"Is that animal or human blood?" Enzo queried, as calmly as one might ask, *'milk or sugar in your coffee?'*

"Both," Kara replied.

Standing at a safe distance behind Enzo, Ava reached out for the edge of the nearest support; a dainty table holding a gaudy, but undoubtedly priceless vase. The orange china wobbled. She withdrew her grasp.

Cyrus laughed, a hysterical giggle reminiscent of a hyena. Daphne maintained her robotic smile and distant stare. Was the robot routine because someone had the sense to compel her? Or had shock made the poor girl glitch?

For the longest stretch of time, Enzo said nothing. Finally, he loosely gestured at where the four vampires detained his nephew, and said, "Release him."

Cyrus claimed his arms back with a violent jerk. "That's it? No lecture, Uncle dear? No reprimand, no threats?"

Wishing she'd stayed in the kitchen, Ava took a step back. But Enzo turned to her before she could shuffle another inch.

"Go upstairs and gather your things. We need to leave now."

"Okay." But to obey, she'd have to walk right by Cyrus, who had fixed a ravenous stare on her.

247

"Leave to go where?" The blood-streaked maniac enquired.

"Ava." Enzo motioned at her to move.

Ava reached his side before survival instinct cut off her ability to walk. Fixated by the globule of blood hanging from Cyrus's chin—and how it readied itself to snap free and smack the tiles under his filthy boots—she missed Enzo reaching for her. When his cool fingers enclosed her wrist, she started.

Cyrus smirked, making a point of running the pad of his thumb slowly over his bloodied lips before sucking it clean. "How do you do it, Uncle? How do you resist the call of her blood?"

"Hold your tongue, Cyrus."

"But she smells delicious."

"Cyrus!"

"The penguins are my favourites," Daphne suddenly said, vacant gaze still blankly staring ahead. "But I like the giraffes, too."

Enzo escorted Ava across the hall. Unsure of how her legs found the strength to function, she half hid behind his back as he tugged her along.

"Go where?" Cyrus roared as Enzo herded her up the stairs.

Enzo waited until he reached the landing before turning to glare down at his nephew. "The Enclave called."

Cyrus's bravado immediately evaporated. He visibly rounded in on himself, swiping at his chin and righting his torn, skewed jacket. "The Enclave?"

"Yes."

"Uncle—I—I."

"Kara. Take Daphne to her room and have her cleaned up, please."

"Yes, Mr Paladino."

"Kurt and Carlos. Did you take care of the scene?"

"Yes, Mr Paladino," two voices answered.

A nod of approval, and Enzo urged Ava forward.

"What about me?" Cyrus wailed.

"What about you?"

"The Enclave—I—I didn't mean to, Uncle!"

"You never do, do you, Cyrus? Yet, here we are—again."

Enzo practically shoved Ava inside her room. He slammed the door, guarding it as she turned to face him. "I'm sorry you had to see that."

"So am I." She'd fully expected Cyrus to lunge. The sulky teenager had vanished. In his skin, a manic killer squatted, relishing the terror he roused. "Is that him at his worst?"

Enzo shook his head.

"Why do you allow Daphne to stay with him? He'll kill her, Enzo."

"He won't. He's never killed a woman—not once."

Cold comfort. Ava hugged herself. From outside her door, Daphne's voice queried about the penguins' feeding time. "Don't worry, you'll see them soon," Kara promised with her unfailing cheer as she led Cyrus's piteous girlfriend along the hallway to her room.

"Why did he react that way—when you mentioned the Enclave?"

"He thinks they've learned about whatever it is he's done. Three, maybe three-hundred-and-fifty-years ago, Cyrus slaughtered twenty-seven men in one night. As punishment, they imprisoned him for twenty-seven weeks; caged him in a sensory deprivation cell and fed him only once a fortnight." Enzo left the door to stand before her, gently taking her shoulders.

For a wholly sane being, such an incarceration would be torturous. For Cyrus, it must have been hell. No wonder the prospect of a repeat had struck such terror into him. "He thinks they'll imprison him again?"

"Yes." Enzo took her chin, tipping her face up. "Forget about Cyrus. We have a more pressing issue right now."

"I know." It hit her once more; the perfectly natural urge to rest her cheek to Enzo's chest, wrap her arms around his granite middle, and

249

gobble up the comfort from his presence. How could what she felt be wrong?

Iz's words echoed, the angry insistence Enzo had compelled her, and how Ava needed to stamp her feelings down, twisting confusion tighter.

"Is your bag packed?"

Nodding, Ava inhaled again to find purchase in ever-increasing turmoil.

"We should go. We can talk about what lies ahead once we're on the plane." Enzo leaned in, and with care, placed a soft kiss on her forehead. "Tie back your hair," he said softly. "It'll be windy."

The exit he'd left unprotected had been in full view the night Ava had partied with tequila. Enzo brought her down to the basement, across the tiled sweep of the pool area, and to the door right beside the sauna and steam room. When he pushed it open, she staggered against an assault of noise, wind, scent, and bright sunshine.

The deafening whomp of rotating helicopter blades overpowered any chance of hearing birds or waves, but as Enzo took her elbow and led her towards the helipad, Ava drank in gulps of biting sea air, the lush scent of greenery, and the tang of seaweed and brine.

Enzo hoisted her up and into her seat with ease. She'd never flown in a helicopter. She couldn't even remember when she'd last been on a plane, and at a loss with what to do, allowed Enzo to fasten her belt and slide on her headset.

He took the seat beside her and donned his own headpiece. "Comfortable?"

Ava blinked at him. Comfortable? No. Ready to crap her pants? Yes. Wondering why they weren't driving to Dublin Airport? Double yes.

It took a few moments before the helicopter worked up the steam to lift off. An involuntary squeak escaped her as it glided upwards, slowly turned its rear to the coastline, and swung out to sea. Confused about why they flew away from the coast instead of inland towards the airport, she jabbed her thumb over her shoulder. "The airport's that way."

Enzo smiled at her. "We're flying to the Isle of Man. A plane is waiting for us there."

And he didn't mean a passenger plane that they'd be sharing with dozens of other passengers, did he? No. Enzo Paladino possessed his own swanky jet, no doubt tricked out with cream leather seats, two-inch thick carpet underfoot, and a team of personnel to cater for their every need.

Dizzy from lift off, sensory overload, and the absurdity of her situation, Ava closed her eyes.

'Tell him you're done,' Iz's demand whispered.

But Ava wouldn't—couldn't. She'd remain at Enzo's side until the very end, fighting for Martha, and for everything else—the enormity of which rushed her with such frightening overwhelm, her lungs closed up.

Enzo's soothing touch rested on where she clutched the edges of her seat. "I know, Ava," his voice crackled. Even though interference and the clamour of flight brayed louder, his empathy smacked her right in the centre of her chest, spreading heat behind her ribs. "Breathe, Ava. Just breathe."

So she did. She took one breath after another, and when curiosity finally overtook trepidation, it encouraged her to part her eyes and look out.

Sea, everywhere. Tiny white horses galloped across the water. Embellished by a clear sky, the spread of blue glistened and sparked. Ava had imagined a helicopter flight to be bumpy and unnerving, but the pilot held them so steady, she almost believed they travelled by road. If he flew low enough, could she lean out and trail her fingers through the surf?

Enzo hadn't let go of her hand. He delivered a gentle squeeze, urging her to look at him.

"It's not as bad as I thought," she said, her voice an odd blend of buzz and crackle. "How long will it take?"

"Another twenty minutes."

"And where to then?"

Enzo tapped his lips, tipping his chin towards the pilot.

A top-secret destination. It had to be, she supposed. The Enclave hardly advertised the location of their clubhouse. What would happen once she got there? What form would their questioning take? She couldn't lie to them, so if she blurted out Enzo's secret, had he a plan to handle the fallout?

Don't, she warned herself. *Don't try to control this fucked-up situation. It is what it is. Just go with it.* Otherwise, the alternative promised panic. Trying to manage an unmanageable situation would bring nothing but hysteria. Today had already reached epic shit show levels. If she allowed anxiety to gallop away with her, she'd be a useless, blubbering mess.

Ava spent the rest of the flight watching the view. Sea thinned to land as a patchwork quilt of greens and browns flew beneath them. Within minutes, the approach to Ronaldsway Airport stole her ability to breathe all over again. The sight of the ground rushing up to meet them had her desperately pressing on an imaginary helicopter brake.

A bump announced their landing. Enzo removed her headset, unfastened her seatbelt, and with a motion for her to remain sitting, hopped out of his side, and reappeared at her door.

Shaky legs just about kept her upright as they ducked away from the swooping overhead blades. Buffeted by the wind, Enzo pulled her under his arm. Ava clung on, soaking in his security. Did he know that if he let

252

her go, she'd crumble into a million pieces on the tarmac and blow back out to sea?

Ahead, a jet—all sleek lines and elegant angles—waited, engines already whining. They hurried up the steps and entered a luxurious cabin before she remembered to draw in lungfuls of precious fresh air again. All too quickly, the door slid shut, sealing them inside with a satisfying suck.

Airborne once more, Ava stared out the window, wondering if the strange sensation mushrooming behind her breastbone was the urge to laugh hysterically, or cry until she passed out.

"Greece."

Attention pulled inside the cabin, she shifted to face where Enzo sat opposite her. "We're flying to Greece?"

"Athens, to be exact."

"Oh. Okay." She'd never been to Greece, but admitting it aloud seemed childish in the face of what lay ahead.

As they rose higher into the blue, the land below shrank. The Irish Sea sparkled once again, but the view held no charm. A sudden thought jerked her upright. "Iz!" she said. "My phone. I left it behind. What if she rings? If I don't answer, she'll think something's wrong." But would Iz call? After the argument they'd had, it would take her days to cool off. Or maybe not. She might stick to her guns and insist Enzo the bad guy, and Ava a stupid idiot for falling for him.

"I'll call Iseult and let her know."

"No," she said. "Don't. It won't help matters."

Where his arm availed of the padded rest, Enzo rubbed his thumb and index finger together; a tell of anxiousness she'd come to recognise. "What did you argue about?"

Too frazzled to lie or dodge the subject, Ava sighed a low, "You."

The jaw tick returned. Enzo flicked his gaze to the window, hardness lining his expression. "I'm sorry. Is there anything I can do?"

"No. We probably just need a little space. We'll sort it out."

"She doesn't trust me." His statement, not a question, carried regret.

Ava shuffled in her comfy seat. If Enzo fished for details, he wouldn't get them.

"It's understandable," he said, before she could offer a comment. "I'm a Paladino."

"It doesn't matter. She should trust me to know my own mind."

Ava didn't register the approach of the flight attendant until the man, who looked like a young James Dean, appeared at her side. "What can I get you?" He smiled between them.

Ava shook her head at the idea of food or liquid passing her lips. "Nothing for me, thanks."

"Chamomile tea, please," Enzo butted in. "And something light to eat."

"I'm not hungry," Ava told him.

"You must keep your strength up. You've eaten very little today."

Tea, crackers, cheese, grapes, and the ubiquitous snack-pack of pretzels landed on the slim tabletop a moment later.

"You let me know if there's anything else you need," James said with a chipper tone that had Ava thinking he should meet Kara.

"Tequila?" she muttered.

"Of course."

"I was joking!"

But James had already shot off. When he returned with three fun-size bottles, winked, and set them down beside her tea, Ava couldn't help but laugh.

Enzo, too. And savouring the rare smooth serving of Enzo Paladino's humour, she no longer required the alcohol version.

Despite her resistance, she slowly made her way through the snacks. Under Enzo's insistence, she drank one serving of tequila, and soon after, sheer exhaustion tugged her into a dreamless sleep.

The white noise of the cabin kept racing thoughts at bay, and when she woke to Enzo's gentle touch, it was to hear they were about to land. At some point, he'd covered her with a throw; cashmere soft, and azure blue. She longed to stay beneath its warm, cloudy comfort, but responsibility and a whole lot of unknown waited.

They landed twenty minutes later.

Ava followed Enzo down the jet's steps, across more tarmac, and into a waiting car.

"Where to now?" she asked as it pulled away.

"The hotel."

23

Is this how A-list celebrities experience travel? Ava wondered.

Carted from mansion to helicopter to plane to car to hotel had required zero effort from her. No faffing about with heavy luggage, no fumbling for passports, tickets, and boarding passes. No squeezing into tiny commercial airline seats and breathing in the same stuffy air as all the other germ-ridden passengers before disembarking like an army of dishevelled ants to scramble for baggage. She hadn't suffered a single worry about transfers, coaches, or directions to the hotel, had she lost her passport along the way, where had she stuffed her phrase book, and was it safe to drink the tap water. Instead, she glided upon the smooth Paladino stream, admiring the view as Enzo steered the entire operation.

They'd arrived at the hotel two minutes ago; an obnoxiously grand, shiny, gold-trimmed affair, with polished floors reflecting crystal chandeliers. As Enzo spoke to the receptionist—in flowing Greek, of course; no phrase-book for Mr Paladino—Ava studied the affluent residents milling about the lobby. In her boots, jeans, simple blouse and blazer, she stuck out like a sore thumb. Enzo fitted in perfectly with his crisp charcoal pants and black shirt. He leaned against the reception desk with such ease, it wouldn't have surprised her to hear he owned the place.

"This way," he announced, key in hand as he cupped her elbow. All day he'd been escorting her with the same gentle touch.

"Why is there only one key?" she asked as he steered her towards the lifts.

The hall porter trailed them with their bags. Enzo grabbed the elevator door to keep it open, inviting the young man to ride up with them—and to avoid answering her question. If he'd manipulated them into a one-bed situation, Ava silently promised she'd blockade herself in the bathroom for the night.

More luxury appeared when the suite door swung inwards. Ava ignored the finery as Enzo tipped the porter.

Alone, and as Enzo turned the interior lock with a decisive snap, she folded her arms. "One room?"

He crossed the living area, winding between a smoked glass coffee table flanked by two virgin white couches, to yank the curtains together. Beyond them, Athens sparkled; a pretty mess of lights. The view quickly disappeared. "The bed is yours, Ava. I won't be sleeping."

"Why?"

Busy ensuring he hadn't missed a gap, Enzo reminded her he didn't need to sleep. "And I'm not leaving you out of my sight," he added. "So yes, one bed, one suite. And neither of us will leave it until the morning."

Ava turned away, pretending the abstract art behind her held interest. *And neither of us will leave it until the morning.* He meant the suite, not the bed, but the thought licked her insides with enticing warmth.

257

Out of his sight, she fanned her hot face, and found the bedroom. Yup. Big enough to house a family of five. Plonking onto the enormous bed, she flopped backwards.

Too much, too fast, her brain whined. She had to agree. One minute, she'd been tucked away in Martha's room, happy with her lot. The next, in Athens, preparing to meet the Enclave to defend Enzo.

The digital clock on the nightstand announced the time as nine-forty-three. In just over twelve hours, she'd face an inquisition. No matter how she framed her situation, the fact remained that Enzo had brought her to his home against her will, and while she currently resided under his roof as a *'protected house guest'*, she was, to all intents and purposes, his abductee.

To add to the problem, her abductor had talked her into reanimating a thirteenth-generation witch—one who would scupper whatever evil plans brewed within the bowels of the Enclave.

To protect Enzo and herself, she'd have to lie. And without a doubt, the Enclave had systems in place, which would detect those lies.

"Shower," she quickly decided. If she could avoid thinking about what lay ahead, she might not lose her sanity before dawn.

Enzo paced the expansive living room area, arguing on the phone. It wasn't Italian in which he conversed. While Ava didn't have a word of Greek besides *ouzo* and *mousaka*, from what she'd heard, she didn't think he ranted in the native tongue either. Regardless of the language, the conversation had him agitated. Quietly grabbing her bag, she returned to the bedroom and threw it onto the luggage stand. Whatever shit he dealt with, she didn't want to know; she had enough on her plate, thanks very much.

As Ava tugged out her pyjamas a little too aggressively, her silk tarot pouch tumbled free. Would a quick reading clarify or muddle matters? "Clarify. I hope."

Not wanting to be disturbed, she brought the deck into the bathroom, flicked the lock, and lay the cloth on the vanity unit. As she shuffled, she decided to work with the same spread as her previous reading; current path, what is hidden, what lies ahead.

"No point in trying to fix what's not broken, right?" she asked her reflection, now understanding the odd glances downstairs. Her sleek ponytail had slumped into a lopsided mess. Loose strands jutted out, embodying *finger-in-an-electrical-socket* chic. Complimented by panda-eyes from sleeping on the plane with her make-up on, she looked like she'd been dragged through a ditch backwards. "The state of you," she tutted at herself. But her street-urchin style could wait.

Although tricky to ground and centre with her thoughts so hassled, Ava took a few deep breaths, called out to those watching over her, shuffled, and dealt.

The 2 of Cups, 7 of Swords, and the Tower.

"Again?" she whispered at the Tower.

So, chaotic upheaval remained in her future. For her current path, the 2 of Cups represented union, typically a heart-based one. The last time she'd read her cards, the 2 of Swords had appeared in the position, mirroring her indecision. Now she had sweet harmony in its place. The message pointed towards her and Enzo.

If Iz were standing beside her, she'd snort, and likely flush the card down the toilet. But Ava smiled, kissed her index finger, and pressed it over the image of the happy couple. "Thanks for one friendly message."

The 7 of Swords in the *'What is hidden?'* position stole her warm and fuzzies. It warned of sneaky tactics, someone stealing an unfair advantage. The card often appeared when clients battled with manipulative colleagues at work. It also starred in partnerships where one partner gaslighted the other.

Waylen Kane immediately came to mind.

259

Previously, she'd had the Moon warning of illusion and fear. The 7 of Swords offered a downgrade for the skulduggery, but it continued to alert her to someone sneaking around out of sight, manipulating for personal gain.

Ava slotted the cards back into the deck. Wrapped up safely, she tucked them into her suitcase once more, and flipping a one-eighty on her shower decision, opted for a bath instead.

She contemplated the reading while soaking in vanilla scented bubbles.

The 2 of Cups gave her hope. She and Enzo worked in harmony now. They'd nurtured trust, and because of it, supported each other. With whatever tomorrow might bring, she knew without hesitation that Enzo would protect her. The card also represented love; a blissful union. It was a message she always enjoyed seeing for her clients, and for once, it was nice to get it for herself. Aware of the sudden goofy grin on her face, she scowled it away.

Next, she tackled the argument with Iz.

The echo of harsh words continued to sting, but Ava couldn't ignore her friend's concerns—however unfounded they might be. While she trusted Enzo, and certainly didn't believe he'd tricked her into anything to abuse her witchery, she couldn't cave to the heat between them. Not yet, anyhow. Once the eclipse passed, successful outcome or not, she'd know exactly where they stood. April 21st would yank up the blinds and allow illuminating daylight to spill into their world again. If Enzo made it clear he wanted her, she'd explore what developed between them—but until then, no more almost-kissing. No more anything that would flame the sparks constantly igniting between them. "Easier said than done," she moaned, and slid under the bubbles to drown a groan.

Resurfacing, she grabbed the roll-top edge. Her splint clacked against the ceramic, reminding her to apply more balm before bed. The healing salves had worked wonders, and while she wouldn't risk damaging tendons by removing the splint too early, the prospect of facing the Enclave with a visible disability—no matter how small—made her suddenly uncomfortable. She didn't want anyone assuming her incapable or weak. When she declared her ability to find Martha, it had to ring with confidence—*she* had to stand before them with confidence. Unfastening the protective binds, Ava threw the splint aside and flexed pruning fingers.

The water had cooled before she climbed out. The luxurious toiletries collection included a body butter that smelled good enough to eat. Buttered from head to toe, somewhat relaxed after the bath, and swathed in a fluffy white robe, she dropped into the swivel chair positioned by the dresser in her bedroom. Entertainment channels offered several English programs, including movies. Perusing the menu, Ava swished from side to side as she worked through the list, reckoning a mindless movie would help her to fall asleep.

Enzo knocked before she could decide. He entered with a tray and an expression she chose to ignore.

"What is it with you and food?" she asked kindly, watching as he set it down. "Have you a secret feeding fetish?"

"The only fetish I have is ensuring your good health and well-being, Ava."

A bowl of steaming jasmine rice and vegetables sat under the cloche. "Something light," he said, sitting on the end of her bed. "Eat a little, please."

Realising she'd had nothing hot to eat for the entire day, she obliged.

As Ava worked her way through the portion, Enzo twitched and fidgeted. In a most un-Enzo like manner, he studied the room, fiddled with his shirt cuffs, briefly examined his nails, and spent a short while squinting at the ceiling.

261

Ava scraped up the last of the rice, swallowed, dabbed her lips with the napkin, swivelled to face him, and pulling up her bare feet to tuck them under the robe, said "I'm ready for whatever it is you'd rather not say."

"We need to talk about tomorrow."

"We do."

He'd been labouring on the farthest corner end of the bed, but slid over to sit opposite her. "Waylen Kane has proposed employing truth magick on you."

"What kind of truth magick?"

"Edyta—she holds the other seat in our faction—says he's requested the use of deer's tongue serum."

"Oh, shit." Ava had never used it herself, but Nessa had a tincture of deer's tongue in her special collection. Mixed with herbs promoting communication, when applied correctly in ritual, it packed a truth-blabbing punch.

Fiddling with the robe belt, Ava scrolled the length into a coil. Hasty packing hadn't included nullifying herbs, and there was little chance they'd be able to procure any before ten o'clock tomorrow morning.

"We can't risk the Enclave learning of our true intentions," he warned.

"But if they use that stuff on me, I won't be able to lie."

Enzo nodded, his scowl black as a November night as he watched her roll and unroll the belt. "I have a suggestion."

"Tell me."

"You won't like it."

"I haven't particularly liked much of anything up to this point, so what difference will another inconvenience make?" she asked, the question coming out a little narkier than intended.

He stood, and as if his palms sweated, wiped them down the outsides of his thighs. Not liking this sudden anxious state one bit, Ava unfolded her legs and returned her feet to the floor. "It's something *that* bad?"

262

"Yes."

What? she was about to demand, when the answer hit her itself, as sharp and jolting as a wet fish to the face. "Compulsion." The only way she could stand before the Enclave and speak without missing a beat, was if Enzo compelled her to forget all about flipping Martha's witch switch.

Ava had yet to see Enzo look so pained as he stared down at her. "It may be our only solution."

Ha! Ava imagined Iz barking as she grasped her mugwort charm. *You defended Enzo earlier, insisted on his trustworthiness, but now faced with the ultimate test, you're faltering, aren't you! See? I told you!*

The old one in question sat again, folding heavily with a grunt. "I don't want to, Ava. I really don't. You, of all people."

A weighty *but* hung in the silence.

But it's the only way.

But we have no time to plan something else.

But we can't risk them learning our intentions.

And they couldn't. If the Enclave—Waylen Kane in particular—discovered the truth behind her involuntary stay in Paladino Palace, and how Enzo wanted to reboot his witch niece in order to outwit him, Ava could already envisage she and Enzo up and vanishing like a fart in the wind.

A sudden recall of the 7 of Swords waved for attention. Maybe she and Enzo were the ones who needed to take the unfair advantage? Someone in the Enclave worked dastardly deeds, so why shouldn't they fight like with like? It might level the playing field. "I think we need to consider it."

Enzo gripped his head, raven locks sprouting between his fingers. "Surely there's a spell you can work?"

"Without ingredients, a grimoire, *time?* No. There's not."

263

He looked up at her, eyes dark with regret. "I don't want to hurt you, Ava."

When a vampire compelled a human, it called for a simple stare and command. But witches were a different story; it would hurt her—a lot. Her subconscious would fight him with every step. But typically, witches didn't agree to compulsion. If she entered into the intrusion with trust, it might be easier for them both. "You can undo it, right?"

"Yes. Of course. That goes without saying."

"And the Enclave won't be able to tell?"

"If they suspect I've compelled you, it would take days to prove it. The process is—" He fell short. A look of disgust twisted his expression. "I won't allow it to happen. And they won't risk wasting time holding you when you could be searching for Martha."

"So what would you compel me to believe?"

"Ava." He sighed, slumping once more.

"Tell me, Enzo."

"That I approached you," he said to the floor, "proposed your help in finding Martha in exchange for payment, and you agreed. I'll leave in the incident with Larsen, and how I protected you." His head lifted. "Neither will I remove the journeying this morning. They need to know we made contact and have a lead."

"But you'll erase everything to do with your actual intention?"

"Yes."

"What about Paladino Palace? You can't tell them we're living there."

"No." Enzo stood again. "But I'll have to choose somewhere in the surrounding area. Too many have seen me in Calnaloch. I have to say I'm situated nearby."

"Okay. So, we're lying about Dunfarr. What else do we need to cover up?"

It was almost midnight before Enzo had assured himself they'd covered every angle. He wanted to wipe as little as possible from Ava's mind. The more left intact, the more detail she'd recall, and the less suspicion they might raise. She'd suggested writing exactly what needed to be compelled in and out of her mind, and with sheets of hotel stationery already filled, he re-read the entire lot for the third time.

Ava sat opposite him, gently swivelling the chair. She'd shaken off the robe an hour earlier to reveal a cotton pyjamas set of black shorts and a tee sporting a colourful cartoon pony covered in tattoos. Above the image, sparkly letters stated; *'I Heart Death Metal'*.

Despite her stifling a yawn twice in the last ten minutes, he stalled, repeatedly reading over his notes.

But she knew his game.

"Enzo, the quicker you do this, the quicker it will be over."

He lowered the sheets. "Perhaps there's another way."

"Not when time is against us, there isn't. We're in a bind. This is the best solution. It's not ideal, but right now, we have little choice."

Vanilla and cocoa butter perfumed her skin. Every time she folded or unfolded her arms, crossed her legs, or pulled them up into the seat, a waft would tease him.

Separation would serve him best right now. Their heated moment on the library couch earlier that day insisted on replaying, driving him half feral with the want to finish taking the kiss Waylen Kane's call had interrupted. He hadn't ever thought himself a possessive man, but Ava O'Keefe had unearthed an innate longing to root himself firmly by her

265

side. If he were eloquent, he'd tell her, but actions came easier to him than words.

"Enzo," she said softly.

Without realising it, he'd been staring at her, lost in her eyes. In the low light, they'd turned a shade reminiscent of green aventurine. He'd once gifted Martha a necklace crafted from the gemstones. "You're right," he said, blinking to end the daydreaming and return to reality. "We are in a bind, and this is the only solution."

"Exactly. It is what it is." Ava gathered up her hair, and twisting it into a rope, threw it over one shoulder. The action drew his attention to unprotected fingers.

He motioned at them with a frown. "Where's your splint?"

"I took it off. I don't want to walk into the enclave court tomorrow with any sign of disability. I'll look weak if I do."

"You're anything but weak, Ava."

She argued with a grimace, shaking her head. "It's better for me this way. I need to feel confident when I stand before them."

"I'll be by your side. I won't leave you, I promise." And he would cut mercilessly through anyone who dared to separate him from her—Waylen Kane, especially.

"I know," she said so matter-of-factly, it briefly stunned him.

Enzo reached for the edge of her chair's seat, fingers brushing the outside of her thighs as he took a grip. With one swift tug, he wheeled her towards him until their knees grazed.

Startled by his boldness, the lips he ached to taste popped apart. "What are you doing?" she whispered.

Leaning in, he palmed her jaw as the other hand cupped the rear of her head. "I'm about to cause you pain, and I need to know that you understand my feelings for you before I do."

"But—"

266

"Words aren't my forte, Ava. Please, just this one demonstration of my affections."

Her breathy "Okay" had barely trailed free before he moved.

The kiss formed with a careful first brush of lips.

Enzo listened to her body, ready to pull away the moment he sensed discomfort. Gifting himself a few quick seconds of contact, he broke the soft connection. Between them, millimetres of space offered her the opportunity to withdraw. But instead of stiffening and pulling back, Ava pitched closer, instigating the second kiss.

He met her, desire rising as abruptly as hers. When his tongue tipped her bottom lip, she opened for him.

Despite his longing, he hadn't anticipated what kissing her would provoke.

As if detonating internal explosives, their connection swarmed his skin with a fever he hadn't felt since his human years. The urge to possess her raged hotter than ever, claiming his limbs and possessing his control.

Lurching upright, Enzo tugged Ava to her feet with him.

Clutching her to his chest, he spun them as one, tipping her onto the bed, where he grasped her wrists and pinned them above her head. Delirious from the silkiness of her skin, how her racing pulse tapped a frantic rhythm beneath his thumb, and how every stroke, caress, and taste urged the beat faster, Enzo groaned into her mouth.

Ava responded with a whimper, kissing him deeper.

Divinity laced the perfume of her skin, the scent he'd fought against for so long liberating memories of rich berries, plummy wine, and a tease of spice.

When she tugged against his hold, he quickly broke it, afraid he'd hurt or frightened her, but unrestrained hands dived for his body, grabbing his waist to draw him closer. She murmured his name, and when she squirmed beneath him, directing his arousal to the growing heat between her legs, it threatened to unravel him entirely.

Stubborn sensibility interrupted.

Enzo stilled, groaned aloud at his sudden but necessary restraint, and broke their fevered kiss.

Ava came to her senses at the same time. She swallowed, eyes rounding as she too realised how impassioned they'd become. A soft laugh escaped. "I think you've made your affections quite clear, Mr Paladino."

Shifting his lower body, he lifted it away from searing temptation. "And dare I say you also, Miss O'Keefe?"

Before he could risk savouring her warm, sweet mouth again, Enzo swiftly shot to standing. Ava propped herself up on her elbows, cheeks flushed, lips swollen, eyes almost black.

He put out his hand. She took it, allowing him to pull her upright.

"Promise me something," she said softly, stepping aside to create a safe distance between them. "When you compel me, take away the memory of that kiss."

The request immediately vanquished the warmth skimming his perpetually cold skin. "Ava . . ."

"Until we're done with the Enclave."

Hope reignited.

"It will be easier for me. Don't ask me to explain why, please. I need to forget it."

"I'm a bad kisser?"

She smiled at his attempt to find humour. "Awful. Thirsty dog awful. Sloppy washing machine awful."

Enzo clutched at where his heart failed to beat but somehow pulsed for this witch. "I'm mortally wounded," he croaked.

She laughed, shaking her head at him as distracted fingers rose to skim the lips he'd devoured. "Promise me?"

"I promise."

"Okay." Ava motioned at the papers lying on the floor. They'd fallen when he'd thrown her onto the bed. "Let's get this over with." Unhooking her necklace, she placed the charm on the dresser behind him. "Don't forget to tell me to put this back on as soon as you're done. Otherwise, I won't understand why I'm not wearing it in the morning."

Which wouldn't end well for him, the unsaid truth warned.

Ava folded her arms and, with a tight inhale, tried to smile. "Ready when you are."

Enzo waited in the living room until Ava fell asleep.

Impatience slowed time as he counted five minutes of steady, deep breathing. Once assured she wouldn't rouse, he returned to her room, carefully slipped under the covers, and slowly enveloped her in his arms, fitting her back snugly to his chest. Her willingness to allow him to compel her had lessened her pain, but nonetheless, tears had sprouted as she'd fought her witch instinct to repel his vampire intrusion. It took fifteen minutes of repeated force before he finally breached the barrier. A minute longer and he would have called a halt.

Once hooked into him, Ava sat in silence, cheeks and eyes glistening. She looked straight through him, not at him—which had bothered him greatly. He'd seen the same expression countless times over his centuries, and with the exception of only one other occasion, the blank, far-away gaze had never brought him distress.

His beautiful witch had been smart to insist he write everything down. The torment of compelling her had erased his own mind. Without guidance, he would have forgotten most of the fabrications. And as promised,

269

he'd compelled into hiding the memory of their kiss. Above all the other commands, it had been the hardest to speak aloud.

Enzo buried his face in her hair, inhaling deeply. He craved carrying a piece of her in every cell of his body, wanted her scent tattooed on his skin so the greedy, covetous creatures amongst the gathering would recognise his claim—Kane, especially.

Whatever the warlock planned, Enzo feared Ava lay at its epicentre. But without knowledge of Kane's machinations, could he truly protect his witch?

24

Sleepy muscles tingled as Ava stretched and rolled over. Still half asleep, she patted for the comfort she'd been enjoying, but its absence shunted her fully awake.

Mid-yawn, she realised the strong arms, broad chest, and butterfly kisses had formed part of her dream. She couldn't recall sexy time—just cuddling. Hopefully, that meant she hadn't moaned a certain name aloud—especially as the man who'd dominated her dreams possessed wicked hearing.

Despite soft light filtering through the edges of the heavy curtains, the clock on the nightstand announced the time as eight-twenty. Automatically checking for her mugwort charm, she shuffled upright. Exhaustion had won last night. She vaguely remembered starting a movie, but she must have fallen asleep during the opening credits.

Conscious she'd abandoned the remote somewhere nearby, Ava turned to the pillow beside her.

It didn't hold the device. Something else took its place; a head-sized dent, and lying in its concave, a single, coal-black hair.

Ava lurched away from the lonely strand, scrambling to recall the previous night. Enzo had brought her food. They'd talked about the meeting, but then he'd said goodnight and left, taking the tray with him. After, she'd grabbed the remote, snuggled down, and fallen asleep. Had cuddling against him *not* been a dream? "Oh, shit." Quickly yanking up the duvet, she noted her top and shorts still in place.

A soft knock sent the covers smacking down. "Yes?" she answered, a little too shrilly.

"You're awake."

"I am. Come in."

As if afraid she cavorted around the bedroom naked, Enzo cracked the door open by an inch. "We need to leave soon," he announced, stepping in once assured of her decency. "Will you take breakfast before we go?"

Concern over his possible presence in her bed last night evaporated as she took in his attire. A black three-piece suit with a white shirt, raspberry red tie, and a matching silk handkerchief poking out from the breast pocket. The formality had nerves sparking immediately. "No, thanks."

"Tea?" Tension roosted upon him, too. Crow's feet forked out from his eyes as he glanced at where she clutched the sheet to her chest.

"Yeah, sure. Green tea if it's there. If not, whatever's available. I don't mind."

A trademark Enzo nod, and the door clicked shut.

Wishing she'd known about the enclave court wardrobe requirements, Ava slipped out of bed. As she passed the television, she spotted the remote lying beside the room service menu. *No*, she quickly reasoned with her over-active imagination and its immediate conclusion. *Enzo*

272

may have come in to check on you, seen it discarded on the pillow, picked it up, and safely stowed it beside the television once he'd turned it off. The stray hair probably fell off his clothes. And the head dent is yours from rolling over during the night. "Correct?" she whispered to herself. "Correct." Mystery solved. Or so she'd keep telling herself.

Thanks to the missing enclave-dress-code memo, she'd packed poorly. Ava tugged black jeans, a mesh-knit jumper—also in black—and a red tank top from her case. Footwear options offered her sturdy, low-heeled boots, or slightly tatty canvas flats. "Boots," she said, and scanning the chosen outfit, realised she and Enzo would walk into the enclave court wearing matching colours.

Once dressed, she applied enough make-up to mask her death-warmed-up complexion. After, she battled through a few rounds of scooping and knotting her hair into order. In the end, she opted to leave it down—preferring Waylen Kane to see she'd made no kind of effort.

Satisfied with her appearance, Ava faced herself in the mirror. "You can do this," she told her reflection. But it was Iz's assurance she needed to hear, not her lame, pithy one that failed to rouse even an ounce of confidence.

Tea and Enzo waited in the living room. He'd obviously dined on paranoia for breakfast. When she reached to open the curtains and check out the one and only time she'd probably ever see Athens, he told her to leave them shut.

"Prying eyes," he said.

He'd left her tea on the table separating the blinding-white couches. Afraid to go anywhere near the pristine fabric, Ava scooped up the mug and sipped while standing.

"How did you sleep?" he asked.

"Great, actually. I guess exhaustion caught up with me. Did you stay awake?"

"I did." The dazzling couch didn't repel Enzo. Although, he did perch on its edge, elbows planted on his knees, fingers loosely clasped as he contemplated the impossible gleam of his black shoes.

Tension ratcheted up with every sip she took and twitch he made.

"I'm nervous," she said, thinking they'd be better off admitting the truth.

Enzo looked up at her, unmasked regret slanting his eyes. "I'll be with you the entire time."

"They won't question me alone?"

"No. You'll face the room at the foot of the reeve's chair." He motioned a semi-circle. "The factions will form a half circle around you."

"And you'll be in your seat?"

"Yes. To your left. You'll be able to see me, don't worry."

But she *was* worried. Ava set the mug on the silver tray, realising her stomach didn't appreciate tea sloshing around its already gurgling insides. "And I should answer everything truthfully, right?"

"Yes." Enzo rose, a column of sombre black. He didn't meet her eyes as he straightened his waistcoat. "You have nothing to hide. *We* have nothing to hide."

By the time they left the suite and rode the elevator down to a basement carpark where a BMW with tinted windows waited, Ava vibrated with nerves. She slid into the back seat, stomach sour, palms clammy, and legs jittery. Enzo slipped in beside her.

The driver hid behind a partition of opaque glass. An enclave employee, she guessed, wiping slick palms over her denim-clad thighs. "I think I'm going to be sick."

"You're not." Enzo leaned around her, grasped the waiting seatbelt, drew it across her body, and snapped it in place. He didn't bother with his own, but shifted sideways on the seat to face her, where he scooped her hands together before lifting her knuckles to his lips. "Look at me," he insisted.

"Now would be a superb time to compel me to be calm," she whispered.

"Ava."

"I'm deadly serious." If he even looked like he might agree, she'd whip off her charm necklace and let him bleach her brain of anxiety.

"I won't leave your side. I promise. The Enclave simply needs to hear the truth from you. Whatever they ask, you answer honestly."

"What if I say something wrong—something that could get you into trouble?"

Enzo draped a length of her hair over her shoulder. "I have done nothing warranting punishment. You came to me voluntarily, despite what Waylen Kane believes."

"I did," she confirmed, hoping he'd keep touching her hair, hands, or whatever. The physical contact eased her panic and allowed her to think straight. "I agreed to work with you and entered your home willingly. You're paying me for it, so it's an official business transaction."

"It is."

"I'm not with you under duress."

"You're not," he confirmed.

"And that's the only assurance they require."

"Correct." Enzo offered her a smile, but it lacked his usual certainty.

Ava sucked in another breath and released it in a loud whoosh. "Keep talking to me, please? I don't care about what—just keep my brain busy so I can't freak out."

He tipped his chin towards the window. "Did you know Acropolis means *'high city'*?"

Although dulled by the heavily tinted glass, it was hard to miss the Acropolis sitting proudly above the spread of Athens when she twisted around to look. "I didn't."

"It was originally built for military defence, but when the Persians invaded, the Greeks holding the fort abandoned it out of fear. Xerxes and his army destroyed it."

"Were you there?" she joked.

"I missed it by a few centuries."

Enzo plied her with facts that went in one ear and out the other for the entire twenty-minute drive. But his diverting chatter worked. When the driver rolled to a stop in an underground carpark, the urge to puke, faint, or run away as fast as she could, had eased.

He took her hand to help her out of the car. As soon as she straightened, he gently pulled her in, lips brushing her ear. "Is your necklace somewhere secure?"

"Yes."

"You're sure? I can't trust Kane."

"You can trust me," she told him, easing back, even though she wanted to cling to him like a toddler on the first day of school. "It's protected."

"Bene," he murmured, and before she could withdraw fully, hooked her around the waist.

Enzo led her to a cramped service elevator. They rose in silence, and when the door slid aside with almost comical jerking, they emerged into a poorly lit, spartan corridor. Grey linoleum underfoot, flickering fluorescent lights overhead, and ashen walls streaked with rust stains. Not the opulent enclave setting Ava had presumed.

The walkway curved, delivering them to a mammoth steel door flanked by two men wearing bulky navy jumpsuits. One hauled a bunch of keys from his belt, wrestled with the lock, and over hinges pleading for oiling, instructed them to step through.

Fresh morning air greeted Ava. Starved of the luxury, her lungs fed with sudden greed as she glanced around.

They'd entered a compact courtyard, flanked by towering walls of red brick punctuated by petite arched windows of leaded glass. Where sky hung in a square high above, spire-tipped pinnacles scratched at the low-hanging cloud. All sharp-angled and imposing proportions, the Gothic structure loomed over her, silently judging.

They weren't alone in the courtyard.

In a blatant *them versus us* move, a group of individuals gathered to one side. From beneath bricked arches, curious glances flicked her way. Some were discreet, others not so much. Those less polite appraised without shame, raking both her and Enzo with their judgement.

Enzo's cool touch seeped through her layers. "Ignore them."

Happy to obey, Ava swung her eyes skyward again, clinging to the security of his closeness. *This will all be over soon,* she promised herself.

"Ah, our guests are here."

The glib greeting oozed from the shadows, followed by a figure who strode towards them with an air of self-importance.

Enzo stiffened.

In response, Ava lifted her chin, despite her heart shifting into fifth gear.

"Waylen," Enzo greeted with a tone icy enough to swivel a few more heads in their direction.

But their summoner locked his stare onto Ava only, flagrantly blanking Enzo. "This must be Miss O'Keefe." Waylen came to a stop before her, a puff of breeze from his swooping arrival delivering a waft of something bitter. The scent was familiar, but not recognisable enough for her to name. "Welcome."

"Hello," she replied, leaving her hands hanging loosely by her sides instead of offering one in greeting.

Ava scoped a quick inventory of the infamous Waylen Kane. Only a few inches taller than her, a stocky build that suggested a love of food over the gym, ashen skin, a weak jawline, and a defined chin dimple. His most noticeable feature was his eyes; a startling forest green commanding his appearance. But unlike Enzo's warm caramel eyes that possessed the ability to compel her, instinct warned her not to stare into Waylen's gaze.

"Thank you for agreeing to meet with us," Waylen said, indicating the '*we*' with a flourish towards those at his rear.

"Did we have a choice?" Enzo queried testily.

Waylen's pasty smile landed briefly on Enzo. "You could have declined."

Amusement snorted in reply.

"Miss O'Keefe." Ava almost flinched as the sharp gaze latched onto her again. "We appreciate your gracious acquiescence to our summons. While we find ourselves in less-than-congenial circumstances, I extend my—"

"Le mie più profonde scuse," Enzo cut in, slapping one hand over his silk handkerchief with dramatic regret.

Waylen's simpering expression hardened into a scowl. "Your deepest apology for what, Paladino?"

"It seems I missed the vote securing your position as reeve." From across the courtyard, a low chorus of amusement tittered. "Are congratulations in order, Kane?" he queried with faux sincerity.

Annoyance curled Waylen's top lip. "I'm merely welcoming the witch."

"As if you own the goddamn place. Please" —Enzo flapped for Waylen to step aside— "can we get on with this farce of a meeting?"

Waylen wheeled around and stomped away. The cluster of members waited until he'd stormed past them before trailing under the archway.

Ava glanced up at Enzo. "Is it wise to piss off the man who'll soon be interrogating me?"

Open disdain melted as Enzo threw her a subtle wink. "All part of the game," he whispered.

Beyond the arch, Ava and Enzo entered a dreary vastness. A grand cathedral stripped of its former glory opened before her. Ava gaped up at the naked structure; a sky-high dome ringed by stained-glass windows, supported by looming walls of rhino-grey stone. Rooted into the grimy tiled floor, hulking pillars rose like petrified tree trunks. Besides the paltry circle of glazing above, no other natural light graced the space. The scene was a far cry from how she'd imagined the infamous enclave clubhouse.

Beneath a film of age and neglect, a mosaic of black and white patterned the floor. It drew her attention to a raised level—perhaps where the altar had once stood. A simple wooden plinth sat on the pale marble, holding a boxy high-backed chair.

At the foot of the platform, and to where Enzo's touch directed her, a half-circle held twenty-one chairs; three for each of the seven factions. Although smaller than the reeve's seat, they were equally utilitarian-looking. Bluntly carved, with flat seats unadorned by cushions, Ava imagined the Enclave all knew the joy of plank-arse after a long meeting.

"You'll stand here," Enzo said quietly, leading her to a few feet from the plinth's edge. Stepping in close enough for their clothes to brush, he blocked her view as members shuffled into their respective places. "Ava," he barely whispered, a furtive move catching her chin to arrest her skating gaze. "I'm right here. Answer truthfully, stay calm, and remember to breathe, okay?"

"Uh huh," she choked out, wishing she could cling to him like a koala.

Enzo pivoted on leather soles to where a trio of seats waited. A tall, slim woman with vibrant chestnut hair already occupied the chair on the right. Edyta, Ava guessed. Enzo sat left of her, and when Ava noted the space between them, the glaring absence bolstered her courage. For Martha. She would do this for Martha.

On her nearest right, the first trilogy of seats forming the semi-circle was empty. Enzo had told her the angel faction rarely attended meetings. All breeds of non-corporeal beings fell under their rule, yet only angels held enclave seats. Angels had the power to switch between corporeal and non-corporeal, so how did the Enclave know for sure they didn't attend meetings? If Ava were an angel, she'd sure as hell—*heaven*—use her invisibility to spy.

Next in line, Waylen dominated the centre of the warlock faction, now wearing a bland grey robe over his clothes. His group governed witches and sorcerers, which was why he'd demanded Enzo explain a witch in his service.

Next, the shifter members, all three eyeing her with benign interest. Ava knew a few members of Calnaloch's sparse shifter community and found them an easy-going, friendly lot.

The fae contingency whispered amongst themselves, angular faces turned away from her as they conversed. Faes represented goblins, elves and the other numerous *'secondary'* members of their community. During her mum's teenage years, those secondary members had banded together to demand their own trio of seats on the Enclave. But their campaign amounted to nothing when the Enclave voted a landslide refusal.

Demons were next in line. All three sat in silence, their burly forms resulting in elbows and knees kissing as they squeezed together. The faintest trace of sulphur came from their direction.

Nymphs claimed the second-to-last section. As Ava's gaze reached them, they each gave her a respectful nod. Nymphs and witches fought for the earth. Their common respect for Mother Nature bound them together, so Ava replied with a tiny smile. Would the factions vote during this process? If so, the kind head-tilts of assurance from the nymphs gave her hope.

Finally, the vampire faction. She'd sensed Enzo's stare on her while scanning the gathering. When she locked onto him again, his silent promise of protection rang loud.

"Shall we begin?" Waylen rose, sucking all attention in his direction as he took centre stage. Despite how he represented her community, she already thoroughly disliked him. "Enzo Paladino. We have summonsed you here today in response to allegations of abduction, imprisonment, and coercion of Ava O'Keefe, a member of the witch community."

Enzo held stoically rigid.

Waylen turned to her next. "Ava O'Keefe. We have summonsed you here today to deliver your own response to these allegations."

Taking her cue from Enzo, Ava met Waylen's unnerving stare without blinking.

"Mr Paladino. What is your response to the allegations?"

Enzo casually cleared his throat. "I deny all allegations."

"Miss O'Keefe. How do you respond?"

"Mr Paladino has not abducted, imprisoned, or coerced me."

Waylen clasped his chubby hands, a look of satisfaction rousing a smile.

So. . .that was it? She and Enzo were now free to leave?

Hope quickly shrivelled as Waylen spoke again.

"I propose the use of truth magick. All those in favour?"

As hands rose, Ava gaped at Enzo in panic.

It's all okay, his answering nod told her. *Stay calm.*

The bitter odour clinging to Waylen suddenly named itself; *deer's tongue.* Ava had once dug the truth herb out of Nessa's box of Stuff-You-Don't-Touch, sniffed it, and immediately gagged.

281

Waylen hadn't expected refusal. Before hands had even fully lowered, he'd already withdrawn a petite brown bottle from his robe's pocket.

She stiffened as he approached, sweat quickly building between her shoulder blades. What if he asked her about non-Enzo-related stuff? What if she involuntarily blabbed everything about the necklace?

"Seven drops," he announced, withdrawing a dropper from the bottle. "Under the tongue, please."

Thoughts as wild as feral cats erupted. But before Ava could herd them together, her lips had parted and tongue lifted.

Waylen deposited seven drops of the vile, bitter serum. Instantly, all decorum scattered.

She retched, slapped her hand over her mouth, and doing her best not to throw up, breathed through the rancid taste. She'd take a gallon of Iz's mouldy sock tea over deer's tongue serum any day.

It took a long, wretched moment to gain control. Tears streamed, her nose ran, and her throat burned raw. Ava tugged her cuff over her hand to wipe her face, but Enzo appeared before her, his raspberry handkerchief proffered. She took it with rasped thanks, and dabbing her cheeks and nose dry, kept the little piece of him clutched in her grasp.

Within seconds, a blanket of invisible threads settled over her. Soft as a cloud, it drifted down from the crown of her head, smothering her thoughts. Rigid muscle softened. Breath came without restriction, and her heart slowed.

"I think we're ready." Waylen's voice came from far away. "Ava, can you identify this man?"

Ava turned toward the question. As if viewing a black-and-white movie, the edges of her vision clouded, casting a soft romantic light on where Waylen stood behind Enzo. "That's Enzo Paladino."

"What is your relationship with Mr Paladino?"

"He's paying me to locate his missing niece; Martha Paladino." Ava smiled at Enzo. He looked so handsome in his fancy suit with broad shoulders filling it out perfectly.

"How did you come to this arrangement?"

"He asked me, and I agreed."

"Where is your home, Miss O'Keefe?"

"Apartment twenty-six—"

"Not the full address; the town will suffice."

"Calnaloch."

"Are you living there presently?"

Ava glanced behind her, wondering if a seat was available. She felt a little rubbery-legged. Sleepy, too.

"Miss O'Keefe. Are you living in your apartment in Calnaloch presently?"

"No. I'm staying with Enzo," she answered with a wistful sigh. "His house is *enormous*."

A collective titter prompted Waylen to cough loudly. Silence fell.

"Are you staying there of your own free will?"

"Hell, yeah. It's *way* bigger than my apartment, and it has a *really* nice kitchen."

"Has Mr Paladino ever denied you permission to leave his home?"

"No." Ava frowned over at him. "Why would he do that?"

"Do you wish to return to your own?"

"No. Not until I find Martha. Then I'll go home. But I'll miss the kitchen. There's a library, too. Candles *everywhere*," she said, motioning wildly to impress upon them the volume of candles. The gesturing tilted her slightly off-balance.

"Where is Mr Paladino's home?"

"Objection," Enzo said loudly. "Not relevant."

283

"Carlingford, in County Louth," Ava answered anyway. "It looks out over Carlingford Lough, and the view is amazing."

Enzo tutted annoyance.

"Shit," she whispered, curling her traitorous lips over her teeth. "Sorry."

Waylen rounded the row, coming to stand before her again. She inched away from his approach, and once again turned to consider sitting on the plinth's edge.

"Kane, allow her to sit," a voice said.

"She's fine as she is," he replied.

"I probably should sit," she told him quietly. "I feel a bit wobbly."

"I have a few more questions. Then you may sit."

Holding back the urge to sigh, Ava muttered an, "Okay."

The questions kept coming. She continued to answer.

Occasionally, Waylen cut her off. A few times, he asked her the same question, but in a roundabout way. "You're repeating yourself," she told him, and making a get-on-with-it gesture, tutted at his inadequacy. It drew another ripple of laughs.

When he peppered her with questions about Martha, she told him all about the journeying spell, and how she'd connected with Enzo's niece, but couldn't yet identify her location. "I've already figured out what to do, though. The next time, I'll use less grounding magick." Ava gestured for Waylen to lean in. "Just don't tell Enzo. He'll say no."

"Kane, this circus has gone on long enough."

Ava tilted back to see Enzo on his feet. "There's a circus here, too?"

Laughter echoed around the room. Waylen clapped, demanding order, but the male nymph spoke up, his voice as melodic and light as trickling water. "Paladino has clearly not coerced the witch, Kane. They have a legitimate agreement."

A round of agreement echoed.

"One of our members is missing," a voice blocked by Waylen's stout form added.

Ava peered over Waylen's shoulder to see one of the demon faction gesturing at Martha's empty seat.

"You should support this collaboration, not waste their precious time," his deep voice demanded.

"The nymph faction agrees. Send them on their way."

"Can we first vote on a date for Martha's seat to be resigned?"

"Yes, that's a far better use of this gathering."

"It would certainly be more beneficial than this nonsense."

With voices coming from all angles, Ava grew dizzy. No longer caring whether it would be rude, she stepped back and clumsily lowered herself to sit on the plinth. "Room is spinning," she murmured, grasping her head.

Cool hands covered hers, and when she looked up, Enzo had dropped to one knee before her. "I'm here, Ava."

Beyond them, a heated discussion filled the enormous space with clamour. "I'm so thirsty. Did I drink tequila? I don't remember, but I think I'm drunk."

"It will pass. Sit here for now."

"Can we go home?"

"Soon, Ava. Soon."

Another vote took place. Ava blinked against the feathery view of hands rising into the air. She lifted hers, too, fighting to make her heavy arm obey. "What are we voting for?"

Enzo kindly pulled her vote back down onto her lap, spotting where a corner of his silk handkerchief peeped out from her fist. She clutched it against her chest, preventing him from reclaiming it. "No. It's mine now."

Another one of his beautiful smiles appeared. Enhanced by the black-and-white movie filter, his eyes and teeth dazzled. "You may keep it."

"It smells of you," she explained, pressing it to her nose and breathing in deeply. "Sorry about telling them where your house is."

"That's okay."

"But it is a *really* beautiful house."

"It is."

A sharp clap from Waylen made her jump. Enzo kept his hold on her, but turned to where Waylen now had his back to them. A small tear marred the hem of Waylen's gloomy robe. Ava nudged Enzo to point it out, but he put his finger to his lips.

Waylen blabbered on, a monologue she couldn't follow thanks to cotton-wool filling her head.

Tugged back down to earth, heaviness swamped her body. Astringency flooded her mouth. *Not tequila,* she realised, trying to gather enough saliva to wash down the rotten taste; *deer's tongue!* Oh, shit. What had she blabbed? But her blurred memory refused to remind her.

Enzo continued to hunker before her, palms cupping her elbows, thumbs brushing the soft flesh of her inner arms. He'd twisted away to listen to the animated discussion, gifting her a view of his neck. Surely he wouldn't be touching her so tenderly if she'd said something she shouldn't?

Distracted by his neck tendons flexing as he watched the proceedings, she leaned in. This close, his scent swirled around her. Would he mind if she rested her head on his shoulder? Bone-tiredness swamped her body, along with a vein-shrinking thirst. She wanted to return to Paladino Palace, drink ten gallons of water, and sleep for a week.

The lure of Enzo's solidity proved too difficult to fight. Ava tipped forward, and registering her little grunt as her forehead met granite, slipped away from the Enclave and Waylen Kane.

25

Enzo held Ava against him as the vote announced Martha's seat secure until April 21st; the day after the eclipse. Relief rushed him, but he didn't succumb to release. Instead, he maintained composure, scooped Ava into his arms, and stood.

Kane's charade hadn't gone the way he'd hoped. Anger scoured his pasty face as he glared at where Enzo cradled Ava safely. But a flick of switch and he replaced the fury with a mask of sympathy. "Due diligence, Paladino," he explained away the summons and interrogation. "I'm sure you understand."

"I had thought us sharing a mutual trust, Kane."

"We do, we do, but—" Kane tipped his chin at where enclave members filed out of the hall, blaming the circus on their demands. "Word got out you have the witch. I had no choice but to play this role today. No hard feelings, eh?"

Enzo bit down before replying, "No, of course not."

"Let me know when you locate Martha. And—" A meaty paw landed on Enzo's shoulder. "Do reach out if there's anything you need. I take it," he whispered, fanning Enzo's face with foul breath. "You haven't forgotten our agreement?"

"You'll have my vote," Enzo lied with ease.

"Excellent." His gaze lowered to Ava. "Please apologise to Miss O'Keefe on my behalf. I took no satisfaction from the affair."

Like hell he hadn't. Kane had enjoyed every posturing second of the farce—up to the moment where he realised he'd failed to secure whatever it was he desired.

Sudden possessiveness steeled Kane's gaze. He reached out to where a length of Ava's hair draped over one cheek. "But we have to be seen following enclave law, despite our personal desires. It is what it is, correct?"

Enzo jerked, yanking Ava aside before Kane could touch her. *It is what it is?*

"Paladino?" Kane queried with a look of wariness.

"If she wakes now, she'll startle," he said. "She's been through enough today."

Kane's suspicion narrowed further; the green-eyed slant reminiscent of a reptile. "You're protective of her."

"She's valuable. Without her, I risk never finding my niece."

The warlock grazed Ava's body with one more covetous stare, and drawing himself up, puffed out his chest. "Keep in touch, Paladino."

"Of course." And with his final lie muttered, Enzo wheeled away, securing Ava with a possessive grasp as *'it is what it is'* echoed.

289

Ava slept the entire way back to the hotel, and for three hours after. Enzo lay with her, cradling her stillness to his.

Kane's comment had filled him with violent dis-ease. No matter how he tried to rationalise how the viper and Ava shared a liking for an uncommon saying, nothing calmed his agitation. Neither could he forget how possessiveness had hooded Kane's greedy gaze. Whatever game the warlock played, Enzo stood on the sidelines, ignorant of its purpose.

Securing Ava tighter, he inhaled her scent. Traces of vanilla lingered—not enough to overpower the remnants of bitter deer's tongue, but sufficient to replay a far more favourable memory; their kiss. He smiled into her tresses. His witch hid a passionate side, one he anticipated teasing out, and hopefully, soon.

Confusion over why she crawled up out of a hangover when she couldn't remember drinking, formed Ava's first waking thought. Her mouth had turned to sandpaper, and her throat a scorched desert. She also had a blinding headache and a sour stomach. Scrambling to recall just how hard she and Miss Tequila had partied, she cautiously opened her eyes.

A strange room, afternoon light, and the distant hum of a busy city. "Where in the hell am I?" But as she slowly peeled herself upright, remembrance returned; the Enclave, Waylen Kane, and a dose of deer's tongue.

290

A glass of water waited for her on the nightstand. Not caring if her stomach sent it straight back up again, she chugged it down. "Enzo?" she croaked, nervous of the silence beyond the bedroom. "Are you here?"

He didn't even knock. A flurry of startled air, and Enzo stood over her. "I'm here."

"We're at the hotel," she stated the obvious. "I don't remember leaving the court."

Enzo took the empty glass and returned it to the nightstand. At some point, he'd removed his jacket and waistcoat, and with his sleeves rolled up to the elbow, her stomach flipped in a far more pleasant way. "Waylen's posturing put you to sleep." His weight settled onto the bed by her knees.

"It's all a bit fuzzy." Much like the night she'd made an idiot of herself only a few short days ago, the enclave interrogation session replayed in jumbled, foggy nonsense. But until the deer's tongue—along with whatever else Waylen had blended into the serum—wore off, the finer points would evade her. "It went okay, right? I said nothing I shouldn't have, did I?"

"You answered every question."

"But did I mess anything up?"

Enzo found her shin under the duvet and gave it a gentle squeeze. "Of course not. How are you feeling?"

"Rough. Are there any painkillers in this fancy suite?"

"Yes. I had some sent up, even though I wasn't sure if you'd want to take them."

"I'll take the drugs, please. And water. Gallons of it."

Enzo dutifully darted off and returned with a box of paracetamol and two bottles of water. Ava took two tablets and guzzled down the first half-litre bottle.

"Are you hungry?"

291

Still sipping, she shook her head, waiting until she caught her breath to ask what time they'd be leaving.

"As soon as you're ready. My pilot is on standby."

"Okay. Let me grab a quick shower and then we'll go." She didn't want to spend a minute more than necessary in the city where the Enclave congregated. Until Enzo's jet kissed the clouds, she feared a summons, demanding they return for further questioning.

"I'll wait for you in the living room."

As soon as Enzo left, Ava threw off the duvet. It wasn't until she'd padded around the end of the bed when she cottoned on to her bare legs and feet. Enzo—presumably—had divested her of boots, socks, jeans, and jumper. Heat rushed to her cheeks at the idea of him peeling off her skin-tight jeans. It normally took a hefty tug to yank them off at her ankles. How had she not woken? And had he seen her underwear? Whipping up the hem of her tank top to remind herself of the briefs she'd put on that morning, she sighed in relief. Simple black ones. A quick check beneath her top revealed a black bra. They weren't a matching set, but at least she'd been organised enough to colour-coordinate her underwear. "Don't think about it," she murmured, spotting where he'd thoughtfully placed her folded jeans on top of her suitcase. Her jumper, he'd draped over the back of the chair at the dresser. Socks and boots waited beside it. "Gah! Don't think about it."

A thorough brush of her teeth removed the worst of the lingering bitterness in her mouth. Panda-eyes blinked at her while she scrubbed. Had her make-up run while standing before the Enclave, or while she'd slept? Whichever, between melted mascara and enclave-induced sweat, her entire body itched for a hot shower.

Flashbacks of the interrogation played as she doused herself in creamy suds. Waylen had pushed her hard about Martha. He'd persisted with questions about Enzo keeping her captive in his home, too—the home

292

whose location she'd stupidly blabbed. "Oh, crap." What if enclave members turned up at the lough house? Enzo would be *pissed*.

With the grime washed off, Ava exited the shower enclosure and reached for a sheet-sized fluffy towel. As she tugged it off the rail, a scrap of paper fell loose, fluttering to the floor. The hotel logo filled one corner, and when she bent to pick it up, noted her name in her own handwriting.

'Ava. Check your suitcase', the cryptic note ordered.

Swaddled like a burrito, Ava returned to the bedroom and flipped open her case. A quick search through her few clothes revealed nothing, but when she unzipped the interior pocket holding her tarot deck, an envelope waited.

Her name appeared on the front, with a *'Read Me'* instruction underneath, again in her writing. As an added security measure, her signature covered the sealed flap.

Equally intrigued as confused, she sat on the bed, slid her nail under the edge, and ripped.

She'd written herself another note.

'Enzo will explain everything on the plane. Trust him. Don't freak out. Everything is okay.'

The note wasn't alone. Also tucked into the envelope, the 2 of Cups tarot card waited. Ava stared at the enigmatic mail. Why couldn't she remember writing this, or going through her deck to find and remove the 2 of Cups? She fully understood the significance behind the card; her burgeoning relationship with Enzo and the trust that grew between them, and she couldn't deny her own scrawl or signature. But as if someone had wiped the entire event from her mind, she— "Oh, *fuck!*"

Fingers immediately flew to her mugwort pendant. It hung in place. Had she allowed Enzo to compel her?

Rising to her feet, still grasping the pendant, Ava read the note again. *'Enzo will explain everything on the plane. Trust him. Don't freak out.*

Everything is okay.' She'd double-underlined *'don't'*, knowing this moment would instigate just that—a massive freak out. But easier written than obeyed.

Flinging off the towel, Ava hurriedly dressed. She yanked on the black jeans again, but grabbed the last clean item of clothing from her case; a grey hoodie. As she slid it on, her fingers met another piece of paper hidden in the sleeve.

'Stop freaking out! Everything is fine. Trust me.'

The command sedated her enough to finish dressing, fix her hair, slap on a little make-up, ensure she'd left nothing behind, and exit her room calmly.

When she entered the living room, Enzo paced the wall of curtained glass. He'd donned his waistcoat and jacket again, and with his own bag waiting on the floor by the couch, he simply murmured, "Ready?" to which she replied, "Yes."

Thoughts toppled over each other as they drove to the airport. Enzo queried her silence with a couple of pointed looks, but each time she replied with an, "I'm tired, that's all." The same driver who had delivered them to the hotel and enclave meeting chauffeured them out of the city, and as much as Ava wanted to blurt, *'You compelled me? And I let you?'* she knew better. So, with teeth clamped, she stared at a busy Athens afternoon, labouring to keep her breathing steady.

The airport neared. Thinking she'd never get out of the damn car and into the plane, she lowered the window a few inches. Even if it did stink of aviation fuel, she craved air.

Enzo remained equally mute beside her. Sitting close enough that their elbows and outer thighs brushed, she registered each of his minute shifts of discomfort. Just as they passed the main terminal buildings to where hangars housed private jets, he abruptly stiffened.

294

With measured slowness, he turned to her, pointedly glanced at where her charm hung beneath the neck of her hoodie, and dragged his stare back up to lock with hers. *'You know?'* his panicked squint queried.

'Yes,' her replying blink answered.

Not another look or word passed between them until they'd vacated the car, collected their bags, stepped inside the jet, and fastened their seat belts. As Athens dropped away and clouds skated by the window, Enzo leaned towards her. "How, Ava?"

"I left notes for myself."

He rose from his seat to pivot and land on the one beside her. "When? I didn't leave your side!" Realisation struck. "You asked for tea."

Ava shrugged. "I don't remember. All I know is that I have two notes telling me to trust you, that you'll tell me everything, and that I'm not to freak out."

"And . . .do you—trust me? Or are you freaking out?"

Glancing over her shoulder, she wondered if James Dean's lookalike was onboard again; tequila wouldn't go amiss right now. "Did I readily agree to it?"

"You did." Where she fiddled with the belt buckle, Enzo gathered up her anxious fingers. "I was the one who resisted."

"Why did we do it?"

"You'll understand everything when I reverse it."

"Whoa—*reverse* it?"

"You insisted."

Removing her hands from his, Ava shoved them into the pouch pocket of her hoodie. "I did?" A necessity to erase the compulsion he'd placed upon her meant that what she currently accepted as fact wasn't accurate. But how much of it? *Don't freak out. Trust Enzo,* a whisper reminded her. "Am I completely oblivious to the truth right now?" she asked.

"No. We hid only what was necessary to protect you—*us.*"

295

"So I lied to the Enclave?"

"You spoke your truth."

She'd spoken *her* truth. Typical vampire word-play. "Tell me one thing I lied about."

Regret tilted his lips down. "My home."

"In Carlingford?"

He nodded.

"What about it?"

"It's not in Carlingford. It's on Dunfarr, off the coast of Calnaloch."

"You live—I've been living on *Dunfarr?*" But Carlingford Lough formed clearly in her mind's eye; how the morning sun sparkled brilliantly on the water of the glacial fjord. In the evening, the retiring day would highlight coastal vegetation against a copper sky. She could even picture the flat garden running down to the shore and the sensation of spongy grass beneath her bare feet. "There's no house in Carlingford?"

"No."

"But I can see it; the water, the sky, the garden. Even how the grass—"

"Feels beneath your bare feet," he cut in. "You described it to me. We made notes. You can see sunlight on water, and how the setting sun silhouettes the foliage, correct?"

She nodded, shocked by how brightly her memory of this fictitious place shone in her mind.

"We agreed to keep the bulk of truth in your memories. The house is real. But it's on Dunfarr island."

"What else is a lie?" How sitting this close to Enzo had her struggling not to inhale that subtle cologne he wore? How she'd dreamt of his cool, hard body pressed against hers while she slept? That they'd almost kissed on the couch in his Dickens library? Maybe, in reality, she hated him. Could the Enclave interrogation have been her chance to escape? If Enzo feared he'd lose her, of course he'd turn to compulsion. But how had he removed her charm—or convinced her to take it off?

Inflating doubt prompted her to lean away from him, the armrest of her seat digging into her hip as she widened the space between them. Iz had worried Enzo had compelled her. Had he manipulated her all along? Did she sit here, ignorant to the entire situation, a stupid, willing fool who allowed velvet-brown eyes and breath-thieving smiles to draw her in?

"You're freaking out." Enzo stood, retreating to the aisle to give her more space. "What can I say to prove I have done you no harm? That my—*our*—intentions are honourable."

She clutched her charm. "Did I willingly remove this?"

"Yes."

And if she wanted the truth shoved back in, she'd have to unclasp it again. *Don't freak out,* her stern note reminded as the 2 of Cups materialised behind her eyes. *Trust him.*

Desolation crumpled Enzo's expression. "Ava, I would never—*have* never—betrayed your trust. The truth we hid is—"

"*You* hid. The truth *you* hid."

"Yes, but with your guidance. One moment, I'll show you."

Enzo darted to the rear of the cabin, where he'd stowed their bags in an overhead locker after boarding. He tugged his free, rummaging frantically before withdrawing a sheaf of folded sheets. When he handed them to her, she recognised her handwriting amongst his astonishingly beautiful copperplate script. She'd added in random words, expanding on a description, or crossing out a line to restructure it. The first page detailed the Carlingford house's location, the next bore Martha's name on repeat. She wanted to read it all, but panic had her eyes skittering, unable to absorb more than a few words at a time.

"You insisted I undo the compulsion. If you don't trust me to, I won't, but the whole truth is now hidden from you, and in order for us to proceed, I'll have to tell you."

"In which case, it still demands I place my faith in you."

Enzo lowered himself to perch on the arm of the seat on the opposite side of the aisle. Regret sagged his normally proud shoulders. Where his hands hung between his knees, fingers twisted. "Back to square one," he murmured.

Doubt battled doubt. Ava flicked over the pages again, then beyond the jet to where they'd risen above puffy, cotton-ball clouds. *Listen to your gut, pet,* Nessa would say, if she were here. But it was hard to consider that tiny whisper when confusion and fear raged. "Iz thinks you compelled me."

"Not before last night. I swear on Martha's life."

But Martha was already technically dead, so how valid was that promise? "She said you fooled me into liking you. Maybe she's right."

"Much like I know you don't employ love magick, I don't compel affection."

Ava believed him, but was it only because of his vampire influence?

Slamming the heel of her hand to her forehead, she groaned. Uncertainty grew legs by the second. If she allowed this confusion to spiral, she'd never clamber her way back to reason. Even if she studied what they'd written, it proved nothing when potentially composed under Enzo's control.

Realising she could assume nothing as factual, suspicion corkscrewed her sanity faster than she could scramble for logic.

"I need a minute." Ava flung their supposed compulsion plan onto the empty seat beside her, unlocked her belt, and lurched upright. "Where's the bathroom?"

Enzo gestured to his right.

298

She brushed by him, and locating the narrow door, ducked into the tiny cubicle and snapped the lock into place.

In the weeks after her mum had died and the O'Keefe curse had made its claim on her, Ava had suffered crippling panic attacks. One of the quickest ways to control her breath and centre her thoughts was to splash her face with cold water or dunk it into a full sink. The minuscule sink in Enzo's jet didn't cater for face-dunking, so she settled for splashing instead. It quickly arrested tight, erratic breaths.

A pale, dripping countenance greeted her when she met her reflection in the mirror. Droplets clung to her hair, and the make-up she'd flung on that morning gathered under her lower eyelashes. But she'd gained control of her racing heart and thoughts again.

Her predicament all boiled down to one simple question. Did she trust Enzo Paladino?

Yes.

But also, no.

Iz had sown that seed of doubt.

A paper-towel dispenser spat out a soft, thick napkin. Ava dabbed her face, wiping away the dark rings around her eyes. She blotted her hair dry, and moistening the napkin further under the tap, clamped it to the rear of her neck. "Mum," she whispered. "I could really do with your help right now."

Enzo claimed he'd only compelled her once, and was ready to whip it all out again. But how could she know for sure this wasn't all part of his game? Iz had warned he might have coerced her long before she had the mugwort charm, meaning he'd only have to utter one word and she'd willingly remove it. Was she eyeball-deep in manipulation? Or prior to last night, had she known every truth and wholly trusted Enzo?

Mum, she pleaded. *How can I trust my gut instinct?*

You can't.

299

The sudden realisation snapped her eyes open. Enzo's compulsion coursed through her, compromising memories, emotions, and intuition. She knew exactly how to prove it—and how to irrefutably test his promise to reverse the lies.

Shoving the water stopper into place, Ava filled the basin. She needed her own blood for the spell, but spinning around to survey the poky cubicle, found nothing sharp enough to pierce her skin. A pat down of her body offered no inspiration, but as she swept upwards and brushed her charm, realised her necklace's clasp held potential.

Unhooked and in her grasp, she dragged the tiny gold edge across the pad of her index finger. It took firm pressure and a painful twist, but the clasp eventually bit in. A drop of blood welled. Ava held it over the water, squeezing to encourage enough of a flow to form a scarlet cloud. She didn't have time to craft a chant with rhyme or finesse, so bluntly called on the water to repel manipulation as she gently stirred.

After three clockwise turns while murmuring the incantation, she watched her blood slow against the flow. Within seconds, it rotated in the opposite direction.

The competing currents declared her body bore the effects of mind-control. But now came the real test. She'd tell Enzo to remove his compulsion, and when he was done, she'd repeat the spell. If the blood continued to swirl anti-clockwise, she'd know the truth.

Ava sucked the tip of her finger, and wrapping it in a piece of towel, unlocked the door.

She emerged to find Enzo standing in the centre of the aisle, statue-still, braced against flanking headrests. His nails had pierced the leather padding.

"Why can I smell your blood?" he croaked.

Ignoring his question, Ava displayed her unfastened mugwort charm. "Undo the compulsion."

26

The act of reversing compulsion hurt like a bitch. Ava clenched against a swarm of wasps piercing her brain as Enzo tried to breach her mind. Every witch-cell in her body screeched and thrashed in retaliation. If she'd calmly accepted him, unfailingly trusted him, she wouldn't be hissing and writhing. But she couldn't even trust herself at that moment.

Peace floated down when he drilled through the final barrier. His voice formed her new surroundings; a soothing murmur as formless fingers plucked at threads to unbind the truth. After the agonising pain, she sank without hesitation into the lull of his whispers.

The more he unfastened the invisible locks, the more Ava recognised the sense of returning to her true mind and body. When heavy eyes flickered open, she couldn't deny the shift in her being, despite its subtlety.

Enzo knelt before her, gently stroking her cheek. "Ava."

"I'm okay."

"I'm sorry. I know it hurt. Can I get you anything, do anything?"

"No. I just need you to wait here," she told him hoarsely, rising on unsteady feet.

Inside the poky bathroom, she performed the spell once more. Although still dizzy, she sighed in relief as her blood flowed in tandem with the clockwise motion stirred into the water. He'd cleared her of all compulsion. Every thought, memory, and emotion she possessed were hers—including those already catching her breath.

Ava fastened her charm in place, and once the rust-tinged water disappeared down the plughole, splashed her face again.

Enzo looked like someone had kicked his puppy when she emerged from the bathroom. Hunched on the edge of his seat, sorrowful eyes watched her walk through the cabin.

"You didn't lie to me," she said, sinking into the support of the comfy leather.

"No. I wouldn't—and haven't."

"I wasn't sure, and I needed to be."

"I understand. I would feel the same were I in your position."

Still slightly off-kilter, she recognised her body's cry for grounding. As if her anchor had come undone, it felt as if she floated aimlessly. Being airborne didn't help. *Food*, she muttered over the jumble in her head. Hot tea and preferably something carb-laden would centre her.

"Ava." Enzo's thumb brushed her knee. She opened her eyes, unaware she'd even closed them. "Talk to me, please?"

A sigh partially herded the scattered mess. "I remember it all. I know now why we did it. We were right. It *was* the best course of action."

"Do I have your trust again?"

"You do." Ava twisted to scan the noticeably attendant-free cabin. "I need to eat."

"What would you like?" He immediately shot upright.

"Tea, and something sweet, please?"

"Of course. One minute, tesoro."

She waited until he'd ducked out of sight to drop her face into her hands.

That kiss.

Oh, that *kiss!*

It refused to leave her thoughts—along with how being caged beneath him had lit her insides.

The memory ignited a fresh explosion of butterflies. Touching where he'd grazed her throat with his teeth, Ava bit down on her lip to halt an erupting groan. Everything else; all the weighty consequential facts, like Martha's rescue, reinstating her witch power, and Cyrus the blood-thirsty maniac? Nothing but a sidebar. All she could think about was that goddamn kiss. No wonder she'd told him to compel it out of her mind for the meeting. She'd have blabbed it for sure.

Enzo returned in a puff of wind, bearing a tray with tea, a fresh apple pastry, more pretzels, and a pot of fruit salad. "Will this suffice for now? As soon as we get home, I'll cook you a proper meal."

"This is perfect, thank you."

It would almost be preferable to blame compulsion for her lust-drunk thoughts. At least that way she could claim her inability to focus on the grave situation completely unrelated to her damned stupid hormones.

Internally squirming against the awkwardness stalking their space, Ava ate in silence. Meals with Enzo were usually chatty, enjoyable affairs. Not this uncomfortable muteness made all the louder by the white noise filling the cabin. Acutely aware of his stare, she busied herself with picking apart the pastry and chewing each mouthful slowly.

A weird juxtaposition of two different Avas played havoc. On one side, she had the compelled Ava, who knew nothing about The Kiss.

That version of her quietly fancied Enzo, but maintained a strict *'Don't Shit Where You Eat'* policy. But on the other, she had the real Ava, who bounced like a sugar-buzzed toddler every time the memory of their passionate lip-lock replayed. Why wasn't she writhing against the enormous task awaiting her? Why did her damned mind only want to fixate on clambering onto Enzo's lap, and ordering him to kiss her anarchic brain into silence?

Her tiny sigh cracked his patience. As she struggled to peel the cellophane lid off the fruit salad tub, he swooped in, nabbed it from her, whipped off the seal, and holding the snack hostage, said, "Please, Ava. Your silence is killing me."

Yeah, well, thinking about that goddamn kiss is killing me. "I remember everything."

"Wasn't that the point?"

"*Everything*, Enzo," she said, finally daring to look up at him.

"You're upset about our kiss." He handed over the fruit cup.

Ava dug out a red grape. "That's not it." *Not entirely.*

"What is it, then?"

Although Enzo didn't even know how to whine, enough desperation strained his tone for her to appreciate how her reticence bothered him a lot. "This" —she motioned between them with the grape— "is a distraction we don't need. I have ten days to sculpt and perfect a spell to rescue and reconnect Martha. Once the eclipse passes, and I go back to my life, and you to yours, things will be very different for us both."

"How different?" he asked quietly.

Ava bit into the fruit. Stored in a chilled unit, the cold stung her teeth, making her wince. "Reality will have kicked in."

"A reality where you assume I shall walk away and never think of you again?"

"We lead incredibly different lives, Enzo."

"Let me ask you this, then. Will you think of me? When the wards lift and you're free to leave Dunfarr Lodge, will you never look back?"

Ava swallowed the juicy coldness. "I don't want you to leave. Neither do I want to never see you again. And if I did—wait, sorry. Dunfarr Lodge? You named your tardis of a mansion a *lodge?*"

Enzo landed in the seat beside hers once more. "Let me make myself clear, Ava. I have no intention of leaving you or Calnaloch when our business concludes. I want to insert myself into your life, and I hope you would like to do the same in mine. Of course our lives differ, but we will learn to compromise, to evolve, to navigate *this*" —he mimicked her *between them* gesture— "as one. My feelings for you are genuine, not a manipulation for my personal gain. Can I restrain myself for ten days? Yes. Will I find it easy? No. But I respect your wishes, and I can't argue with their reasoning.

"Vampires and witches rarely align, especially not emotionally, but after centuries of treading this earth alone, I refuse to ignore this serendipitous bond. I also refuse to allow the assumptions of others or the inconveniences of our daily lives to dictate my heart's desire. My needs are simple. I want you. I want us. And that's all there is to say."

The impassioned speech concluded with a concise nod of *'so there.'*

"Except for one final matter," he quickly added. "The previous owners named the house Dunfarr Lodge. When I purchased it, it never crossed my mind to rename it *Paladino Palace.*"

It took Ava a moment to remember how to work her tongue. "You said you were no good with words."

"That was not an eloquent declaration."

"From my viewpoint, it was. Here's me trying to be all practical and reserved, and you just rip your heart out of your chest and slap it down beside my tea and fruit salad to demonstrate your affections."

A smile softened his lips. "That would make for a violent and bloody statement." Enzo leaned in, taking her chin. "I shall control myself for ten days, but before I declare a vow of chastity, I demand the sustenance of a kiss."

"One single *chaste* kiss," she said softly, already fixated on where a flirty little smile played at the corner of his full lips.

"The chastest, mia bella strega."

As limited as Ava's Italian was, she understood his murmur. She'd never been called anyone's *beautiful witch*, and before her breathy sigh could trail off, Enzo had captured it. Despite his restraint, the kiss left her dizzy and hungry for more.

He remained in the neighbouring seat while she ate the petite serving of fruit salad. Although he faced forward, he occasionally stole a glance at her. Each look grazed her with warmth and contentment, as if exposing his heart had settled peace in his bones. The Enzo Paladino sitting beside her wasn't the same man who had orbited her first few days in his home with tense, jerky movements. He'd hidden himself efficiently with his air of marginal tolerance and fading patience back then. She'd assumed him aloof and sober, but now saw beyond that Knight of Pentacles mask. He possessed the charming and passionate energy of the Knight of Wands; an alluring sensuality that had a delectable low-down heat simmering once more.

"Is there anything else you'd like?" he asked as she popped the last piece of fruit into her mouth.

Ava bit into the pineapple. "No, thanks. This was perfect."

With her hands no longer occupied, Enzo claimed one for himself. He clasped it between his, and with a smile still dancing around his lips, closed his eyes.

She settled back with him, the one now stealing appreciative glances. How had something so amazing become entwined with their chaotic

306

situation? Her mum always said that whatever was meant for her would never pass her by, regardless of the lesson it taught. Ava hoped the lessons with Enzo would be positive, life-changing ones. The persistent Tower card warned of catastrophic collapse, but if they tumbled down together, surely it wouldn't hurt as much?

The return journey followed the same route as their outward. Just before ten o'clock, they landed in Ronaldsway Airport in the Isle of Man. After an efficient disembarkation, Enzo helped her into the helicopter. Within a few minutes, they rose into a pitch-black sky, canting towards Calnaloch.

Not since her mother's death had Ava experienced such a tense and exhausting two days. Her fight with Iz seemed like weeks ago, and their botched efforts to locate Martha, equally distant. Wishing she could turn off her non-stop thoughts, she tried to doze, but a windy night buffeted the helicopter, leaving her too nervous to hide behind closed eyes. As pinpricks of light announced the east coast of Ireland, worries looped, muttering about Iz, and if she'd called.

So much of what Iz had said continued to hurt, the comment about how she'd prefer Ava with Finn over Enzo especially.

Iz didn't do irrational. She was always the person to hit pause in moments of crisis and keep a level head, so Ava couldn't stop picking at why she'd reacted so explosively. Had she learned something about the Paladinos? Something that rendered the entire family irredeemable in her eyes? Iz's harsh words had reflected protectiveness. For her to have spoken the way she had, pointed at Ava being under threat. But threats

307

already smothered her, and all Ava could do right now was focus on her priorities; rescue Martha and reconnect her to her witch lineage.

The coastline neared. Ribbons of light marked the busy roads in and around Calnaloch, with the town itself a glittering web. They approached from a northerly direction, and as shapes took form in the dark night, Ava picked out the formation of the Hag's Nose hooking the water. Perched on its hump, and lit by a dramatic blue spotlight, she admired Calnaloch's Martello tower.

Knowing she'd never get to see it from this angle again, Ava shifted in her seat, absorbing the view. Its twin sat further out to sea on the Heath, but in darkness. Ava often wondered why the towers spread along Ireland's east coast had been left to decline. A yearly ritual of lighting fires from one tower to the next would connect communities and remind them of the strength of togetherness.

Despite tiredness and sentimentality fogging her brain, a sudden realisation slapped her fully alert. Before she could grab at Enzo and direct him to look, the pilot announced they were about to land. As they dipped towards Dunfarr, the tower vanished from view, but her awareness had already solidified into a confident knowing.

Aware she couldn't blab in front of the pilot, Ava waited until Enzo had her bundled inside the house. As soon as he shut and locked the only unwarded door, she blurted out her discovery. "Martha wasn't saying *'our'*. She was saying *'tower'*. She's in a Martello tower—the circular brick walls, the damp surface, remember? The witches are being held in a tower!"

Enzo glanced toward the Hag's Nose. "You think she's *here*, in Calnaloch?" Startled disbelief notched his volume higher. "She's been here, this close to me, all this time?"

Afraid he'd actually bolt out into the darkness on a rescue mission, Ava grabbed his arm. "No. Not here. Whoever has them wouldn't be foolish enough to keep the witches right under our noses. But knowing they're hidden in a tower makes locating them much easier."

Enzo dropped the bags to dig out his phone. "The authorities need to search now."

"Wait." Ava stalled where he frantically swiped. "They won't be visible. Even if they were in the Hag's Tower, we wouldn't see them. The cloaking magick that's shielding them hides them from actual sight, too."

"So you and I must search for them."

"Enzo." Ava applied more pressure when he moved to scroll through his phone again. "Listen to me. The kind of spell required to break through that cloaking takes time to craft. I'd also have to cast it over and over, on site, at every tower, until I find the right one."

Understanding formed. Enzo lowered his phone. "For which we don't have time."

"No. It could take weeks. There are almost thirty towers along the east coast alone."

His hope withered.

"But" —she hurried to appease him— "I can try picking up on energy signatures or traces of witchcraft. And if that doesn't work, we could consider asking the witch communities beyond Calnaloch for help."

"What can they do that you can't?"

His earnest question filled her with warmth. It wasn't fair to compare Enzo to Finn, but on the occasions Finn had seen her doing her witchy thing—even something as simple as wafting sage around her apartment—he'd always responded with the same reaction; a minute shake of head and a half-grimace suggesting she should be embarrassed with herself.

A few months into their relationship, war had almost erupted in the town when a developer applied for planning permission to build warehouse units and a filling-station on a prime piece of land by the town's entrance. The few acres had been arable land for decades. After the landowner died, the family gave Calnaloch locals consent to cast thousands of wildflower seeds into the soil. For many years, it existed as an unofficial wild garden. Local primary schools brought the pupils onto the land to appreciate and teach. Nature enthusiasts filmed and photographed, and once, a well-known high-fashion publication came in the height of blooming season to capture models wearing haute couture amongst the butterflies, corncockle, and cornflower. When the last remaining family member sold the land and the developer swooped in, the prospect of having the haven ripped up to accommodate a filling-station and warehousing units, brought the town's witch community together.

One night, they gathered en masse to cast an obstruction spell.

Less than a week later, the developers pulled their planning request, citing a re-evaluation had proved the land inappropriate. Ava, Iz, and dozens of witches celebrated on the land that night, but while walking up the town on her way home, Finn had met her. He'd laughed, informing her their *'little spell'* had made feck-all difference. *'Seriously, Ava,'* he'd said. *'Do you honestly believe a few rhymes and dried herbs have the power to put off an entire development company?'*

Refocusing on Enzo's question, and not her past, Ava told him covens might be willing to craft and cast spells on their local towers. "We'd need to do it all in one go, though," she told him. "A sort of spell-casting carpet-bombing."

"Will the covens answer your call?"

Ava shook her head. While a workable solution, it came at a heavy price. "Not mine, no. Felicienne is the only person who'd have the sway to herd the covens into working as one."

"No," he said, instantly dismissing the idea. "Then she'll know you're here."

310

"She will. And why." And because Felicienne never did anything out of the kindness of her heart, she'd demand full disclosure. She'd then take over entirely, and slot herself into the eclipse-working. The prospect had a shiver skittering down Ava's spine.

"No," Enzo repeated, with sharp decisiveness. "I don't want that woman involved in our business."

As if suddenly realising they'd returned to his home, Enzo blinked at their poolside surroundings. "It's late," he said, turning to where the bags had slipped from his grasp to land on the ornate tiles. "And you're exhausted. I also promised you a meal."

"It's too late to eat."

" I'll make something light."

Ava dragged herself downstairs once she'd deposited her bag and used the bathroom. Enzo had whipped up an omelette. It waited on the table, along with two thick slices of buttered toast and a mug of tea. "When I go back home," she told him, sliding into her usual bench-seat at the table, "I'll never get used to cooking again. You're ruining me with every meal you make."

"Well, then, perhaps I can continue to cook you the occasional meal?"

Looking up at where he scrubbed the pan in the sink, back facing her, she smiled. He'd changed out of his suit, replacing it with a pair of Levi's and a grey t-shirt. Her view of perfectly fitted jeans and lean muscle shifting beneath cotton almost distracted her from noting his cautious tone. "You hate the smell of food."

A tiny noise that sounded like a laugh got lost in a cough. "It's no longer an issue."

311

Ava forked a piece of the omelette. He'd mixed tomatoes, mushrooms, and spinach into the fluffy egg, and her stomach grumbled in anticipation. "But when you don't eat it, why go to all the bother of cooking?"

"I enjoy the process. And feeding you is not a bother. It's a pleasure."

Glad he busied himself with cleaning, she ducked as her cheeks flared. "Uncle?"

Cyrus had crept to the open doorway with such stealth, Ava jumped. She walloped her knee off the underside of the table, rattling cutlery and crockery.

"Sorry," Cyrus said to her.

Enzo whipped up the tea-towel, and turning to face his nephew, blotted suds off his hands. "What is it?"

"I was wondering if the Enclave made a ruling."

Lowering her attention to her food, Ava opted out of the conversation. Enzo continued to allow Cyrus to believe the Enclave knew of his most recent infraction. If it prevented Cyrus from killing again, she'd play along, too.

"It remains under discussion."

"But—" Cyrus inched further into the kitchen. "What did they say?"

"Not a lot besides mention of an Observation Order and the oubliette."

Cyrus visibly flinched. Even from where Ava chased a piece of mushroom around her plate, she saw the jerk from the corner of her eye.

"It would only be for a week, though, right?"

"You slaughtered a defenceless animal, too, Cyrus."

"I didn't mean to."

"And it's not your first infraction." Enzo threw the tea-towel aside. He came to the table, and tugging out the chair across from where Ava sat, leaned on its curved backrest. "You'll know as soon as the Enclave make their decision."

312

"Did Reeve Ortega speak to you alone?"

"Not once."

"Okay." Cyrus tugged at the hair curling over one ear. "Goodnight, Uncle. Goodnight, Ava."

"Goodnight, Cyrus."

Enzo rounded the chair and sat. Ava waited until he finished tracking Cyrus's return to his room before quietly asking, "What's an Observation Order?"

"When they put a team on an individual who repeatedly commits offences. Based on the severity of any subsequent infractions, punishment can range from the oubliette to death."

"The oubliette is the dark cell, right?"

Enzo nodded.

"How long will you keep this up?"

"Until I can get my own men here to watch him. Hopefully, it will keep him restrained until Martha is home with us."

Poor Martha, she thought, returning to her meal. Whether she realised it, a lot balanced on her safe return and reanimation into a witch—almost as much as rested on Ava bringing her home in the first place.

27

The following morning, Enzo waited until Ava had eaten and safely tucked herself away in Martha's room before departing the house. Cyrus stayed in hiding, waiting for an enclave ruling. Daphne remained with him. Torn between sending the unfortunate woman on her way and risking Cyrus's retaliation, or leaving her in his nephew's company to suffer further mind manipulation, Enzo had faltered before turning the boat away from the jetty.

He hadn't slept once Ava had gone to bed. He'd tried, but after an hour of staring up at his bed's canopy, surrendered to wakefulness and abandoned his room. A wander of the house, a flick through several of Martha's grimoires, and a few hours of reading in the library, saw him through to the dawn. Throughout those quiet hours, he'd made a plan, and waited patiently until the house lay in order before leaving.

Iseult had replied to his request to meet with a one-word answer:

Iseult: Fine.

Aware of the attitude she'd bring to their meeting, he faced into the brisk wind warning of an incoming storm, reminding himself to be patient. Ava confronted an enormous challenge and needed her best friend in her corner to face it. In Athens, she'd talked in her sleep the night he'd compelled her; pitiful sighs and murmurs, pleading with Iseult not to fight. He could do little to help with witchcraft, but perhaps he could orchestrate peace between the two women.

Enzo moored the boat at the harbour, and with fifteen minutes to spare before his meeting with Iseult, walked towards the crest of the Hag's Nose. The Martello tower came into view as soon as he passed the former lighthouse cottages on the seafront. Situated on a hillock of grass, he first noted the vegetation sprouting from its roof. As he further neared, he studied the entrance; approximately twelve-feet above ground and bricked shut. The concern his niece lay trapped inside had him tempted to leap onto the roof and punch his way through. But locals were out in their droves before the forecast storm rolled in.

Enzo strolled three measured laps of the tower, studying the structure for any sign of weakness or recent disturbance. With no visible clues, he retreated, perching on a nearby wall to further contemplate from a distance.

Whoever accessed the tower—whether it be this one, or one further along the coast—he couldn't disregard the possibility of an underground tunnel. The structures idled since the latter half of the 19th Century, and in the passing decades, tunnels may have been dug to access the interiors

315

for smuggling. With Calnaloch's rich history, a visit to the local library would assist, and if necessary, a call to the town's historical society.

Content with his tower observation, Enzo headed for the Lighthouse Cafe. At eleven o'clock on a Tuesday morning, it would be busy with mothers and young children. Hopefully, the crowded public space would place Iseult at ease.

Not a single table remained free when Enzo entered. He placed an order for an espresso and found a spot at a narrow counter running one length of the cafe's sandstone interior wall. Tucked into the corner, it would allow them to speak freely, but also give Iseult the reassurance of being visible.

She arrived three minutes early, a thunderous expression landing the moment she located him in the crowd. Weaving her way through buggies and tables, she flashed thin smiles at those who greeted her. When she came to where he stood, he immediately understood her fight with Ava had been far more significant than he'd assumed.

"Where is she?" Iseult immediately demanded, stepping into his personal space without hesitation. "I called, and she didn't answer."

"The Enclave requested our presence. We flew out the day before yesterday and returned late last night. Ava is safe in my home. She has the phone by her side. You can call her right now, if you wish."

Iseult cocked a *'we'll see about that'* glower at him, and lifting the flap of her satchel bag, dug out the phone he'd given her. As soon as Ava answered, Iseult asked where she was. Over the pitch of dozens of conversations and a wailing baby at a nearby table, Enzo just about caught Ava's reply of, "In Enzo's home."

Iseult cut her off before she could say more. "Where were you yesterday?"

"We had to attend an enclave meeting. Iz, can we talk?"

"Not now. I'm still pissed at you."

316

Iseult hung up so abruptly, Enzo had to bite down not to snap at her rudeness towards Ava.

"Did you compel her?"

"Ava worked a spell to answer that query for herself yesterday. Her mind is free of compulsion. I am not controlling her." He itched to add on that if Iseult would only bury her prejudices and talk to Ava, she'd learn the facts for herself.

"So?" Iseult shoved the phone into her bag. "You called me here. What do you want?"

"Ava is upset. She needs her closest friend right now."

"Wow." Open disdain roused a bark of laughter. "How *dare* you" —a black fingernail poked him in the centre of his chest— "tell *me* what *my* friend needs. Who the fuck do you think you are to stand there and act like Ava's welfare is *your* concern?"

While Enzo had only held one brief face-to-face and three phone conversations with Iseult, she hadn't displayed such open animosity towards him up to that point. Aware it would benefit neither of them to be spotted conversing, Enzo cut straight to the chase. Platitudes would not calm whatever boiled her blood. "Speak freely, Iseult. Say whatever it is you wish to say."

"Let Ava go. I don't care what she's doing for you. Tell her you no longer require it."

"Ava won't agree. She has fully committed."

"Isn't that convenient?" Iseult laughed without humour once more. "But here's the thing. When Ava learns the truth about you, she'll realise the mistake she made, and then you'll discover just how powerful the witch you're manipulating *really* is."

"What truth, Iseult?"

317

Ava's friend scoured the nearby tables for signs of anyone listening. Assured of privacy, she held his stare with confidence. "The truth about how you're responsible for her mother's death."

Startled by the accusation, Enzo reared back. "I had *nothing* to do with Aoibheann O'Keefe's death."

"Keep pretending that, Mr Paladino, but Nessa O'Keefe and I know better. I'm just sorry I didn't hear sooner—*before* you fooled Ava."

"I have neither manipulated Ava nor hidden anything about her mother's death. I had no part in—"

"Save it." Iseult flashed a palm to silence him. "I know how much your kind love word-play, so let me make it clear. You may not have been present at her murder, but Aoibheann died because of you and your damn family. That," she said, jabbing him once again, "makes *you* responsible."

Enzo grabbed Iseult's hand and discreetly drew it down between their bodies. Although he wouldn't hurt her, he kept a tight enough grip on her wrist to remind her of how he could. "I don't know who killed Ava's mother," he said in a harsh whisper, "so mind your tongue, Miss Boleyn. Your attitude has already worn my patience thin."

Almost nose to nose with him, Iseult's eyes narrowed, glistening with pure hate. "But you do, Mr Paladino. It was your charming *Mrs* who murdered Aoibheann."

Stunned into rigidness, Enzo barely registered Iseult yanking her hand free. "Giulia is dead," his seizing throat croaked. "Centuries ago—long before . . ."

Iseult hitched her bag strap more securely onto her shoulder. Once more, she laughed, a bitter bark of amusement. "Necromancy is alive and thriving, Enzo Paladino. Much like your wife. She killed Ava's mother, and your current involvement with Ava means she'll come for her too. We both know exactly what she wants. And when she—"

Enzo didn't wait to hear the rest of Iseult's dire warning. He blew through the crowd, out the door of the cafe, and straight for where he'd moored.

Confusion spun his world into a clamour of light and noise as he struggled not to move at inhuman speed. A trawler had docked, trailed by hungry seals and squawking gulls. Between the wail of tired winches, the shouts of harried men, and the surrounding activity of the busy harbour, his senses rebelled against overload. He'd believed Giulia dead—centuries ago. On the night he'd turned Martha, Giulia had been fifty-four. He'd wed her when he was forty-two, and she only twenty-one, and despite the horrors of Martha's rescue, he hadn't failed to notice Giulia's youthfulness. She'd obviously been working with death magick, and he'd refused—

"Look where you're goin', will ya?"

A young but rugged face filled Enzo's vision. Utterly disconnected, he'd walked straight into a man heaving a net off his trawler and onto the pier.

"My apologies."

The jolt returned him to the present, and with another apology, Enzo sidestepped the tangle of netting and hurried for his boat.

Iseult's tirade suggested she knew nothing of Aoibheann's death until Enzo had Ava in his home, which meant Nessa had told her after the fact. Nessa O'Keefe liked to portray herself as a batty crone, but in truth, she was a sharp, gifted witch—one whose knowledge Enzo couldn't disregard. Neither could he ignore the threat to Ava.

Thoughts swimming with wild and frightening conspiracies, he leapt aboard the boat, turned the ignition, and aimed the bow at Dunfarr.

If Giulia had survived centuries through the maleficence of death magick, Ava was already at a terrifying disadvantage. Should he tell her? Revealing Giulia's involvement would mean admitting his part in Aoib-

319

heann's death—however small his role. The knowledge would repel Ava. He'd lose her forever.

Dunfarr neared. Despite clamouring fears and thoughts, one fact clarified with chilling certainty; the person who lay behind his niece's abduction.

Only one witch possessed the power to subdue Martha—the woman he'd once called his wife.

Enzo found Ava where he'd left her; deep in research at the desk in Martha's room.

"You're back early," she said, wincing as she manipulated her stiff neck. He'd intended on being away longer. His itinerary in Calnaloch had included a forced run-in with Felicienne to gauge what she'd learned during his and Ava's absence. But Felicienne could wait. "There's a storm coming in. I didn't want to get caught out with the high tide."

Ava studied him, a tiny frown adding further creases to her already troubled brow. "Did something happen? You have that look about you."

"What look?" he queried, assuming a nonchalant pose against the apothecary cabinet.

"A *'shit has hit the fan'* look, but you're trying to pretend it hasn't."

Enzo found the strength to smile. "I didn't know my face could portray such complicated expressions."

Ava set down her pencil, and rolling out her shoulders, sat back in the chair. "What's up, Enzo?"

"It seems Manus Larsen wasn't the only necromancer interested in your necklace."

She shrugged, lifting her chin towards the glass doors behind him. An agitated wind whipped around the eaves. "What can they do? I'm safe here, right?"

"Of course you are."

"If anything, *you're* the one who needs to stay at home. If they're suspicious enough, they could follow you."

"True." Enzo plucked at his tie knot. He hadn't sucked in a breath since 1525, but as if redundant lungs suddenly craved oxygen, he loosened the restriction pressing against his throat. "How is your research going?" Judging by the despondency clouding her eyes as efficiently as the approaching storm, not to her satisfaction.

"You know that saying about bringing a fist to a gunfight?" Ava cast a worried frown at the notes she'd made. "Well, that's how I'm feeling right now."

"Why?" Enzo approached the desk, rounding it to scan her research.

"I'm fighting dark magick with light. It works in a Disney world, but not in reality."

Enzo grasped the back of her chair with one hand, and leaning forward, braced his other on the desk. She'd made copious notes, but many she'd scored through. A number of sigils she'd also scribbled over, frustration reflected in the wild pencil strokes. "So, what do you suggest?"

Ava propped an elbow on her notebook, and resting her chin on her palm, angled her face to where his hung temptingly close. At first, he read the mischievous smile as a flirtation, but with a deliberate swing of eyes, her gaze landed across the room. "That."

Momentarily distracted by the nearness of the sweet lips he ached to taste once more, it took a few seconds before he followed her pointed look.

The ebony cabinet.

321

Instinct lifted him fully upright, tongue already forming a refusal. But Giulia Lombardi skulked with her depraved, magickal practices. If he wanted Ava to have the power to stand against her, she needed to fight like with like. "You told me you don't practice dark magick."

"It doesn't mean I haven't worked with it."

When he looked down, Ava offered him up a guilty smile.

"When mum was alive, I dabbled with it a little. We both did. Mum was cautious with what she taught me, and we were always hyper aware of what we worked. But after she died, Nessa found out, lost her shit, and made me swear I'd never practice it again, so . . ."

So, Ava didn't avoid dark magick out of fear or principle, but because she'd made an oath?

"Did you enjoy working with it?"

She paused to consider her answer. "It's a very different experience."

Enzo turned to prop himself on the edge of the desk.

Ava sat back again, bringing her pencil with her. She fiddled with it as she spoke. "White, light, good—whatever label you want to put on the magick I use, it's like eating only healthy food every day. While it may not be the most exciting, you know the good it does in your body. Whenever I practised dark magick, it felt more like feasting on carrot cake. Not exactly healthy, but far tastier, as long as I didn't overindulge."

For her to feel that way meant someone along the O'Keefe lineage had practised dark magick. It had to be in a witch's bloodline for them to coalesce. Her mother, perhaps? "Did your mother practice dark magick?"

Ava shook her head. "It was me who went to her, not the other way around. She said no at first, but I guess she was worried that I'd try it anyway, so she agreed to work it with me and supervise."

"So it's in your bloodline?"

"Somewhere, yes. But I don't know who, or when." Ava tapped the pencil end against her lips. "Can you unlock the cabinet?"

322

He could. But he needed to weigh the consequences of allowing Ava O'Keefe into Martha's collection. Aoibheann had supervised her daughter as a curious teenager. But as a vampire, he possessed nothing with which to control the capable adult witch looking up at him from under her lashes. If the darkness sucked Ava in, he might lose her to the same path Giulia tread. "May I think about it?"

"Sure. But, Enzo?"

Peeling his stare away from the innocuous cabinet, he replied with a cautious "Yes?"

"I'm not planning on embracing the dark side. I just want to see what my options are, the different methods I can use to reach Martha. So far today, I haven't achieved much, but I did discover this."

Ava stretched across the desk to tug one of Martha's oldest grimoires towards her. Written in English, many of the pages had faded beyond legibility, and some had succumbed to age so severely, they resembled tissue paper. She gently spun an open-page spread to face him. "Do you want the science bit, or will I skip to the good part?"

"Skip, please."

"We may not need Martha present here to flip her witch switch. I've more research to do, but there's a solid chance I can restore her power regardless of her location. To fuel that connection and make it breach-proof calls for a slice or two of carrot cake. Hence—" She smiled, sending another grin in the infernal cabinet's direction. "A request to explore what's in there."

28

After lunch, Ava ploughed into research with such focus, she lost track of time. It was only when Enzo appeared to remind her about food when she lifted her head and realised the afternoon had surrendered to evening—a wild, dirty evening. Deaf to the outside world, the balcony doors framed an image of a wicked storm chucking sheets of rain. Such severe gusts raged, they chased water sideways across the panes. "When did that blow in?"

"Twenty minutes ago," Enzo told her.

He'd changed from his earlier shirt-and-tie outfit to jeans and a black t-shirt. As he neared the desk, a wisp of his cologne teased, along with soft cotton hinting at the leanness of what lay underneath. Ava dragged hungry eyes down to her notes.

"Any progress?"

Humming a yes, she splayed her hand on the grimoire she'd pulled from a cramped shelf earlier. "I'll need your help with this one, though. It contains a few advanced siphoning spells, but they're all in Italian."

"Of course. After dinner?"

"Yes. If you're up for it. I can wait until tomorrow otherwise."

"Ava, I want to assist. I already feel entirely useless."

Pushing the chair away from the desk she stood, trying to hold back a smile. The translation would take some time, meaning they'd spend most of the evening together. "You're not useless," she told him. "Far from it."

Enzo tutted disagreement.

As they made their way down, she remembered to ask about using the gym. Her addled brain left her exhausted enough each night to sleep reasonably well, but she missed physical exercise; walking on the beach especially. When wrangling with a decision, she always found striding the shoreline helped her to gain clarity. If she could plug into music and pound Enzo's fancy treadmill for a while, it might help to create space within her cluttered thoughts.

"Whatever you need, Ava. You don't need to ask either. What's mine is yours."

Unsure of how to reply to such a heartfelt statement, Ava murmured a quiet, "Thanks." Following Enzo into the kitchen, she took her place at the table as he made a beeline for the oven.

A moment later, he placed another masterpiece before her. Ava gaped at the stuffed aubergine brimming over with rice and cubed vegetables. Chunks of melting goat's cheese sat on top. The sight made her mouth instantly water. "Enzo, this looks amazing."

"Thank you. I enjoyed making it."

Hesitant to cut in and ruin the perfect presentation, her cutlery hovered. "Did you cook a lot in the past, or is this something you've only done recently?"

"In the past." With his habitual modest serving of wine, Enzo took his usual place opposite her. He sat with her for all her meals, now. Ava preferred it this way; they got to talk, and she could untangle her brain by tangling his. "In my later years, especially. The food back then was quite different, of course, but I always enjoyed the art of taking raw ingredients and coaxing them into a meal."

He studied his wine as he spoke, a tell Ava recognised. When Enzo shared moments from his past with her, memories that continued to trouble him sent his gaze down. When he recalled positive experiences, he never hesitated to look her in the eye. She wondered what circumstances or stories lay behind his love of cooking. "How did you make this?" she asked, preferring his eyes on her than drowning in his Chianti.

He took her through the process, surprising her with how simple the meal was to make. She occasionally watched cooking videos online, but always thought herself too impatient to create such fancy dishes. Her repertoire lacked imagination, but Enzo had inspired her to be braver and more confident in the kitchen.

Just as she savoured the last bite of his latest delicious creation, Cyrus and Daphne appeared. Daphne went straight to the pantry to root for snacks. She'd talked Cyrus into watching a movie, and chatted excitedly about their planned evening. Cyrus leaned against the island in silence, expression blank.

"Come and watch with us," Daphne said to Ava, emerging from her foraging with an armful of treats.

"Another night, thanks." Ava smiled up at her. "I've a lot of work to do."

Daphne fired disapproval at Enzo. "I don't know anyone who makes their accountant work as hard as you do. How can you even need that much accounting?"

'An accountant?' Ava silently queried Enzo with raised brows as Cyrus stared mutely at his mismatched socks. "I don't mind," she told Daphne. "There's a lot to be done, and I enjoy it, so . . ."

"But can't you take a night off?"

"Daphne." Cyrus broke his silence to nudge her out of the kitchen.

"She works too hard," Daphne insisted on arguing as they disappeared.

"I'm an accountant?" Ava queried as Enzo tipped back his remaining mouthful of wine. "Whose idea was that?"

He lifted his chin in the direction of Cyrus's departure, but aimed his smile at her. "You don't like mathematics?"

"Let's just say my maths is as good as my singing."

"Well, in that case, you're fired."

"Hurray!" She threw her hands up. "Can I leave now?"

Although she joked, a tiny flicker of disappointment crossed Enzo's face. She immediately wanted to take her jesting back.

"Mr Paladino?" Kara entered the kitchen. She'd obviously been outside. Wet hair clung to her cheeks, and her top was almost soaked through. "The storm is picking up. Shall I drag the boat in?"

"Merda," Enzo muttered, quickly rising. "La barca. I forgot about it. We'll do it together."

Kara retreated, her shoes squelching on the tiles as she walked away.

Enzo followed, but as he passed where Ava sat, brushed her shoulder with a light touch. "I won't be long,"

"No rush. I'll be upstairs," she said, the catch in her voice audible.

Alone in the kitchen, she pressed the backs of her fingers to her hot cheeks. Damn that man. And damn her horny imagination already pic-

327

turing his shirt soaked through, muscles flexing as he heaved the boat out of the water.

Trying to ignore the images, Ava distracted herself by tidying up. As she kneed the dishwasher door shut, trees flailing in the wind beyond the glass caught her eye. The unnatural silence continued to unsettle her.

Approaching the doors, she watched loose leaves scuttling across the grass. Plant debris skated alongside. The detritus tumbled into a corner of the garden, joining the pile already formed; a sizeable drift of twigs and leaves. Struck by how odd it was to watch the violent dance while totally cut off from its sound, Ava didn't realise someone studied her until movement reflected in the glass alerted her to a figure in the doorway at her rear.

Max.

Instinct spun her with a jerk. *Fire!* an inner voice cried as she noted the purposeful threat of his stance. "Are you looking for Enzo?" she asked after a protracted pause, in which he stared coldly at her.

"No."

Her heart drummed so rapidly, the thrumming lodged in her throat. Enzo battled the storm. Between his distance, the whips of wind and lashes of rain, he wouldn't hear her panic, nor if she screamed.

But Max already knew that. He'd bided his time for this exact moment.

They moved in unison, but Max had vampire speed on his side. Her blast flew wide, the fiery surge evaporating mid-air as he slammed her to the glass. He pinned her in place, clutching her ponytail to wrench her head aside and expose her neck. In the milliseconds it took, she hadn't even had time to draw a sufficient breath to cry out.

A pinch of fangs.

Ava yelped against the stab, but the pitiful squeal barely reached a whisper.

328

And yet . . .

A deafening roar. A violent wrench.

Abruptly unpinned, Ava fell, landing hard on her knees.

Across the room, Cyrus had already slammed Max to the floor with one hand clamping his throat. Where he'd smacked the vampire down, the tiles beneath him had smashed. "Animale schifoso!" Cyrus spat.

The sting of vampire venom registered. Ava grabbed her neck, swiping against the burn. When she pulled her fingers away, only a scant smear marked her skin. But the tear was enough. Max had tasted ample of her to want more, and her freed blood stoked his hunger.

A blur of frenzied snarls and roars exploded. Ava scuttled backwards, cowering against the wall, her fingers crushed to the two pinholes in a bid to block her scent and ease the piercing sting.

Cyrus and Max battled in a manic whirlwind. Sound-tracked by smashing glass and crockery, the tornado whipped across the kitchen.

Ava wanted to scream for Enzo, but shock had captured her breath. It had all happened so fast, her brain hadn't yet progressed beyond the fright of Max's appearance reflected in the glass.

The rabid vampire lunged for her again, eyes wild, snarl viciously hungry. Clawed fingers swiped so close they stirred wind across her cheeks. As Cyrus wrenched him away, she finally found the ability to scream. It poured from her in one piercing, ragged shriek of terror.

Enzo's roar breached the mayhem. The violent tornado came to a brutal stop. A loud crash announced Max landing on the kitchen table, face up. Enzo braced him in place, and with a guttural cry, Cyrus ripped both Max's heart and throat out with a swift, bloody yank.

Detached from her body, Ava registered the shift in her environment as Enzo hauled her up into his arms. Unable to tear her eyes from where Max already turned grey, breath rushed from her stricken lungs as her attacker softened like a soaked sponge. He desiccated into lumps, fine

329

puffs of dust billowing from his sleeves and neckline as he deflated into nothing more than a pile of clothes. Where feet had filled his boots hanging inches off the floor, the unsecured footwear landed with a heavy—and strangely comical—thud.

"Ava!" Enzo's horrified expression blocked the view. He grabbed her chin, forcing her to face him and not the disintegrated vampire.

"Is she hurt? Did he hurt her?" Cyrus yelled.

Where she continued to clamp her neck, Enzo gently prised her fingers away. Her heart persisted with slamming against her ribs. Every limb shook, and just as her knees unlocked, the room tipped and blurred.

When the stomach-churning spin ceased, Ava found herself lying on the couch in the library, Enzo leaning over her. The rapid change of location exacerbated her woozy vision.

"It's over, Ava. It's over."

Cyrus hovered over her, too, clasping his head with blood-stained fingers. "Dimme che sta bene?"

"Sta bene. È solo sotto shock."

As if a magickal incantation, hearing Enzo say 'shock' immediately halted her brain glitch. Mind and body re-calibrated with a sickening lurch. "I'm—I'm okay."

"Ava."

"Yeah. I'm here. I'm okay." Enzo's hand remained on her neck. Hers lay over it; clammy fingers pressed to his dry, stone-cold digits. If Cyrus hadn't . . . If he'd been a couple of seconds later. . . "It happened so fast," she murmured. "I couldn't even—"

"Shh," Enzo hushed before delivering an order to Cyrus.

Cyrus dashed out of the room. She squirmed to sit upright, but Enzo held her down.

"No. Stay. Give yourself a moment."

330

Cyrus reappeared with a dinky first-aid kit. He cracked it open and took out an antiseptic wipe, quickly passing it into Enzo's waiting hand. In a move Ava had read enough times in smutty novels to forever associate with steamy bedroom antics, Enzo tore the square packet open with his teeth.

"Um, it's okay, I can—"

"Lie still," Enzo commanded, and bending over her, carefully dabbed her skin. "He only nicked you."

"I know. It barely stung."

Cyrus hissed like a feral cat as he flung the kit onto the coffee table. "Bastardo. La morte era troppo poco per lui."

Enzo's reply grunted agreement with whatever Cyrus said about Max being a bastard and something to do with death.

"Thank you." Ava gave him a shaky smile.

A call from the hallway broke the tension. "Cy?" Daphne sang. "Where are you?"

"Take care of her," Enzo ordered. "I've got this."

Cyrus aimed a final glare at where Enzo dabbed at Max's fang marks, spat another slew of Italian curses, and called out a, "Coming!" to Daphne.

"Cyrus?" Enzo stalled him on his way out the door. "Grazie, nipote. Grazie."

Cyrus barely nodded in reply, but Ava caught the flash of elation in his eyes before he disappeared.

"I'm okay, really." This time, Enzo allowed her to sit up, but he stayed squished beside her on the couch. She took over from where he had the wipe pressed to her neck. It bore only a tiny smudge of blood when she pulled it away. "See? It's nothing."

"I shouldn't have left you alone."

"You couldn't have known."

331

"I should have," he snapped, but just as abruptly, his expression crumpled. "*Two minutes.* I wasn't even gone for two minutes. If that damned wind hadn't been so loud!"

Max would have found another moment where you'd left me alone, she argued in silence. But now reduced to a heap of ash on the kitchen table, he'd lost that chance. "All's well that ends well, right?" she quoted a saying of Nessa's.

Enzo's scowl only thickened at her glib comment.

"Enzo, I'm okay, really," she assured, plucking at his sleeve. The storm had soaked him through. "You should change. You're soaking wet."

"I won't catch a chill, I assure you."

"Vampires are chill-proof?"

Enzo scooped up her hands, and bowing his head, brushed them with kisses. He muttered something in Italian; the comment trailing off with a pained sigh.

She wouldn't dare say it aloud anytime soon, if ever, but if Cyrus hadn't ripped Max off her—

"Sweet tea," Enzo announced, as if he too had the same thoughts and needed instant distraction. "Let me make you a hot, sweet drink."

Ah yes. The Irish cure-all. "Okay, thanks. And, if you're still up for a little translation work, we can—"

"No, Ava. No work. You need to rest now."

"Rest means thinking," she told him, flicking aside any idea of moping around like an invalid. "I don't want to sit around replaying what happened. It's over. I'm fine. Let's just forget about it."

Where the storm had messed up his hair, damp locks hung over clustered brows. Ava studied the mussed up strands begging to be corralled into place. She hadn't noticed the scattering of grey hairs in his sideburns before. A meagre few had sprouted near his hairline, too. Luckily for

Enzo, he'd never have to worry about grey hair, but he'd have made an incredibly sexy silver fox.

Cool fingers captured her chin. "You should stop looking at me like that."

"Sorry." Swinging heavy eyes to where the first-aid kit had landed, Ava silently chastised herself for staring.

But despite his warning, Enzo enticed her back to him.

Humour softened the tension that had been lining his face. "Not for another ten days—after which, I demand you look at me that way at least once every day."

"Hmm." She pushed out a sigh. "Such hardship."

His wily thumb brushed her bottom lip, a slow, deliberate touch declaring he also required her kisses daily.

"Enzo," she warned, resistance already frittering apart as invisible cupids nudged them together, thinning their distance to mere inches.

Voice hoarse with want, his nose brushed her cheek. "Dolce tentazione."

Oh, yes. Such sweet temptation...

"Dirty clothes!" She hadn't meant to blurt aloud the first distraction she could think of, but it tumbled free as she overpowered the naughty imps and sexy vampire with a gentle shove.

The *sweetest* of sweet temptation. She'd quickly forget Max if Enzo pressed her into the cushions and seared her mouth with another one of his kisses, but she had rules to abide by, and a hundred things far more important to do than play tongue-twister with hot Italian vampires.

"Laundry," she clarified, flapping him out of her way and swinging her feet to the floor. "I'll put on a wash while you change, and then we'll make tea and work on translations."

Before he could reply or argue, she scuttled out the door and took the stairs two at a time.

333

Where she'd found the strength to deny Enzo, Ava didn't know, but she deserved a shiny gold trophy for her restraint.

Yet again, Enzo lay awake, alert eyes piercing the thick darkness of his room. The same wretched thoughts ran in a loop: If Cyrus hadn't heard Ava's heartbeat racing, if he'd been a split second later . . . If only he had known about Giulia and the wickedness she'd embraced to remain alive. If only he'd learned sooner about how it connected him to Ava's mother's death . . . If Iseult or Nessa told Ava before he could. If Ava walked away; cut him out of her life entirely. . . "Fanculo," Enzo muttered, driving the knuckle of his thumb into the centre of his forehead.

He couldn't lie to Ava. When Iseult had first told him, his initial reaction had been a selfish one; keep the revelation a secret. But he'd witnessed enough of life and relationships to know how secrets only created a cancerous rot between people.

Giulia had Martha. It made perfect sense now—especially how Martha's cry of 'Tell Enzo it's—' had been so brutally cut off with his neck being snapped.

Giulia had somehow learned he had Ava. While Giulia wouldn't risk losing her chance with the necklace again, he, her ex-husband, was a loss she'd willingly accept. But what plans did she concoct for Ava? Giulia was one of only a select few who knew about Martha's extensive lineage. If she connived to take Ava's necklace for herself, did she plot to use Martha? Could Martha's power overwhelm Ava? Had he tasked Ava with arming the one witch who could potentially kill her?

Enzo grunted, and with another foul mutter, rolled onto his side, facing where Ava's room lay across the hall. In just over a week, the

334

eclipse would commence. Danger crept ever closer for his bella strega. He wouldn't dare to leave the island again—not even the house. From now on, he'd ensure Ava was in sight, or close hearing range.

If Cyrus hadn't caught the sudden racing of her heart, if he'd been a fraction of a second later ripping Max off her. . .

An anxious mind twisted sleep into a familiar nightmare. Enzo found himself reliving the night he'd turned Martha. Once more, he fought the primal urge to feed on her, block out the perfume of the blood she'd purposely spilled to entice him. But her pleading urged him closer, coaxing him across muddy ground like a serpent.

He begged her not to ensnare him, but present-day Enzo screamed and thrashed in as much vain as past Enzo.

Martha's sweet blood washed over his tongue. He yanked her closer, burying his mouth against the fountain of hot, sacred nectar. She cried out, and as he drew straight from the artery, the form in his arms changed.

Suddenly, he was no longer drinking, but kissing. His lips lavished a neck, a warm, young neck, caressing skin as he savoured Ava's unique taste. Wet, sticky ground had also vanished. In its place, his bed; soft, enveloping, heated by Ava's passion.

Short, panting breaths filled his head, her desire raging as hungrily as his. He moved to claim her mouth, but the haze of his carnal need dissolved, interrupted by her *actual* struggle to breathe.

Enzo reared upright, grabbing for Ava, already terrified of what he'd see; her neck ripped open by his fangs, her fingers clutching at the wound. But his bed lay empty, sheets cool, and free of blood.

335

Disorientated, he clambered out, staggering as he lurched aside.

Labouring breaths persisted; a steady draw in, a heaving pant out.

He hadn't dreamt the struggle. Although faint, somewhere in the house, Ava fought for breath. Her heart pumped, but it wasn't fear-induced.

Enzo grabbed his trousers, and whipping them on, hurried down to the basement.

Kara stood outside the gym, her rigid stance easing when she realised it was he who shot down the stairs. "Mr Paladino," she greeted quietly.

"Is she alright?" he asked equally softly.

"Yes. I heard her come down, so I've been standing here since. She's on the treadmill."

At three-twenty in the morning?

The door hung only a few inches ajar. Enzo approached, cautiously peeping through the gap. Now closer, he could not only hear Ava's straining lungs, but the tinny music coming from the headphones she wore. The sportswear he'd asked Kara to procure for her were already in use; a form-fitting set of charcoal-grey running gear with neon-pink stitching around the edges. She'd tied her hair up, but the tail end of her ponytail had turned slick from where it brushed against the sheen of sweat on her back.

Although the belt sped, Ava straddled it, feet balanced either side as her forearms took her weight on the control panel. "You can do this," she murmured to herself crossly. "You're an O'Keefe witch. You can do this."

Not a 'one-more-mile' pep-talk, Enzo guessed.

"You can restore Martha's power. You *can*. And you have to."

Ava straightened to take a drink from a water bottle, also neon-pink; the same colour as the hair-tie holding up Kara's voluminous blonde ponytail.

336

So, he wasn't the only person suffering insomnia thanks to rampaging worries. Enzo inched away. Although he wanted to stride in to assure Ava she was, without doubt, entirely capable of restoring Martha's power, Ava needed to believe it herself first.

"You can do this. You have to. There's no other option." Another pause, punctuated by three more swallows of water. "Too much hangs in the balance if you fail."

Enzo didn't want her thinking that way; believing she held full responsibility for locating and renewing Martha so his niece could claim the reeve title and secure the future integrity of the Enclave. *But that's what you've asked of her. You laid that weighty task upon her.* Lowering his head, regret slid his eyes shut.

"I won't fail."

The sudden change in tone lifted his head.

"I *have* got this. I'm a goddamn O'Keefe witch. And I have access to a power no-one else has." Joyful realisation released on a soft laugh. "Fuck you, doubt. And fuck you, insecurity. And to the next vampire who thinks I'm a happy meal? Fuck you too, buddy."

Enzo met Kara's look of amusement. He brought a finger to his lips, warning her not to make a sound.

Feet hit the treadmill again. "I have got this. And, Iz? You're wrong about Enzo. You'll see."

Enzo slipped away, returning to his room.

Half an hour later, Ava returned to hers. She hummed to herself in the shower, and shortly after, he fell asleep to the gentle rhythm of her peaceful slumber.

337

29

Ava couldn't blame Felicienne's wards for her new and sudden onset of deafness. The cause sat opposite her, expression grooved with regret, eyes lowered to the floor.

Would a point come at some stage between now and the end of time, when Enzo would reveal another shocking truth and she'd just shrug, and say, *'Really? Wow! Imagine that?'* Would she eventually become inured to secrets and revelations? Or would every instance of someone uttering the words, *'We need to talk'*, or, *'I have something to tell you,'* result in her losing the ability to speak and hear?

The breakfast Enzo had delivered sat on the coffee table. Curls of steam had already waned, and the butter had disappeared into her toast. Before he'd said, *'We need to talk'*, he'd dragged over the armchair, his avoidance of taking a seat beside her a warning of dire incoming news.

338

Now, still awkwardly perched, he continued to stare at his leather loafers, shame rendering him mute.

Disconnected, Ava watched as her shaking hand reached out, grabbed the mug, and lifted it to her lips. Lukewarm green tea registered. She took another sip, followed by a gulp. It finally chased down the lump blocking her voice.

"So, your ex-wife is still alive. She murdered my mum, and Iz knows, but Iz told *you*, not me, and your ex is probably coming for me now, and is also most probably the person who abducted Martha." Not her finest sentence, but her brain appeared as scrambled as the egg congealing on her breakfast plate.

"Yes."

"Were you—were you there—when my mum was . . ?"

"No." Enzo's contrite eyes flicked up. "I didn't know Giulia was still alive—if that's even what she is." Disgust blanched his already ashen skin. "I had no idea of the connection between her and your mother. I wasn't there when Aoibheann died, Ava."

"Then why did you say you had a hand in her death?"

"Because Giulia was—*is*—my responsibility."

"I don't understand."

"In the years after I turned Martha," he addressed his shoes once more, "I searched for Giulia. I knew she'd never stop craving Martha's power. I also wanted revenge for everything she'd put us through. But—" His head hung lower. "I gave up after twenty years. I presumed her dead. Until yesterday, I never once even entertained the possibility she continued to walk this earth, ruining lives with her wickedness. I should have known," he said, slamming the heel of his hand to his forehead. "I saw her that night—the night I turned Martha. I hadn't laid eyes on her in thirty years, but she hadn't changed. She remained the youthful twenty-one-year-old girl I'd married. If I'd paused to question it, I would have

339

recognised the darkness she'd consumed. I would have understood her capabilities and never ceased hunting her. Instead, I foolishly assumed her out of our lives." Profound regret twisted his lips as he lowered his hand to look up at her. "Throughout all that time, she's been hiding in the shadows, piecing together whatever it is she plans for Martha."

Ava parked that particularly worrying detail for later. "But you didn't know about my mum, right? You're as shocked as I am to learn that Giulia's still alive—and to blame. Correct?"

He nodded, but it carried none of his typical Paladino-ness.

"So you didn't have a hand in anything."

"But *I*" —he poked himself square in the chest— "should have ended her life centuries ago. *I* was aware of how desperately she wanted Martha. *I* chose to believe her dead."

Ava set down the mug. "Look, it's your choice if you wish to carry guilt for that oversight. But don't sit there and say you're responsible for my mum's death when you're not. If you actually were, I'd leave here immediately, regardless of who's out there waiting. And the next time we met, I'd reduce you to a pile of ash. Understood?"

Shaking out her hands to rid her body of trembling, Ava stood. "*This* is why Iz is pissed off at me. She blames you, but is mad at me because she knows I trust you."

And have fallen for you, a quiet little whisper added.

"*I'm* the one who has the right to be pissed off. *Me*," she said, poking herself as she shuffled out from the tiny gap between the couch and coffee table. "Iz" —the same finger swung toward Calnaloch— "knew about my mum and never told me! What kind of friend keeps secrets like that, huh?"

"I do believe," Enzo said cautiously, a brief flash of palms declaring his neutrality, "that Iseult just recently learned of this. I got the distinct impression your aunt told her only after you came here."

Ava huffed out a sharp laugh. "So *Nessa* plied me with lies for years? Fed me some bullshit story about warlocks and sacrificial magick?"

Regret thinned Enzo's lips.

With the secret exposed, the cloak of deception unravelled further. A wider understanding became apparent.

"She knows Giulia has been out there all this time," Ava realised aloud. "And how she's hankering after the necklace. No wonder she's been so anal about me warding my home, my car, all the goddamn offices I've worked in over the years—even Iz's shop. Fuck! I've been susceptible to that crazy bitch all along! What was it going to take for Nessa to tell me the truth?"

Ava marched over to the balcony doors, angry breaths steaming the glass as she stared past the coastline towards Wicklow. "Did she know about Giulia long before my mum died? Did she choose not to warn her, either?"

When Enzo didn't offer an opinion, she wheeled around, hand out held. "Dial Iz, and give me your phone."

"Ava," he said calmly.

"No," she insisted, flicking impatiently. "Phone. Now."

Enzo sighed, and withdrawing his phone, dutifully called up Iz's name. When he handed it to her, Iz hadn't yet answered. Three rings droned out before she did.

"What?" she snapped, as waspish as Felicienne on her bitchy best day.

"Enzo had nothing to do with my mum's death."

"Ava? Is that you?"

"And if you'd told me instead of keeping it a dirty little secret like Nessa has for the goddess knows how long, you could have saved Enzo and me a fuck-load of time and energy. You owe Enzo an apology. Whatever prejudiced bullshit Nessa fed you, she's wrong, and you'll apologise to Enzo for speaking to him the way you did. You also owe *me* an apology. I'm a grown woman, and I know myself better than anyone. No-one—not you, Nessa, or anyone out there knows what Enzo and I are trying to do here, so stop inciting hatred against the one person who's striving to do good!"

"Ava. I'm—"

"No. *I'm* pissed at *you* now, so this time, *I* get to hang up." Ava stabbed the screen into black, but she felt no better as Iz's plea fell abruptly short. It wasn't Iz who deserved her anger; it was Nessa. Iz had reacted out of love for her friend, and if Ava were moving freely around Calnaloch, Iz would have told her face-to-face about Giulia.

But Nessa knew.

Nessa had clenched the secret for years. Maybe even hidden it from her mum, too. The guilt Enzo battled lay upon the wrong shoulders. If anyone deserved to writhe in shame, it was Nessa.

Tears blurred the colourless afternoon. Sea and sky blended into a sheet of grey, and where mist rolled up the coastline, the land beyond Calnaloch disappeared into the fog. "Why does everything keep getting more and more messed up?"

"Ava." Enzo appeared behind her, circling her with his arms. He tugged her shoulders to his chest, resting his cheek against the side of her head as he held her close.

She wanted to resist, but her craving for comfort didn't care about rules. Sliding her hands over his forearms, Ava leaned into his strength, knowing he could take her full weight with ease. "I'll call Iz tomorrow. I'll have cooled down by then."

"You need your friend."

"That's what's killing me. She's the one who stays sane when we're all losing our shit, and now she's the one losing it."

"She's worried." Enzo's lips brushed her temple. Although subtle, she could hear him inhaling. Bliss trailed out on its release.

342

"Iz and I will talk. It'll be fine. But Nessa? That's something else entirely. All this time, she said nothing. How could she have done that?"

Enzo squeezed her a little tighter. "You know why."

"I can't—won't—accept my protection for a reason. If she'd warned me about Giulia, we wouldn't have been stumbling around here like blind fools trying to figure out who has Martha. Not only that, but hiding the truth puts me in danger. If Giulia finds me, it'll only take minutes for her to cut me down."

The hold securing her tightened.

"Nessa knows better than to leave me exposed—especially to someone who fights with dark magick. I don't understand why she hid it."

"Fear, mia amata."

"Fear of what?" Despite the comfort of his hold, Ava shuffled around to face him. "That I'd freak out? Run and hide?"

Enzo swept her face with a gaze that had the power to make her instantly forget all her troubles. "You're no coward, Ava O'Keefe. My guess is that your aunt fears what you've already chosen to do."

"Which is what?"

His sneaky little moves bumped her shoulders against the glass. Where their clothes brushed, sparks fizzed—and not because of static electricity. "The cabinet," he said, not lifting his heated gaze to swing it towards the pretty piece of furniture hiding Martha's baneful collection.

But Ava found herself unable to resist its lure. "She's afraid of me fighting like with like," she realised, aware she coveted its contents with growing curiosity day by day.

Enzo captured her chin, forcing her to meet the depths of his sombre eyes instead. "As am I."

"I can handle it."

"Which also concerns me."

"Why?"

343

His hips made contact, pressing her fully against the cold glass. Sandwiched between two cool walls, Ava suppressed the delicious shiver it sent through her.

"What does mia tam—mat—whatever it was you said, mean?" she asked, ignoring the other, far more crucial questions.

"Mia amata," he repeated, as fixed on her mouth as she was on his. "It means my beloved."

"Your beloved?" she whispered, aware only her breath separated their lips.

"Yes. My beloved," he said lightly, "whose wishes I shall respect." Enzo pulled away, a cheeky smile tilting the lips Ava wanted. "Unless you've changed your mind."

She scowled up at him. "I haven't." *Almost, but not entirely.* And even if she had, for being such a tease, she'd deny him the kiss she also desperately desired.

Enzo flattened one palm to the glass, half trapping her in the tiny space. Taking her chin, he brushed her lips with the pad of his thumb. "We have work to do."

"We do. So you should quit your flirty moves, mister."

Impressed by her self-control, Ava ducked away from him, heading for the desk.

Damn Enzo Paladino and his sexy flirtations. But he had quenched her anger a little. Nessa deserved an earful, but for now, the urge to smash something had subsided.

"So," she said, rounding the desk, hoping she sounded all business-like again. Enzo remained by the balcony doors, one shoulder taking his weight as he slung one ankle over the other and folded his arms. Somewhere, Michelangelo's spirit sighed at the perfection. "Will you open that cabinet for me?"

344

Alone in his room, Enzo faced the view of Calnaloch. Martha's instructions to unbind the cabinet waited on the dresser. But the weighty consequences of what he might unlock rendered the innocuous page as dangerous as the infernal cabinet's contents. All the unsealing required was an incantation, one he'd used himself under Martha's guidance before. Yet, once the inlaid doors swung open, he'd cross the line upon which edge he now faltered.

What if Ava didn't have the control she claimed? She'd worked dark magick under the supervision of her mother, but as a gifted adult witch, did she possess the strength not to tumble into its insidious embrace? His knowledge of witchcraft would make even the most inexperienced witchling laugh, so how could he ever hope to keep Ava safe? And yet, without Martha's armoury, Giulia would certainly cut Ava down. He'd witnessed witch warfare over the centuries, and on only a handful of occasions had he seen light magick win over dark.

If he'd known Giulia lay behind Martha's disappearance, would he have brought Ava into his world? Selfishly, yes, because realistically, only she possessed the gift to overpower Giulia and free Martha.

But selfishly, no, too. Because without warning, his bella strega had bewitched him so wholly, he wanted a full lifetime with her—not just these scant few weeks that could potentially come to a grim end.

Enzo closed his eyes, tipping his face to the heavens in a plea for divine wisdom. Overriding all these worries, the one he struggled the hardest to shove down clawed its way up again; from whom had Ava inherited her dark magick?

345

The deeply unsettling answer whispered from the shadows, but as before, he refused to acknowledge the unwelcome reply.

Ava hovered by his shoulder as he spoke the short incantation. Once completed, he removed the petite brass key from his pocket and tucked the page away again. Excitement had Ava holding her breath as she watched him slide it into the lock and twist. When the latch snicked open, a low gasp rushed free.

"It's open?"

The elation in her eyes cautioned him to snap the lock back into place, speak the sealing chant, and forbid her to even look upon the damned cabinet again. But he said, "Yes," instead, and stepping aside, allowed her to drop to her knees and swing apart the doors.

A long moment passed before she reached in and withdrew the first grimoire. Bound in aged black leather, Martha had secured it width-ways three times with a thin length of braided hair. Ava settled it on her lap.

"I can feel it," she said quietly, palm hovering over the cover. "It reminds me of dread; the minutes before an exam begins, or sitting in the waiting room at the dentist."

Enzo ached to tell her to put the book back, but he had to trust she had enough experience to understand the force of what lay in her lap.

Carefully, she rolled the tail of the bind between her thumb and forefinger. "Is this hair?"

"Yes."

Hesitant eyes lifted to where he stood over her. "Dare I ask what from?"

"A demon."

346

"Gross." She grimaced, and quickly wiping her fingers on her sleeve, set the book down beside her. "Okay, so there's a lot in here. Can you give me a run through?"

"Only a partial one." Enzo lowered himself to his hunkers. "This," he said, pointing at the coarse wooden box occupying half of the bottom shelf, "is where Martha keeps the enchanted objects. I cannot tell you their individual uses, unfortunately. The grimoires here" —he gestured at the dozen tomes lining the middle shelf— "are all devoted to dark magick. And these three—death magick." Martha had secured the trio in a cloth cover, held in place by a length of knotted cord. From it, she'd hung crystals, amulets, and sprigs of dried herbs.

"They can stay there," Ava said, shaking off a shiver. "It looks like Martha has them bound good and tight, anyway. And this top shelf?"

"A collection of solitary spells, enchantments, and sigils. She gathered them from dozens of witches and warlocks over hundreds of years, so their origins are too vast to trace."

Martha had neatly stacked the scrolls and loose sheets. Some bore jagged edges from where they'd been ripped from grimoires. Others showed the ravages of time, while the stack with blackened tips, Enzo recalled her saving from a fire in Führer Headquarters in 1945.

"I can't give you the specifics of what they contain. We'll have to translate them individually."

Ava circled the centre of her forehead as if staving off an ache. "Can you sense it?"

"No." He shook his head.

"It's intense."

"Martha often said the same."

"I'm not sure where to begin, but I instinctively selected this one," she said, gesturing to the book she'd withdrawn, "so lock it up and I'll begin."

347

"Lock it fully?" he queried.

"Yes. With the sealing ward lifted, it's a lot harder to ignore. I won't be able to concentrate with that constant hum."

Enzo gladly shut the doors, turned the key, and uttered the spell to secure it. Ava got to her feet while he did, taking the black volume with her. She set it on the working table, and from a drawer of the apothecary cabin, withdrew a pair of cotton gloves. Before she opened the book, she took a moment to herself, closing her eyes as her lips moved in silence. When she finished, and caught his curious stare, she answered his unspoken query with one word; "Protection."

Enzo had watched Ava work before, but this time, solemnity weighed her actions and expression. She slowly turned from one page to the next, her movements cautious enough for him to fear something malevolent waited to leap out and attack. A few pages in, she reached for the notebook on her desk, and setting it beside the grimoire, jotted down a string of sentences. "Most of it's written in English," she said, "but is this Greek?"

Enzo leaned in. The passage she pointed at, sitting alongside an elaborate illustration of which he could make neither head nor tail, he recognised as Cyrillic. "Russian."

"Oh. Shit."

"I can translate."

A hint of jealousy weighted her sigh as she said, "Of course you can." But her seriousness evaporated as she turned to him with a smile. "Tell me. Is there anything you can't do, Mr Paladino?"

"Non riesco baciare la mia bellissima strega."

Her tiny laugh tempted him to prove himself wrong and take the lips he longed to possess. "Ha. *Bacio* means kiss, so I can just about guess what you said."

"Who taught you the Italian for kiss?" Abrupt jealousy demanded.

"A friend," she teased, and leaning in, whispered, "Baciami il culo."

Enzo tutted. "Such profanity."

"I told you; I learned all the bold words."

30

B olstered by a new arsenal, Ava located Martha later that evening. Despite what she'd assumed about Giulia occupying a Martello tower far from Calnaloch, the spell proved her wrong.

"Tutto questo tempo," Enzo muttered, slowly shaking his head at where the Calnaloch tower glowed on the map Ava had spread out on the working table. "All this time."

An obliging member of Calnaloch's history society had loaned Enzo the map. Dated 1923, it displayed a slice of the east coast, with each tower drawn by hand. Although crude, the illustrations were large enough for the fiery trail of smoke to surround Giulia's hidey-hole. A wavering ring of orange light now circled Martha's location.

"Right under our noses," Ava agreed. She'd used a spell Enzo had translated from the black grimoire. During the casting, the air had filled with a wicked stench of sulphur, but as the glow now faded, the foul stink waned with it. "Because Giulia knew we wouldn't assume her

350

foolish enough to keep the witches this close? Or because she enjoys being a brazen bitch?"

"The latter," he answered, absentmindedly brushing the sensitive spot between her shoulder blades. So far, there'd been no more almost-kissing, but Ava's restraint didn't extend to dodging gentle caresses.

Whenever possible, Enzo narrowed physical distance, even if it simply meant his knee or arm touching hers when they sat together. When moving through the house, he consistently put his hand to the small of her back or cupped her elbow. If close enough, he'd sometimes touch her face by lightly grazing her jaw or tucking loose hair behind her ear. If he needed to stress a point, he'd take her chin, so she would meet his eyes and read the earnestness in their brown depths. With anyone else, Ava would have found it clingy. But with Enzo, it felt so uncontrived, she wondered if he was even aware of the propensity—or how it soothed her. "We can't launch a rescue mission, Enzo."

Pained agreement came with a grunt.

"If Giulia discovers we've located Martha before eclipse day, she'll cloak her so tight, I won't be able to reach her at all."

"I know."

"A rescue demands we also lift the cloaking spell. But then I'd have to figure out what magick Giulia has used to sedate the witches, and counteracting it will take considerable time—time where I'd be exposed; an easy target for Giulia's dark magick—not to mention the creatures skulking around Calnaloch."

Enzo didn't need a detailed explanation for why a storm-and-rescue wasn't tenable. But it didn't stop his scowl from flicking between the map and the spot on the wall where beyond, the tower sat on the head of the Hag's Nose. If he bolted, he'd be gone before Ava could blink.

"As awful as it sounds," she pushed, hoping he listened to reason, "it's safer for all of us if we leave Martha there."

"Lo so, mia amata."

Yes, he knew, but would it keep him by her side?

The smoke evaporated. Where it had circled Giulia's lair, orange powder dusted the yellowing parchment. Ava had used Marigold-leaf powder. While typically utilised for protection and prophetic dreams, the plant also helped to discern the culprit behind a theft. With Martha effectively stolen from Enzo, the sunny petals—ground with his blood and a handful of demonic ingredients—had proved a potent spell.

Ava hadn't relished the idea of tapping into demon energy. Like everything witchcraft-related, it took practice to control and master. Working with its dark energy had left her jittery inside, as if she'd eaten too much sugar on an empty stomach.

Wafting away the final dregs of sulphur, she said, "I wonder how many witches she has trapped in there now?" Iz's last report from the previous Friday had declared seven, but Ava guessed it to be higher by this point. Giulia most likely planned on channelling thirteen witches, and with the eclipse due in eight days, she still had plenty of time to abduct another six.

"I'll make enquiries."

"Or," she said, brushing remnants of yellow dust off the map, "I could call Iz."

"Are you ready to speak to her?" Enzo asked, passing her the map's protective cardboard tube.

"Without biting her head off? Probably not."

"Leave it to me, then. It might be best if you and Iz don't talk for another day or two."

Ava waited two days.

Just after ten on the Friday night, Iz called the spy phone. Enzo had arranged the time by text.

Hiding out in her room, Ava curled up in the armchair. She wasn't sure whether she'd cry or snap when Iz answered. Emotions battled, but she couldn't tell which had the greatest control. Yet, when the phone finally rang, her mind went blank.

"Hi," Iz said immediately.

"Hey."

An awkward silence stretched out before Iz broke it with, "Can I go first?"

To Ava's surprise, she suddenly realised she didn't want an apology. She just wanted things between her and Iz back to normal. "Yes."

"I'm sorry, Ava. I really am. Nessa told me about the Paladino connection to your mum, and I lost it. You're right; she has a prejudiced slant on what happened, and if I'd heard the truth, I wouldn't have gone off on you like I did. I'm—" Iz's solemnity wobbled. "I'm sorry for what I said, especially the stuff about Finn. It's no excuse, but I was scared for you, and when you spoke about Enzo the way you did, I panicked. From where I stood, all I saw was you trapped by a Paladino, and because we can't talk face-to-face, I was afraid that it wasn't you, but a compelled version of you. You said I have to trust that you know what you're doing, and I do, I swear."

Unsure of where to begin her own speech, Ava fiddled with the zip on the cushion in her arms. "Iz, I—"

353

"I miss you, Ava," Iz barrelled on. "And I'm worried sick about you. There's a fuck-tonne of strangers in town, everyone's on edge, Felicienne is stirring shit, and Finn's hounding me non-stop. I had a dream the other night that I walked into the stockroom and found you sitting on my Goth throne, smiling. All this shit was over. You were home safe, and I was so happy, I woke up sobbing. Ever since, every time I go out back, I'm wishing like mad that you'll be there. I'd give anything to see you. I hate not knowing what's happening; the stress you're dealing with, the pressure, the threats. And then I go off on one and say things you don't deserve. I'm a crappy friend. You were right to—"

"Iz. Catch your breath."

"Sorry," Iz whispered, sniffing against tears. "I hate myself. I wish I could take back that awful conversation. I was a bitch."

"Let's forget about the shitty conversation, okay? What you said came from a good place."

"I really didn't mean it to come out the way it did. I love you. You know that, don't you? These last few days have been shite. I'm so sorry. I really am."

"I know, Iz, I know. Look—" Ava clutched the cushion tighter, hoping that squeezing it would lock down the secrets she longed to blurt. "I can't tell you what's going on here, but I assure you; Enzo hasn't compelled me. He did, briefly, but it was for my safety, and I made him do it. After, he reversed it, and that's when I worked a spell to ensure I was completely free of compulsion, which I am. So, I promise you, I'm not under his control; I'm here willingly. Once this is all over, you'll understand everything."

"I believe you. I do."

"Good."

Iz pulled in a steadying breath. "It's hard being ignorant of what you're going through, Ava. One half of me wants every detail, but the other doesn't, and then I feel guilty for avoiding what you're having to deal with."

"No, Iz. No guilt. Do you hear me? It has to be this way."

"I know, but it doesn't make it any easier."

"You'll just have to suck it up," Ava told her kindly.

"Okay." Iz's tone firmed as she flipped to down-to-business mode. "Of more importance. How are you doing? Are you okay there—wherever *there* is?"

"I am, honestly. Enzo is taking really good care of me, and this is definitely the safest place for me right now. I'm finally making progress with the spell. There's still a lot to work out, but I'm hopeful I can be ready in time. If I can pull this off, it will do a lot of good—more good than you and I will probably ever realise. But if I don't—"

"You *will* pull it off," Iz cut in. "You're Ava O'Keefe. You've got this."

Iz's words banished fragile self-belief. As if steeling Ava's bones, they even perked her up out of her slouch. "Thanks, Iz."

"I'm here for you, Ava. One hundred, no—one *thousand* percent. No more freak outs, I promise. Sane, rational Iz is back."

Ava laughed softly. "Good. I missed her. And I need her. I'm scared about what lies ahead."

"I'm sure you are, but I believe in you, my witchy friend. And. . ." Her voice softened with careful humour. "Ancient vamps don't go to the trouble of abducting any old witch, you know. They only pick the absolute best."

"No pressure, so."

"You've got this, Ava. You'll kick ass. So, tell me; is there anything I can do for you?"

"Yes." Ava braced in fear of the update. "What's the latest count of missing witches?"

Iz tutted. "I guessed there was a connection. It's eleven as of yesterday."

"Eleven?" Giulia had worked fast in the last week.

"Two more to go. Am I right?"

"Probably." Ava sighed. "This is hard—not being able to tell you." Especially as it happened right under Iz's nose.

"It is, but I need to keep answering Felicienne's incessant questions with an honest *'I don't know'*. If she gets a whiff of me hiding information, she won't let it go."

"She's hounding you that much?"

Iz grunted, an accompanying creak of leather announcing she'd heaved herself off the couch. "The Italy charade is over. She cornered me in the shop this morning with a theory you're on Dunfarr. Allegedly, Enzo owns the house on the island. She said he paid her to cast warding spells around it two months ago. She reckons he has you chained up in the basement, barely keeping you alive on mouldy bread crusts and stagnant rain water. Don't tell me either way, but I wanted you to know. I warned Enzo earlier, too."

"You spoke to Enzo?"

"Yeah. When he texted me, I called him. We had a chat. I needed to apologise to him, and he accepted it—graciously. A lot more graciously than I deserved."

The sound of running water placed Iz in her kitchen, filling the kettle. Ava squirmed deeper, closing her eyes so she could imagine herself sitting at the table. Iz would make a pot of strong tea and they'd spend the next few hours sorting out all the world's problems as they munched through her biscuit stash. "Yeah, Enzo's that kind of guy."

"So it seems." Iz gave a quiet laugh. "Okay. We've only ten minutes left, so brace for an information burst."

"Hit me."

"Finn and Felicienne are the tightest BFFs you've ever seen. Finn has morphed into Mr I Believe, and honestly, as annoying as he was before,

356

I preferred him as Mr I Don't Believe. Felicienne made him a mugwort charm. He showed it to me yesterday, boasting about how he's now vampire proof."

Ava groaned, and rolling her eyes to the heavens, thumped her forehead.

"He's got round-the-clock surveillance on your apartment, and had the balls to think he could confront Nessa. Thankfully, I got wind of it while he was on his way to Ballinastoe, so I warned her."

"And?" Ava laughed as Iz snickered.

"The car mysteriously broke down halfway up the Sally Gap. He had to wait two hours for a tow."

"You're joking."

"Nope. He knew it was Nessa, too. All of a sudden, he has a newfound respect for witches, so when you get home, you need to be ready. He already has it in his head that you'll clap eyes on Finn two-point-oh and fall madly in love with him."

"Did he say that?"

The kettle clicked off. Iz filled the waiting mug. "Oh, he was a *fool*, Ava," she mimicked. "He was too scared to believe before, but now he knows the truth, and he *wholly* accepts you. You're the *only* woman for him. He wants you and all your beautiful witchery back."

Ava cringed, huddling tighter. "I'm not the woman for him."

"No, you're not." Iz's tone softened. Ava listened as the cutlery drawer opened and Iz dug out a spoon before stirring her tea. "But I'll let him figure that out for himself. Is the subject of you and Enzo off-limits?" she asked cautiously.

Ava smiled. "There's not much to say."

"You're not together?"

"We're waiting."

"For?" Wood dragging against tile declared Iz taking a seat at the table.

357

"Reality. When things go back to normal, we'll see how we fit into each other's lives."

"So he's staying in Calnaloch?"

"Uh-huh. Yeah," she half-whispered.

Iz laughed. "Oh, girl. You have it baaaad."

Ava patted her pinking cheeks. "I think I do."

"And he does too, clearly."

"Uh-huh," Ava agreed, fanning herself with her free hand. "Tell me what else is happening in Calnaloch."

Iz laughed at the clumsy subject change, but happily filled her in on the growing number of strangers skulking around their town. Anna had a spike in business with all the people wandering into her shop looking for the tarot reader. The Cauldron had its fair share too, but Iz had perfected her 'get the hell out of here' scowl, so most of those who walked in, did an about-turn and left.

Concerned about Giulia's presence in the town, Ava asked if there'd been any odd activity. She guessed Giulia smart enough to operate below the radar, but with Calnaloch on high-alert, all it would take was a witch picking up on warding energy to draw attention to the Martello tower.

Iz only commented on an increase of gatherings in Rune Park, and the shifter community deciding to get out of dodge until things calmed down. "General consensus blames the incoming eclipse for all the weirdness," she clarified. "No-one suspects anything else."

Which provided the perfect cloak for Giulia's nefarious business. "Let me know if something strange happens, okay?"

"Strange like what?" Iz queried.

"Occurrences you and I would label odd for Calnaloch."

Iz agreed with a low hum of concern. She then announced she'd spoken to Nessa. "I clarified a few things," Iz told her as Ava recognised the clink of the biscuit jar lid. "Nessa didn't say much in reply, but she was fairly quick to shove me out of the house with a mumble about no-one knowing the full truth."

"What the hell does that mean?" Ava wondered.

"No idea," Iz said around a mouthful of biscuit.

Unfortunately, the timer trilled just then, warning them of only seconds left. Quickly arranging their next call, they swapped goodbyes and love.

Ava remained in place, unfolding her legs as she allowed their conversation to percolate. Relieved she and Iz had cleared the air, she slumped deeper into the seat. As teenagers, they'd fallen out a couple of times, yet had always made up within a few hours. This argument had differed. It had haunted Ava for the entire week. Even with Enzo stuck to her, the disconnect had blared, and with each day, the stony distance between her and Iz had lengthened. She and Iz liked to joke they were sisters-from-other-misters, and in truth, they both loved each other more than many blood sisters did. Now they'd reconciled, Ava's world had resettled on its correct axis again.

Ava smiled, clutching the phone to her chest. The peripheral bullshit with Finn and Felicienne they could deal with. And once eclipse day passed, Ava would hold a long-overdue discussion with Nessa. But bolstered and focused once more, right now, she had only one task to tackle.

Grinning, she hauled herself out of the deep seat. "Okay, O'Keefe. You've got some serious witchery to craft. Get to it, girl."

359

39

A routine fell into place as the days trickled by.

Ava would come downstairs in the morning to find her breakfast ready and waiting. Enzo would sit with her while she ate, then retreat to Martha's room with her to translate, debate tactics, or read in silence while she worked. He unlocked the cabinet whenever needed. Ava quickly learned it prompted grim muteness which only doubled in intensity when she rooted through the enchanted items—or as she liked to call it; *the box of fun things*. Only when she'd returned the items to their slots, and Enzo had sealed the cabinet shut again, would his shoulders soften and morbid scowl ease.

Throughout the day, he'd bring her lunch, tea, snacks, and water. He'd disappear at five, and shortly after, entice her downstairs for another one of his delicious meals. In the evenings, she'd try to relax for an hour or two, but typically found herself drawn upstairs to Martha's room to continue where she'd left off. Once ten o'clock arrived, she'd force herself to call it a day. If frustrated or anxious, she'd retreat to the gym. Some of her best ideas had come while plugged into music and drenched in sweat.

Now more settled in Paladino Palace, her meditation practice had also stabilised again. Her gran and mum hovered in the quiet space, their gentle energies directing her towards solutions, and sometimes, steering her away from considerations.

Since Athens, Ava hadn't yet had the urge to unwrap her tarot deck. Every day, she palmed the cards to say hi, but experienced no intuitive poke to shuffle and draw. The concern she'd pull the cataclysmic Tower persisted. Twice in a row already promised shit going south. A third appearance would annihilate her confidence. Gut instinct told her she'd calculated a safe and stable method to reach Martha undetected. She'd also almost finalised how to dial into twelve deceased witches, link them as one, and harness their witch lineage. But the last step—how to unlock Martha's metaphorical witch fuel-tank and pump the power in—continued to evade her. At this delicate stage, a gloomy trio of tarot cards could tip her over the edge.

Although Cyrus and Daphne remained in the house, they'd morphed into two quiet mice, emerging on tip-toe when they thought no-one around. Ava had seen Cyrus only once since the night Max had bitten her, and all he'd said was he hoped she was okay, and if she needed him for anything, to let him know. On the few occasions he'd left the island, Enzo's four additional men had trailed him. Still under the impression the quartet were an enclave observation team, Cyrus had been keeping his temper in check. Enzo had said he wasn't confident it would last.

Earlier that morning, Ava had met Daphne in the kitchen, but just like the previous two times they'd chatted, Ava found Daphne strangely subdued. She queried it with Enzo, worried that Cyrus had compelled

361

his girlfriend so much that he'd altered her personality. But Enzo assured her Cyrus hadn't compelled Daphne since the horrific zoo incident. *'I'm watching her,'* he promised. *'Cyrus will let her go soon.'*

So, yes; peace infiltrated Paladino Palace. But the tranquillity unnerved Ava.

As every day passed, the sense of the world holding its breath increased.

Iz had nothing to report from the town. Felicienne hadn't darkened the door of The Cauldron in days, and Finn, Iz told her, had stopped asking questions.

Calnaloch would soon darken under the eclipse. Now was the time for last-minute retaliation, not the calm lapping Ava's world like a lazy summer tide.

She contemplated the stillness while sipping a fresh mug of tea, admiring a rare cloudless night sky hanging over the glassy sea. A full moon beamed down, its form mirrored to perfection in the water. Not one rogue white horse churned its surface. "Even you're faking it," she murmured. "The calm before the storm, huh?"

Enzo had left her alone to take a call. His expression upon noting the caller could have curdled milk. Ava had asked who it was, and he'd replied with a muttered, *'Trouble'.* Someone from the Enclave, she guessed, most likely that lecherous warlock Waylen Kane. She hoped to never see him again. "Never *ever*," she whispered, shaking off a shiver of repulsion as she turned to face the pile waiting on the desk.

Thirty hours remained. In that time, she had to finalise a way to connect Martha with her witch ancestors, unlock the padlock securing her witch tank, and figure out how to ram the power of twelve dead witches into its confines. The hours trickled away at speed. If she didn't have a Giulia-proof plan by noon tomorrow, the Tower literally would come crashing down on them all. "So quit stalling," she ordered herself. "Time's a-wastin'."

Enzo reappeared not long after. So focused on a promising conduit spell she'd unearthed, Ava didn't realise he'd returned until movement from the corner of her eye made her startle.

He didn't react with his usual smile at her jumpiness. A *Major Shit Has Hit The Fan* expression scoured his brow. Ava marked her spot on the page with her fingertip. "What is it?" she asked with unmasked reluctance.

"If I ask you to stay up here until I return, will you respect my request?"

Fear immediately scorched her veins. "You're leaving the house? This close to eclipse day?"

"No. But we'll have a visitor. It would be best for you to remain out of sight."

Ava forgot about marking her place. Shying away from the news, she shrank into the chair. "It's not Waylen Kane, is it?"

"*Cristo*, no."

"Is it an enclave member?" she asked, palming where her heart clattered.

Enzo shook his head.

If it wasn't Waylen Kane, or one of his fellow faction members, she didn't care who came calling so late on a Tuesday night.

But Enzo obviously did. Annoyance, and what she suspected to be distaste, thinned his lips.

"I'll stay up here," she promised.

363

"Thank you."

"Enzo?" she called after him, suddenly guessing who the caller might be. "Is it—?"

"Please, Ava," his disembodied voice cut her off from the stairwell. "Remain here until I return."

"Okay."

But curiosity nibbled as Ava contemplated her suspicion. She said she'd stay *'up here'* but not specifically *where* up here. And when *'up here'* simply translated to *'not down there'*, so long as she didn't place a toe on the ground floor, she wasn't really breaking a promise, right?

Abandoning the desk, Ava hurried down the stairwell. Breath held, she waited by the door, ear cocked.

Yup.

A clack of heels on marble. A snarky sniff following—no doubt accompanied by a haughty flick of lengthy hair.

Felicienne Alarie had come a-calling.

Ava gave them a head start, then crept out onto the landing. A careful peep over the railing granted her a view of the empty hallway below. Max's replacement, a whip-thin vampire with hair so black it shone like a mirror, had vacated his usual station.

Conscious of how even a loud breath would alert Enzo, Ava eased back, hovering close to her bedroom door. A quick shielding spell would have hidden her presence, but it required sage, and Enzo would catch on to her game the second he got the whiff.

Conversation in the library had already kicked off. Although Enzo spoke with more composure than the five-foot-nothing of ire before him, his patience wouldn't hold.

"You have absolutely *no* right, Mr Paladino. Who the hell do you think you are coming to our town and taking command of our most valuable witch?"

"You've changed your tune," Enzo replied. "Not a week ago, you spoke about your *most valuable witch* with heated disrespect."

"Which leads you to assume you have the right to take her?"

"I have taken no-one."

"I know Ava's here. Don't assume me a fool. I want to talk to her now."

"If Ava were here, I can't imagine she'd be inclined to speak with you. You're not exactly her greatest supporter."

"Ava and I have an understanding."

Yeah, the one where you're a bitch and I'm the selfish witch who won't bow down to you, Ava thought with a smirk.

"We share a history, one upon which you have no right to comment or make assumptions."

"And yet, here you are, making assumptions about *me*."

"Do you understand what is at stake here, Mr Paladino? There are thirteen witches missing—fourteen, including Ava."

Shit. Giulia had her full complement. With thirteen third-generation witches under her control, she was now locked and loaded, ready for eclipse day.

"Ava's duty lies with serving her kin, not parasites!"

"Name-calling doesn't suit you, Felicienne."

Ava smiled to herself. Enzo could talk rings around the High Priestess for hours. She'd end up leaving with the same number of answers with which she'd arrived and not realise it until the door hit her ass on the way out.

"Your petty, selfish desires have put the lives of thirteen young people at risk. Ava is the only one who can help our community."

"I'm aware of what Miss O'Keefe can do for the missing witches, and I'm sure wherever she is, unless she's incapacitated, she's already working to free them."

365

"If Ava weren't incapacitated," Felicienne spat, "she'd have reached out to me by now."

"I admire your confidence."

Enzo, Ava pleaded with a glance to the ceiling. *Don't poke the bear!*

"Mr Paladino. If Ava doesn't reappear on Thursday to assist me with locating and freeing our missing witches, I'll ensure she's cut off entirely from our community. Are you prepared to carry the weight of that consequence, too?"

'Here we go again,' Ava mouthed. She'd lost count of the number of times Felicienne had flung that threat at her.

"You'd cast out your most valuable witch?"

"Where is she, Mr Paladino?"

Enzo didn't reply.

"Ava!" Felicienne had reached her tether's end. "Ava, I know you're here! Come out now!"

"Holler all you please." Enzo sighed. "But you're wasting your breath. And assaulting my eardrums."

"Ava! *Ava!*"

Movement from Ava's left revealed Cyrus. He held a finger to his lips, and coming to where she stood, nudged her inside her room. Downstairs, Felicienne's pitch reached chandalier-shattering level.

"Who in the hell is that?"

"Felicienne Alarie, High Priestess of the town's coven. She's looking for me," Ava whispered.

Cyrus tipped his chin towards her bedroom window. "The witch who erected the wards?"

She nodded.

"If you won't tell me where Ava is, I'll hand this matter over to Waylen Kane!" Felicienne's warning echoed up the stairs. "I'm sure the Enclave

366

would be interested to learn how a member of the vampire faction has abducted and compelled a witch into his service."

"Unfounded accusations don't sit well with the Enclave, Felicienne."

"Listen here, you smug leech. If you wish to carry on living undisturbed out here in this gaudy monstrosity of yours, I advise you to release Ava O'Keefe. Otherwise, we can make life very unpleasant for you—starting with me revoking the shelter wards I placed!"

Cyrus mouthed a shocked 'ooh!'

"So, not only do you come to my home spouting racial slurs and accusing me of abduction," Enzo said with a dangerously calm tone, "but now you're threatening me?"

A wicked smile thinned Cyrus's lips. He winked, and before Ava could grab him, he'd vanished.

She darted out the open door after him. If he broke his murder-hiatus streak, it would be her fault.

"Uncle?"

Ava closed her eyes. *Please, Cyrus,* she begged, gripping the railing in fear.

"Cyrus, I'm busy. We'll talk later."

"This is the witch who bound me here, isn't it?"

"Cyrus—"

"Who are you?" Felicienne snapped over Enzo's protestation.

"Cyrus Paladino, the vampire you've trapped with your filthy witchcraft. Whatever my uncle told you about me, it's all lies. Don't believe a word of it."

"Cyrus. Upstairs now, before I—"

"I want out of here!" Cyrus yelled. "You can't keep me imprisoned like this. It's not fair!"

"I—I crafted those wards for *you?*" Felicienne asked with sudden uncertainty. "But you're a vampire, not a witch."

"A vampire who was once a witch," he lied.

"Cyrus, how many times have I told you to stay in your room?"

"Fuck your orders. Let me out, do you hear?"

"I'll lift the wards," Felicienne quickly announced. "But on one condition."

"Name it," Cyrus said. "Anything to get away from my uncle."

"Felicienne, don't you dare!"

"Is the witch Ava O'Keefe here?" she asked, ignoring Enzo.

Cyrus laughed, a hysterical bark of mania. "Ava O'Keefe?"

"Yes. Ava O'Keefe. Is she here?"

"Ava O'Keefe," Cyrus sang, sounding unnervingly like he had the day he'd returned from the zoo wearing animal innards. "That little witch is the *reason* I'm locked in here, you idiot!"

In the silence, Ava could picture Felicienne's eyes bugging out. "You—she—"

"*Enough!*" Enzo's yell jolted Ava. "Cyrus, back to your room, now!"

"No. I want out of here! Tell her to lift the wards."

"Cyrus, to your room. I won't say it again."

"I hate you!" Cyrus roared. "She's just one stupid witch! Fuck you all!"

Cyrus burst out of the library, flinging the door back so hard it bounced off the wall. A clatter of crushed plaster hitting the floorboards followed. He stomped up the stairs, cursing and huffing, rounding off his performance with a final roar of "Fuck you all!" before joining Ava at the railing. "Good performance?" he queried quietly.

"Impressive," she said in a barely there whisper.

Cyrus twirled his hand, impersonating a dramatic stage bow in reply.

"Felicienne," Enzo said evenly. "If you're quite finished with disturbing the already fragile peace of my home, insulting me, and threatening my safety, I think it's time you leave."

"What does Cyrus want with Ava?"

"Nothing good, trust me. But the more pressing concern at this point is that you've just angered my nephew. He's past his snack time, and you're a delicious bag of witch blood tempting his insatiable appetite."

"You have until tomorrow, Mr Paladino," Felicienne announced with a sharp sniff.

Both Ava and Cyrus backed away as a click of heels tracked her stomp across the wooden floor of the library. She emerged into the hall.

Enzo strode ahead of her, opened the outer door, and with a tight gesture, urged her to remove herself from his premises. But before she could fully stomp by him, he snatched her arm, jerking her against him. A squeal escaped. "I don't take kindly to threats, Miss Alarie. Speak to me like that again, and my retaliation will be positively biblical."

Felicienne staggered out the door. Enzo slammed it behind her.

"Bravo, Uncle." Cyrus clapped. "I haven't heard that *'positively biblical'* threat since 1767."

Enzo ignored Cyrus to stare up at Ava.

"And," Cyrus added, "the destruction *was* positively biblical." Whistling *'The Ride of the Valkyries'*, he pivoted away for his room.

Ava took over his spot to lean on the banister.

"I asked you to stay upstairs." Enzo sighed up at her.

She motioned at her lofty position with a grin. "This is upstairs."

"You heard it all, I presume?"

"Cyrus may have briefly confused her, but Felicienne will be back," she warned, making her way down.

"Perhaps we should co-operate with her?"

Ava snorted. "Over my dead body."

"Ava, she has threatened to cut you off."

"Pfft." She flicked away the empty warning. "Felicienne threatens to cut me off at least twice a year, and she hasn't yet. Besides, I'm a solitary

369

witch, so by nature, I work alone, therefore, nothing from which to ostracise me."

Enzo sighed as she walked into the library ahead of him. Felicienne's overpowering perfume lingered, a heady blend of patchouli and vetiver.

"She's pissed because she knows there's some serious magick about to go down, and as High Priestess, she's not involved. It's killing her, compounded by the fact it's *me* who'll be doing the magick."

"I don't like her threatening you."

Ava plonked onto the couch. Enzo sat, too, but on the edge, so he could knead the tension cording his neck. Slouched against the cushions, Ava wondered if her little human fingers would have the strength to massage the knots away. Did vampires even get knotted muscle? Probably not. But it wouldn't hurt to try. A few drops of oil, Enzo braced between her thighs as she worked from behind on his shoulder muscles, and—

"Ava," he said a little more forcefully. "Are you listening to me?"

"Yeah. Sorry, what did you say?"

"What about The Cauldron?"

Having missed his point because her brain insisted on crawling into the gutter at every opportunity, Ava frowned at him.

"She could coerce Iseult into barring you from The Cauldron."

"Oh. No. She won't. And even if she tried, Iz would just laugh at her. She's a solitary, too, so Felicienne can huff and puff all she likes around her, but it won't make any difference."

"What about your clients?"

"Okay, Enzo." Ava sat forward, taking his arm to urge him to face her, otherwise, the expanse of his shoulders would continue to distract her—not that his handsome face didn't hold an equal power. "Listen to me. Felicienne's threats are empty, so forget about her bluster. She wants in on the eclipse magick, that's all. It reflects badly on her that I'm not in her coven, and with all the activity in town right now, word has spread far

370

and wide about the missing witches—including me. My money is on her yanking down the shelter wards. Besides that, she won't risk retaliating against you personally.

"When I do my thing on Thursday, you yourself can meet the witches at the Martello Tower and take them to Felicienne's home. Whatever rot she spouted at you today, she'll quickly withdraw. You'll have saved her reputation, be in her good graces, and all will be wonderful in her spite-filled world again."

"And what about you?"

"I'll still be the ungrateful, selfish witch who won't join her coven or allow her near my necklace. So like I said." She smiled. "All will be splendid in Felicienne Land. Order restored."

"Despite the good you'll have done?"

If I can do it, she almost said.

"Surely she'll treat you with more respect once she learns you single-handedly saved the witches?"

Ava smiled at his optimism. "I think we've a better chance of seeing pigs fly."

"Non capisco quella donna. I don't understand that woman," he translated.

"Felicienne wants only one thing. As long as she can't have it, she'll remain pissed off."

Enzo pulled her hand onto his lap before lifting it to his lips. "She's a fool."

Ava shrugged. "It is what it is."

A flicker of tension set his jaw clenching. "Are you sure the necklace is safe? Can she locate it with a spell?"

"It's perfectly safe. She can't access it, ever. I'd tell you where it actually is to put your mind at ease, but the magick protecting it prevents me."

371

Enzo frowned at her as he absent-mindedly delivered another cool kiss to her knuckles. She immediately wanted to shuffle closer to him and rest her head on his shoulder. "Ask me where it is."

He obliged with a quiet, "Where's the necklace?"

"In the boot of my car. Ask me again."

"Where's the necklace?"

"In the tincture cabinet in Iz's shop."

"Where's the necklace?"

"Stashed in the chimney of my bedroom upstairs. We could play this game all night," she told him, fiddling with where his folded shirt cuffs bunched around his elbow. What she really wanted was to trace the veins on the underside of his arm, but touching of that nature would only lead to forbidden kissing. "And you'll never get the same or correct answer. When Manus Larsen had me, I even told him you had it. The protective magicks pour lies out of my mouth. It's physically impossible for me to state where the necklace is—just as it is for Felicienne or anyone else to locate it."

Ava had learned to decipher the Paladino grunts, and the one he gave meant *'fine'*. But a sulky fine.

Shuffling off the soft cushions, she got to her feet. "I'm almost at the finish line with the siphoning spell, so let's forget about Felicienne for now."

"Va bene."

"Va bene," she repeated, doing her best Marlon Brando impersonation.

Enzo stood with a look of amusement as she tried to mimic the actor's down-turned mouth.

"I'm gonna make you an offer you can't refuse," she carried on, leading the way out of the library and towards the stairs. "And you're gonna take it, or tonight you'll be sleeping with the fishes."

372

"I'd rather be sleeping with you."

Ava faked a shocked gasp, even though she preferred that option too. "Ragazzaccio," she tutted.

"Not naughty enough," Enzo grumbled in reply.

32

The day of the eclipse arrived.

Ava woke before the sun had even shed its duvet, and rolling over, tugged hers over her head, hoping darkness would trick her brain into going back to sleep.

It didn't work.

Denying her rest, it immediately fired into action, beginning with the spell-casting order. Its recital of the steps kicked her wide awake within seconds.

Just before lunch the previous day, she'd finalised the entire complicated spell. She and Enzo had then spent the afternoon considering every possible hitch. By the time they took their places at the dinner table, she had a ready solution for each one—except for swarms of flying fish. Allegedly, during a hybrid eclipse in October 1986, a shower of fish had rained down on a remote Alaskan town, slapping residents unconscious. Fish-showers aside, Ava had fallen into bed after midnight, confident she'd nailed the spell and contingency plans.

But.

"Don't," she groaned at herself.

Doubt poked her with a bony finger. *But what if you've missed something? But what if you've messed up an order, or incorrectly created one of the thirteen sigils that would form the working circle?*

If she had, the spell would instantly crumble.

One more run-through, anxiety pleaded.

"Okay, fine," she surrendered with a sigh, and shoved down the duvet. Grey pre-dawn light seeped through the cracks in the drapes. "Goddess. It's way too early."

The clock on the mantel announced six-fifteen when she passed it en route to the bathroom. Five-and-a-half hours until the Moon passed between the Earth and the Sun. If all went to plan, this time tomorrow, she'd be comatose in her own bed, sleeping off the rigours of what lay ahead.

The idea didn't exactly thrill her.

Normality waited, and with it, uncertainty over what might happen between her and Enzo.

With the shower fired up, she reached out to test the temperature. Her hand shook as water streamed over it. "Come on. You've got this," she told her jittery self.

She showered without products, and once dried off, ignored her usual treat of scented body lotion. Witches had their own rituals before heavy spell-casting. Ava's preference was to fast for the twenty-four hours before, wear only cotton clothes, and avoid all cosmetics, creams, and lotions with perfume. If Nessa were here, she'd have had her bathing in unheated rain water while turning her nose up at Enzo's fancy shower.

Dressed in black cotton leggings and a plain black tee, she studied her reflection in the bathroom mirror. "You've got this," she assured herself, and scooping up her hair, tied it in a ponytail.

She sat to meditate at seven, quickly sliding into the in-between where her mum and gran waited. Sombre energy drifted around them. Normally, she'd talk to them, but it wasn't a morning for chatter. Instead, she soaked up their presence, and before parting ways, asked them to smooth the path for her connection to Martha's ancestors.

When she blinked back to awareness, the clock had zipped forward to eight.

Remaining in place, she rubbed where the skin around her neck already tingled. The nearer the eclipse drew, the more it would hurt. Eventually, she'd bleed.

She hadn't told Enzo yet. Typically, anyone present when she worked eclipse magick anticipated one thing, but what they got, they never expected. Deciding advance damage-control wouldn't go amiss, she heaved herself out of the chair.

Enzo was waiting for her in the kitchen when she entered. She set the basket holding the secateurs, cotton gloves, and cloth she'd consecrated the previous evening on the empty table. Both he and it looked forlorn. The previous day, he'd made her a light lunch, and since then, she'd only consumed water. The lack of food didn't bother her; she didn't have the stomach to eat, and wouldn't until late tomorrow. But his expression suggested the fact didn't sit easily with him.

"I'm not hungry," she reassured, "so don't worry."

"Did you sleep?"

"A few hours. You?"

"No." Enzo turned away to take down a glass and fill it. "Do you have the list of herbs?" he asked, passing her the water.

376

Ava handed over the sheet. Thankfully, he didn't need a lesson in how to cut herbs for a working; Martha had trained him well. Picking up the basked he asked, "You'll be in Martha's room?"

"I will."

With his distance granting her a few safe moments to talk to Cyrus, Ava hurried back upstairs. When she knocked on Cyrus's door, he answered it, dressed only in jeans. Daphne was noticeably absent.

"Can I talk to you for a minute?"

"Si."

Cyrus widened the gap, and she stepped inside. "Enzo's in the greenhouse," she told him.

Understanding she had something important to say—and out of Enzo's earshot, Cyrus elbowed the door shut.

A scar puckered the skin above his left hip-bone. The memento from his human life suggested a blade-wound, and its jagged edges a poorly executed attempt to sew the severed skin together. Not wanting to stare, Ava dragged her gaze up, only for his crossing of arms to arrest her attention as low light reflected off the silver barbells piercing his nipples.

When she met his eyes, he cocked his head fractionally, a tiny smirk making her wish she'd remained in the hallway to deliver her request.

"I need your help with something today."

'What?' a half-assed shrug queried.

"When I'm working the spell later, things will turn gnarly. I need you to ensure Enzo doesn't interfere. He can't break the circle, no matter what happens, okay?"

Curiosity narrowed Cyrus's eyes. "What will happen?"

"I. . .may bleed."

"You *may* bleed?"

Holding in a sigh, she confirmed, "There'll be blood."

377

Cyrus rounded her to sit on the edge of his unmade bed. Adorned in black satin sheets with a scarlet trim, it, and the rest of his room, looked every inch the cliched vampire nest. A mess of plump cushions in deep plum tones cluttered the foot of the bed. The black-and-plum colour theme bled into the drapes, while walls layered in flocked black wallpaper also carried accents of the rich mulberry hue.

Above, a large mirror formed part of the ceiling. Not only did it capture the disarray of Cyrus's bed, but where he sat watching her.

"I can handle a little blood," he said, drawing her out of a scene where she lay looking up at herself—but on Enzo's bed, and with Enzo. "As can my uncle. So what's the problem?"

"He's faltering. He had a moment last night and tried to call off the whole thing."

Cyrus tutted. "I knew he would."

The nightstand to the left of the bed held an assortment of clutter, including a Manga comic and an empty wine bottle. "So, if it comes down to it, can you—will you try to. . ?" Ava lamely gestured a clutching motion.

"Restrain him if necessary?" Cyrus translated.

"Yeah," she said quietly.

Leaning sideways, Cyrus stretched out, propping himself half upright on one elbow. "How bad will it get?"

"It'll look worse than it really is."

Not believing her bullshit, he snorted. "You think you can get my sister home safely?"

"Yes."

"Then I'll do what you ask."

"Thanks."

Ava cast a pointed glance at the second nightstand. It held only a brass oil-lamp. The typical human necessities; tissues, phone charger, water, a book—were noticeably absent. "Where's Daphne?"

"I sent her home."

"Oh." *Lucky Daphne.*

"Is that all you wanted?"

"Um, yeah, thanks." Taking the hint, Ava retreated to the door, slipping out with another whispered thanks.

She hurried down to the kitchen again, grabbed her liquid breakfast, and, with an about-turn, headed up to Martha's room.

Half way up the stairs, her ears popped.

She stalled, wincing against the high-pitched ring that followed.

"What the hell?" she muttered, stretching her jaw to counteract the reverberation. She hadn't experienced ear-popping as a side effect to fasting before. Perhaps it was the building eclipse energy.

Or the start of trouble.

Shrugging off the concern, Ava focused in on her first task. The previous night, Enzo had promised he'd clear a working space on the floor of Martha's room for her. She emerged from the stairwell to find an altered layout. He'd shoved all the furniture to the outer edges, leaving more than enough room for her to construct the complex circle she needed to draw.

After a sip of water, she walked a lap of the boards and picked the spot to begin. Her ears continued to ring, but the pitch had already softened. She poked at one while grabbing her notes and chalk, and crossing to the north position, hunkered down.

The waking morning promised a clear day. Wispy cloud skittered across the sky, driven by a frisky wind. It danced over the balcony, throwing around the winter detritus that had gathered in one corner. Brittle leaves scuttled over the flagstone, and where they hit the glass doors, pattered like rain.

Hungry gulls squawked.

Ava looked up, briefly envying their freedom as they hovered on the wind's coat-tails. When a curious robin landed on the railing, puffing up its red breast before delivering her a sweet song, it distracted her even further.

"Oh, fuck!" Ava shot to her feet, dropping her notebook. The chalk fell with it, snapping in two. "Enzo!" she yelled, darting for the stairs. "Felicienne revoked the wards!"

More practised with panic management than she, Enzo had his team of vamps surrounding the perimeter of the house within minutes. He then made a string of calls, his Italian orders delivered calmly, but with an edge of urgency. When he hung up, he dialled another number. "Speak to Iseult," he ordered, handing her the phone.

Iz launched straight into action as soon as she heard about Felicienne's retaliation. "That bitter bitch!" she raged. "Okay, don't worry. I'm on it. Enzo's crew will need to hold the fort for a while, but we'll be there as fast as we can. Right now, you have to protect yourself. Throw up whatever shields you can, okay?"

"Okay."

Despite the gravity of their situation, Iz paused to smile. "I guessed you were on Dunfarr. I sensed you were close."

Before Ava could say a proper goodbye, Enzo bundled her back up- stairs. It wasn't an exaggeration to guess dozens of witches, warlocks, and every creature in-between worked location spells to find her. On eclipse day, there was always a last-minute scramble to grab her. One year, they had caught her out, forcing Nessa to stuff her into the back of a friend's van and drive her around Leinster for the hours leading up to the eclipse.

They'd ended up in a car chase through the busy town of Enniskerry before Nessa had dodged the stalkers.

Quickly gathering the necessary to shield herself, Ava got to work. Unfortunately, with every minute they neared eclipse time, her energy signature would sing louder. No matter the shields raised or cloaks draped, each rotation of clock hands would lure those hunting her closer.

Enzo paced, muttering in Italian while Ava ground protective herbs. Curses grumbled as he marched over and back in front of the doors, with Felicienne's name punctuating the blasphemies. The High Priestess had undeniably earned the crown for Most Vindictive Bitch. Ava couldn't wait to see the shock on her puss once she learned she'd put the rescue of fourteen witches in jeopardy with her nastiness—if Enzo didn't kill her first, of course.

Eight-fifty.

Ava noted the time and drew in an inhale. Like all the previous breaths she'd sucked in, it didn't do much to settle the nerves sparking in her stomach. The eclipse was due at twelve forty-seven, and would last four minutes. For those two hundred and forty seconds, Ava needed absolute focus. If the house, or she, were under assault, things would go south fast.

One problem at a time, she told herself. Everyone else might lose their heads, but she had to remain calm.

With a circle drawn, she stepped inside the protective boundary, and lowered herself to sit cross-legged. Energies of the five elements swirled around her as she crafted a shield. But even as the invisible layer formed, intensifying magick pushed against the constraint. She had two hours at most before the shield would fall away. Once it disintegrated, she'd be a flashing neon sign, yelling a loud, *'Here I Am!'*

Noting Enzo's strained expression when she opened her eyes, Ava kept the fact to herself. "I'm protected now," she told him. It wasn't exactly a lie.

"How can I help?" he asked as she returned to her feet and crossed over to the working table.

Items spread across its surface. Yesterday, she'd had the foresight to lay out everything. With each ingredient ready and waiting, including those for all her contingency plans, her efficiency left him redundant. "Keep me focused," she said. "If shit kicks off outside, unless I can hear it, I don't want to know. I have to get this circle drawn, and it'll take a while."

Enzo appeared beside her on soundless feet, nudging her around to face him. "We can call this off."

"Nope."

"I can search other avenues to reconnect Martha."

"Enzo, we're not having this discussion again." Reaching around him, Ava tugged over the basket he'd filled with fresh herbs. "Someone will flip Martha's witch switch today, and it needs to be me. The Goddess only knows what shit Giulia has planned if she gets to her first. I don't even want to think about the fuckery she'll cause with Martha's power racing through her crusty veins. We also need to yank the witches she's channelling out of her clutches," she added, rooting out the cuttings of thistle and St John's Wort. "Chances are they're already in bad shape. There's also the enclave issue. Do you really want that asshole Waylen getting the reeve seat?"

"There are ways around these issues." Enzo plucked an exceptionally vicious thistle-cutting out of her hand. It, and the St John's Wort, would help to infuse strength in Martha. Enzo's niece would need it to face off against a necromancer while adjusting to witch energy flowing after centuries of disconnect.

382

"Not without me channelling eclipse power. We'd be fools not to make the best use of today's energy."

Enzo cupped her face. "Amore mio," he whispered, resting his forehead against hers. "I'm sending you into the lion's den."

"I volunteered," Ava reminded him. "Besides, I have claws too, you know."

But not as wicked as Giulia's, the creases of his frown worried.

Ava clutched the front of his shirt. "It would be better for me if we handle today one step at a time. I know how risky this spell is, but if you start freaking out, I'll start freaking out."

Enzo took her chin, angling her precariously close to kissing distance. "No freaking out."

"Good. Because I need you to—"

His mouth cut her off.

Ava hesitated, afraid she'd lose herself in him at a time when her focus needed to be elsewhere. But his soft, careful brush of lips promised he simply wanted a taste—not to devour her.

Leaning in, she kissed him back, and although lips and tongues mingled for only a few seconds, it was enough to make her insides heat.

"Interesting way of distracting me," she commented as he wisely created space between them.

"I thought so too."

A little stunned, Ava steadied herself against the table. "You're breaking the rules, you know. There's a while to go yet before you have the green light to kiss me like that."

Smouldering brown eyes fixated on her tingling lips. "Rules are made for breaking," he told her, and with a wink, returned to his post by the balcony doors.

383

Less than fifteen minutes later, Ava sensed the first tendrils of searching energy. They scraped down her spine, goose-bumping her skin so severely it stung. "Any sign of Iz yet?"

Enzo scoured the stretch of garden and spread of sea with intent. He turned to look at where she chalked the sigils, his keen vampire senses immediately picking up on her discomfort. "No. What can I do to help?"

"Nothing." Doing her best to ignore the scratching between her shoulder blades, Ava carried on sketching.

"How are they breaching your shields?"

"With every minute the eclipse energy builds, so does my power. It's like turning up the volume on the radio. Eventually, no matter how hard we try, nothing will mute the sound."

"But they can't psychically attack."

"Not yet."

A quiet buzz announced a message. Enzo checked his phone. "Iseult is on her way. She procured a boat. And twelve witches. She says Nessa should be here before eleven."

"Nessa?" Ava's head shot up. Did she come to help or hinder? Today was *not* the day for a showdown between Enzo and her aunt.

Enzo read her mind. "Don't worry. We'll be civil. There are more important matters to deal with."

"You don't know Nessa," she murmured, turning her attention back to her notes.

White dusted Ava's fingers, and the hard floor already had her knees aching, but she still had seven more sigils to draw, and the outer ring of the circle to construct. Wishing she'd had the foresight to bring the

384

iPod so loud music could block out the world, she returned to sketching. Kara had taken the iPod off the island to upload all of Ava's favourite music, and The Sisters of Mercy would distract her nicely right about now. "Can I ask a favour?"

"Of course."

"Music would help. I left the iPod and headphones on my bedside locker. Could you—?"

Ava hadn't even finished her sentence before the requested items appeared before her. "Wow." She laughed. "You're fast."

"Only when necessary," Enzo replied, trying to lessen the tension with a wiggle of eyebrows. Scowls, he pulled off to perfection, but his eyebrow acrobatics made her laugh louder.

Ava scrolled for *Floodland*, her favourite Sisters of Mercy album, and shoving in the earphones, nudged the volume up as the first track began. "Much better."

Before she got halfway through the album, the surrounding air thickened. Pausing mid-sketch, Ava tentatively felt out the invisible curtain. "Iz," she realised, hitting pause and tugging out the earbuds.

Enzo confirmed with a nod. "They arrived a few minutes ago. They've already spread themselves around the island's perimeter."

"I can feel them."

But as easily as Iz and company had sailed from Calnaloch harbour, so too would those hunting her. Loud music cut Ava off from the situation outside, but Enzo's sudden jolt into rigidity a few moments before had suggested unwelcome arrivals had landed in advance of Iz.

385

"The ones that came before her?" she asked quietly, twisting to check the time with the mantel clock. Ten-fifty; two hours remaining.

"Dealt with."

"Okay." Ava shoved the buds back in and returned to the music. *'On days like this, in times like these, I feel an animal deep inside,'* she sang along to *'This Corrosion'* in her mind.

The animal inside her already stirred.

Like a sleeping cobra, it had uncoiled slowly over the last while, and unimpressed by the wall of muscle and bone containing its power, squirmed angrily.

Ava tilted her head from side-to-side, easing the tautness in her neck. *Soon,* she promised.

It all kicked off at twelve-thirty.

Ava had just finished the circle and was walking it inch-by-inch, triple-checking she'd drawn every symbol and sigil correctly when Enzo's frantic gesturing caught her eye. She whipped out the earbuds, cutting off The Cult.

"What is it?" But she could already hear. Outside, shouts and roars rose.

"More have arrived," he told her, motioning she remain in her circle when she moved to step out of it.

But worried for Iz and Nessa, Ava came to where he stood, peering down at the chaos unfolding by the water's edge. "Shit." More boats had arrived. Three men already waded through the shallows, heading straight for where the witches braced to fight.

A missile hit the balcony doors.

Ava yelped, instinctively ducking. But an explosion of glass didn't follow. Under the protection of the witches, the pane refused to even crack.

"Stand back," Enzo warned all the same.

Unhooked from music and the focus of forming the circle, Ava registered the increasing power streaming through her body. It heated her bone-deep, sparking beneath her skin. For those desperate to reach her, she sang like a siren, enticing them closer, promising their every desire.

A mental pat-down confirmed her fear as she moved away from the glass doors. The buffer she'd cast had cracked, and in places, already fallen away. Great chunks of her lay exposed. Beyond her physical form, where Iz, Nessa and the other witches had erected an outer shield, it too fragmented.

It wasn't their fault.

Her power uncoiled at a speed and strength far greater than their intent, and it already stretched out to taste freedom.

These final few minutes were the most dangerous.

As the out-of-sight chaos grew louder, panic twisted her gut. "What's going on out there?"

"They're outnumbered. They're fighting back, but they've lost their formation."

Another bang rattled the doors. Enzo remained in place, watching the battle below.

"Is anyone hurt?"

"No," he told her, shifting to a different angle. "I can see Iseult and Nessa. They're holding their own."

If the witches couldn't keep control of the shield they'd raised, it would only be a matter of seconds before an intruder found a way through to attack.

387

Ava contemplated entering the circle and raising another cloak. With her power already humming loud enough to make her ears ring, she could commence the working earlier than planned. But it would deplete her energy, and the Goddess knew she needed every last drop for what lay ahead.

"They're regaining control," Enzo announced, nose almost touching glass. "They just need to . . ."

Need to what? she was about to ask, when an ice-cold sting sliced through her left forearm.

Ava cried out, snatching at where pain flashed. A sizeable cut parted her flesh, immediately welling blood.

Enzo shot to her side, shock rendering him mute as he gaped at the wound.

Before she could warn there'd be more, the second struck with vicious speed; a twin slice on her right forearm.

Ice swarmed, a layer of arctic wind meeting the desert heat of her rising power. The conflict of temperatures immediately rattled her body. "Has to be someone close," Ava squeezed out through gritted teeth as Enzo dropped to his hunkers with her. "On the island."

"How are they doing this?" he yelled.

Another merciless cut ripped through her thigh.

Ava screamed against the pain. Blood oozed, quickly soaking into her cotton leggings. She didn't have enough hands to slam over the slashes, and as a fourth stabbed her left thigh, pain dropped her onto her ass. "Enzo!" she pleaded. "Do something!"

He retaliated with a blur of action. Through a haze of pain, Ava watched as he flung open the doors and darted out onto the balcony. A second later, he blew into the room, snatched something off the coffee table, and with a jerk, fired it out into the morning.

The assault came to an abrupt end. Wounds snapped shut and the icy chill evaporated.

Ava gasped against heat rushing her body again as she heaved herself onto her knees. Although her human eyes lagged Enzo's pace, she understood what he'd done. "Death by frisbee?" she croaked. Earlier, he'd brought her more water and a fresh glass, balanced on a circular silver tray. The tray was now missing off the coffee table.

"Amputation," Enzo replied, slamming the doors. "But if a severed hand doesn't dissuade them, it'll be their head next." Helping her upright, he winced at the blood streaks.

"I'm okay," she promised, fighting to steady her breath. "How are we doing for time?"

"Twelve minutes."

"Okay." Ava grimaced at her sticky palms. "No time for delays so, but I need to wash this off."

"I'll come with you."

After a hurried scrub of hands, sound-tracked by the low drone of chanting witches, Enzo called for Cyrus and Kara. They appeared on the landing in a blast of air, expressions grim. The normally chipper Kara spoke gravely, her stance alert as she reported to Enzo in Italian. Cyrus delivered his account, gesturing towards the rear of the house.

Ava didn't need a translator to understand things were grim. "The safest place for me right now is inside the circle," she told them. "I can shield myself once I'm inside."

They returned to Martha's room in a group. The earlier yelling had ceased from outside. Witch-chant rose loud and clear, defiance in the thirteen voices.

Ava immediately stepped inside the circle.

Enzo, Kara, and Cyrus took position a few feet back, angled with both her and the balcony in their sights. Cyrus shifted place to ensure Enzo stood in the middle. Ava didn't miss the tiny nod between him and Kara; he'd roped her in for backup should Enzo buckle.

"Four minutes," Enzo stated.

Outside, an eerie silence had descended.

Beyond the low hum of witch-song, songbirds and squawking gulls hushed. Movement in the celestial heavens pinched out the brightness of day, laying a premature but brief night upon the land.

Heart galloping, mouth dry, and hands already clammy, Ava sucked in a tight breath. *Here we go.*

33

Invisible barbs bit into Ava's skin as she gathered everyone's attention with a firm, "It's time." She swiped at the stinging, surreptitiously checking her fingers. They came away blood-free. "So, once I begin," she told the three onlookers, "no loud talking. And under *no* circumstances must anyone breach the circle."

"Understood," Enzo answered.

"No matter *what* happens," she insisted.

A tight nod. "Si."

Cyrus threw his uncle a look of doubt.

'Don't fail me, Cyrus,' she pleaded in silence. If he did, she'd stake him herself.

Ava lowered herself to sit, settling her hands, palms up, over her knees. "Goddess be with me," she murmured, and closing her eyes, shut out the external world and retreated within.

Rapidly building eclipse power coursed beneath her skin, breaching the usual blackness behind her eyes with rippling streams of gold. As if sensing imminent release, its accompanying hum grew louder.

Aoibheann and Evelyn were near, announcing their presence with a warm press of energy on each shoulder. *'Mum, Gran,'* she greeted. *'Stay close.'* And then, reaching into the void, she called out to Martha.

A response echoed back on the third try.

Latching onto the wispy thread with which Martha endeavoured to bind them together, Ava wound the silvery cord around her right wrist. She looped it twelve times; one for each lineage of Martha's ancestry.

With the grip secure, Ava crafted a protective shield next. She worked quickly, chanting the complicated rhyme while mentally drawing the sigils to bind and buffer. Disconnected from her physical form, she pictured herself standing on the seashore; feet rooted, arms raised as she drew potent power down from the heavens.

The first blow came sooner than she'd hoped, but she'd expected Giulia's retaliation. With Martha's connection secure, the shield in place, and the hum of eclipse energy singing higher, the attack bounced off her walls.

Whatever magick Giulia had used to subdue Martha, Enzo's niece writhed in pain. Ava diverted a prudent current of her power through their cord. Martha responded almost immediately, and peace washed over Ava. *'I've got you,'* she promised. *'Hold on for me, Martha. We've a wild ride ahead.'*

Ava sat cross-legged inside the circle, a myriad of smoking herbs partially constricting Enzo's view. Her breathing came in controlled inhales and exhales. Despite her lips moving, no sound escaped. As she wove her magick in the in-between, her fingers twitched.

Ninety seconds remaining.

The scent of blood pierced the pungent haze. Enzo started against the familiar bouquet as a uniform loop of tiny puncture wounds appeared around Ava's neck. Blood quickly welled, sprouting dark red drops. They formed thin streams, trickling over her collarbone before disappearing into the neckline of her t-shirt. Sure he hallucinated, Enzo blinked against the macabre chain suddenly looping her throat. The coil of barbed-wire pierced her delicate skin, its jagged prongs viciously hungry. "Che cos'è questo?"

Cyrus suddenly blocked his view. "No, zio. È normale," he whispered.

It didn't look *normal* to Enzo.

"Mi aveva avverito," Cyrus revealed.

The news didn't calm Enzo. "She didn't warn *me*," he replied, glaring at his nephew, but when Enzo moved to shove him aside, Cyrus clamped his arm.

"No," he warned. "You can't stop it now."

Night swamped morning. The temperature had dropped in the last few minutes, and with it, a wind had picked up. As the eclipse peak neared, light shimmered around Ava. A dazzling inner stream poured into her being through the crown of her head. Between the shimmering glow and smoke haze, Enzo lost clear sight of her form.

393

He now understood why Ava always insisted the necklace safe. It never left her. The ugly inheritance permanently lassoed her neck. Hanging in the centre of her breastbone, the gemstone powering her incredible magick radiated silver light. The moonstone, no larger than a grape, sparked and fizzed.

Time.

Ava's head fell back, her body turned rigid, and the force channelling through her body erupted.

Chaos had descended upon Ava's make-believe shoreline.

With Giulia scrabbling manically at the shield, the onslaught of twelve witch lines forming a current so intense her veins scalded, and Martha bucking against her captor's choking binds, Ava raced to siphon, direct, and infuse while fighting off the frenzied necromancer.

Containing eclipse power normally took all of her strength and focus, but corralling a dozen ancient witches while the celestial energy scorched her insides, already threatened her consciousness.

She yelled for her mother and gran. The moment Giulia had retaliated, she'd lost sense of their gentle touch. Without their grounding hold on her, she feared total disintegration. *'Mum, Gran!'*

No response came.

Gritting against pain, Ava funnelled everything she had into driving Martha's ancestor power through the channel Giulia fought to obliterate. Seconds slid by, each one closing the door on her only chance to resurrect Martha as a unicorn witch. Giulia parried with blast upon blast of dark, noxious magick. Through it, Ava could hear the screams of the witches feeding her. The suffering they endured had to be monstrous.

394

Tendrils of sludge snaked around Ava's ankles. A rotten stench of sulphur oozed with the binds. Although Martha's box of fun things had gifted her arsenal with demon magick, Ava couldn't wield it with the same efficiency as Giulia. As suffocating vines crawled up her body, her hold on Martha's cord, and the channel with which she siphoned a dozen witches, faltered.

Only seconds remained before the eclipse would wane. Once its full strength tapered off, Ava would fade with it.

Fear sparked.

Conscious of how easily it could overwhelm her, she honed in on Martha's pain and the pitiful screeches of her fellow witches. She needed the fuel of anger. If Giulia hijacked the working and diverted Martha's ancestors through her captive witches, the necromancer would have a power flowing through her veins no-one could ever temper.

'Fight with me!' Ava yelled at Martha's ancestors. *'Choose the side of good!'*

Her plea stirred a reaction. Giulia's reptile-like coils loosened.

'Yes! That's it—fight!'

Ava drew on every ounce of her remaining strength. In one tremendous gulp, she sucked in the final watts of eclipse energy, drove them through her cord to Martha, and with an undignified yank, heaved the Paladino ancestors forward, cramming their power in one brutal shove down the channel.

The force created a vacuum. As if a turnstile battered by two opposing gusts of wind, Ava spun out of control.

Giulia's demonic energy, the roar of a dozen wakened witches, Martha's vampire nature howling against a coup, and thirteen young captives being drained of their life force crashed down and through Ava.

She inhaled to scream, but Giulia descended, plunging her into a foul, sticky darkness.

The mist blinding Ava to her surroundings slowly cleared.

She made out tiny pinpricks of light first.

Inch by inch, they expanded, revealing themselves as fairy lights looped from rafters above her head.

A blend of scents registered next; lavender, jasmine, and verbena.

As if emerging from a tunnel of thick spiderweb, the view widened, revealing a familiar scene. Dried herbs and fairy lights, purple and indigo walls, crochet lace framing a tiny window, and below it, benches layered with aubergine velvet cushions. It looked exactly like her gran's caravan.

Someone had placed her in a seated position. Ava could see her knees, and where her hands rested on her thighs, but disconnected from her body, couldn't actually feel herself. *'Move'*, she ordered her hand. As requested, it rose. She turned it over in the fading haze, and curling her fingers in to her palms, dug her nails in. No sensation.

"Hello, pet." Suddenly occupying the empty bench she'd just studied, Evelyn O'Keefe smiled over at her.

"Gran?" Ava blinked twice to clear the illusion, but Evelyn didn't vanish. Instead, she remained, grey hair glistening in the sun beaming through the window at her rear. "Gran—is that you?"

"Yes, Ava, love. It's me."

Unable to make sense of the scene before her, Ava wondered what had her brain cooking up the nonsense. Dreams didn't normally present such vividness. Was it death? A side-effect of her spirit leaving her body?

Everything about her gran's caravan was exactly how she remembered; the scents, the colours, the way gran's crystals reflected the sun and sent sparks of light shooting across the curved walls. Evelyn's equally

396

comforting presence was exactly as Ava recalled, too. When her wavering hand reached out, even the bangles on her wrist jangled.

Fuck! Not a lovely dream. She'd died! She'd kicked the goddamn bucket on the floor of Martha's room, which meant that Grade-A bitch Giulia had won, and—

"You're not dead, pet," Evelyn announced. "And mind your language, missy."

Ava watched her grandmother's veined hand rest on her knee. No accompanying touch came with it. "I'm not dead?"

"You're not." Evelyn clucked her tongue with a familiar *'don't talk nonsense'* tone. "You're in the in-between."

"Why?"

"You absorbed a lot of power. Our bodies can only hold so much."

"So, I'm not dead, but I *am* dying?"

"Resting, not dying."

Ava hoped Evelyn spoke the truth. If she were dead, it meant leaving behind more than she was ready to let go; Enzo, Iz, Nessa—her whole life.

Beyond the window at Evelyn's rear, the landscape sparkled, not unlike when Aeylor the fae had drugged her with fairy glitter and turned Calnaloch into a sparkling eye-scorcher. Unease rolled through her. What happened to her on the other side while she sat here? The last thing she remembered was Giulia's toxic magick swallowing her whole. Did she still battle, or had she lost?

"When can I go back? I shouldn't be here."

"Once you're healed."

"When will that be?" Ava demanded.

"Soon, pet."

Ava only realised then she wasn't actually speaking. As Evelyn had answered, she'd done so without moving her mouth. "I messed it up, didn't I?" she said, reaching up to see if her lips moved. They didn't. "I couldn't hold off Giulia, and now I'm lying on the floor in Enzo's home and he's probably losing his shit."

"Oh, you held her off. Don't worry, mo chroí."

"So, it worked?"

Evelyn smiled at her. "Of course it did. Martha has the matter in hand now. You can rest here with us for a while."

"Us?"

"Ava, sweetheart."

As unconscious hallucinations went, this one really did take first place. When a form took shape beside Ava, she spun to see her mum looking at her, as full of life as Ava remembered—not the grey-skinned corpse she'd wailed over in the morgue. "Mum?"

Although they flung themselves at each other, no warm arms enveloped Ava. Instead, a wave of pure, unconditional love washed over her, sending tears to her eyes and filling her heart with such longing, it hurt. Okay, maybe death wasn't so bad—if it meant being reunited with her mother.

"Not death," Aoibheann whispered, breaking their intangible hug. "Ava, love, do you know how proud I am of you?"

Ava drank in the vision before her. This image of her beautiful mum was the one she'd hold on to from now on. Not the memory swamped in grey coldness, sound-tracked by her sobs and the stench of morgue chemicals. Aoibheann shone. She had reformed beyond death; warm, pink-cheeked, eyes glistening, and smile beaming. "I miss you so much, Mum."

"I know, sweetheart. But I'm always with you. I'm by your side whenever you call, whenever you think of me."

"I've felt you. Sometimes, I can smell your perfume."

Aoibheann smiled. "We're never far," she promised.

398

"Is it true? Was it Giulia who . . ." A faint, far-off call breached the cosy space. Ava turned in its direction. "Enzo. He's calling me."

"We don't have much time, Ava."

They didn't. Ava could already feel the pull urging her towards the arched teal door that would lead her down from the caravan.

"Ava." Aoibheann pulled her attention from the beckoning exit. Urgency crowded her features. "You must choose life, do you hear me? You have more work to do, my sweet girl. Don't let your life go."

"Why would I let it go?"

Ava!

Enzo's plea grew more panicked. But as desperate as he sounded, so too did Aoibheann.

"Choose life, Ava. Do you understand?"

"No, but I have to go, Mum." The body she couldn't feel rose to standing. Invisible cords jerked, coaxing her away from her mother and grandmother. "I don't want to, but I don't think I have a choice." The little door to her rear creaked open.

"We're always with you, pet," Evelyn said.

The two women who had shaped her life faded. Ava could see straight through her gran, to the plump velvet cushions at her rear. "Five more minutes!" she pleaded to whatever force separated them.

"I love you, Ava."

"I love you too, Mum, but please, just another few minutes! I'm not ready to say goodbye again! Mum! Gran! *Please!*"

The caravan's interior shrank, swallowed by the sudden darkness through which Ava found herself falling. Her cry of "five more minutes!" persisted, along with Aoibheann's plea.

"Choose life, Ava! *Choose life!*"

34

Enzo hadn't slept in three days.

He'd barely fed either. Feeding meant leaving Ava's side, and his whole world had reduced to one crucial thing; the muffled thud of a human muscle.

Elbows on the bed beside her knees, aching skull braced by palms, and eyes closed, he listened as Ava's heart continued to fight. Sometimes, his mind played tricks; dragged out the pause between each beat to fool him into thinking she could no longer wage whatever war raged inside her body and mind. For a short, but painfully frantic moment, he'd turn rigid, plead with whatever forces listened not to take her. And then he'd hear it; blood pumping through valves and arteries, courageous and stubborn, just like his bellissima strega.

400

Iz and Nessa both insisted Ava would wake. After the eclipse passed, once day reclaimed its rightful place and the celestial forces retreated, they had burst into his home, yelling for her. But she'd already fallen by then, her consciousness stolen by the immense power she'd channelled—and whatever Giulia had thrown at her. Enzo had breached the circle, scuffing chalk-lines and sigils as he drew her onto his lap, terrified by her dead weight and thin breaths. The necklace had already vanished, sealing the wounds it had created on its retreat. But blood stained her neck and throat, and as he'd cradled her limp form, calling her name over and over, it dried in her hair and clothes.

Nessa had been the one to brave his wrath by kneeling beside him and insisting he release Ava to the witches' care. He'd carried her downstairs, laid her on her bed, and stood to one side as Nessa and Iz tended to her. Prepared in advance, Ava's aunt had come with a myriad of herbs and oils. She and Iz worked calmly, their gentle murmurings in contrast to the panic seizing his dead heart and desperate mind.

Despite their promises, three days later, Ava hadn't woken. Colour had returned to her cheeks, and her heart certainly beat with the steadier, louder rhythm he'd come to cherish in the last few weeks. But despite his soft pleas and kisses, she stayed away, lingering in the world to which her mind had taken her.

Hunger pangs clenched Enzo's insides. He winced against the stab, and opening his eyes, straightened. At five in the morning, the house carried only the sounds of alert vampires. The witches slept; Nessa and Iz in the guest room down the hall. Downstairs, Cyrus occupied the library, an occasional creak of leather and quiet flick of page as he read. Martha wandered the greenhouse. Although he couldn't hear her murmuring, he knew she talked to her precious plants, misting their leaves as she showered them with love.

401

"You'll be no good to her half desiccated with hunger, Uncle," Cyrus commented from the library. "I can hear your insides eating themselves from here."

"I'm fine," Enzo told him, even as another griping pain twisted.

Cyrus snorted.

"Alright," Enzo surrendered. "Come and sit with Ava. I'll be quick."

Martha's return had settled Cyrus. The sulky teenager had disappeared, replaced by the subdued boy, who happily orbited his sister. As Enzo hurried downstairs, he heard her return indoors. To assist her recovery, he'd employed a donator; a human who readily gave their blood to vampires. Contracted under strict terms and conditions, the young man currently slept, but he'd left a pint of his nutritious O positive in a sealed black glass jug in the pantry as requested.

Enzo lifted down two glasses as Martha sat at the table, but she waved off the offer and told him to drink the lot.

"Ne hai più bisogno di me," she told him.

Perhaps Enzo did need it more than her. The second the first mouthful washed over his tongue, his stomach almost clambered up his throat to guzzle it down. He drank half in two greedy mouthfuls, but sipped the remainder, already feeling strength return.

Locked in on Ava's heartbeat, Enzo took a moment to study Martha.

She looked a hell of a lot better than when she'd first stumbled over the threshold of Dunfarr Lodge, propped between Kara and Cyrus. Chunks of her hair had fallen out, once plump cheeks clung like tissue to her face, and where Giulia's binds had trapped her in place, blood stained her wrists and ankles.

Martha hadn't healed as quickly now she bore both witch and vampire blood, but only that morning Enzo had noted the first marked improvement. As she sat opposite him, inhaling a cutting of jasmine bloom,

402

further healing was evident. Colour blossomed in her full cheeks, and healthy hair formed a thick braid down her back.

"How are you adjusting?" he queried.

Martha smiled to herself. "Slowly. With my vampire capabilities diminishing, I need to learn patience with this weaker form. But with my original self restored, I somehow feel stronger than ever."

"Please don't rush to Athens, Martha. The Enclave can wait."

"They most certainly can," she agreed, gesturing he share his meal. She took a few sips before sliding the glass back to him. "Besides, there's a certain witch upstairs I wish to acquaint myself with. I'm curious to meet the woman who has stolen your heart."

Enzo laughed at her mischievous smile. He would never deny his love for his bella strega. "Ava is excited to meet you, too."

Martha herself had called the Enclave to announce her release and safe return. She'd obviously caught Aurelius Soto in a genial mood. To facilitate her recovery, he'd agreed to push the reeve election out by a week, and formally accepted her candidacy for the role. With the significant changes Martha had undergone, Enzo relished the prospect of watching stunned faction members—Waylen Kane, especially—when she presented herself and her restored abilities.

Only minutes after the eclipse had passed, Kane had called Enzo, demanding to know only one thing; Ava's location. A thorough scour of Carlingford village had revealed how Enzo had duped him, and in response, he'd left an angry rant of a voice message. Enzo had ignored the threats contained in every other call, text, and voicemail since. Only hours ago, he'd replied for the first time with a simple four-word answer.

Ava is with me.

403

The ensuing silence since warned of trouble. Kane's retaliation would require careful handling, but both Enzo and Martha were ready. He just hoped Ava would agree to the protection of his home when he travelled to Athens in four days. Nothing would convince him to leave her wandering the streets of Calnaloch in his absence, vulnerable to whatever Kane planned.

"I have a good sense of Ava already." Martha revealed, setting down the fragrant bloom. "The psychic connection we shared opened her to me. She's powerful."

"She is."

"But she lacks faith in herself."

"At times, yes." Enzo paused, catching a faint rustle of cotton. Cyrus, the sleeping witches, or Ava? "She refers to her legacy as a curse."

Martha's eyes lowered. "That, I can understand."

Although tethered to the steady beat from Ava's room, Enzo reached across to rest his hand over hers. "Martha, is this not what you wanted? Have I forced my will upon you again?"

"No," she quickly answered, grasping his touch. "You never forced anything upon me, Enzo. How many times must I tell you? I was the one who coerced you into turning me, and this—"

"No, Mum! Five more minutes, please!"

The slurred plea lifted Enzo from his chair.

"Go," Martha urged. "Go."

Ava tumbled down the steps of the caravan, a frightening sensation of falling backwards, tensing every muscle in her body. She fell, and fell, an endless dive into blackness, all the while pleading for five more minutes.

A flail flipped her over.

Ground rushed towards her.

Screaming, she threw out her hands.

With a violent jerk, she snapped awake. A blurry figure leaned over her.

"Ava?"

"Enzo?" she croaked, blinking gritty eyes. "Am I dead?"

"No, amore mio."

"I fell."

"You did. But you're in your bed now. You're safe. It's over."

Awareness stretched beyond the handsome face looking down at her. "How did I get here? I fell from the caravan. My mum . . ." The hazy line between dream and reality sharpened.

"The caravan?" Enzo queried.

Ava took a moment to catch her breath and separate jumbled memories into their correct slots. She hadn't dreamt her mum and gran. The lengthy fall and almost landing marked her return to consciousness. But had what Evelyn told her about defeating Giulia and releasing Martha been true? "Did it work?" she asked, moving to shuffle upright. "Did I release Martha? Is she okay? What happened to Giulia? What about the—"

405

Enzo hushed her back onto the pillows, sitting by her side to ensure she remained horizontal. "It worked. Martha is home, safe and well. The witches are all recovering with their respective families by their sides."

"And Giulia?"

"How are you feeling? You've been asleep for three days."

"Three days?" Although noting his avoidance of the Giulia subject, news she'd been asleep for so long shoved the concern further down the queue. "So, it's Sunday?"

"Monday. Almost six in the morning."

With no obvious pain suggesting an injury, Ava patted her chest. "I feel okay," she said, shuffling her legs to ensure her limbs responded in full. "Was I hurt?"

"The magick took a lot out of you. You collapsed as soon as the eclipse waned."

"I barely remember what happened." Memories blended together, a jumble of pain, darkness, and the scorch of eclipse power consuming her body. Alongside, the agony of those Giulia channelled.

Enzo smiled down at her. "For the best, perhaps."

Perhaps. But the memories wouldn't hide for long. Once Ava fully recovered, they'd return. She'd record her experience then; document every step of the working in her grimoire. "But Martha's okay? She has her witch abilities again?"

"Yes."

"And the captive witches are all safe and well?"

"They are."

"And Giulia?" she prompted once more. "Where is she?"

Regret doused Enzo's smile. "She fled. Cyrus and Kara reached the tower only moments after the eclipse passed, but she was already gone. While they brought Martha back here, I notified Felicienne. She and her coven freed the remaining captured witches."

406

Groggy from her extended involuntary sleep, and battling a heaviness warning her battery still required substantial charging, Ava struggled to process the bad news. Giulia remained free, and no doubt, already plotted revenge.

"Nessa and Iseult are here," Enzo announced, breaking in on disturbing thoughts. "They've been caring for you, too."

Ava gaped up at him. "Nessa's *here?* In this house? But—how? I—"

"I'm sorry." Enzo tutted at himself. "Too much information, and too soon. I should have taken my time with you."

"No," she said, propping herself up on her elbows. A lot had happened in the last three days, and she needed to hear it all. "Start at the beginning," Ava demanded. "But maybe take it a bit slower. My brain is still fried."

Ava had worked her way up to sitting by the time Enzo had filled her in on all that had taken place. An all-over ache persisted, as if she'd run a marathon, or tumbled down a flight of stairs. Although her cotton-wool brain had cleared, a mild headache lingered behind her eyes. "So, Giulia got away Scot-free?"

"Don't worry. I have a team of thirty scouring for her."

"They won't find her. Look at how efficiently she hid for centuries." Staring beyond Enzo, Ava contemplated Giulia's escape. "And she's probably planning not to emerge for another three years."

He frowned at her specificity.

"The next eclipse," she clarified.

Immediate denial scoured his expression. "No. Impossible. She won't come near you—I won't allow it."

"Somehow, I don't think she'll be asking for your permission."

He softened at her tiny smile. "No more talk of her, please," he said, and leaning in, captured her chin. "We have far more pleasant matters to discuss, my bella strega."

Elbowing him away, Ava clamped her mouth, and with an emphatic head-shake, mumbled, "I haven't washed my teeth in three days. No kissing," from behind her palm. In fact, her body odour had to be noticeably bitter at this stage. "You should go. I need to shower. I'm sure I stink."

Before Enzo could argue, the door to her room burst open.

"You're awake!" Iz yelled, and like a drunk bird, took flight, landing on the bed beside her. Hauled into a tight hug, Ava's "oof!" disappeared into Iz's blonde locks.

"You're awake! Oh, thank the Goddess!"

Pinned down, Ava laughed. "Iz, I need to breathe!"

"Nessa!" Iz shouted, scrambling to her knees. "Ava's awake!"

Hit by a barrage of questions, Ava tried to answer as best she could. But between Iz's interruptions and the hugs she delivered every few seconds, most of what she answered went unheard.

Finally composed, Iz clasped her hands to her chest and heaved out a long, loud sigh. "Thank the Goddess. I've never petitioned her as much in all my life. At some stage, I think I may have even promised her my firstborn."

"Iz," Ava chided, shifting to resettle herself against the pillows.

"Kidding." Iz winked, and turning to scowl in the direction of the room she'd been sharing with Nessa, muttered, "Where the hell is—"

"Right here." Nessa appeared in the doorway. Dressed head-to-toe in flowing black and silver, and her wild grey hair an explosion of curls, she looked every inch the mad crone. "Hello, pet."

Although Enzo had been facing Ava, he shifted around to sit beside her, making it clear he wouldn't vacate the room for the incoming awkward conversation. Nessa had been under his roof for three days. Obviously, they'd barely conversed during that time.

"Nessa," Ava greeted tersely.

"How are you feeling?"

"Like I've been slammed by a bus."

Nessa nodded in understanding.

"In more ways than one."

Enzo threw a sideways glance at her as Nessa twitched with guilt. Ava hadn't expected anger to erupt, but now Nessa stood before her—well, hovered in the doorway looking guilty as sin—weeks of amassed one-way conversations tumbled up her throat.

Nessa took a step further into the room. "We'll talk once I'm home."

"We will," Ava promised. "About *everything*."

Nessa tugged her cardigan tighter. "I'm glad you're awake, pet. You'll need to take it easy for the next day or two. Iz, make sure she rests."

Iz stiffened beside Ava. "You're leaving?"

Purposely blanking where Enzo sat beside her niece, Nessa replied with a curt, "Yes. This is no place for me. Or you," she added, aiming the barb at Ava.

"Nessa!" Iz snapped.

"This is *exactly* the place for me," Ava replied.

Her aunt fired a baneful glare at Enzo, and with another tug of cardigan, turned and left. "Come and visit me when you're ready," she said.

Iz jerked to roll off the bed and follow.

Ava grabbed her arm. "No, don't. Let her go."

"She shouldn't have said that," Iz argued.

Enzo stood, smoothing down his navy sweater. Happy to dwell on his handsomeness over Nessa's snark, Ava smiled up at him. But she recognised the look settling on his expression. *Orders incoming.*

409

"Iseult, perhaps you could help Ava to take a bath. While you do, I'll prepare breakfast."

Iz tipped her forehead. "Yes, sir."

"Amore mio," he directed the next order at Ava. "Iseult must stay with you. You're not strong enough to bathe alone."

"Sir, yes, sir," she said with a smirk.

He tutted at them both, but humour broke through, gifting her a full force Enzo Paladino smile.

Iz waited until he'd left the room before turning to Ava. "I think I've just been turned hetero."

"That's the power of the Paladino smile," Ava sang. "No-one's immune to its magick."

35

I z sat with her back to the vanity unit while Ava soaked. Shakier on her feet than she'd realised, she'd needed Iz's help with making the short journey to the bathroom—although she did kick her out before undressing and lowering herself into the water. Iz didn't need a close encounter with her toxic pits.

"This house is amazing," Iz commented, studying an array of creams and lotions lined up on the floor where she sat cross-legged. She'd found them while nosing around the bathroom and currently lathered her hands in Shea butter. "I can see why you were happy to stay here."

Still distracted by the earlier terse encounter with Nessa, Ava muttered agreement. "What secret is Nessa keeping?"

Iz pursed her lips as she sniffed a bottle of body-lotion.

"Clearly, she hates the Paladinos," Ava continued, "but she can't blame them for Giulia's actions, so there has to be something she's not telling us."

411

"I agree, but until she sees fit to tell you, you'll be in the dark."

Ava scooped up a handful of suds and blew them towards the ceiling. "I don't like not knowing."

"Who does?" With all the pots and bottles sampled, Iz took a photo of two she planned to hunt down online. "I'll bet this stuff costs a fortune."

Although Ava enjoyed the hot soak, her empty stomach begged for food. She was also excited to finally meet Martha in the flesh. Having being hooked into each other psychically, they each already knew the other, but meeting face-to-face would seal their bond. Ava hoped they could spend a few hours together in Martha's room. She remained curious about so many of her possessions, not least the contents of the *'infernal cabinet'*—as Enzo had christened it. Now she'd danced with dark magick, it had piqued her interest. With patience and care, she believed she could blend a few techniques into her own practice. It would be nice to discuss it with someone who wouldn't immediately dismiss her inquisitiveness like Nessa would.

"I can smell toast," Iz groaned. "I'm starving." She quickly restocked the cabinet, and once done, grabbed a sheet-sized towel off the heated rack. "C'mon, Prune Lady," she said, holding the towel out. "Don't stand up too fast."

Already revived, and smelling a lot sweeter, Ava wrapped herself in warm cotton and leaned against Iz as she carefully stepped out of the bath. "I can't wait to go home," she admitted, dabbing her neck dry. "I miss my apartment so much."

"This place is fabulous, but yes, I get it. Home is home. How soon do you want to leave?"

"Tomorrow," Ava said, accepting a bottle of orchid and neroli body-lotion.

Iz threw her a look of uncertainty. "Will you be strong enough?"

Ava smiled. "Probably not, but that won't stop me."

Enzo's niece had been waiting patiently in the kitchen, and with Enzo, Cyrus, and Iz present for the significant moment, the room stilled in suspense.

As Ava and Martha clung to each other, Martha whispered she had no words. Ava agreed. What could be said? They'd shared an experience beyond description; *How are you?* and *Thank you!* would reduce it to something insignificant.

Once they'd both gathered themselves, Martha eased Ava out of the tight hug to grasp her shoulders. Martha's smile and sparkling eyes reminded Ava of Saturday morning tarot lessons, afternoons foraging for herbs, and midnight tales around a dancing bonfire. From the moment they'd first connected in the astral plane, a kinship had formed.

Ava studied the woman before her, almond eyes a shade lighter than Enzo's, cheekbones a model would die for, thick braided hair a luminous silver, and a slender form hiding the power of her combined vampire and witch lineage. She already knew she and Martha had forged a connection distance would never sever. As sisters of the craft, even if Enzo slipped out of Ava's life, Martha would remain.

"Mia sorella," Martha whispered. "My sister."

"Come," Enzo said, foreseeing the incoming meltdown as Ava swiped tears off her cheek. "Sit, amore mio."

A spread worthy of a five-star breakfast buffet lay in wait.

Iz had already taken a seat. Shimmying with excitement, she whipped up a platter of pancakes and slapped two onto Ava's plate before piling three onto hers. "Are we the only two eating?" she asked, reaching for maple syrup with one hand, and the plate of bacon with the other.

413

"Two-and-a-half," Martha replied. "I'm still adjusting to the act of eating solid food, so I'll nibble."

"How does that work?" Iz queried, slathering her pancakes with syrup. "Will you need both blood and food, or will you have to choose one over the other?"

"It will take a few years, but my vampire capabilities will slowly wane. Until then, I can nourish myself with either option."

Cyrus announced he was going to bed. He bent to give Martha a one-armed hug. Contentment briefly washed his expression as Martha rested her head against his shoulder. She murmured something softly to him. "Ti voglio bene," he answered.

"Anch'io ti voglio bene," she replied affectionately, patting his arm.

Cyrus's violent, petulant tendencies had retreated with the return of his sister. As Ava watched the tender exchange, she wondered how long his peace would hold. She also wondered about their plans to remain in Calnaloch. With Martha due to face the Enclave, responsibilities could demand her presence in Athens for months. Would Cyrus travel there with her, or would Enzo be saddled with babysitting once more?

Enzo settled beside her, spooning berries and melon onto her plate. She still needed convincing he didn't harbour a feeding fetish. As if hearing her thoughts, he stole one of her raspberries and popped it between her lips. "It pleases me to care for you. Get used to it."

As the food slowly disappeared, conversation turned to the Enclave. Martha had made plans to travel to Greece on Thursday evening for the reeve vote on Friday morning. With Iz present, they kept details to a minimum, but anticipation had Enzo and Martha exchanging smug little glances. As much as Ava never wanted to set foot in the eerie place again, she longed to be a fly on the wall for the Grand Reveal. The expression on Waylen Kane's pasty face would be worth it. Maybe Enzo would take a picture for her.

"However, before I leave," Martha announced, "I'm throwing a party, here, tomorrow evening. We have a lot to celebrate, and I expect you both to attend."

Iz lowered the plate of bacon. "A party, here?"

"Yes." Martha chewed slowly, but not in thought, more as if her jaw needed time to remember the act of masticating. "Nothing too elaborate. A low-key event."

Ava wondered if Martha's idea of *'not too elaborate'* resembled Enzo's. If so, it called for a fancier outfit than anything she had upstairs. *Another reason to go home tomorrow,* she thought.

"I accept," Iz said.

"Me too," Ava added. "But I will need something nice to wear, so—" She turned to Enzo. "I think I'll go home tomorrow."

Worry shadowed his eyes, but he nodded, and softly brushing her jaw, said, "Of course."

Ava heard the unspoken *'however'*, but left it unchallenged. Whatever condition or argument Enzo planned to attach to her departure, he'd reveal soon enough.

After breakfast, Iz announced it was time for her to leave. Once packed and ready to go, she and Ava stood in the hallway, an argument almost erupting when Iz insisted she'd fill Ava's empty fridge and pantry. "Your cupboards are channelling Old Mother Hubbard," she reminded her. "And your apartment needs an airing out, too—once I break through Nessa's spells, of course." Mimicking martial arts moves, she did a slow-motion high-kick, followed by a, "Hi-ya!"

"Iz, you have The Cauldron to take care of. I'm more than capable of shopping for food."

"I've closed it for two weeks," she announced, returning to a normal stance. "I need the break. Anyway, with all the customers from the last few weeks, I've more than enough financial padding for me to take three months off, so a fortnight won't kill anyone."

"Yes, but—"

"And," she butted in. "The entire town awaits your return. Are you ready for all that attention in the fruit and veg aisle?"

Ava quickly rethought her argument.

"Nope. Didn't think so." Peering over Ava's shoulder, Iz checked the kitchen door remained shut. "Plus," she whispered, "Finn."

"Yeah, yeah, okay," Ava hushed her with a flap. "Thanks. I accept your kind offer."

"He's been texting me," she said. "I can give you another few days if you don't want him to know you'll be home tomorrow."

"No, it's fine. If he drives by my place, he'll see the lights on, anyway."

"He has a billion questions."

Ava groaned. As much as she'd longed for her return to reality, it came with issues she'd rather avoid. A hard chest met her back. Two arms encircled her, and Enzo's lips brushed her ear.

"And I have a billion distractions."

"I'll bet you do." Iz snorted a laugh. "Get a room, you two," she wailed as Ava squealed against Enzo's tickles.

Once released, Ava grabbed Iz into a final hug. "See you tomorrow, Iz. I love you."

"I love you, too. Take care of my girl, Enzo," she called out as Kara met her on the front steps.

"Always," he answered.

As the motorboat growled into life outside, Ava and Enzo returned to the kitchen. Enzo had already cleared up. "I wanted to help," Ava said, frowning at his vampire efficiency.

"We have more important things to do," he said, and, taking her hand, gestured to the garden she'd spent weeks admiring from behind glass. "It's time you breathed in sea air," he told her.

The first blast of fresh morning air made Ava's head spin. Stopping in the doorway, she grasped Enzo's arm to savour the precious moment. Did the outdoors always smell so rich and sweet? Did the tang of sea brine habitually lace each inhale? Overcome by the scents of unfurling leaves and blossoming buds, Ava almost swooned. "I've missed this."

Enzo led her through the garden, watching with unmasked joy as she caressed spring growth and sampled delicate perfumes. When they rounded a bank of shrubs and an impressive greenhouse appeared further ahead, she almost squealed.

A masterpiece in Victorian design, the elaborate structure sat in a small clearing, flanked by silver birch and rowan trees. "This is unreal," Ava said, noting the prolific growth inside. "Iz needs to see this. She'll flip."

Humid air layered with dozens of scents greeted her when they stepped inside. Ava immediately recognised the everyday herbs witches stocked. The healthy, bountiful plants occupied the first aisle, but when she rounded to the next, a range of more specialised plants appeared.

Enzo walked with her, naming those he could remember. Swiping her index finger and thumb across leaves, Ava breathed in the unique scents raised by her touch. She sampled harmless berries and flowers, and with the plants they couldn't touch or taste, admired by sight only.

He waited until they'd strolled every aisle before steering her against a cast-iron upright supporting the domed roof above. Pained restraint laboured a sigh as he cupped her face, tracing her cheekbones with his thumbs.

Ava admired him, too, trailing the hard lines of his body; marble perfection beneath his cashmere sweater.

"You have bewitched me," he murmured.

"Body and soul." She smiled. "And I love, I love, I love you."

Recognising the Austen quote, he laughed softly with her. "I'm Mr Darcy to your Elizabeth Bennett?"

"I think so." Tugging him a little closer, Ava said, "We have overcome a lot of pride and prejudice in the last few weeks."

"That we have."

"And?" she dared to ask, "what happens now?"

A cool thumb brushed her lips. Eyes fully black, Enzo leaned in, a hair's breadth keeping his lips from hers. "I never wish to be parted from you from this day on."

No longer the witch in his service, Enzo claimed her with a searing, hungry kiss. *My lover*, it declared. *My amate, my bella strega.*

Ava strained up to take him with equal intent. Sandwiched between him and the ornate upright, she melted into hot putty, a strangely delicious juxtaposition of her heat colliding with two steely-cold forms.

Where the curve of her skull met the iron upright, Enzo slid his hand in between, grasp possessive as he angled to take the kiss deeper.

Earlier, inhaling air for the first time in weeks had made her dizzy.

Moments ago, the scents of the greenhouse had threatened to spin her vision.

But the way Enzo kissed her now, how he asserted ownership—it had Ava close to spinning off into the ether.

A cold touch met her smouldering skin. Ava gasped against the maddening relief. Ravenous fingers tugged her shirt free of her waistband, spreading out on her lower back before skimming her ribs and cupping

418

one breast. Ignited anew, she leaned into him, desperate for him to rip away the cotton separating his skin from hers. "Enzo," she pleaded.

Abruptly, only one iron structure held her upright.

Enzo had leapt back, expression pained as he tilted his face to the curved glass above. A moan broke free, followed by a sweep of the tongue she'd been entwining with her own, swiping over his front teeth. As his jaw tipped open, she sought what had ripped him out of their clinch. But his fangs hadn't dropped. "Enzo?"

Bliss crossed his face, wiping out the torment. Lowering his head, he dragged his forefinger and thumb down either side of his mouth, and pinned her with such a ravenous look, her bones liquefied all over again. "This is what you do to me," he said, a wicked smile making her want to repeat it.

"Then come back here and finish what you started."

Enzo closed the gap with one wide step. "Not here." Feather-light kisses danced over her lips, cheeks, and eyes. "You deserve so much more than rushed and clumsy. I will worship you slowly," he whispered, tugging her to him again. "Diligently, perceptively. Our bodies will learn to recognise each other's touch, how we each unravel and pleasure the other."

Sure she was about to self-combust, Ava dropped her forehead on his shoulder. "Enzo, you're killing me."

"Anticipation," he murmured, skimming her ear with his tongue and sending a pulse of hot shivers down her spine, "is a wonderful aphrodisiac."

"I don't think we need any kind of aphrodisiac," she mumbled into cloud-soft wool.

Enzo dug her out from his chest, framing her face once more. Amusement bowed his lips. He took more satisfaction from her frustration than

419

was fair. Maybe she should hold him off when the time came; give him a taste of his own agonising medicine.

As if reading her scowl, he laughed before delivering another kiss. A more reserved one this time, but still hot enough to make her quickly scrap the idea of resisting him. No-one had ever made her this flushed and flustered. This level of desperate need was a novel experience for her.

"Now. About Wednesday," he said, grounding her back into harsh reality.

"What about it?" she asked warily, fixing her shirt with one hand as Enzo took the other to lead her out of the greenhouse.

"I would like you to stay here while Martha and I are in Athens. You'll have better protection in my home than yours."

As Enzo held back the exit door, Ava ducked under his outstretched arm. "The eclipse is over, Enzo. The scroungers have scuttled off to their lairs. No-one's interested in me anymore."

"Not true," he said, gently squeezing her hand. "Waylen Kane maintains a worrying interest in you."

She slowed to a stop. "Why?"

Weeks of confinement with Enzo Paladino had granted Ava the opportunity to learn his ways. One aspect she admired was how he refused to coddle her. Even if he knew it would upset her, he never brushed over facts, or patronised her by promising *'everything will be okay.'* So when he answered with a troubled, "I don't know," she accepted the warning without arguments.

"Okay. I'll stay here on Wednesday night, and I'll wait until you're home before I go again."

Enzo pulled her in, and with a quiet, "Thank you," kissed her forehead before resuming their walk through the gardens towards the house.

"Is Waylen planning another interrogation?" she wondered.

"I don't know what he's planning. He called within moments of the eclipse passing, demanding to know where we were."

"He knew we lied about Carlingford?"

"Once he scoured the village and found no trace of us, yes."

"Shit."

Enzo hummed agreement. "His interest in you troubles me. I'll sound him out while I'm in Athens, but in the meantime, I want you protected."

"He'll be pissed when he learns the whole truth, Enzo. What's to stop him from hauling me back there for another grilling? He'll blame you for compelling me, and punish me for agreeing to it."

"There will be no punishments," he stated angrily, halting their walk again. "I acted for the greater good, and as soon as Martha takes the reeve seat, every faction member will come to learn the truth. Kane's day of reckoning has come. No longer shall that viper spread his malignant ways amongst the Enclave. Martha and I shall eradicate his filthy rot and restore integrity. No more interrogations, Ava. No more summons."

"Okay," she said calmly, taking his hands in hers. "Deep breaths, Enzo."

"I don't breathe," he reminded her, but with a smile.

"Then think about your happy place."

Tense shoulders softened. With purposeful slowness, he grazed her body with a heated look, ending his travels on her lips. "Much better," he agreed.

"If this" —Ava motioned at herself— "is what motivates you, I clearly need to start taking more advantage of the fact."

"Please do, mia bellissima strega."

"If you insist."

Enzo slid his arm around her waist and pulled her in for another kiss. "As much as I would like to spend the day with you in my arms, Martha

421

has threatened untold misery upon me if I keep you all to myself. She's waiting for you upstairs."

Ava inhaled against a rush of excitement, clutching his sweater as she turned to squint through the morning light towards the upper storey of the house. "Now?"

"Yes."

But she didn't immediately release him to dart away, partly because of the distraction of being pressed against him. "Where will you be?"

"Right here. I have business to take care of, but I won't be leaving the house."

And partly, she realised, because old habits die hard. "Sorry," she said, shaking her head. "It's going to take time for me to remember I'm not in constant danger anymore. Don't stay here on my behalf. If you have somewhere to be—"

Enzo tightened his embrace before she could fully peel herself away. "Cara mio, the only place I need to be is here, with you."

Tucked away with Martha, it took fading light and a cross stomach before Ava realised how much time had slipped away. With kind patience, Martha had spent hours touring her precious space, sharing every detail about her vast collection. They flipped through grimoires, studied scrolls, and fiddled with enchanted objects. Martha even detailed the contents of her box of fun things from the cabinet. If Ava had known half of what the seemingly innocuous items could do, she'd have worn gloves to handle them—double-gloved, even.

422

Squirming against the corkscrew-shaped item that could render a man infertile, Ava flapped at Martha to return it to the pile. "Enough," she pleaded with a laugh. "Before I need brain bleach."

Martha planned to take her most precious items with her when she left, but the majority she would leave behind.

"Come and go as you please," she told Ava. "Whatever you require, if it's here, please avail of it."

Which included access to the cabinet.

Sitting on the ground before it, Martha slid the chest of enchanted objects back into its nook. "About these," she said, motioning at the grimoires dedicated to numerous branches of dark magick. "You need to study them."

Ava shied away, sucking air through her teeth. "Yeah, I think I'll leave those be."

Martha disagreed with a tight shake of head. "Ava, you cannot deny dark magick runs in your blood. You wielded it with proficiency. I felt it," she said, patting her breast bone. "Don't ignore your inheritance. Dark magick holds beauty in its depths, and wielded with integrity, it's a powerful force."

"I have no training," Ava explained. "And Nessa won't help. She'll outright refuse. If I go it alone, I'm afraid of wandering off the safe path."

"I will guide you." Martha reached over to rest her hand on Ava's knee. "I'll be your anchoring light. But I can only take you so far. At a point in the future, you'll need a dark magick practitioner to take over. When the time comes, I'll find you the right person."

Ava contemplated the offer, a strange mix of dread and excitement fizzing as she glanced at the row of ancient grimoires. "I wish I knew who I inherited this from."

"Of course you do." Martha sighed. "But your family prefers the truth to remain buried."

"There has to be a record somewhere. The Enclave are duty-bound to record every supernatural birth and death, right? Surely there's an O'Keefe family-tree penned into some crusty tome."

"Now that you say it . . ." Martha considered the suggestion, absentmindedly massaging and flexing her hands. She'd complained earlier about feeling constantly chilled. With her body shifting from undead to living, it would take months before her temperature regulated. "I'll speak to Aurelius," she decided. "Discreetly, of course. He should be able to set me in the right direction."

"The right direction of what?"

Both women startled at Enzo's arrival. It appeared Martha's vampire hearing had already declined. "Enzo." She laughed at her own jumpiness. "I shall have to fit you with a bell."

"I had to ask him to cough his arrival," Ava told her, and reaching out to accept Enzo's hand, allowed him to pull her gently to her feet. She winced as pins and needles stung. "I jumped out of my skin more times than I can count over the last few weeks."

"You must both be hungry," Enzo said. "Dinner is ready."

"I am," Ava admitted, happily leaning against him as he kissed her forehead. "We lost track of time."

"We did," Martha agreed, rising a lot more gracefully.

"What do you wish to discuss with Aurelius?" Enzo asked as they descended the main stairs.

Ava paused her appreciation of savoury aromas drifting up from the kitchen. "The source of my dark magick." When no comment followed, she stole a sideways glance at him. "I'd like to know who I inherited it from."

"Of course. But with all that's about to happen over the next few days, it might be best not to place yourself in any kind of spotlight for the time-being."

424

"You're right," she realised, slowing as she stepped onto the hallway tiles. Enzo insisted Waylen Kane wouldn't retaliate against how they'd fooled him, but what if other enclave members took offence? "I should probably lie low for a while."

"It would be for the best."

36

Almost a month after Manus Larsen's goons had hauled her out of her home, Ava finally slid her key into the lock, and with a whispered, "I'm home!" eased open her brand new door.

At first, she cautiously walked each room, testing the air for lingering negative energy. But Nessa and Iz had kept her sanctuary locked tight. Once satisfied she was safe, Ava threw open the windows, changed into jeans and a t-shirt, and set about scrubbing.

By that evening, she'd cleaned her entire apartment, stripped and remade her bed, mopped all the floors, and tended to her lonely plants. An unseasonably warm April night lingered outside. With the balcony doors flung open, fresh air had finally chased every last drop of staleness away.

Unable to sit still, Ava moved between the rooms, grinning like a fool as she adjusted and touched her belongings. Rose incense burned in her bedroom while Sandalwood sent lazy streams drifting towards the ceiling in the living room. Her home smelt like home again, and she couldn't stop breathing in the welcome familiarity.

Unable to forget that Finn's CSI crew—not to mention Manus Larsen's thugs—had been in her private space had prompted a thorough sage-cleanse. Nothing had gone missing, and thankfully, the journals she'd filled ranting about Finn remained hidden in a shoebox at the top of her wardrobe. If Enzo had been any later in getting to her apartment and compelling Finn away, he'd have found them. Perhaps it was time to burn those particular memories.

While attempting to recreate Enzo's stuffed aubergine perfection, Finn called. Ava didn't pick up, but texted him while keeping a close eye on the oven, watching goat's cheese melt with enticing intent.

> Will catch up with you tomorrow. Need a quiet night in.

> **Finn:** Okay. I'm glad you're home. I was worried sick. Look forward to seeing you.

Ava put the phone on silent and left it face-down on the island beside the pile of post she still had to tackle. She didn't relish the idea of seeing Finn. If what Iz said about him doing a one-eighty on her witchery was true, she knew how intense he'd be—and persistent.

The prospect of seeing Enzo excited her *way* more.

Lifting the dish out of the oven, Ava wondered what they'd talk about now grand rescues and complicated magick were no longer the hot topic. "Maybe we won't be talking," she told her meal. "Maybe we'll be too busy doing the mattress mambo."

427

For her first attempt, the meal turned out delicious. Her presentation wasn't as perfect as Enzo's, but it tasted almost as good.

Positioned at the counter, she admired her balcony while eating. A blaze of colour filled the space. That afternoon, she'd received four separate flower deliveries, each from a family grateful to have their missing member safely returned. The gratitude in the accompanying cards had moved her greatly. Ava remembered only too well the horror of waiting for news of her missing mum. How every hour had stretched on more painfully than the last, and how, when her phone had finally shrilled, it hadn't been the news for which she'd prayed. Thankfully, for the families of Giulia's victims, their prayers had been answered.

As if annoyed she darkened a bright day with sad thoughts, a sudden breeze whirled through the balcony doors, rattling the metal chimes hanging above the opening. They shook with a disharmonious clang. "Okay, sorry. Happy thoughts, Mum. Happy thoughts."

But happy thoughts led her to only one subject, and by the time she'd cleaned up, her impatience to see Enzo had her twitchy.

Enzo hadn't given a specific time for his arrival, only that he wanted to give her space after being away from her home for so long, so it would be evening before she saw him. But as Ava fussed with her hair in the bathroom mirror, she worried their separation had already reminded him of the life he'd lived without her—a life where he hadn't promised himself to a small Irish town and an O'Keefe witch. "Stop!" she muttered at herself. Since when did she obsess over men?

With the evening cooling, Ava retreated to her room to find a light sweater to throw over her dress. Enzo would show when he showed. And until then, she'd behave like a normal person. "Not some Victorian damsel suffering an attack of the vapours over a gentleman caller," she said, returning to the kitchen.

"An attack of the vapours?"

428

The gentleman caller stood on her balcony. An almost replica of the night he'd first appeared—suit and all—the sight brought Ava to a clumsy stop in the doorway. Once again, her heart thudded and mouth turned dry. But this time, the old one's presence didn't sear her veins with fear. Something far more delightful shot through her body.

Obviously, Enzo had squeezed in his visit after a photo-shoot for Hottest Man On The Planet magazine. The trademark three-piece Paladino suit graced his form; a navy so deep, it could be mistaken for black. A silk tie, the same midnight blue, speared the centre of his dazzling white shirt.

"Buonasera."

Ava swallowed, and half found her tongue. "You're here."

"I am." Enzo pushed himself away from the railing's edge and strolled towards the open doors, raking her from head to bare feet.

He looked *ravenous*. And the Goddess help her; she hungered for him just as acutely.

A few steps towards him took Ava to the edge of the island, but there she paused.

She wanted to drink this moment in. Once she invited Enzo across the threshold, they'd dive on each other so fast, she wouldn't have the time, or the ability, to think.

Enzo came right to the opening. Like magnets, they automatically strained to connect with each other, but Ava held her ground.

"You have to invite me in."

"I know," she said, clenching against the heat in his tone. This moment deserved to be dragged out for as long as possible; it was far too delicious to rush.

Taking a grip of the counter behind her, Ava leaned into its support. "You're dressed to the nines."

"I wanted to look good for you."

You'd look better naked, her lustful tongue almost blurted, but she swallowed it down and replied with a far more ladylike, "You always look good."

Enzo held her with a growing smile, one layered with heat.

"It's a warm evening," she said lightly, even though her heart whirred so fast it vibrated in her throat. "Too warm for that many clothes."

Long-restrained desire stretched across their divide. Enzo's gaze seared as he acknowledged her invitation. One of his sinful smirks appeared, and with tantalising slowness, he removed his jacket, eyes never leaving hers as he casually threw it aside. It landed on the bistro table.

Heart nearing explosion-speed, Ava pulled in a breath.

Sex with Enzo Paladino.

This was one of those moments in life where an event would draw a definitive line between before and after. *Before* Enzo Paladino took her to bed. *After* Enzo Paladino took her to bed. The journey to the after, she anticipated with such yearning, she had to swallow before she could speak again. "What about that tie? Isn't it uncomfortable?"

"Terribly." A flick loosened the knot. With male-stripper proficiency, Enzo slid it out from under his collar, taunting her with the whisper of silk against cotton—inch by maddening inch. "You also appear to be overdressed."

Ava grasped the hem of her sweater and slowly peeled it up. While not as sexy a manoeuvre as his, she did manage to remove it without catching her hair.

"Bellissima," he said with such throaty desire, need sparked harshly enough to loosen her knees.

"Your shirt," she said, her request barely audible to her own ears over the racing of her heart.

Slender fingers obeyed, but only unfastened the top button. "Your dress," he parried.

Ava reached under her arm to open the zip. Cool air washed against scorching skin. The convergence manifested as a shiver, forcing her to briefly close her eyes. When she parted them, he'd undone every shirt button. Transfixed by the tantalising reveal, she watched as he made a deliberate show of freeing his shirttails from his waistband.

"More," she whispered when he stalled, purposely waiting for her command.

White cotton parted, baring the full glory of Enzo Paladino's bare chest.

Already hypnotised, Ava took a step towards him. "Holy shit."

"Ava." The pained utterance drew her wonder up. Enzo spanned the open doorway with outstretched arms, exposing his torso further. Muscle flexed as he clenched the frame. "For the love of god," he growled, "invite me in."

Close to disintegrating with desire, anticipation, and the tiniest flutter of fear, Ava took a final bracing inhale. Sex with Enzo. Was she truly ready for it? Her tongue seemed to think so. "Enzo, please come in."

Arms lowered. A grunt of satisfaction rumbled. One foot swung over the threshold, and Ava's breath bottomed out.

Enzo blurred towards her. Before she could blink, he'd pinned her beneath him on her bed, her dress already ripped away.

"Mia bella strega," he said, lips crashing against hers. "Finally."

Enzo kept her captive in her bed until lunchtime the following day.

Ava savoured every blissful moment of the confinement until the need to shower finally demanded attention. He followed her into the bath-

431

room, and even though she didn't think her body capable of producing another orgasm, he coaxed out one more as the water ran cold.

With her bones as loose as the silk tie still puddled somewhere on her balcony, Enzo carried her back to bed, ordered her to stay, and after a short while, returned, balancing a tray piled with food and fresh coffee.

He sat beside her while she ate and sipped, taking the opportunity to study her room. Whatever his gaze paused on, she told him the story behind it.

Halfway through an account of a school-trip to Paris, where their French teacher had fainted at the top of the Eiffel Tower, Enzo's head tipped fractionally to one side. Ava recognised the tell; he'd heard something she couldn't.

"What?" she asked with undeniable reluctance. Even if the world was about to come to a violent end, she refused to move out of her bed today.

Enzo waited, a tiny smile growing.

She nudged him. "Enzo."

A loud rap landed on her front door.

"Shall I get that for you?" he asked lightly.

Grinning, she took another bite of toast smothered with butter and honey. "Yes, please. And you can tell whoever it is that I'm too weak-kneed after all-night sex with you to leave my bed."

"My pleasure."

Enzo sprang from the bed with such anticipation, she nearly choked.

"Unless it's Finn!" she hissed after him. "Enzo!"

It was, of course, Finn. "What the—who the hell are you?" he snapped.

"Fuck!" Ava shoved the tray aside and scrambled out of bed to hide behind her half-open door.

"May I help you?" Enzo asked, all sweetness and light.

"I'm looking for Ava."

"I'm afraid she's indisposed."

"Sorry—who are you?"

"Enzo Paladino. And you're Detective Delaney, correct?"

Silence.

"I'll let Ava know you called."

"No." A thud announced Finn preventing Enzo from shutting the door. "I want to see her now. I'm sure you can appreciate how worried I am about her well-being. You've had her locked up in your home for the last few weeks, and now you're in *her* home, alleging she's not available."

"It's no allegation, detective. It's a statement of fact. Ava doesn't wish to be disturbed. She's resting."

"Resting or not, I want to see her. *Now.*"

"And *I* said—"

Ava darted out into the hall. "Finn, I'm here. I'm right here. And I'm fine."

Anger scoured Finn's expression, but it quickly shifted to relief. "Ava."

"Hi. Everything's fine. I'm fine. See? All in one piece."

But a barely dressed piece. She'd leapt out in nothing more than her Fleetwood Mac t-shirt. It just about covered her lady bits. Pillow-tousled hair, lips swollen from a night of Enzo's hungry kisses, and no doubt, a pronounced glow from all the amazing orgasms she'd had, succinctly declared why Enzo had announced her as *indisposed*. It didn't help the man in question wore only his black silk boxers, gifting Finn an eyeful of every other inch of his body—the perfect body Ava had spent the night enjoying.

Finn's brief reassurance swiftly darkened to anger. With a subtle move, she tugged the hem of her t-shirt down.

His pissy glare flicked between her and Enzo. *'You're with him?'* it screamed.

"As I said, detective. Ava is indisposed. Perhaps you could call another time?"

A vein bulged on Finn's forehead. Before it could erupt into a full-blown aneurysm, Ava quickly promised she'd call Finn tomorrow. "We'll talk then, okay?"

Finn snorted in disbelief at the scene before him, fired another scowl at Enzo, and withdrew his foot. "Tomorrow, Ava."

"Yes, tomorrow."

Enzo shut the door with measured grace. Satisfaction oozed as he padded towards her.

"Was that really necessary?"

"Simply stating what's mine," he told her, and scooping her up, carried her back to bed.

Iz arrived later that afternoon. Enzo said goodbye with another knee-trembler of a kiss, promising he'd return later to bring her to the party. Ava suspected he would have stayed only he needed to feed. Between them, they'd used up a lot of energy in the last twenty-four hours, and she didn't have a stash of blood in her apartment.

"We should try to sleep tonight," she told him, grabbing the open ends of his tie.

Enzo allowed her to tug him in for another kiss. "That sounds very boring," he said, smiling against her mouth.

"But necessary for the human."

"As long as you're in my arms, I don't care," he said, backing away with a grin and a whisper of, "and naked."

Already opening the wine she'd brought, Iz smirked when Ava returned to the kitchen. "I see you're having a little trouble walking. Saddle-sore, are we?"

"In all the best ways."

"I'll bet," Iz said, her dirty laugh hitching as she popped the cork out of the bottle. "So, how amazing is vampire sex?"

"Better than you can imagine," Ava told her, sliding her butt onto the stool. She accepted the glass Iz held out.

"I want details," Iz warned.

"Oh, you can't handle the details, trust me."

Iz chuckled away to herself as she poured her own glass, and with the day warm enough to sit outside, they retreated to the balcony.

Ava glanced at where Enzo's tie had fallen, inwardly clenching against the thrilling rush of memories their night, morning, and afternoon, reignited. Yes indeed, life before Enzo Paladino had taken her to bed, and life after. There most certainly *was* a difference.

"Have you talked to Nessa?" Iz asked, forcing Ava to focus on less pleasant subjects.

"Briefly. A quick call to say I'm home."

Iz pinned an *'and?'* look on her.

"And I told her when I'm ready, we'll talk. I'm still too pissed with her right now. I'll say something I'll regret, so I need to cool down first."

"Speaking of needing to cool down . . ." Iz savoured another mouthful of wine and popped a crisp in her mouth. "Finn called over. He stormed into my house like a goddamn bull."

Ava cringed.

"He was furious, my friend, ranting about you being under compulsion and Enzo being an arrogant son of a bitch. Were you actually almost naked when he called?"

"I wouldn't say *almost* naked. I had a t-shirt on, and Enzo was wearing boxers."

Iz pouted. "Poor Finn. You've crushed his fantasy."

"A fantasy he cooked up all by himself. And he'd better watch what he says. If he starts accusing Enzo of compelling me, there'll be trouble. Especially if he blabs it to Felicienne. Have you seen her yet?"

"Nope."

"Is she avoiding you?"

"Avoiding the whole town, I reckon. She said too much nasty shit about you when you were missing, and now she's facing a backlash. I heard Ciara Brady's parents ripped her a new one right in the middle of Strand Street yesterday. No-one's seen Felicienne since."

"Well, ain't karma a bitch?" Ava sang, reaching for the crisps. Despite all she'd eaten that day, she remained ravenous. Vampire sex really did burn a lot of calories.

"Right." Iz clapped a call for order. "Tonight. What are we wearing? And what, in the name of the Goddess, does one bring to a vampire party? Blood? Virgins? A box of bats?"

37

"Low-key?" Iz whispered as she and Ava gaped at the transformation for Martha's *'nothing-too-elaborate'* party.

The gardens of Paladino Palace glowed under strings of dainty lights, lanterns, and enough candles to light a small nation. A marque occupied a chunk of the lawn, furnished with a table large enough to seat twenty more than their paltry gathering of five. A gentle breeze curled through the open sides, fluttering the layers of white and cream linens draping the table. It skated through the setting, enticing the candles in a trio of wrought-iron candelabras to dance. As flames stretched and flickered, sparkling crystal and gleaming silver twinkled. Beneath the candelabras, delicate wreaths of ivy, primrose, and forget-me-not added a subtle splash of colour. The scene looked more like the bridal party table at a wedding than a simple family celebration.

The spectacle didn't end there. Dotted around the floor of the marque, giant fish bowls held tea-lights floating amongst rose petals. Two Gothic-style standing candelabras flanked the entrance, both strung with ivy.

Between the abundance of rippling candles and linens, and the peaceful music coming from somewhere off the patio, the scene appeared other-worldly.

"That's not a CD playing," Iz murmured, nudging Ava to turn around.

Positioned on the far side of the patio, a string quartet played, complimenting the magical backdrop. Ava recognised the tune; a current pop hit, but with a classical twist.

"What do you think?" Enzo asked, motioning they follow him inside the marque towards an impressive drinks table.

Martha had ducked in ahead of them to tweak cutlery and reposition chairs. On arrival, she'd told Iz she wanted to steal her for a while. Ava hoped it didn't include a tour of the greenhouse without her being present. She couldn't wait to see Iz's reaction to the abundance of Martha's rare plants.

Ava spotted Enzo's fancy tequila, but her favourite party tipple seemed at odds with the elegant setting. Tonight wasn't a night for drunk dancing or flirting with the outrageously sexy man waiting for her reply. "Um, it's beautiful. Stunning. It's just—I don't know. I don't have words. How did you put this together so fast?"

"We have our ways," Enzo said lightly. "What would you like to drink?"

Ava chose a respectfully demure white wine. With Enzo and Martha planning to leave early in the morning, she'd agreed to stay for two nights—neither of which, Enzo had informed her, she'd be spending in her *old* room. If she hit the tequila, chances were, she'd flop onto his fabulous four-poster bed half unconscious and rob herself of all the fun. "And water," she added to her order. No drunken antics tonight. She wanted to enjoy and remember every minute.

Iz asked for champagne, and as Enzo deftly opened the bottle, Iz rested her head on Ava's shoulder with a sigh of open longing. "Two nights won't be enough in this place."

Enzo had asked Iz to stay so Ava would have more engaging company than a bunch of vampire sentries. Cyrus wouldn't travel to Greece, but he wasn't the kind of guy to sit around and chat over a plate of cheese and crackers, or enjoy a sauna. With all the entertainment provided in the basement, their two night *spa break*, as Iz had christened it, would fly by.

"Is this all for us?" Iz asked, scanning the spread of platters.

Olives, cheeses, fruit, crackers, and breads occupied one side of the table, with tapenades, pesto, and chutneys on the other. Did Enzo really think she and Iz alone could eat all that food? Martha still preferred blood to solid food, so at most, might nibble a little cheese. "All that food could feed us for a week," Ava agreed.

"So stay for a week." Enzo winked.

"We just might," Iz said, accepting her champagne. "Cheese, Aves?" she asked, reaching for a plate.

"Not just yet, thanks." The boat ride over had left Ava slightly queasy. She couldn't blame the rocking motion; it was simply her fear of being on water that had turned every muscle rigid and her stomach sour. Somehow, she'd have to get over her aversion. Many boat trips lay in her future, and she didn't want to find herself swamped in a cold sweat every time she came to the island. Maybe she should ask Enzo to compel the fear out of her. He could then teach her how to swim. Suddenly enamoured by the idea of being wrapped around him in his fancy pool, she hid her smile against the rim of her glass. Yes. Swimming lessons with

439

Enzo sounded like a wonderful plan. Although, they might not get a lot of actual swimming done.

"Dance with me," Enzo said, drawing her out of the distracting daydream. He took her glass and set it on the table.

Iz had already loaded a plate and plonked herself into a seat. She wouldn't be budging for a while.

As they stepped onto the patio, Cyrus appeared from the kitchen. He saluted them with his tumbler of whiskey, heading to where Martha called out to him.

"You've thought of everything," Ava said, admiring the fairy lights strung over the makeshift patio dancefloor. "Ever considered a career in event management?"

"This is all Martha's doing," Enzo told her, pulling her in. "She keeps close tabs on our network, disguising her information-gathering as extravagant parties. It's another reason why she'll excel as reeve. She has a way of bringing people together, and keeping those who should be distant, apart." Enzo had foregone a jacket and tie for the evening, but still remained devilishly handsome, dressed in a black shirt and charcoal trousers. He skimmed her cheek with his nose as she pressed herself closer to him. "You look stunning, mia bellissima strega."

"Thank you. You're quite the handsome dance partner yourself."

They danced in silence for a short while, content to sway in each other's arms as a warm night and soft music drifted around them. As they rotated, Ava took in the view; Martha and Iz already deep in conversation at the table. Cyrus chatting to Kara, their attention on his phone. They both laughed at whatever they watched.

"Cyrus seems different," Ava commented quietly. "Calmer."

Enzo glanced over at his nephew. "For now, he is. But it won't last. He's bored here. Martha will need to take him away soon or he'll revert to form."

"Will he go to Athens with her?"

"No," he said, fingers trailing up and down Ava's spine in a most distracting way.

Ava could understand why Cyrus needed to remain behind. With his dislike for rules and decorum, he'd probably cause untold trouble. Besides, he still believed the Enclave knew about the incident at the zoo. "Where will Martha take him?"

"He's happiest in Italy. He has a circle of acquaintances there. They'll keep an eye on him when Martha can't. Speaking of Italy." Enzo took her chin, wanting her full attention on him, and not on his unstable nephew. "I'd like to take you to Florence."

"Florence? When?"

"When you're ready. Once you're settled into your routine again."

Ava fiddled with his open collar, entranced by the hollow at the base of his throat. "For how long?"

"A few days, a week, a month. Whatever you'd like. It's a beautiful city, brimming with art and history. You'll enjoy it."

"Oh. So, we'd be sightseeing?"

Enzo captured her busy hand, laughing at the smirk she tried to bite down. "There are many sights I long to see, yes."

"Such as?" Meeting his heated gaze, Ava held her nerve. Enzo brought out a boldness in her she hadn't known existed.

"This dress," he whispered, drawing her close as he ran both his hands over her ass and gave it a gentle squeeze, "pooled on the floor around your ankles. This hair," he continued, sending a warm thrill through her as he threaded it through his fingers before clasping the rear of her neck, "spread out on my naked chest."

Ava had to remind herself to breathe as he leaned in and seared a line of kisses from her earlobe to her shoulder.

"And this," he murmured, gently tugging at her bottom lip with his thumb. "Caught between your teeth right before you cry out my name and come undone."

"Enzo." Ready to melt into a hot puddle around his feet, Ava closed her eyes.

"I'm killing you?" He preempted with a chuckle.

"In all the good ways."

Enzo's lips landed on hers, delivering a kiss hot with promise. Remaining behind closed eyes, she hummed in pleasure. Enzo kissed her like no man ever had. Every stroke of lips and press of tongue declared his passion, his need, and his claim. Unfortunately, being undead meant he didn't suffer the pesky need for oxygen.

Ava pulled away, laughing at her involuntary gasp for air. "When you kiss me like that, I forget how to breathe."

"I know a remedy," he replied, brushing his lips over her cheekbones. "Practice."

"I'm down for that."

Enzo trailed his fingers along her arms, lifting her hands so she'd loop them around his neck. "You're glowing tonight, cara mia."

"It's the candles," she told him, kissing his jaw.

"No, it's you. There's a light in your eyes I haven't seen before; elation."

"Yes, I'm happy," she agreed, stroking the hair at the back of his neck. In the fading evening, his eyes were almost black as he smiled down at her. "Martha and I talked a lot yesterday. She helped me to see the good I achieved, and how my power isn't a curse. For the first time in my life, I'm really starting to believe it's a gift. I did something good with it. I brought about positive change. It's never had that kind of impact before."

Ava didn't know if vampires could shed tears, but Enzo looked like he might in that moment.

"The world feels different," she admitted, shrugging because she couldn't really explain how. "I feel both lighter and stronger."

"That your possibilities are endless," he said, as if he too experienced the shift.

She nodded. "It's unfamiliar territory for me, but I like it."

Enzo drew a circle at the base of her spine. "You discussed dark magick, too," he said. "Martha told me."

"She wants to help me explore it," Ava confirmed. "It's strange," she said with a smile. "We hardly know each other, yet there's a bond between us, something deep. Ancient, almost. Ancestral, maybe?"

"Your witch kinship?"

"It's something beyond that. I don't know, I can't explain it. But, whatever it is, I know I can trust Martha to guide me through figuring out my magick. Nessa has always pushed against the idea, and I'm so angry with her right now, I'm not sure if I'll ever truly trust her again."

"It will take time. But she's your family, Ava, and at the heart of Nessa's actions lies the urge to protect you."

Ava wondered what Nessa would say if she were to hear Enemy Number One defending her. "I know. Time, though. Lots and lots of time."

The quartet moved onto a new piece of music, a haunting melody with an Italian sound. Enzo murmured satisfaction and wrapped her against him. "Perfetta."

It *was* perfect. Ava closed her eyes, resting her cheek on a firm slope of pectoral muscle. Everything had turned out better than she could have ever hoped. She'd worried about how she and Enzo would slot into each other's lives, but now on the other side, realised it would happen organically. Her fears of shoe-horning were ill-founded. They'd simply complement each other's life, not complicate.

Unbidden, a reminder of three tarot cards flashed.

443

No! she snapped at the urgent little poke that followed. She'd spent most of her life fearing the worst, and for the first time, inspiring promise lay in her future. Self-doubt didn't appreciate how she'd suddenly chosen to ignore its annoying little whispers, but it would soon learn she had no space for uncertainty in her life any longer. Especially when it fought to derail her happiness with dread.

It was a dud reading, she told herself for the umpteenth time, *distorted by sticky energy from a dirty deck.*

Earlier that evening, after Iz had left to go home and change for the party, Ava had finished the last of her unpacking. Before leaving Paladino Palace, she'd safely stowed her tarot deck in a pocket of her suitcase. Although under pressure to get ready for the party, she'd unwrapped the deck, unable to disregard the sudden urge to shuffle and draw. She should have ignored the call, or at least grabbed a deck unsullied by all the heavy energy she'd carried around for the last few weeks. But she'd foolishly shuffled while asking what lay ahead for her before dealing three cards.

The Tower, the 10 of Swords, and the 8 of Cups looked up at her from her bedspread. *Chaotic upheaval! Betrayal! Moving on!* they announced. The dire message, spear-headed by the stalker Tower, had prompted her to scoop up the cards, shove them back into the deck, and plonk it on the slab of selenite on her altar.

Ava refused to accept destructive Tower energy lay in her future. Despite all the odds, they'd rescued and restored Martha. Yes, Giulia was on the loose, but it wasn't likely she'd crawl out of her crypt until the next eclipse. So what chaos did the Tower indicate? As for the 10 of Swords and its message of endings and betrayal? Who'd stab whom in the back? Not she and Enzo, that was for sure. The kindest card, the 8 of Cups, signified moving on from a friendship or relationship for the better good. *Definitely a dud reading. Forget about it.*

"Amore mio?" Enzo stirred, catching her chin. Concern tightened his features as he looked down at her. "What is it?"

"Nothing, really. It's just hard to shift from being on red-alert to this," she answered, lifting her chin to the glorious night twinkling around them as they slowly rotated to gentle music. "Life after the eclipse. It'll take time for me to adjust."

"I'm here," he told her, gathering her in close again. "Share your worries, Ava. Whatever your thoughts, no matter how insignificant you may believe they are, I want you to share them with me."

But now wasn't the time to admit a spur-of-the-moment tarot reading gnawed at her happiness. Not when Enzo was about to leave her for a few days. Once he returned, and she went home, she'd prepare a proper reading, using a fresh, fully charged and cleansed deck. *Yes*, Ava decided, tightening her hold on Enzo, *a dud reading*.

After another long while of dancing, the waiting feast called. Iz and Martha had disappeared, so Ava took a seat at the table with Enzo, filling a plate with food.

Cyrus reappeared with a book. Quieter than earlier, he chose to move away from them, slouching once he took a seat at the far end of the table.

Ava and Enzo talked about the upcoming enclave vote while she ate. Enzo had no doubt Martha would secure the seat. He'd been speaking to Edyta, and it appeared it wasn't only the vampire faction who questioned Kane's behaviour. "He's dug a hole for himself," Enzo said, reaching for the champagne bottle nestled in a bucket of ice. "And made more enemies than allies."

"Can he be kicked out?" she asked.

445

"One can hope." The champagne bottle held less than half a glass. "I'll fetch another," Enzo told her, and dropping a kiss on her head, left the table.

Ava watched him go, spotting Martha inside the kitchen.

Iz wasn't with her. They'd toured Martha's room earlier, but Ava hadn't seen Iz for a while.

Glancing over at where Cyrus sat, she recognised his demeanour warning he wouldn't welcome company, but she got up from her seat, regardless.

He'd been peeling grapes.

A macabre little pile of torn black skin sat on a side plate, uprooting memories of the day he'd arrived home dripping in blood. With another grape flayed, he popped it in his mouth and bit down with a snap.

His mood had shifted. Martha had spent most of the evening with Iz, and Ava guessed Cyrus didn't like it.

"Everything okay, Cyrus?"

"Peachy."

Clearly not. Trouble brewed. Ava checked the house again. Both Martha and Enzo had vacated the kitchen. "Have you seen Iz?"

"No," he muttered, as much as to say he had no interest in anyone or their whereabouts.

Cyrus's mood wasn't her problem tonight. They were here to celebrate, and Ava had a greenhouse stuffed with plants to show Iz.

Beyond their candlelit space, night had swallowed the garden. Ava peered in the direction of the greenhouse. Had Iz beaten her to it and found it herself? She'd really wanted to see her expression as she gaped at Martha's collection for the first time; it really was the stuff of herb porn. "Tell Enzo I'm in the greenhouse," she said, and leaving Cyrus to his pile of grape-skin, ducked out of the marque, cut across the patio, skirted the string quartet, and hurried towards the shadowed lawn.

446

Soft grass tugged at her heels. Ava quickly pulled off her shoes, squealing when cold grass kissed her warm feet. Further ahead, a soft light glowed from inside the greenhouse. Iz had already found her way inside using the torch on her phone. "Spoilsport," she tutted, reaching for the door.

A day of sun had the interior air heavy with scent. It momentarily caught Ava's breath, the pungency bringing tears to her eyes. "Iz, you ruined my fun," she called, slipping back on her shoes. "I wanted to see your surprise."

Iz didn't reply.

"Iz," she called louder, coughing against the surprising strength of plant vapours as she rounded into the aisle containing the most poisonous specimens.

Iz was on her hunkers further ahead, back turned to Ava.

"What are you doing?" Ava asked, wondering how Iz could see in the dim light. Ava herself could barely make her Iz's form.

"Come see this," Iz murmured.

Ava neared, registering the strange hoarseness to Iz's voice. "You changed?" she queried, noting how she now also wore black. "Iz?"

Without turning, Iz motioned for Ava to step closer.

"You ruined all my fun," Ava said again kindly. "I wanted to—"

"No. *You* ruined *mine*."

Iz rose, but Ava realised too late it wasn't her friend.

The figure wheeled around, a hand shot out, and before Ava could jerk out of reach, a warm, wet bind slithered around her forearm, locking her in place.

The air thickened, immediately scalding the back of Ava's throat and stealing her voice. Death crept over her, a second skin of marrow-deep dread, tight with cold and hopelessness.

447

Startled vision flickered, suddenly clarifying the figure standing before her. Ava didn't recognise the face, but the sense of malevolence she knew too well.

Giulia!

Such beauty, she caught herself thinking, but depravity shone in the woman's startling blue eyes; a summer sea polluted by the poison of death magick.

Ava moved to yank herself free, but Giulia's grip bit tighter. She'd fastened herself to her forearm, ice-cold fingertips embedded in the soft flesh below Ava's elbow.

Against her will, Ava mimicked the same hold on Giulia's arm. The witch had bound them together with a slick, bloody rope.

No. Not a rope.

Innards.

An intestine so fresh, the iron tang of blood filled Ava's nostrils. She wanted to scream, lash out, fight, but whatever herb Giulia burned, it overwhelmed her ability to retaliate.

A glint in the low light yanked Ava's fright down and to her right. Giulia gripped a blade, the steel reflecting a slice of russet fur. A dead fox lay where she'd been hunched moments before.

"You ruined *all* my fun." Foul breath came with Giulia's statement, delivered with a voice ravaged by time and the blackest of magick. "I chased the necklace for centuries. Followed its intended path for hundreds of years. It should have been Martha's, but she chose to rid herself of her power to stop me."

Internally, Ava screamed and flailed, but trapped by whatever filthy magick Giulia wielded, her body remained frozen and vulnerable.

"And then it made its way to the O'Keefe line."

A stuttered, "N—no" worked its way up Ava's throat.

448

Giulia leaned in, tracing the tip of her nose up her cheek. "I can smell him on you."

"N—no, s—stop."

"He'll mourn you." Greedy eyes flicked to the base of Ava's throat. "The O'Keefe line ends with you," she rasped, tongue darting out to taste victory. "I'll finally take what's mine."

The first plunge of blade didn't register. But the force of Giulia's punch bowed Ava, driving breath she no longer controlled out of her lungs. Doubled-over, she suddenly faced the ground, watching as blood splattered on her shoes. Giulia's hand gripped the knife's handle, with the blade itself hidden—buried in Ava's flesh.

Sharp nails clamped Ava's throat, and with a cry, Giulia yanked her upright.

Ava blinked in shock, struggling to catch up with spiralling chaos.

It was supposed to be Iz. She was supposed to be showing the plants to *Iz*, not staring into the eyes of a madwoman!

Giulia licked her lips, focus on where the necklace would appear in the seconds before Ava's life winked out. "Now."

A violent jerk and the blade sliced upward for a second time.

Pain flashed, searing hot. Ava choked on her own cry.

Giulia laughed, a wheeze of delight.

The greenhouse blurred. Billowing light feathered the edges of Ava's vision as coldness bit.

From behind Giulia, movement stirred the shadows. A darker fog formed, hovering above the dead fox; two women.

'So soon?' she cried out to her mum and gran. They'd said she had a long life before her, that she had so much yet to do. *'Mum, you were wrong!'*

Aoibheann's face formed, expression twisted in horror. She gestured wildly, but what could Ava do? A third jerk had already sealed her fate. Giulia's blade had sliced again. *'Mum! Help me!'*

449

The world exploded. A blast of glass and plants, screaming and pain.

Wrenched from Giulia's bind, agony slammed. Ava hit the ground, face down in her own blood.

So much of it.

Warm and sticky.

Was it all hers, or had the fox bled out, too?

Ground rushed away from her as a cry breached her shock.

"Ava—*Ava!*"

Ava had never witnessed such terror on Enzo's handsome face. Would he listen if she told him not to worry, that although she'd be gone soon, he'd be okay?

As screams and hollers raged, Ava drifted behind closed eyes. Too much pain. She could feel where her blood drained from her body, hot pulses marking its exit on to the greenhouse floor. Where it flowed out, cold rushed in, settling into her bones, wrapping her in death's shroud. They were too late. *'I'm dying.'*

'Choose life.'

'Mum, no. It's too late. It's over.'

'Choose life!'

"Ava. Open your eyes, Ava!"

Enzo's command ripped her mum away. Behind him, the night spun and dipped. "Enzo," she whispered, coughing as blood rushed up her throat. "It hurts."

"Take my blood." His wrist appeared in her fading vision. Twin holes pierced his skin. "Take it!"

Two little drops. A scarlet cure-all. But they'd forever alter her, distort her magick beyond recognition. "C—can't."

"Yes, you can! For the love of god, Ava, *take it!*"

Blood erupted from her mouth instead of refusal.

'Choose life!'

"Ava." The wrist hovered over her mouth. "Take it! Don't choose death. Stay, cara mia. Fight. *Fight!*"

'Choose life, sweetheart.'

'Ava, pet. Choose life.'

'What kind of life, Gran? You know what his blood will do to me. I'll transform into something irrevocably broken. I won't be me. He loses me either way. I lose either way. Let me choose death. Please.'

Aoibheann's ghostly face loomed closer. *'You don't belong here, Ava. Not yet.'*

'Mum?'

'You don't belong. And I don't want you here. I won't welcome you, do you hear me? I'll go. You'll be alone.'

'Mum, what are you saying?'

"Ava, open your eyes! Drink, please!"

"Just give it to her!" Iz screamed. "Why are you even asking? She's dying, Enzo!"

'We'll stay if you choose life. We'll always be with you. But if you choose to die, you'll wander here alone, forever. We'll never meet again.'

"Cristo, Ava!"

'Mum, no!'

'Listen to him! He needs you. This world needs you, Ava. Now is not your time to leave it, so choose life. I never had the choice, sweetheart; it was taken from me. Do this for me. Choose life for me!'

A swirl of faces hung over her; the tissue-thin apparition of her gran and mother as they pressed against the veil, contrasted by the vividness of Iz, Cyrus, and Martha's horrified expressions.

And closest to her, Enzo. Anguish had twisted his features beyond recognition.

"Ava," he pleaded. "My bella strega. Don't do this. Don't choose to die. Stay for me. I beg of you."

451

"Ava!" Iz screeched. "Take it for fuck's sake!"

'For me, sweetheart. For me, please!'

'Mum?'

'Choose life, Ava! Before it's too late!'

38

THREE MONTHS LATER

A raging bonfire silhouetted Ava's hunched form. Finn watched from Nessa's kitchen window, the view fractured by yet another cracked pane. Ash flecked the splintered glass, further distorting the scene. Nessa had lost so many windows in the last three months, she'd given up replacing them. Sheets of plywood were cheaper. The cottage already looked like a tenement with half its windows boarded up.

"Here." Nessa handed him a flowery mug with a chipped handle.

Tea, no milk. He hated black tea, but whining seemed petty. "How long has she been out there?"

"Since four."

Finn glanced at the clock on the stove front. Ten-thirty at night. "Jesus."

"There's no wood left." Nessa tutted, joining him with her own mug. Hers had milk. "She's gone through a year's worth already."

"So, what's she burning now?"

"Nothing. She's raising the fire herself."

"All this time? Since four o'clock?"

"And hasn't even broken a sweat."

"Fuck." The mug came down onto the draining board, sloshing tea over the side. Finn flicked the scald away before licking his hand.

God help him, but he fucking hated Enzo Paladino. The bastard had saved Ava's life, but had ripped every sweet, good part of her out in the process. Finn barely recognised her anymore. She was a woman possessed by something demonic, a violent force her fragile body couldn't contain.

At war with the world around her, Finn had witnessed Ava's shouts blowing out windows, exhales of agitation ripping trees out of the earth, and when frustration drove her to tears, pipes buckling and taps exploding. Nessa's home bore the scars of fire, flooding, and hurricanes, but she shrugged off each and every assault.

'It's just stuff,' she insisted every time. *'Rather Ava wreck my home than the alternative.'*

Finn found it hard to believe Ava had willingly chosen to take Paladino's blood. Iz had told him she'd been seconds away from dying before she'd caved. Sometimes he didn't believe Iz, or any of them, not even Ava. Why would she voluntarily choose this life? She wouldn't, *couldn't* have. Paladino had made her take his blood. He'd compelled her. He must have. The Ava Finn knew, would *never* have opted for this horrific existence.

Nessa jabbed him with her elbow. "Go on out and talk to her."

"She doesn't talk back."

"She doesn't need to. She just needs to know you're here for her."

"It's not *me* she wants."

Nessa tutted again. "It is. She just doesn't know it yet."

Finn folded his arms. Sometimes, on good days, Ava talked to him. When she did, it built his hopes up all over again.

Ava may have been the one who had ended their relationship, but Finn had been the one to ruin it with his ignorance and impatience. His cowardice had pushed her away, made her believe he thought her practice and abilities a load of bullshit. In truth, he'd been terrified. Calnaloch was a town like no other, and when he'd first arrived, he'd thought the entire population needed psychiatric help. But now he knew better.

He still loved Ava. He didn't think he'd ever stop. Yet *he* was the one to blame for this mess. His fear had led her straight into the path of the vampire who appreciated her gifts. Paladino knew Ava's worth. He'd never once doubted her, and Ava had recognised that respect and confidence.

Despite Nessa's insistence, Finn feared Ava wouldn't ever take him back. She'd told him as much. It was the damned vampire for whom she cried, and Finn couldn't understand why, not after what he'd done to her.

"*You're* here, *he's* not," Nessa added with a testy sniff, stooping to pick up the wet towels piled in front of the washing machine. There'd obviously been another plumbing incident that day. "She'll forget about him eventually," she said, shoving the sodden load into the drum.

Whatever about Ava forgetting, Finn agreed that his presence had to count. Paladino had fled. He hadn't been seen in months. For all his supposed love for Ava, the second she'd really needed him, he'd fucked off and left her. The selfish prick couldn't handle the warped version he'd created.

Iz didn't agree. Enzo hunted Giulia in revenge, she'd told him. And Ava needed space to find control without him around, meaning Enzo hadn't left her. *'Far from it'*, she'd snapped. Allegedly, he regularly came to the boundary line, and would watch over Ava for hours on end. But if he *could* cross it, Finn wondered, if Nessa yanked down the wards keeping him and his filthy kind out, would he actually help Ava? No. The fucker wouldn't.

Finn abandoned the bitter tea. Nessa was right. *He* was here, and Paladino wasn't. It would take time, but Ava would trust him again. She'd come to realise who was the better man—who *truly* had her best interests at heart.

A mixture of balmy July weather and Ava's wild inferno warmed the night when Finn stepped out the back door. He made his way down the sloping garden to where the ground levelled out. Beyond, the Ballinastoe Woods formed a jagged slash against navy sky. Sun had baked the earth all day, and the scent of dry pine tickled his nostrils.

Finn slowly lowered himself onto the log beside Ava. She didn't acknowledge his arrival. Practice had taught him not to speak first, so he sat in silence, hands clasped, elbows on his knees. If she wanted conversation, she'd start it. If he instigated chat, he risked her getting up and walking away.

Nothing but ash lay on the earth inside the fire pit. Fluffy white petals scurried around the base of the updraught, dancing like cherry blossom in spring wind. Yet above them, flames roared ten feet into the air; angry, ravenous, violent tongues, straining to consume the night sky.

Finn stole a glance at Ava's profile, catching what he'd expected; a blank expression, eyes staring into nothingness, raging flames reflected in the dead gaze. Unnerved, he looked away.

When they'd first brought Ava home, Nessa had confidently promised everyone she'd have Ava *'Back to herself in no time'*.

May dragged by with daily reports stating no improvement.

June rolled around with Ava's wild power continuing to cause endless havoc. Nessa insisted she'd fix it.

456

'I know what I'm doing!' she argued. *'And if you'd all be patient for five bloody minutes, you'd see for yourselves!'*

But she continuously failed. No matter what Nessa tried, Ava couldn't control her distorted magick.

'It has a mind of its own', Nessa finally admitted.

By mid-June, Finn had lost faith in Nessa's methods entirely, and ignoring Iz's warnings, approached Felicienne for help. He hadn't received the answer he'd expected.

'Ava O'Keefe always thought she was too good for this coven. Now she knows the truth, she can suffer the consequences of her pride alone,' Felicienne had snarled before slamming the door in his face.

Finn hadn't spoken to Felicienne since, but half the town had already cut the High Priestess off, so he doubted one more would make a difference.

By late June, Iz began to argue the case for Martha Paladino's help—offered, no doubt, by Paladino himself. Iz and Paladino remained in constant contact. Finn didn't like it, but Iz didn't give a shit.

'Who I talk to is none of your business,' she'd said. *'And for your information, Enzo and Martha are both working to find a way to help Ava, so keep your prejudiced opinions to yourself.'*

Thankfully, Nessa refused Martha's assistance. The Paladinos had caused this nightmare, and they were sorely mistaken thinking the O'Keefes would accept their help to crawl out of it.

So, here they were, three months later, almost at the end of July. The only change Finn could see was Nessa's cottage nearing total destruction, and the Ballinastoe Woods close to disappearing if Ava didn't stop burning every piece of wood in sight.

"This helps."

Finn almost started against Ava's quiet statement. She hadn't spoken to him in over a week. The last words they'd exchanged had been angry

457

ones. She'd yelled at him to go away. He'd begged her to listen to him. She'd screamed at him to leave her alone, and another window had exploded. "The fire?" he asked softly, already tensing to stand and leave.

But she didn't snap at him to go. "I don't feel so angry," she replied after a strained pause.

He took his time answering, too. "That's good."

She shifted, tilting her head as if her neck ached. "Is it?"

"Maybe you just need to let the anger pour out until there's none left."

"When it dies, I die. That's all I am now—uncontrollable anger."

Ava wanted a conversation he didn't know how to navigate. Finn glanced over one shoulder. Usually, whenever he got anywhere near Ava, Nessa watched, ever-hopeful of a reunion. But she wasn't at the window spying on them. Instead, he saw her leaving the kitchen, heading for the hallway. Iz, he guessed. She'd texted him earlier to say she'd be up later. Iz would handle this better than he. She'd know what to say. "I'll be back in a sec."

Towels already turned lazily in the washing machine. The sudsy load rotated with a comical sloshing, almost drowning out the voices from the hallway. Finn crossed the kitchen, realising it wasn't Iz who'd arrived.

"Not without what I came for," a man said impatiently.

Finn turned immediately rigid. *Paladino?*

"And like I already said—no," Nessa snapped in reply.

"Listen to me, Nessa O'Keefe."

"No, *you* listen to *me*," she whispered loudly.

Finn darted to the half-open door, straining to listen. It wasn't Paladino. The accent had a British twang. *More's the pity.* Vampire or not, he'd kick the shit out of Enzo given the chance.

"You have no claim here, do you understand? You have no rights or authority under the roof of my home, so take your threats and—"

"I have *every* right."

458

A creak announced the front door widening. Combined with the threat in the stranger's voice, it urged Finn out into the hallway. "Ness? Everything okay here?"

Caught off guard, Nessa faltered. She'd been attempting to close over the door on the visitor. Flashing a fake smile, she released it. "Fine, love, fine. Go on back out to Ava."

"Who's this?" Finn tipped his chin at the stocky figure blocking the entrance. He appeared agitated. Flushed cheeks warned of fading patience, but it was the desperation in the man's emerald green eyes that caught Finn's attention.

"Waylen Kane," the visitor announced, raking Finn over with a look of derision. "And you?"

"Finn Delaney. *Detective* Finn Delaney."

Kane dismissed his title with a sneer. "Stay out of our business, son. It's way beyond your jurisdiction."

Finn took a step towards him. "I'm not your son, and this is very much my business."

Nessa grasped his arm to shove him back towards the kitchen. "Finn, love, leave it. Keep an eye on Ava for me, please."

Refusing to budge, Finn ignored her plea.

"Nessa," Kane said, the sudden calmness in his tone layered with malice. "We both know I'm the only one who can fix what that bastard has so *perversely* damaged."

Nessa shook her head, gaze flitting across the carpet as she inched away. One ragged corner bore a scorch mark. The boards beneath held more damage. "I won't allow it. No. No way."

"I'm not asking for permission," he said, oily tone slick with warning.

Anxious hands twisted. "Give—give me more time. I can fix it. I know I can."

459

Kane took a step further inside. "You've had more than enough time. I warned you tonight would be the deadline—that I wouldn't leave without what I came for."

"No," Nessa whispered.

"Why are you making this so difficult?" Kane asked kindly, shrinking the gap she tried to create. "You know I have the power to claim what I want."

Finn had witnessed Nessa taking the full brunt of Ava's assaults. She'd barely flinched. Once, after Ava had flung her across the kitchen, Nessa had shuffled to her knees, swiped her bloody nose, and with a laugh, asked, *'Is that all you've got?'*

But this Nessa was afraid. She cowered.

Taking one wide step, Finn placed himself in front of Ava's aunt. "You should leave, Mr Kane. Now."

"Stay out of this, boy."

Nessa gripped the back of Finn's t-shirt, shielding herself behind him. A rattle announced her bumping against the hall table. The impact toppled the lamp on its cluttered surface, dousing the hallway in flickering light. "Please, Waylen, go."

"Not without Ava."

Ava?

Finn instinctively straightened, asserting his presence as he reached behind to nudge Nessa farther aside. "What do you want with Ava?"

"None of your damned business," Kane snarled.

Although distorted by blinking light, blatant menace carved Kane's expression. Finn suddenly wished he hadn't left Ava alone. Whoever this man was, he belonged to Ava and Nessa's world, a being from whom Finn couldn't defend himself, Nessa, or ultimately, Ava. "Ava's not going anywhere with you. She belongs here, with her family. With *me*."

Eyes narrowed, a reptilian squint warning Finn to run, grab his girl, and never look back.

"I *am* her family. Ava is my daughter."

THE END

Need more of Ava & Enzo?
Become a member of my exclusive Readers Lounge, and unlock content you won't find anywhere else! *Members get Turning Moon: A Novella for free!*
Visit www.julieembleton.com

Acknowledgements

I would like to extend my gratitude to the following people, all who have contributed to the creation of Moonstone & Mugwort. First, to my family. I'm grateful beyond measure for your love and support. Abby, you're my why. I love you, Moomin.

Marianne and Beatrice, where would I be without your unfailing encouragement and demands for the next book? Thanks for being my champions. You both deserve all the wine and cheese.

To Miriam Maddock, my author buddy who knows exactly what I'm going through every step of the way, and keeps me motivated when I need that shove. We'll have that Scottish castle someday, my friend.

To Linda Ganzini, a truly beautiful soul. Thank you for checking, and where necessary, for correcting my poor Italian.

Many thanks to Frank Whearity of the Skerries Historical Society for sharing his research on the Martello towers of Skerries. There may be no definitive proof of smugglers digging tunnels into the towers, but I still like to believe they exist.

To my Instagram and TikTok fam. Thank you. Some days I think I must be insane, and then I jump online and you're all there to remind me that we're insane as a collective, so that makes it okay.

Finally, to you, my beloved readers. It's the beginning of a new adventure with this Oath & Legacy series. Thank you for sticking with me for the last twelve years. Here's to the next twelve, and all the fun and madness it may bring.

About the Author

Julie Embleton is a dark fantasy author from Dublin, Ireland.
She writes tenacious, kick-ass females who can rescue themselves (thanks very much), gutsy heroes with tender hearts, and heinous villains who thrive on chaos. Her stories weave suspense, romance, and magick, mostly with happy endings, though she's not above the occasional cliffhanger.

Born and raised in Ireland, Julie lives by the shores of the moody Irish Sea, north of County Dublin. When not writing, she's often found with her second great love: tarot. Julie doesn't just write about magick—she lives it, working as a professional tarot reader and guiding others in her holistic mindfulness practice. If you're curious, you can explore more about her other passions at creativesoultarot.com

Julie's dark fantasy books transport readers to moody, magical worlds filled with strong characters and supernatural intrigue. Join her Readers Lounge for exclusive updates, sneak peeks, and all things fantasy at juli eembleton.com

Love dark fantasy and behind-the-scenes bookish fun?
Become a member of Julie's exclusive Readers Lounge, and unlock content you won't find anywhere else! *Members get Turning Moon: A Novella for free!*
Visit julieembleton.com

Visit JulieEmbleton.com

Dive into the **Turning Moon** series, a contemporary world where wolves, vampires, and witches defy prejudices, join forces, and fall in love. The heroines are feisty, the heroes gutsy, and the villains heinous.
Available in e-book, paperback, and audio.

Travel between realms with the captivating **Coveted Power** series, an epic coming-of-age fantasy, where sorcery, treachery, and love straddle medieval and contemporary worlds.
Available in e-book and paperback.

Oath & Legacy weaves a spellbinding dark fantasy series where ancestry and duty walk hand in hand, for better or worse. With vampires, witches, demons, and fae at its heart, the series brims with betrayal, devotion, and forbidden longing.
In this world, every choice echoes through generations.
Available in e-book, paperback, and audio.

Enter a dystopian world where supernatural beings fight for survival, defy prejudices, and find unexpected love. **Rogue Assassin:** A standalone dystopian romance.
Available in e-book, paperback, and audio.

Become a member of my exclusive Readers Lounge, and unlock content you won't find anywhere else!

Members get Turning Moon: A Novella for free!

Visit julieembleton.com